Abe's Legacy

Marjorie P. Dunn

Best Wishes
Marjorie P. Dunn

*To Victoria (Vikki) and Alexander (Alex) Bonser —
my grandchildren.*

By the same author:

For the Love of Children
The T'alli Stone
The Reluctant Traveller

Front Cover:

*Remains of Broadhead Wheel Mill, on the Loxley, near Little Matlock:
workmen searching for ther tools.*

Abe's Legacy

Marjorie P. Dunn

The **Hallamshire** Press
1998

Acknowledgements

Thanks to Philip Marshall and Frank Westwood for their help.
Also special thanks to my husband Bob for his support, encouragement
and help in writing this book.

Published by The Hallamshire Press
The Hallamshire Press is an imprint of
Interleaf Productions Limited
Broom Hall
Sheffield S10 2DR
England

Typeset by Interleaf Productions Limited and printed by
The Cromwell Press, Trowbridge, Wiltshire.

British Library Cataloguing in Publication Data:
A catalogue record for this book is available from the British Library

ISBN 1 874718 42 3

Chapter 1

Within the valleys of the gritstone peaks which lie on the borders of Derbyshire and Yorkshire, men lived their simple but hard lives, then passed on into obscurity. Some made their mark while others were merely players in disastrous incidents, the gravity of which the outside world had little comprehension.

Who now can say with certainty where history and fiction entwine, and at some future date when long-buried foundations are exposed, perhaps we can be forgiven if we let our romantic imagination run wild at what might have been. The wild moorlands and peaceful valleys through which we tramp hide many secrets, concealed by verdant growth, and we pause for a brief moment's reflection before passing on.

On the fertile sloping fields which lie between Storrs and Bradfield, men toiled in the heat of the August day in order to complete the work which nature had enhanced so abundantly. However, that same heat was becoming increasingly more oppressive as the afternoon wore on and first one man then another looked skyward in trepidation. One heavy cloudburst at this stage could ruin the entire crop or at least lower the value of the yield.

Edward stopped for a moment, leaned against the wheel of the last dray-load of hay and looked apprehensively towards the darkening sky. The harvest was almost gathered in but it was some distance to the farm from the field and he knew that it wouldn't be long before the impending storm broke, putting at risk all their hard work.

Wiping the sweat from his dusty brow with a rolled-up shirtsleeve, he sighed and eased his aching shoulders once again, for until this last wagon-load was safely inside the barn there was still much at stake. The air was heavy and oppressive, the clouds ominous and beads of moisture gathered on the back of his neck as he waited impatiently whilst the hired hands backed the horse into the wooden shafts of the dray.

'Make haste, lads!' he cried, urging on the tired youths. 'There's still work to do and those storm clouds are building up fast.' Edward moved forward to help secure the animal, and called out to the man who stood above him on the loaded wagon. 'Is everything secure up there, Abe?' he shouted hopefully. 'The horse is ready and we daren't delay any longer.'

Abraham Bagshaw tested the safety of the load with his hay-fork and called down reassuringly, 'Aye, everything's fine up here so let's get back and under cover before the storm breaks. I'll stay up here—you get moving as fast as you can!' With that he lay back in the hay and rested his weary limbs after the day's gruelling ordeal. He freely admitted to himself that the years were beginning to take their toll of him; he was no longer the robust figure of his youth. Staring up at the menacing sky he recalled the numerous other times when, as a child, he had travelled like this, sprawled lazily out on the sweet-smelling freshly cut hay. Now, as always, the heady fragrance invoked in him a deep sense of well being which, if it had not been for the oncoming storm, would have lulled him to sleep. Instead he lay there, simply relieved to be carried back on the dray rather than having to walk along behind it.

Soon the sky became as dark as night and Abe calculated that it would be a miracle if they reached the farm before all hell was let loose. He knew from experience almost to the second when that would be; the decreasing gap between the lightning and the thunder claps was as accurate to Abe as his favourite time-piece. Only when all the hay was secure beneath the rafters of the ancient cruck barn would he allow himself a moment of complete satisfaction. In fact he would enjoy listening to the rain as it beat savagely on the barn roof. He had a favourite perch on the upper floor where he would sit secure in the knowledge that the age-old beams, although well chewed by the worm, were still capable of withstanding the fury of the elements. There was an ageless feeling of safety as he sat there listening to the pounding, knowing that he would be quite dry. In truth he had more faith in the structure of this building than he had in the ancient farmhouse.

Excellent, he thought, the farm was in sight; they had made good time.

Edward, following beside the dray exactly as he had done for many years, was also musing on his inner thoughts, aware that it was impossible to urge the horse on any faster. In spite of the huge load the animal was pulling well but she was a timid creature and obviously disturbed by the oncoming storm. As this was the last dray-load, the older labourers from the village had left a short time before, taking with them their wages and the customary cask of ale and joint of pork, as just reward for their hard work. This age-old custom of an added reward served to ensure that the harvest was completed efficiently and in the shortest possible time. With the end of harvesting some of the men had seen the last of the present year's work. Edward knew that by now they would, to a man, be half way to oblivion and for once their drunken reverie would be accepted by their long-suffering wives as recompense for the wages safely handed over.

The dray finally trundled through the farmyard gate and had almost crossed the rutted yard to the barn when a fork of lightning illuminated the sky. Almost immediately a sharp crack of thunder rent the air and rumbled on for many seconds, terrifying the horse which reared up in panic throwing Edward aside and causing a shaft of the dray to splinter. Then, with a shrill screech, she wrenched herself free, kicking violently against anything which stood in her path and bolted across the broken paving slabs of the yard towards the open gate. Bella barked hysterically at the pandemonium, almost wrenching the chain by which she was fastened from its anchorage.

'Seize the horse before she harms herself!' Edward yelled to the nearest youth. He made to rise from the ground where he had been flung but as he did so the strain on the axle as a result of the horse's violent movements proved too much, and the front near-side wheel began to collapse, causing the dray to list alarmingly and shedding half the load of hay in a heap on the ground.

So quickly had one event followed another that Edward remained where he had been thrown, stunned with disbelief, whilst the two youths stood staring open-mouthed as though spell-bound. It was the pitiful, loud moan which brought them all to their senses. Edward suddenly realised that the noise had not come from the departing horse but from the other side of the dray.

'The Master!' he cried out in alarm, 'He must have been thrown off!' In his haste to reach Abe he almost fell over the upturned hay fork which had also fallen, and cursed out loud; then he saw his friend lying in a crumpled heap on the ground and his stillness warned Edward that there was no time to lose. Bending low over Abe's body he knew even before he touched him that he was powerless to help but whilst ever there was the slightest chance he would not give up. A thin line of blood began to trickle from Abe's ear and mouth, underlining the seriousness of his injuries.

Turning to the nearest youth, who stood as if mesmerised by it all, Edward called out sharply, 'John!' The youth recoiled, still obviously deeply shocked. 'Go and fetch Dr Stone from the village, tell him that there is no time to waste, Master Bagshaw is in a bad way. Take the short cut over the fields and run all the way—there is no time to saddle a horse, and to ride in this weather would be dangerous.' The youth sprang to life and fled obediently in the direction of Bradfield.

Edward felt guilty at the harsh tone he had used to the boy but this was not the time for self approach. Suddenly a blast of cold air heralded the arrival of the storm proper, and heavy spots of rain descended, threatening to soak them. 'Come on, Tom,' he yelled to the remaining youth, 'We've got to get the Master into the barn out of the wet! I know we shouldn't move him but the yard swims with water in a storm, we have no choice.' He tried to shield Abe from the rain with his own body but the intensity of the downpour defeated him. 'Catch hold of his feet, and for God's sake don't let go.' There were tears in Tom's eyes but Edward had no time to sympathise. 'Get a grip on yourself, lad,' he snapped, and the boy's face flushed in bewilderment.

They raised the injured man gently, and eased his limp body the dozen or so yards needed to reach the barn door. It wasn't easy, for though Abe was a lean man he hung like a dead weight, and each jerk and movement increased the possibility of causing further serious damage. 'Set him down, easy now! Then go and fetch something to cover him with.' At the softer tone in Edward's voice the youth hastened to obey, leaving the two older men alone. In the short space of time in which they had crossed the yard to shelter, the rain had become a torrent, soaking them both to the skin. Edward cradled Abe in his arms whilst gently wiping the rain from the unconscious man's face with his sleeve. He feared that Dr Stone would probably be too late to help—all Edward could do was comfort his friend as best he could.

Abe coughed. 'You'll be alright,' Edward said gently, 'John's gone for Dr Stone!' Abe coughed again, causing blood to flow freely from his mouth onto Edward's sleeve as he strove to speak.

'Hush, lie still for a while,' Edward cautioned, aware that there was little time to spare.

With one more desperate effort Abe summoned together what strength he could, opened his mouth and began to talk but it was barely a whisper, and Edward was forced to lower his head in order to catch the faltering words. 'Forgive me,' Abe rasped and his voice tapered off as he gripped Edward's hand tightly before muttering again, 'Forgive me!'

Edward stared down at the pale, stricken face, into eyes which pleaded for reassurance, but he could make no sense out of the dying man's words. 'Hush, old friend,' he admonished gently, for Abe was indeed a friend as well as his employer. 'There's nothing I know of to forgive you for. You have shown me nothing but kindness since I came here.' He thought perhaps that Abe was delirious, drifting into some twilight world that only the dying know. Suddenly he felt Abe's hand tighten, and Edward drew him closer, ignoring his ramblings but aware that his words were getting weaker. 'I forgive you all you ask', Edward whispered comfortingly and hoped this would ease his friend's mind. He was grateful when, several minutes later, Tom returned with a couple of horse blankets, and together they wrapped them gently around the old man whilst murmuring words of encouragement, in the hope that he would rally round.

As they sat, wet and uncomfortable on the hay, waiting for Dr Stone, Edward well realised that if Abe died then his own position on the farm would be in jeopardy. Abe had no relatives and would no doubt leave his possessions to the Parish for the benefit of all in the valley. Not only would he lose his dear friend and kind employer, but also his home and job. Suddenly he became aware that the figure in his arms was heavier, and lay as if resting peacefully. Sadly he had to accept that it was not sleep, but death which had claimed Abraham Bagshaw. There was no longer any need for the Doctor to brave the storm, it was too late, with a deep sense of loss, Edward laid his friend gently down on the straw and bowed his head in grief.

Chapter 2

*E*dward stood before the grey stone fireplace in Abe's sitting room as if warming himself by the heat of the friendly crackling logs, yet there was no fire in the grate today for the weather was mild and dry. He merely sought the comfort that a lighted fire would give, and felt almost like an intruder standing there, just as he had done so many times before whilst awaiting Abe's orders for the day. Here, too, in this same room of an evening he and Abe had enjoyed many a glass of wine together as they played cards, or chess, after a hard day's work. Today, however, it was not the Master who sat in the heavy leather-upholstered chair but a man of the cloth, sifting through a pile of papers which had been taken from the locked drawer of the mahogany kneehole desk.

The man looked up. 'Do sit down, Edward, instead of fidgeting!' he implored, and waited until his instructions had been obeyed before speaking again. 'I suppose', the venerable gentleman continued, 'that it was no secret to anyone that Abe was without a living relative, and so it falls to me, his old friend and confidant to sort out his affairs. Obviously he left a will which, while making many things clear, certainly complicates others, and it is one of a strange nature. I know that in these latter years Abe regretted not having had a family of his own to leave the farm to on his demise. The farm was the only love of his life and he was of the belief that you, Edward, had come to feel the same way about the land and all that belonged to it. In fact he began to look upon you as the son he never had.' The clergyman looked up, his long grey hair shining in the light from the window, he was reluctant to go on. 'Abe trusted me...', he hesitated, 'with many of his inner thoughts as well as his worries. I am no farmer and am content only in doing the Lord's work, so in the end it was natural that he would want you to take over from him.'

The implication of this brought Edward to the edge of his seat. All the anxiety he had felt during the past twenty-four hours left him drained, and he was beginning to despair as to his future. He was now overjoyed. 'Abe was a good Master and a true friend,' he said faintly, afraid to show his true feelings. 'And this is more than I deserve.' His mind was racing feverishly with excitement as he looked intently into the older man's eyes. Was the farm to be his or was he merely to manage it? This latter possibility sobered his thoughts and he waited patiently for the cleric to speak again.

'It is a just reward for the loyalty and companionship which you gave Abe,' the old gentleman continued. 'However, as I said, things are not quite as simple as they may appear, nor may they be to your liking. I was instructed to give you this letter before the will was read out after the funeral. It was written a couple of winters ago when Abe was down with congestion of the lungs.' He held out the letter, and went on. 'He had hoped that by the time of his passing it would not be necessary for you to ever see it—that your circumstances would have changed.'

Puzzled, Edward took the letter without uttering a word and could only guess at the contents as he broke open the seal and unfolded the large single sheet of paper. 'You know the intention of the contents then?' The cleric nodded soberly.

It was as much as Edward could do to keep his shaking hand still as he read the letter in silence. Once the meaning became clear a gasp of astonishment left his lips, he looked questioningly across the desk but saw only pity in the other man's eyes. Then, as if seeking confirmation of his understanding of the words, he read the letter again with greater care.

January 30th, 1862

Dear Friend,

You have served me well both as a friend and employee for the past eight years now, and as I have no living relative to whom I can leave the farm and land I am trusting you with the fruits of my labours. I know you are capable of managing the farm and of looking to the welfare of my other workers.

However, because I do not want, on your demise, for the estate to pass to your unfortunate sister and that worthless husband and family of hers, I make a condition which you will not find easy in your heart to accept.

You must marry and produce an offspring within the first two years of my death, or the farm will go into the hands of the Parish for you to manage. It is my dearest wish that you do not end up a crusty old bachelor like myself. You might decide that these conditions are unacceptable, in which case you may remain manager of the farm for as long as you are capable, but the Feoffees of the Parish will become legal owners and final arbiters in any disputes which may arise. If, at any time, you find this arrangement untenable you will at least have the cottage which is yours in perpetuity upon my death, and I have also left provision for you in your old age.

It is my greatest wish to see you settled and in possession of both farm and land. You may be angry at these conditions but I truly hope that you will come to understand the reasoning behind my thoughts.

I remain your appreciative employer and true friend.

Abraham Bagshaw.

A mixture of dismay and anger at the implications of the will showed on Edward's flushed face. He thrust the letter back angrily into the cleric's lap. 'How could he do this to me?' he exclaimed, all colour suddenly draining from his features. 'He knew that I had no desire to marry, to saddle myself with a woman—let alone a child. This is an insult—marry or the farm and all my efforts go to the Parish! What game was he thinking to play by offering me my heart's desire, to work for myself, at such a high price? Did I displease him so much that he chose to take this revenge? I never knew Abe to be a vindictive man.' There was real anger in his voice now but the older man sat unflustered by the not unexpected outburst. Edward leaned against the front edge of the desk, rigid and drained. 'How could he?' His voice shook with an emotion that took even himself by surprise. 'He must have been ill or something when he made out the will. It's like going back into the last century when some unions had to be proved fruitful before a marriage could take place!'

'Calm down, Edward!' The churchman reproved, 'I can sympathise with you. I too have never married, nor do I regret my decision, but Abe took you in when you were in need and he had no obligation to leave the farm to you. The Feoffees could make good use of the land and its produce on behalf of the poor of the Parish, but Abe wanted you to have it providing it didn't end up in the hands of your sister's family. You have to admit that you have no one else to pass it on to. Sleep on it—you have two years to comply and the idea may not be so obnoxious when you consider its many advantages.' He rose to leave, and gathered his papers. 'You're upset now, both by Abe's death and by the conditions of the will, so why not take a brisk walk to clear your head? I will talk to you again after the funeral, but remember this—no matter what you choose to do, no one except ourselves and the solicitor will know the full implications of the will. It would hardly be fair to a prospective wife if the details were known publicly. I give you my word on the confidentiality of this discussion—that was a promise I made to my friend which I will always honour.'

'There won't be any wife!' Edward shouted angrily. 'Believe me, I shall see Abe buried and leave the area for good!'

Shaking his head, the clergyman made to leave the room once more. 'Sleep on it, my friend,' he called out as he went. 'You have a golden opportunity which is given to few, and farm management work and good accommodation are hard to obtain these days.' Seeing that Edward was in no mood to discuss anything rationally he swiftly left the room, closing the door quickly behind himself to escape further unpleasantness. He lamented the situation for he admired the angry young man and had pleaded to no avail with Abe to be less adamant in his wishes.

'Damn!' Edward exclaimed angrily once the door had closed. This was a sickening blow which had shocked him badly. He strode across to the window and stared gloomily out over the fields to the rugged hills which rose clearly against the skyline. He loved everything about the valley, be it in bright green springtime or the murky dampness of December; neither season nor weather loosed their hold on his affection for the place. Today, however, in spite of the bright, warming sun, the crags seemed to glower back at him mockingly, beckoning him, offering him a challenge. He stormed from the house, slamming the door, then marched across the fields intent on reaching the high ridge and isolation.

He had always been a solitary man, seeking peace in the quiet soft meadows of the valley, or drawing strength from the wild upland moors. How could he expect to find an answer in the hills this time? This was a dilemma made by man. He walked on with such purpose in his stride that for once the profusion of colour and scent of the wildflowers in the hedgerows escaped him. Normally these would have entranced him but not today, he was beside himself with anger and bitterness. Why? He questioned again and again. Why had Abe been so inflexible in his intentions when he had himself scorned the company of women? As single men they had both been happy enough in each other's company, quietly respecting the others beliefs yet maintaining separate, private lives. Now, in death, Abe had destroyed their precious friendship. He could find no room in his heart to understand Abe's conditions in the will, or forgive him his actions. Abe had let him down. It would have been better had he just made him manager rather than tempt him so cruelly this way.

The fields were behind him now, and he crossed the winding stream to reach the foot of the slope which led to the crags above. There they stood, like sentinels, just as they had for thousands of years observing life in the valley below and yielding to no man. Nearing the top he climbed slowly, step after careful step, for he never took chances even when on the lowest part of the rocks, until, when finally he reached the summit, he saw the moorland stretching out into the distance. Turning back to face the slope up which he had just climbed he stared in sombre admiration at the beauty before him.

There was colour in every direction, from the purple of the heather on Bradfield Moor, to the orange berries of the rowan trees on the lower slopes and the verdant green of his own fields. Only one thing marred the scene, his gaze lingered on the dreadful scar made by man in his attempt to dam the tumbling waters of the local streams. During four long years the peace of the valley had been disrupted by the work of the navvies, but now the reservoir was beginning to fill, consuming the fields with its deepening waters. With Abe gone and the valley changing, the future appeared bleak and threatening. Somehow the strength which he normally drew from the view did not come, and he shivered in spite of the warm rays of the sun. It had taken the wind, rain and ice millions of years to form what lay below, yet those same elements could, as they had done to Abe, snuff the life out of a man in seconds.

Edward climbed onto a pinnacle of rock and stared again at the half-filled dam and then beyond to his own broader valley further down. He stood quietly now, pensively gazing at the farm in the distance. Every inch of the land was familiar, the dry-stone walls cherished and cared for. Where else could he find such a place as this, one where he felt at ease, and at peace with himself, bonded to the soil by toil and sweat? He breathed deeply of the musky moorland air and felt the familiar exhilaration creep over him. Over the years he had become part of the land and could no more give it up than he could life itself. To leave would cause him to weep tears of regret until the end of his days, but it was not sufficient to stay and yet know that the land was not really his, when so easily it could have been.

Every cleft and crag had their secrets which they had shared with him over the years and, if he were to leave, it would be as if he had spurned mother nature herself. He could not go! He idly plucked a tuft of soft moss and held it between his sturdy fingers, the green softness feeling like velvet. Would he be like the moss if he married, trapped in the clutches of uncertainty? His feelings were too deep to share, his freedom to walk alone too precious, all he wanted was to cherish the land and he could only do it alone. No! The responsibility and shackles of marriage were not for him.

The thought of possessing this land sent a shiver of delight coursing through his body; the realisation of all his ambitions and hopes was within his grasp and yet his head ached and reeled with the torment of the sacrifice it would demand. He was too old, at thirty, to start again from nothing or to wander without roots, besides, hadn't he earned his place in this valley? He had returned from witnessing at first hand the Crimean War, disillusioned and weak from dysentery he had been taken in by Abe who had trusted him, enabling him to grow strong again in mind and body. Perhaps if he had not been of similar character and temperament as Abe things would not have worked out as well as they did, but they had been kindred spirits. He knew that the villagers thought him to be aloof and surly, but he considered himself to be neither—withdrawn perhaps, but not unapproachable. From the farm hands he had received respect, and from the children smiles, it was the womenfolk who seemed to find him unresponsive and cool towards them. As a result he was neither liked nor disliked by the villagers but looked upon rather as a mystery, yet doing nothing to cause them to gossip. He kept himself to himself, rather as Abe had done, and they in turn had only themselves to blame if he wanted nothing to do with them, for they were a tight-knit lot, full of tittle-tattle, so that Edward preferred to do business in the town rather than mix with them. His cottage lay up the back lane away from the farm, distant enough from prying eyes and fussing women. It suited him well.

The morning breeze ruffled his thick, dark hair. Not one strand of grey was to be seen and overall he was not unattractive with his even, bronzed features, yet there was a sternness about the eyes which forbade unwanted contact. He preferred to be alone, to walk or read in quiet corners. Only Abe had penetrated his solid front, being of similar nature himself.

So! In those last moments of life Abe had begged forgiveness for something which Edward had not understood. Could it have been that on the brink of death Abe had realised the harshness of the conditions, for the fact remained that if he, Edward, wanted to hold on to both the land and farm then he would be compelled to marry.

'What do I want with a wife?' Edward cried out loud. He knew of no woman, free or otherwise, that remotely interested him nor had he any desire to court one. Where then did Abe imagine he would find one willing to be bedded like a sow? He picked up a loose stone and threw it irritably, aimlessly into the bracken; he could hardly expect to make a love match, nor did he want the emotional entanglement which such a relationship would bring. It was quite understandable that Abe wanted to prevent the property ending up in the hands of his sister's husband, although it was not her fault that things were so bad.

On returning from the Crimea, Edward had found his widowed mother dead and his only sister, a simple-minded girl, pregnant yet again by her work-shy husband living in the next valley. The family home in Hathersage had been taken over by another family and there had been nowhere for him to go. He hadn't been a soldier in the Army but had worked as a young stable hand at the Barracks until the outbreak of war and, as a consequence, found himself seconded to the Army helping to ship out horses for the campaign. At first he'd enjoyed scouring the country for horses with his Master, he'd even been excited at the prospect of sailing the oceans of the world and seeing far away places, but no one had prepared him for the terrible conditions he was to endure, or warned him that he would be as vulnerable to disease as were the soldiers. Immediately he had recovered from a debilitating bout of dysentery the Army had promptly shipped him home to Sheffield, weak and unable to work. He began making his way home via

Bradfield when he'd collapsed and Abraham Bagshaw, on hearing from his friend the cleric that there was yet another arrival to drain the Parish Coffers, offered to see the youth, as he needed more help on the farm. For some inexplicable reason he had taken to Edward, found him a room at the farm, and then eventually allowed him to take over the cottage when it became vacant. There he had remained and over the years the pair had become firm friends, sharing their innermost thoughts. Or had they? Perhaps, after all, it had not been quite as mutual a friendship as he thought.

The longer he sat on the rock staring and brooding, the deeper his anger and resentment became until, finally, defiance at his position led him to acknowledge that the only way to keep what should rightly be his was to marry! What he needed, purely and simply was a business arrangement, a respectable woman willing to bear him a child in exchange for security and a comfortable existence. He wanted no emotional ties but would insist on loyalty in every respect. To find such a woman would be no easy task, especially in an area where everyone knew everyone else's business, and to play the courting game would imply more than he was willing to concede.

It was not beyond the bounds of possibility that the parson could find him a wife from another valley, some spinster with no brighter future than to take what she could get. He shuddered, ashamed of his thoughts and rose to his feet, shook his head and started the rugged descent to the fields below, all hope having been expelled and a deep fear for the future slowly consuming him.

That night he tossed and turned, unable to sleep through striving to find another solution, including ways of manipulating Abe's will, but he could think of nothing. When morning eventually arrived he was in a foul mood and in no frame of mind to bid farewell to his dead friend. He stood solemnly and morosely by Abe's graveside, hat in hand, but it was as if a great gulf had opened up, taking with it the memories of happier times gone by. He found it hard to prevent a twinge of bitterness from entering his heart. The man they were burying had become a stranger.

Later, when alone in the farmhouse with Mr Knight of Broadbents the solicitors and the Reverend Elliott, Abe's friend, he once more questioned the validity of the will, but to no avail.

Mr Knight firmly shook his head, 'There is nothing anyone can do to change Mr Bagshaw's wishes. He explained in the letter, I believe, why he was doing as he did. He was of sound mind and at liberty to do as he pleased. The fact remains, unless you marry and produce an off-spring within two years, then the land and farm pass to the Parish. They will keep you on as manager but are not bound to forever, although they must provide for you in sickness or old age'.

Edward found it hard to contain his anger, yet managed to answer politely, but coldly, 'Oh yes! I understand only too well how the land lies, but the situation is as preposterous as it is near impossible. Where, pray, do I find a wife, one willing to marry without affection, affection I cannot give, who will produce a child at the drop of a hat?'

Mr Knight laughed caustically, 'My dear man! You don't imagine that all marriages are made in heaven, do you! Most of our gender are drawn into matrimony by some means or other and you would be surprised if you knew just how many marriage arrangements I conduct in my line of work'. His voice became earnest and confidential. 'Many a man's position in life has been enhanced by a good match, and just as many a father has found an honourable marriage for his daughter.' His voice took on a condescending tone—almost a sneer, 'Even the poor shackle themselves through the foolish act of careless pre-marital consummation'.

This statement did nothing but add to Edward's disgust but he held his own counsel, realising that nothing would be gained by alienating Mr Knight, who, sensing Edward's smouldering anger said, 'Have you thought of advertising for a wife? It is done far more often than you may realise, and not only by a mother in her own social circle by hinting or even outright bribery.' There was no mockery in the man's voice now. 'Indeed, it may be an ideal way of solving your problem! The woman answering your letter would be under no illusion and would have answered out of choice.'

Mr Knight began to gather together his belongings and picked up his hat. 'A word, Sir, before you leave!' Edward called. 'You say it is not unusual for a man to do this? How is it done without it becoming common knowledge?'

'Through the newspapers, with replies sent to a post office box number so that the letters are collected personally by you, without anyone knowing' he replied, placing his hat on his head. 'But I would not have thought a man of your age and standing would need to use such a method. Are there no unmarried females of your acquaintance who would appreciate such an offer?' He made to leave, adding 'If you need help, let me know. I shall of course keep in touch with you regarding the estate, as it does not become your property until you have fulfilled the requirements'. As Edward did not reply, Mr Knight nodded, said good-bye, and left.

'Must I resort to such methods in order to obtain the farm?' Edward begged the cleric who had remained silent throughout the encounter. 'Do you know of any suitable woman not known here in the valley whom I might approach? There is no one locally that I would wish to marry.' His voice became subdued, almost resigned to the inevitable. 'I love this farm and suppose I have no choice, life elsewhere would be no life at all.'

The older man shook his head thoughtfully. 'Perhaps Mr Knight is right but I do see the dilemma you're in, though in all honesty I could not recommend any woman to such a cold marriage. What harm can it do to advertise and see what transpires?'

Throughout the remainder of the day Edward worked on, his mind half on work and half wrestling with his emotions. He was cornered he knew, and would be damned if he would part with all he had worked for and see the fruits of his labour end up in the hands of the Church. Religion had never appealed to him, and if indeed there was a God then he felt more at home with him out in the fields and up on the crags than when seated in a cold, dank building. It looked very much as though, in order to keep the farm, he would have to sell his soul to the devil, even if Satan were in the guise of a woman, and as long as his emotions were not involved he had no choice but to try. So be it! Tomorrow he would go to town and set in motion the business of finding a wife.

However, compiling a suitable advertisement was no easy task, as he found out after supper. Nothing quite conveyed that which he intended, being either too calculating to draw response or too warm, thus offering the expectation of romance, yet he could hardly state what he really wanted from the liaison.

By midnight, his temper getting the better of him, he threw down the pen and took at random one of the drafts, put it in his pocket and retired to bed, vowing to chance his luck with it on the morrow.

The six mile journey into Sheffield went without mishap. Edward had followed the road along the higher contours of the valley side before dropping down into the more populated outskirts of the sprawling town. He was leaving behind the pleasant green fields and riverside mills, heading for the cluttered, dirty streets which wound like snakes between the rows of unhealthy houses and businesses of the area. Beyond, in the distance, a pall of smoke hung in the air and he couldn't imagine a worse place to live, apart from the battlefields—the memory of which occasionally haunted his slumbers even now. He still counted himself lucky not to have been a soldier and so allowed to return home with only memories and the odd internal discomfort to remind him of the ordeal. Many of his companions of those days had fared far worse.

Urging the chestnut mare on through the stench of industry and human habitation he was well aware how fortunate he was to live out in the valley, surrounded by wild moorlands. With no other skills but farming he would be hard pressed to find work except as a poor labourer, or possibly a clerk in the town, but he would also need accommodation. In no way could he sacrifice what he had in exchange for the shabby conditions through which he was now riding. Finally reaching the town, dusty and parched from the long journey, he refreshed himself with a quick glass of ale and a bite to eat at the *Angel Inn*, before proceeding to the newspaper office. The ale had fortified him sufficiently to summon up the courage he needed to enter the office and hand over the draft advertisement to the clerk.

The young man did no more than raise an eyebrow as he read through the draft. 'Allow a week before calling at the Post Office for any replies,' he informed Edward. 'The *Clarion* comes out on a Friday but it often takes a week before some people read it.'

'Thank you!' Edward mumbled, desperately wanting to deny the draft was for himself, but thought it wiser to depart as soon as he had paid his fee. Let the youth think what he liked, they would never meet again.

However, after Edward had left the office the youth chuckled heartily to himself. Here was an article to amuse the reader! Aloud and in a mimicking voice, he read through the advert as he passed into the inner office.

'Wanted,' he said. 'A wife by a young gentleman of good expectations. She must be graceful in her person and amiable in her manner. Property is of no object, but she must be willing to have a child and to be constantly faithful. Respectability is to be insisted upon at all times.

'The gentleman is active and reliable. To balance the innumerable good qualities that he possesses, there is only one drawback which candour obliges him to confess, that of jealousy. This strong feeling will subject the lady to a most inquisitorial scrutiny and risk of reproach if, for example, the offspring had eyes that did not in colour correspond with his own. The gentleman is willing to offer a good standard of life in exchange for an unemotional business relationship with the mother of the child.

'Any lady willing to undertake so awful a task, is requested to address a letter to Box 8, Post Office, Sheffield, to be left 'til called for, after which a meeting will be arranged.'

'Now, now, Albert!' A voice admonished from behind a large desk. 'Leave the poor fellow alone and get on with your work.'

'Go on, Mattie!' Edward urged sharply as the horse once again climbed the mud-strewn road out of the valley ten days later. Damp, clinging drizzle formed a blanket on the mare's coat and she snorted, snatching at her bit as he pushed her forward. 'Go on, gal,' he repeated in a softer tone. It was no day to be travelling really, conditions were bad and matched his mood, but he was impatient to get to town. Since there seemed no sign of an improvement in the weather it was pointless to wait any longer; besides, any further delay could spoil his chances of success.

By the time he had crossed Loxley Chase and reached the mill he was cold, damp and irritable. Steam rose from Mattie's nostrils and she backed away from the mill-owner's familiar pat.

'It's not like you, Mattie,' the man said. 'Don't you like being out in the wet, old gal?'

Edward pulled hard on the bit. 'No, Tom, she doesn't, nor do I for that matter as I'm probably going to town on a fool's errand anyway.' As Mattie had now calmed down, he slackened his hold. 'Do you need anything bringing back? I'll be here before dark.'

Tom shook his head. 'No! Thanks anyway. But it must be important for you to go to town twice in a fortnight? Still, I suppose with Abe dying like that you've got a lot to sort out. Certainly it was a bad do about Abe!' He sighed heavily and, drawing back, allowed Edward to continue his journey.

As he moved off, Edward replied, 'Yes, and I could do without all this bother,' then he spurred Mattie on. The going was easier now on the more level road and he let his eyes wander over the scene before him. He was leaving the ghostly dripping trees behind and the approaching stone houses looked so grey and dismal in the misty morning that he began to regret the decision to travel in such weather. He would be soaked through when he reached town and it was quite possible that there might be no reply to his blunt and cold advertisement when he got there. During the past ten days he had felt a twinge of shame when he recalled the offer he had made and knew that if it didn't work then he would have to make some effort to woo a woman, even if he had little enthusiasm for the task.

Dismounting before the Post Office, he tied Mattie to an iron hook then entered the building and hesitantly approached the counter. 'Have you any letter for Box 8?' he asked quietly, fearing someone would know the reason for his being there. He waited impatiently whilst the counter clerk disappeared, to return after several minutes with a solitary letter.

'I'm sorry, Sir, but there's only one for you.' He saw Edward's obvious disappointment and added, 'But we often get letters to box numbers coming in for weeks after the insertion. If you are willing to pay the postage we could send them on to you?'

Fearing that any other letters might fall into the wrong hands Edward declined, adding quickly, 'I doubt there will be any more under the circumstances, but I'll call next time I'm in town, so if you could save them for me I would be most grateful'. With that he took the solitary letter and left to seek shelter at the *Angel* again where he knew Mattie would be rubbed down and fed whilst he dried himself before a blazing fire. He pondered with nervous anticipation on the contents of the letter, perhaps realising that it would take a rather desperate individual to respond to an advertisement such as his.

On entering the hostelry he observed several drinkers seated at a table chattering amiably about the price of corn and the inclement weather. He chose to sit in a corner by the fire where he could both dry out and read the letter without being disturbed.

The letter was addressed in a neat but uncertain hand by someone obviously tutored but out of practice, a fact which gave him the confidence to open it. Had the handwriting been of a bold or sophisticated nature then he would have been more reluctant to face its contents. He read slowly, strangely affected by the honesty of the writer.

Dear Sir,

I am replying to your advertisement reluctantly, because I fear you will think me unsuitable. I am a woman of poor means due to unfortunate circumstances and recent ill health. I am honest, respectable, and clean of habit being a widow of 28 years with a small child of five years. I am desperate to escape from the terrible conditions in which I am having to rear my child and am willing to serve you faithfully in return for the opportunity to give my daughter a better life. I am capable, when well, of hard work, and am willing to repay with kindness anyone who can help us. I shall soon have no home and will be at the mercy of the Parish. Do at least consider making my acquaintance, I shall not disgrace you.

Your humble servant,
Hannah Hardy.

He was a little taken aback by the frankness of the letter, and although he felt some compassion for the unfortunate plight in which she found herself, he resolved not to suggest a meeting. Besides, he thought, she had a child already and there was just a possibility that other letters might arrive which would be more favourable. However, under the circumstances he felt compelled to acknowledge the poor woman's letter and would enclose a guinea to ease her immediate plight. She appeared to live in one of the poorest neighbourhoods of the town which was no recommendation to her cause, yet he was surprised at her ability to read and write let alone compose such a compelling letter.

Thinking no more about her, other than to post his reply, he finished some other business and returned home determined to make the most of the improving weather and take possession of the farmhouse as soon as he could.

He arrived back just as the sun broke weakly through the clouds and sat for a moment before dismounting, admiring the tranquillity of the view. Even the scent of rain-soaked foliage appeared keener than usual after the confines of the town he'd just left, and he was determined to part with none of it.

Several days elapsed before he could face sorting out the accumulation of Abe's belongings, feeling as though it was somehow an intrusion, akin to prying into the dead man's soul. For the same reason, it took even longer to move from the cottage into the farmhouse. During the daytime he had continued to work at Abe's old desk and had returned each night to the comforts of his small retreat but, realising how inconvenient and impractical this was, he finally grasped the nettle and moved in completely. This done he began exploring each room in depth, inspecting his inheritance, and was dismayed by the neglect which met his eyes. Prior to the accident there had been no reason for him to go further than the foot of the large oak staircase which rose from the centre of the spacious passageway. He had never so much as put a single step upon its treads, nor indeed ever wondered what lay in the upper storey. It seemed that any room not in regular use had been locked up and its contents forgotten, so that dust and spider's webs camouflaged the furniture stored within.

It was no easy task to clear away the neglect of years and he began by throwing open the windows to let in the clean autumn air. Clouds of dust rose as he disturbed books and old papers, causing him to cough and sneeze, and he wondered why Abe had hoarded broken furniture and other useless household items, when there had obviously been sufficient funds to repair or replace each and every article. It wasn't long before a huge pile of rubbish stood ready for burning down in the yard below, watched over almost knowingly by Bella, Abe's black sheepdog.

Occasionally, a room revealed an unexpected item, usually of little value, but there was one exception. In the corner of the smallest of the three bedrooms stood an unusual cabinet which when opened revealed several miniature rooms filled with furniture. It was of no use to him but he was intrigued as to whom it had belonged, for Abe had no relatives. He was surprised too at the quality of the cabinet in which the exquisite miniature furniture lay. He imagined it to be quite old and, on blowing the dust gently from several items, came to the conclusion that no child with clumsy fingers had disturbed these for years. There was little sign of decay or discoloration in the little covers and curtains, and he put this down to the good fit of the doors and windows which had provided such excellent protection. One day when time permitted he would inspect the house and its contents more thoroughly before deciding what should be done with it. In the meantime there were more pressing things to occupy his time so he re-locked the room and promptly forgot about it.

When, a week later, he returned to the town's post office he was disappointed to find that the only letter awaiting him had been written in the same hand as before. It felt quite heavy and he was puzzled on opening it to find that it contained just the guinea and a curt note. With some surprise he read:

Dear Sir,

*Thank you kindly for the guinea which I return. I am willing
enough to work for my upkeep but I cannot accept money given
out of pity by a stranger.*

Mrs Hardy.

Ungrateful woman, he thought, hardly able to believe his eyes. 'Are there
no more letters?' he demanded of the counter clerk.

'Fraid not, Sir!' replied the man, who was quite used to disgruntled
customers.

Edward was undecided over what he should do next. Mrs Hardy had been
his only correspondent and it seemed that so far his efforts to find a wife had
been a waste of time. Should he re-consider Mrs Hardy, notwithstanding her
abrupt response? She did at least appear to be honest with some sense of
pride, even if it was misplaced for someone in her predicament. He, too, had
his pride but the situation was becoming tiresome, and if he was to fulfil
Abe's demand then he could delay things no longer.

He had Mrs Hardy's previous letter in his pocket and decided in
desperation to take a detour on his homeward journey, in order to see just
how bad the conditions were at the address she had given.

Lipton Street proved to be much worse than expected, with numerous
shabby tenement houses, or rather hovels, forming courtyards off the main
street. These were enclaves of miserable, dingy properties fit only for
demolition. His mind recoiled in dismay and he had no desire to meet any
of the inhabitants. No wonder the woman wanted to get away and he could
well understand the desperation in her reply, yet how could she have
expected a gentleman, on seeing such poverty, to take her as his wife?

The house where she lived seemed no different from the others in the
same court, its windows were just as gloomy and the door bare of paint, in
fact it might have never seen paint at all. He shook his head sadly and
gathering the reins to turn the mare's head to leave, he became aware that
he too was being observed. A couple of barefooted urchins had edged closer
in order to admire Mattie, he noticed also, several faces peering through
shabby net curtains around the courtyard.

'Cor, ain't it a big 'un, Mister. Will it kick?' the eldest boy questioned in
a rough voice, as the smaller boy stared wide-eyed from a safe distance.

Smiling, Edward bent down from the saddle and beckoned the owner of
the voice to come closer. 'Do you live here in the court?' he asked.

The lad grinned back, 'Yes, Mister! We both live 'ere'. By now several
more children, equally ill-clad, gathered round, but kept at a distance from
Mattie's nervous pawing.

'Who lives over there at number five, do you know?' Edward asked casually, probing for information.

'Lizzie Hardy and her stuck-up Ma!' came the quick reply. 'She don't let Lizzie play out, an' my Ma ses she's nuthin' to be proud on 'cept she talks with 'er mouth full o' marbles.' The urchin squinted across towards number five, put his hands to his ears, wiggled them like antlers, then stuck his tongue out.

Edward had more sense than to rebuke the lad but he could well imagine why any self-respecting mother would keep her child indoors, away from such riff-raff. A tiny face at the window drew back quickly as though pulled by some mysterious hand, presumably Mrs Hardy's, leaving him with only a vague memory of what he had seen. He reached into his pocket, drew out two half-pennies, bent down and held them out to the eldest boy. 'Here! Take these to the shop and buy something to share.' Beneath the grimy face and hard eyes he saw a glimmer of childish joy, but this was quickly replaced by one of greed.

'Ooh! Ta Mister.' The lad cried, and snatched the coins in case the offer was withdrawn. With that the little group disappeared as quickly as it had come, leaving Edward alone in the yard. He knew, however, that he was being carefully watched by more than one pair of curious eyes from behind the glass of the grimy windows.

Knowing he was thus observed, and feeling rather foolish sitting there, he acted on impulse and dismounted, leading Mattie up to the door of Mrs Hardy's house, where he tapped lightly with his crop on the weathered woodwork. The catch rattled and the door was opened only a few inches by a woman with a pale, drawn face and wide troubled eyes.

'Yes? What is it?' the woman asked hesitantly, then she dropped her voice to a whisper that he could hardly hear and pleaded, 'Please, if you are the bailiff don't let anyone in the yard know why you are here'.

'No, I'm not the bailiff,' Edward answered reassuringly. 'My name is Edward Morton and I'm here in regard to the matter of your letter to me, and my guinea.' The woman's eyes were vacant for a moment, then her pale face flushed with embarrassment and she lowered her eyes. At that moment the gap in the door suddenly widened and he found himself looking down onto the tousled head of a small girl. 'I mean you no harm!' he added quickly, and was rewarded by a shy smile on the face of the child as she looked up at him. It was the face which had been at the window a few moments earlier and he could see from closer inspection that the eyes were candid and clear. She clung to Mrs Hardy's skirts seemingly out of habit, not fear.

Edward smiled in response and then returned his attention to Mrs Hardy. He could not fail to note that, in spite of the shabby and ill-fitting garments on her thin body, she was at least clean, and it was obvious that, although well worn, the clothes had originally been of good quality and style. However, it was not easy to define her character, her pale face showed obvious signs of recent illness but she was not coarse-featured as he had expected, just sallow, drawn and without spirit. If she had been beautiful at some time this fact was now well concealed. Her tired eyes watched him anxiously.

'May I come in, Mrs Hardy?' he asked in a low voice. 'To explain why I am here.' She nodded and glanced quickly at the other houses seemingly fearing the neighbours more than the thought of letting a complete stranger into her home.

Edward tethered Mattie to an iron fitting on one of the window shutters and went inside. Although the kitchen was sparsely furnished, the whitewashed walls were clean and the room tidy, and she had at least made some effort to make it habitable. However, nothing could disguise the dank smell or the evidence of green mould on the outer wall where water obviously seeped in.

It was plain to see that they were mother and daughter; the child stood quietly clinging to the skirt, as before, and looked at him with frank curiosity. He had difficulty in drawing his eyes away from the thin but pretty little face and thought how much healthier the child would look with the bloom of country-fresh air on her cheeks and a good meal or two to fill out her thin frame.

Mrs Hardy waited quietly, more than a little embarrassed by his silence. Only stubborn pride had made her return his guinea, that and the fear of not knowing quite where it would lead. She had been driven by desperation into writing to Mr Morton in the first place and it was only after she had returned his guinea and Lizzie had complained of hunger, that she regretted her impulsive gesture.

He was watching her now and she felt ashamed of her shabbiness. 'I apologise for my rudeness in sending the guinea back when you were being so kind,' she said meekly, wishing that he would leave but sensing that he expected an explanation. 'It was most ungrateful of me!'

Yes, Edward thought, it was rather foolish when she looked half-starved, and the bailiffs were breathing down her neck. He tried again to reassure her. 'It's nothing. I came here to apologise for seeming to insult you, that is all.' It wasn't strictly true but he could hardly tell her that the real reason for his visit was curiosity.

She turned away to hide the confusion which she felt and drew the child closer. 'Whatever must you think of me for writing to you in the first place?' she said quietly. 'At the time I was beside myself with worry and I came across an old newspaper at the house where I do a little washing once a month. I get little chance to read these days, but in doing so happened to see your advertisement.' She was discomforted at this admission and was glad that he could not see her face, which had flushed deeply. 'I don't know why I'm telling you all this—or why you came when it was obvious from my letter that I was unsuitable for…' She hesitated and stopped, glanced at the child and checked her words. She looked up at him suddenly, her face set and the tone in her voice defensive. 'That you felt pity for me I can understand but if you came here merely to humiliate me further then I wish you would leave!'

He was a little surprised by her tone and suspected that, in different circumstances, Mrs Hardy could have a spirit to be reckoned with. It saddened him that circumstances had brought the woman to her present plight. Deciding that it probably would be best if he left, he smiled at the child, took the guinea from his pocket and held it out to Mrs Hardy. 'Please, I want you to take this for the child's sake more than your own. It will buy food for her and help towards the rent.' Sensing that she was about to protest he felt a little annoyed by her foolishness and thought it best to go immediately. Bowing slightly, he wished her good day and turned towards the door. At this the child let go of her mother's skirt and pointed to the window.

'Can I see it?' Lizzie begged, running to the door.

Mrs Hardy forgot herself at the child's outburst and explained, 'It's the horse! She heard you enter the yard but I drew her away from the window when those dreadful children appeared'.

Lizzie became excited and seized Edward's hand. 'Please let me see your horse', she cried.

'There's no reason why she should not, is there, Mrs Hardy?' he asked. 'The other children have gone now.' Seeing the hesitation on her face, he took the opportunity and made for the door before the frown turned into a refusal.

The trusting little hand in his softened the annoyance which he felt at Mrs Hardy's apparent reluctance, and he lifted Lizzie gently up onto the saddle and explained, 'The horse is a girl, and her name is Mattie. Now, what shall I tell her your name is?' His voice was gentle but serious.

'I am Lizzie Hardy,' the child said proudly, holding her head up high. 'What is your name?'

Although surprised by her adult manner he chuckled to himself and replied in similar fashion, 'Edward Morton, but I think you had better call me Mr Edward, don't you?' For several minutes he allowed the excited Lizzie to sit astride the mare, then, lifting her down, he returned her to her mother who had been watching with a pensive look on her face. A look which turned to relief as he mounted Mattie himself and bade them both farewell.

On the long journey back to the farm he tried to banish from his mind the memory of the child's face, particularly the contrast of when first he saw her at the window on his arrival, to that later when it was lit with excitement as she sat in the saddle. No child should have to exist in such conditions, he reflected. His own problems, however, were no nearer to being solved than when they had arisen several weeks earlier, and it was with a feeling of some despondency that he finally returned to the large empty farmhouse.

During the few days following his trip to town he found it difficult to keep his mind on his work; the harvesting was over and even next year's planting had been done, but now he awaited winter with some trepidation. In plain truth he missed Abe more than he cared to admit and for once began to dread the long drawn-out winter evenings alone. He had considered, again with cold calculation, every unattached female in the district but knew that it would be impossible for him to woo any one of them with conviction. It was a damnable business which was beginning to worry him more and more as time went by; it was also becoming more distasteful as he considered the deeper implications involved.

November came and went and with it the work outside lessened appreciably; only the animals demanded his attention, leaving him with time to spare—and time to think. In any unoccupied daylight hours, Edward walked briskly in all weathers up in the hills checking the sheep, but he had no appetite for the quiet evenings alone.

One night, sitting in the gentle light of the fire, his meal dispensed with, he gazed around reflecting on the past. Perhaps over the last eight years he had become selfish and a little complacent, needing no other company but Abe's. The events which had now overtaken them both, left him to reap the harvest of loneliness which he himself had planted, but he knew also he was not endowed with the physical desire, as most men seemed to be, for marriage. Above all he jealously guarded his freedom to do exactly what he wanted at all times. It had been easy to do that in the confines of his small cottage, but here in the rambling rooms of the farmhouse he was strangely disturbed. Taking a book from the cabinet he tried to immerse himself in its contents but his mind wandered constantly, seeking a solution to his melancholy.

He had hoped that by moving to the house he would be able to manage the affairs of the farm better, but the experience was an uncanny one, and somewhere in the process he had lost his sense of direction and purpose. The foreman had preferred to remain in the village in his own large cottage, than move nearer the farm, so that Edward's old home now stood empty and forlorn. It was bad management not to rent the place out and, by letting it stand vacant, it would certainly deteriorate through the harsh winter to come. Perhaps he was too fussy in his choice of neighbours but he had no desire to house any other of the local inhabitants in such close proximity to himself. Another change had also disturbed him; he now needed a housekeeper as well as a wife, for old Annie had given up and retired soon after the shock of Abe's death. The job had been too much for her anyway as was obvious from the state of the house, and it was, he realised, too big for him if he intended to preserve any sense of order in his life.

Once or twice the idea occurred to him to offer the cottage to Mrs Hardy and Lizzie in exchange for some domestic work in the house. However, at the back of his mind he still retained the idea of finding and installing a wife there, rather than have her under his own roof. He had considered every option and concluded that as Mrs Hardy could never be anything more to him than a housekeeper he could not offer them a home. That Lizzie was delightful and Mrs Hardy was probably still capable of producing another child, did nothing to soften his resolve, for the mother was painfully thin, sickly and very proud. She also seemed to have a disturbing streak of stubbornness which, combined with foolish pride, were the two things he disliked most in women.

In the days which followed, however, his mind repeatedly contemplated the shabbiness of their existence, and the grave little face which had watched at the window began to haunt him, making him wonder how they had both fared since his departure. If Mrs Hardy's health had deteriorated further, or worse, then it would be a disaster for the child. These thoughts continued to occupy him more and more as he sat through the long, drab, winter evenings until, in the end, to ease his conscience, he felt compelled to find out how they were. It really was no responsibility of his but somehow they had become just that! Perhaps after all, if Mrs Hardy was willing to take his name and give him a child then the cottage could be hers for life? He could make her an allowance and, in exchange for a little housekeeping at the farm, could educate Lizzie and provide for her future. The thought of having Lizzie's face greet him from the cottage door began to please him.

With a sudden determination, he poked the burning logs and as the embers rekindled, so his spirits rose. Perhaps after all he had finally found an acceptable solution to his problems, and one by which neither he nor Mrs Hardy could lose. Yes, he thought, tomorrow he would send old Jack to Sheffield with an invitation for her and the child to come out to see the farm and the cottage before he made his offer.

Rising eagerly next morning he wrote a brief invitation to Mrs Hardy, then despatched Jack Gray with the horse and trap into the town, and immediately set about tidying up the cottage. Mrs Hardy would no doubt find it a palace compared to the damp hovel in which she now lived but he did not intend leaving things to chance. A fire was lit in every room, food placed in the larder, and freshly washed linen adorned the bed.

For once Edward had slept well and then risen optimistically but, as the day wore on and there was no sign of Jack returning, he began to wonder at the wisdom of his idea. However, it was too late to change his mind now. By mid afternoon the trap had still not appeared and he became agitated. Had they moved away? This possibility hadn't even entered his head, but surely if Jack had been unable to find them he would have returned immediately? Had something untoward happened to Jack on his outward journey, or to the three of them as they returned? He continued to pace up and down the flagstoned floor of the kitchen, unable to concentrate on anything other than the whereabouts of the trap and everyone in it.

He need not have worried, however, for on learning that Mrs Hardy was in the habit of staying out on Fridays until afternoon, Jack had waited for her return. He took the rare opportunity to visit a friend nearby before taking up watch outside the court in Lipton Street. Eventually the pair returned, Mrs Hardy was astonished when Jack approached as she made to enter the house and handed her the note from Edward Morton. She read it with trembling hands, amazed at the content, her first instinct was to refuse point blank to even consider the invitation.

Jack was a little puzzled by the woman's strange reaction to the letter but, having no idea of its content, remained standing politely awaiting a reply. Edward had instructed him to be prepared to bring the pair back to the farm and so he was unsure what to do next. He was also worried about the horse and trap left outside the court and excused himself for a moment to check that everything was alright.

At that, Hannah Hardy entered the house and calmed down. The letter, although unusual, seemed friendly enough, and what she had observed in both Mr Morton and the man who was obviously his employee seemed to offer no threat to her. She pondered on the bleak prospects before her and Lizzie, acknowledging that the guinea he'd kindly given had enabled them to survive this long and, seeing only hardship ahead, decided to take advantage of the situation.

When Jack returned she asked him to wait, quickly gathered a few personal belongings, tidied herself and Lizzie up, and then climbed into the trap conscious that they were being watched by many pairs of eyes behind panes of glass. The party finally arrived at the farm just before dusk.

Edward was at that precise moment about to saddle Mattie with the intention of riding into town in search of Jack. Instead, he greeted the party more warmly than intended out of sheer relief at their safety. 'Thank you for coming, Mrs Hardy,' he said, approaching the trap. 'You must be weary after the long journey?' The chill in the air had left her face pinched and drawn, suggesting that she might have been ill since their last meeting. 'There is a warm fire in the grate and food in the larder,' he announced, holding out a hand to assist her as she attempted to straighten her stiffened limbs in order to climb down.

Mrs Hardy smiled weakly but said nothing as she waited for Edward to lift Lizzie down first. 'Hello, young lady, do you remember me?' he asked in a friendly manner. He was more at home with children than with women and sought to draw the child out. 'Did the pony behave himself, or did Jack have to shout at him?' He turned to help Hannah down whilst awaiting Lizzie's reply.

Lizzie nodded, and looked around her, asking 'Where is the bigger horse—can I see her?'

Edward smiled. 'You shall tomorrow, but now we must get you inside where it is warm. Come!' He did not miss the look of amazement on her face as she glanced about, her eyes missing nothing as she stood by her mother's side. 'If you will do me the kindness of following me, Mrs Hardy, you will find the cottage in which you are to stay is warm and comfortable. I have also provided refreshments which I am sure you must need after your tedious journey, and I am grateful that you agreed to come. I will of course explain everything fully when you have made yourself comfortable.'

Mrs Hardy spoke for the first time since her arrival and was a little hesitant. 'I was out when Mr Gray arrived, and was unsure whether to come or not once I had read your letter; it was also getting late in the day but he assured me that I would be quite safe with him.' She paused as if considering her next words carefully. 'I had not expected to hear from you again under the circumstances and I apologise if I seemed rude and ungrateful at our last meeting.' She had lowered her voice, but spoke sincerely. There was at least some evidence of common sense in her of which Edward approved, and he had to admit that she was neither coarse nor common in her demeanour.

They had crossed the broken surface of the yard and were entering the lane which led up to the cottage when Lizzie stopped suddenly, drawing her mother back by the hand. Her eyes were wide with amazement as she looked at the old holly tree with its clusters of bright red berries. Edward had observed the old tree every year at this time and thought it just another rich part of winter, accepting its appearance without question. To the child, however, who had never seen the scarlet berry clusters amid shiny green pointed leaves it was an enchanting sight. 'Ooh!' Lizzie exclaimed in wonderment, 'What is it?'

Reaching out, he broke a small branch off and held it so that she could see it more closely without being hurt by the tiny spikes of the leaves. 'It's a holly tree and the beautiful red berries are food for the birds, but the leaves have very sharp points which will hurt you. See here!' He deliberately pressed his thumb against a point and showed her the blood which rose like a bubble on his skin. 'Beautiful to look at but that is all. The berries are poisonous if we eat them.' He did not throw the twig away but placed it in the crack of the wall. 'Soon it will lose its beauty, wither and die because it has left the tree!' he explained, kindly.

'Is that why Mrs Green died?' The simple question made him stop.

'Did Mrs Green die?' he asked gravely, half humouring her, half sympathising.

The child nodded. 'Yes, Sir. And now we can't live with her any more.'

'Hush, Lizzie!' Mrs Hardy cautioned gently. 'Don't start all that again. Mr Morton doesn't want to hear, either.' Then, sensing his curiosity she added, 'Lizzie misses Mrs Green. We lived with her and I looked after her until she died, but when that happened, eight months ago, it left us without a home and hardly anything to live on. I became ill also, and couldn't work. I sold everything of value that I had and eventually was forced to take the house in Lipton Street, as no one wanted a woman with a child in tow.' She stopped suddenly and he suspected that she did not wish to continue the conversation. 'But you don't want to know about our troubles, Mr Morton.'

'That is for you to decide,' Edward stated. By now they had reached the cottage and Mrs Hardy said no more. 'Please, go in and find a seat while I light the lamps.' Edward took a taper from a pot and lighting it from the glowing fire, attended to the two lamps which hung from the smoke-stained oak beams of the room. A kettle, which had simmered on the hob all afternoon, was gently steaming and he lifted it and poured the contents into the teapot. 'Make yourself comfortable,' he urged. 'I will fetch the refreshments from the kitchen.' He lit a smaller lantern and carried it into the room at the back of the cottage, leaving Hannah Hardy to gaze appreciatively round the neat, cosy living-room. Lizzie climbed into Edward's chair and within minutes was soundly asleep.

'Let her be,' he said on his return as Mrs Hardy rose to wake her. 'It will be easier for me to explain my offer if she is asleep.'

Taking a cup from him, Hannah's hand shook a little. 'The note was very brief and I was wondering, under the circumstances of our last meeting, why you had sent for me? You said that it would be to our mutual advantage if I came. It really was only at the reassurance of your man that we did so.' She deliberately met his eyes now, and waited. He suspected that she did not entirely trust his motives for inviting her here. 'Where will Lizzie and I sleep?' she asked bluntly.

Sensing her fears he hastened to explain. 'Don't worry, I shall sleep down in the farmhouse, where I live. You will have the cottage to yourself.' She nodded, gratefully. So, he had anticipated her fears correctly and now wondered if it would be better to delay the full explanation until morning.

Seeing her there in the flesh was a different matter to making cold plans in her absence. With Lizzie asleep in his chair and Mrs Hardy on the sofa he found himself with little choice but to stand leaning against the mantel shelf of the chimney, looking directly down on his guest. Her face seemed not as ravaged by sickness as it had appeared in the cold air outside, the soft light of the lamp and fire had smoothed out the effects of her recent illness, but she was painfully thin. He wondered whether he might, after all, have chosen her for a wife under different circumstances. 'I think it would be kinder of me to leave you alone for a while to recover from the journey and to feed the child,' he suggested. 'I have some duties about the farm to attend to and will call back later. Shall we say about eight o'clock?' He indicated the clock behind her. 'Take a look around and amuse yourself as you will. No one will harm you here.'

'No, I don't believe they will,' she replied, accepting with a slight smile, 'and I would appreciate a little time to wash and relax.' With that Edward nodded and left taking one of the lamps with him.

Once alone, Hannah Hardy's curiosity took hold of her and, after ensuring that Lizzie was safely tucked up asleep in Edward's chair, she took down the remaining lamp and left the room to see for herself what, if anything, would give a clue to the mystery of Edward's sudden invitation. It was strange that a dwelling such as this should be without a tenant, yet it did not look uninhabited.

The cottage was surprisingly larger than it appeared from the outside, but then it had been dusk and the area unfamiliar. Climbing a flight of narrow stone stairs which led directly up from the kitchen she found herself on a small landing with a door on each side. Pushing open the door nearest to her, she was surprised to see what appeared to be a neatly stacked mixture of unwanted furniture lining the walls, leaving the centre of the room completely clear. In spite of the obvious lack of use the room, and its contents, smelled quite fresh, due no doubt to the cold evening breeze filtering through the partially opened window. She promptly closed this and left the room.

The door to the other room creaked as it gave way to her touch, making her feel almost an intruder as she entered. A large oak bed dominated the room, whilst the deeply recessed window would, she supposed, give a view of the farm and the hills beyond. She walked to the window and endeavoured to see what lay beyond the glass, but drew back quickly snatching the shutters to, lest she be seen peering out by some passing stranger. She turned back and viewed the room once more noting the tall five-drawer bowed chest, on which Edward had left several items which she might find useful. The room was warm from the fire which he had thoughtfully lit earlier in the day but still she shivered. She had no cause to, unless it was the sight of the great bed with its neatly quilted cover, for the room seemed devoid of fripperies and was more than likely a man's bedroom. Why then had he invited her here and why had such a comely man need to advertise for a wife? She found it hard to imagine herself sharing the bed with the man who, she suspected, did not find her in the least attractive.

Drawing the shawl closer about her bony frame for comfort, she turned and in doing so caught sight of herself in the mirror of a large wardrobe. She went towards it. Within the shadows cast by the lamplight she saw her own reflection for the first time in months. In spite of the soft light, which only partially illuminated her features, she was shocked at the image which stared back at her. She was a shadow of her former self. Recent events had wreaked havoc with her skin, taken the lustre from her hair, and her eyes seemed those of a stranger. She had been too despondent lately to do more than glance in the discoloured old hand mirror back home, and she sank down onto the bed in some despair.

There was no future for her looking as she did now, other than that of drudgery and squalor, nor for that matter were the prospects enhanced whilst she and Lizzie resided in Lipton Street. There were thousands of women in her situation, alone and with a child to rear, so what chance did she have amongst so many? The bloom of youth was gone and it seemed that the only prospect of improvement was to marry some unfortunate widower on the look out for a mother for his large brood of pitiful children. She had made her mistakes in the past, for which she had paid dearly, but for Lizzie's sake she must take an opportunity when it arose.

Lying back on the bed, her eyes staring fixedly up at the ceiling, she was both angry and resentful at her predicament and wondered why Edward Morton had sent for her. A small cry from below brought her back to the present. It was Lizzie, who, waking in the dark with only the firelight for comfort, had become afraid of the unfamiliar surroundings.

'I'm coming!' Hannah cried loudly, her voice penetrating the gaps in the floorboards of the bedroom. She hurried down the steep winding stairs, clutching the lamp tightly for fear that she would trip and let it fall, then she was clasping Lizzie fiercely in her arms, comforting her.

By the time Edward returned, Lizzie had been fed and was tucked up cosily in the large bed upstairs. Mrs Hardy appeared refreshed and more confident.

It was she who spoke first this time. 'I really must thank you for the trouble you have taken, in lighting the fires and leaving such welcome provisions for us. It is some time since either of us have eaten so well.'

'My pleasure!' Edward replied, following her to the sitting room. 'It was simple enough fare, but the simnel cake I had brought up from the village, I thought Lizzie might like it.'

She smiled, 'I'm afraid Lizzie would have eaten it all if I hadn't stopped her. Won't you sit down?' she asked, wondering why he remained in the doorway looking slightly apprehensive.

'Thank you!' He lowered himself into the chair which Lizzie had previously occupied, and stared nervously down at his boots, aware that unless he explained why he had sent for her there was very little else to talk about. He couldn't hedge around the subject indefinitely, and as they knew so little about each other it was up to him to do some explaining. He cleared his throat and considered it best to come to the point. 'You are waiting to hear just why I asked you to come, is that not so?'

Blushing slightly Mrs Hardy replied, 'Not wanting to be unkind I cannot help but think that it is either out of pity, or that you have not yet found a wife?' She had not intended to speak out so frankly or so intimately.

'You are most direct Mrs Hardy, but I don't mind, for now I feel that I can be honest with you in turn without offending you! You must have wondered what possessed me to place an advertisement in the newspaper for a wife in the first place?' It was a statement more than a question, and he watched the colour deepen on her face. 'I will be quite open about it, if you will continue to be so with me. I really have no desire to take a wife but I find myself in a predicament beyond my control, as, so it appears, do you.' She was sitting upright on the edge of her chair now, alert but uncertain what to think or how to react. He blundered on. 'My good friend who owned this farm and land died a short while ago and, as he had no relations, he left the farm to me. I have worked here for years and knew that he favoured me. However, he made a condition in his will which makes things very difficult for me. He stipulated that I should marry and produce an off-spring within two years of his death or the farm would go to the Parish. I may of course work here but will virtually be employed by, and be at the mercy of, the Parish Guardians.' There was a startled look on Mrs Hardy's face. 'Yes! It seems ludicrous but there is no way round it; he did not want my family to inherit unless it was through my direct line. I love this land, Mrs Hardy, and have worked to make it what it is. I can't bear to lose it and don't want to work for someone else.' The flush on her face had gone, to be replaced with a pallor as pale as linen. 'It was just as much a shock and nightmare to me as it must be for you to hear it, and realise that a man could so bind a friend like this. I never intended to marry but this farm is my life and I cannot give it up. Nor could I work here if it were not mine. To be completely frank—I need to produce an heir!' He felt ashamed, and was grateful the light did not shine fully on his face. 'Does that sound wicked, Mrs Hardy?' She made no sound but sat motionless, powerless to utter a word.

He felt drained, almost a stranger to himself as he waited for her reply which did not come. Had he made a fool of himself, he wondered? What did it matter now though, he might as well continue. Averting his eyes from her, he spoke unemotionally, but firmly. 'What I am actually describing is a business deal wherein I offer you the position of becoming my wife in order to bear a single child, and in exchange for this I offer a comfortable home and security for you and Lizzie for the rest of your lives.' His head was beginning to throb as she stood there tense and nervous. 'Yours was the only reply!' he added lamely. Why did the woman say nothing? Turning slightly he glanced in her direction, ashamed of himself and cursing Abe for putting him in this position in the first place. He could stand the silence no longer and, taking it to indicate a rejection, found himself muttering, 'I have been honest with you. I could no more court a woman falsely than I would burn this farm or leave the valley. Lizzie can grow up here in the fresh air and beautiful surroundings without any cares or deprivations such as you are experiencing in Lipton Street. I would respect your right to live your own life providing you did nothing that would bring scandal and disgrace to the farm and our name, and you could live alone and undisturbed in this cottage.'

Throughout Edward Morton's speech Hannah Hardy sat as if in a dream, not knowing whether to despise this confusing, calculating man before her or pity him his predicament. What could she say when all power to think straight eluded her?

As if her continuing silence spoke for her, he felt obliged to bring the meeting to a conclusion and apologised. 'I fear I have shocked you, this proposition must appear outrageous and an abomination. However, I assure you I wish you no harm, tomorrow you will be free to go—please try not to think too harshly of me!' There was emotion in his voice and he raised his head proudly, striving to maintain his self-esteem. 'Take pleasure in your visit—Jack Gray will be available to return you to your home whenever you wish to leave. I bid you goodnight, Mrs Hardy.' With that Edward left and disappeared into the night, relieved to be in the still darkness and hoping that he would meet no one to whom he would be required to speak. Only Bella the sheepdog sensed him and barked excitedly as he crossed the cobbled farmyard.

For an hour Hannah sat without moving. From the moment when she had returned home to find Jack Gray waiting in the trap with the strange invitation, she had been in a daze. She gathered up Lizzie and a few belongings before climbing up onto the cart, but only after they had been travelling for half an hour or so did she really start to question the wisdom of what she had done. The constant fight against hunger and her permanent state of destitution had destroyed her resilience, and she had seized the opportunity to break the monotony of her existence.

Jack Gray's commendations of Edward Morton had banished all deep fears on the cold journey from the town, and the warm welcome she had received had given her reason for optimism. Now it was hard to believe that the man who had been so kind to Lizzie could consider marriage on such cold and calculating terms. He had never once considered her feelings, except inasmuch as she should not think ill of him, but she knew little enough about him anyway to think otherwise.

The fire was getting low in the grate when finally she left the chair and climbed the stairs to the room in which Lizzie slept, innocently unaware of the turmoil in Hannah's mind. For hours it seemed, she lay beneath the soft warm quilt, her child cradled in her arms, recalling over and over again all that Edward Morton had said. Could he be trusted to want nothing more than a child from her and to give her his name? If so, would she be foolish enough to refuse and thus deprive herself of a decent way of life, and a full belly of food for her child? She was ashamed of herself for even considering his offer, yet her future was extremely bleak, and over the last week things had been so bad that she had begun to fear for her sanity. Who would blame her if she accepted this strange offer? Certainly no woman in similar circumstances would turn it down, and she was sure Mr Morton was hardly likely to voice abroad the circumstances of such a marriage.

Secure in the warm, comfortable bed and surrounded by commodious clean furniture, she recoiled at the thought of returning to the damp, dilapidated house in which they had been forced to live. If nothing else she would savour this night and face the future when she woke; until then she would allow herself to dream.

When morning came it brought with it the brightness of the sun, and Hannah Hardy opened her eyes reluctantly, afraid to face the decision which she knew she must make. Turning, she saw that the light which filtered through the ill-fitting shutters was falling on the face of the child who slept peacefully by her side. She was loath to break the spell by rising, although she suspected from the height of the sun that she had slept far longer than normal. Without waking Lizzie, for there was much she needed to contemplate alone, she climbed down from the bed and gently covered the child's face to shield her from the bright sunlight. On opening the shutters, it was obvious why she had been disturbed, for there beneath the window being led along the lane back to their pasture, ambled a long line of cows. They disappeared slowly from sight, leaving a trail of churned mud and dung in their wake, and Hannah wished that Lizzie had been awake to see such a sight.

Once the cows had gone she studied the peaceful scene before her with delight, and quietly opened the window to allow the fresh morning air to enter the room. The air, however, was sharp with frost, and Hannah quickly refastened the window to prevent the room losing what heat remained from the dying embers of the fire. It was too late to rekindle it now, and too late to return to bed, so there was nothing for it but to dress and face the future positively. She sighed, reluctant to leave this strange room which offered such shelter from her worldly cares.

At last! Edward saw that finally the shutters at the cottage windows were pulled back. It was ten o'clock and his nervous surveillance of the cottage was at an end, bringing forward the moment when he must face Mrs Hardy, not a task he relished. The memory of the previous evening's disclosure haunted him. He had sounded callous and uncaring for anything but his own problems, yet on the other hand he had been frank, surely she could see that it was a problem not of his own making, or choosing? It was too late now to draw back, however, and he must endure any contempt which Mrs Hardy might feel for him. He would be patient for a further half hour before calling upon her, by which time she should be dressed and anticipating his call.

As a consequence of his disclosures to her he was convinced the woman would be unlikely to want to take up residence in the cottage, so he intended making one final offer which she might just find acceptable. He was sorely in need of a housekeeper and was willing to offer her this post, the cottage and a small allowance for her services with no strings attached. If she accepted this, after three months she could reconsider his offer of marriage and his own future would be settled. On the other hand, he could hardly turn her out with nowhere to go when the time came, but it was a chance he was willing to take. He was filled both with remorse and sorrow at the hardness of his contemplations, and cursed Abe again for creating the situation in the first place.

He waited the full half hour and then, taking hold of a wooden pail, he headed along the lane towards the cottage where, to his relief, he saw Mrs Hardy appear momentarily in the doorway. Was she awaiting his arrival with equal trepidation he wondered?

On reaching the gate he went first to the well at the back of the cottage for he expected Mrs Hardy would by now be in need of fresh water. The well was overgrown as he hadn't used it for some time and, in brushing aside the dead bracken, he realised that he would have to clear the entrance to the well thoroughly making it safe for her to use. This was just one more task which required attention before spring arrived. He found the steps down to the water slippery with moss and almost lost his footing, but the icy water into which he dipped the pail was crystal clear and free from debris. Mrs Hardy's arms were not as strong as his and she would have great difficulty in lifting out a pail once it was full of water, perhaps, he thought, he should provide some inside storage facility. The farmhouse had a separate supply from a spring which had been culverted to fall into a trough by its back door, but that was too far away to be of use to her.

Lizzie must have seen him from the upstairs window, for by the time he reached the front of the cottage she was there to greet him with a cheery smile on her face.

'Fetch your mother Lizzie,' he said, smiling back and placing the pail down on the doorstep. 'Tell her I've brought some fresh water.' The child obeyed willingly and almost bumped into her mother who, on hearing his voice, had left the kitchen with some nervousness. 'Ah! Mrs Hardy, I thought you might be in need of water. The well isn't safe until I've had some work done on it.' He lifted the pail and made to enter.

'That's very kind of you,' she replied. Then added apologetically, 'I'm afraid I overslept otherwise I would have sought the well myself.' Her manner was pleasant enough yet he was reluctant to enter the cottage uninvited, but the pail was heavy and there was no point in putting it down again. He walked past her leaving her to close the door behind them.

She followed him quietly into the kitchen and waited while he placed the pail on the wooden draining board adjacent to the stone sink. 'It really is thoughtful of you, Mr Morton, and I'm obliged to you for the care you have taken on our behalf. 'I'm afraid I must have appeared bad-mannered last night but your declaration shocked me. The situation in which you find yourself must be an unpleasant one.'

'It is!' he said bluntly. She seemed at least to be carefully concealing any contempt which she felt towards him, and for this he was grateful. 'Have you eaten yet? The provisions in the larder are all for your use, please help yourselves. And please, Mrs Hardy, before you leave, would you be kind enough to allow me the opportunity to discuss the matter again, for I fear I was unforgivably indifferent to your feelings last night. It was unfair of me to put you in such an embarrassing situation.' There was no disdain in her gaze, only a hint of resignation and this disturbed him.

Lizzie stood nearby watching, admiring the long tightly fitting leather boots which clung to his calves. He had a sudden urge to make the serious look on her face change into a laughing one. Before he realised it he found himself giving in to this whim and asked, 'Mrs Hardy, would you like to eat in peace while I show Lizzie the animals? Give her a piece of cheese and an apple, she will come to no harm.'

Hannah Hardy was surprised by his sudden gentleness, and suppressed her own desire to look around the farm in case he misunderstood her intentions. 'I'm sure she would like that, wouldn't you Lizzie?' The child nodded and hopped about excitedly as her mother went to the pantry.

With a piece of cheese in one hand and an apple in the other Lizzie trotted happily down the lane by Edward's side. Hannah watched them from the window and wondered just what kind of man Mr Morton was. He seemed kind enough and Lizzie had obviously taken to him, but she guessed he had a selfish streak within him. Yet, wasn't it purely for selfish reasons that she had accepted the invitation to come, and was considering his offer? She glanced down at the shabby, ill-fitting garment which she had once worn so proudly. Soon it would be in tatters and she had nothing with which to replace it. Who would look twice at her now, or employ her in such a state?

She could see them both ending up in the workhouse. Perhaps there was no future for her, but there had to be a better one for her daughter. Her mind was invaded by a diversity of memories, not just those of poverty and sickness but darker ones which she tried to brush away. Here in the valley she should be safe, free from hunger and poverty, and perhaps eventually be able to put the shadows of the past behind her forever. It would mean putting aside all her romantic dreams—but then they had been her downfall from the beginning. Swallowing hard, she nervously brushed back a strand of hair from her face and admitted his offer was very tempting. If only the price he was asking wasn't so heavy!

The two figures had disappeared from sight, leaving Hannah to stare with sad eyes over the rolling landscape. She could to some degree understand his desperate bid to keep the farm, for when approaching it from the village yesterday she'd been struck by the grey stone farmhouse standing so proudly against the wild wooded hillside. There was untold beauty and grandeur in the landscape, and it was surely a place in which a child could roam without a care.

By the time Edward and Lizzie returned she had composed herself and was prepared to be as business-like about the affair as he had been the evening before.

'Here we are Mrs Hardy, safe and sound from our walk,' he called out cheerfully as he entered the house. 'Lizzie would be happy and healthy out here if you chose to stay, of that I can assure you.'

Ignoring Lizzie's delighted reaction to this, Hannah said kindly, 'I'm sure she would, Mr Morton, and I am willing to discuss your proposition. I have just made some tea, so perhaps we could leave Lizzie here to eat whilst we go through into the sitting room.' Pushing a stool up to the well-worn kitchen table she sat the child down in front of a plate of buttered bread. 'You stay here and eat it, mind,' she said, patting Lizzie gently on the head before following Edward into the adjoining room, where he waited anxiously for her.

He knew that it was up to him to ease the way if Mrs Hardy was to be encouraged to stay. 'I'm afraid I insulted you last night,' he said simply, almost humbly. 'I am not a wicked man, and under normal circumstances such ideas would never have entered my head but I have been forced into this situation. However, after thinking things over during the night I wonder if I might make another proposition, one which you might find more acceptable!' Mrs Hardy said nothing but appeared willing to listen, although it was impossible for him to guess what her thoughts were. 'You are obviously in need of help, and I am so taken with Lizzie that I would like to see her brought up in better conditions. There is accommodation available here in the cottage which I could offer in exchange for work and cooking in the farmhouse. I would, of course, make you a small allowance as well, sufficient to meet your needs. If, say, in three months you still do not feel inclined to marry me then I would have to make other arrangements, in order to fulfil my dead employer's wishes. I would, of course, help you to find other employment and somewhere to live!' He suspected there to be a glimmer of relief in her eyes but let it pass. 'Be honest with me, I beg. Do you think you could be happy here, and will you give genuine consideration to this proposition? If at the end of the three months you agree to marry me, then I would have legal documents drawn up securing both your futures on my demise, the farm to go to our child, the cottage to you and Lizzie.' There was no emotion either on his face or in his voice, and he felt that as a business offer to a woman in such dire straits as she was, the offer was a fair one.

Pleasantly surprised by his generous offer of a trial period, one which could at least get her through the coming harsh winter, she took a deep breath and began to speak. 'Yes, I must confess to being shocked last night, but having thought about it I can see how difficult it must be for you. Times are hard down there in the town, and the valley is so beautiful—it seems cruel to me that your friend has caused you so much trouble. To be honest with you now, I had almost decided out of hopelessness to accept your offer, but was afraid you might expect more from me than I would be able to give! But what would happen if I was unable to produce another child—where would that leave us, and you for that matter? I must know where I stand in those circumstances.'

He was pleased that she had not completely ruled out his offer, and to note that she was capable of shrewd thinking, although he was a little taken aback at the possibility that their relationship might be fruitless. She was, of course, right, for he had never for a moment considered his own ability to create a child, and he wondered if that had crossed Abe's mind at all. 'You're quite right; and I'm grateful to you for that thought. The matter needs more careful consideration; after all there is no guarantee that any other person could provide the child either.' He fell silent, grateful that Mrs Hardy seemed content to let him ponder on this but he was also becoming aware that without legal advice he could well marry and still lose the farm. At last he broke the silence. 'I will discuss the matter with my solicitor and will inform you as soon as possible where we all stand. In fact I will drive you home myself today and call on him. The matter of your housekeeping for me and your occupying the cottage for three months still stands—if you still wish to come?'

She had watched him carefully throughout his discourse and he was not surprised that she had further questions to ask, only intrigued by the warm flush of embarrassment on her face.

'I must ask one more question of you. What if you should desire to have more than one child—would I be obliged to comply with your wishes?' She lowered her eyes, refusing to meet his.

He cleared his throat, trying to cover his own embarrassment. 'I think it very unlikely,' he stammered, 'having enjoyed bachelor life all these years. It is nothing personal but I prefer my own way of life to that of a family man. In any case I would never force you. If that situation arose then I think we could discuss it sensibly but your wishes would be obeyed—not mine.'

For the first time that she could recall Mrs Hardy's face relaxed into a smile. 'Thank you!' she exclaimed gratefully. 'When you have seen your solicitor about the conditions, I would be prepared to work for you and to consider your offer!'

He returned the smile. 'It is I who am grateful for that and apologise if you find me cold and hard. I can't offer you romance, women seem to expect that, or affection—that is beyond my capabilities but I do offer a home, security, and funds to pay for Lizzie's education. It seems neither of our circumstances allow us to choose the direction we would really like to take but by our mutual agreement we could both have peace of mind and comfort in a world that is, as you well know, very harsh. My demands would not be those of a husband, but I do require absolute loyalty as I said before. Nor would I appreciate our arrangement becoming common knowledge.'

'In that case, Mr Morton, I have decided to accept the offer. I shall keep my part of the bargain and no-one shall hear of any of this from my lips.'

There was no doubting Mrs Hardy's sincerity, and he found that for a moment he could say nothing, so strong was his relief at this turn of events. To mask his emotion he took a step forward and held out his hand to grasp hers, saying quietly, 'Thank you—I promise you'll not regret it.' He was startled by his impetuous gesture, and once his emotions were again under control, he said cordially, 'Enjoy the rest of the morning—I will take you home after lunch, say about two o'clock'.

Jack Gray waited patiently, holding the reins whilst Edward handed Mrs Hardy and her child up into the trap. He was unaware of the pact which had been made between his employer and this woman, and even less that she clutched in her purse sufficient money to pay off her debts and buy clothing suitable for country living. He knew better than to question Edward, who usually informed him of decisions in his own good time, and presumed the woman to be a replacement for the housekeeper.

'We will be ready for you on Thursday morning, Mr Gray,' she called out, 'Good-bye!'

Edward climbed in after Mrs Hardy, his mind full of misgivings, though relieved to have set in motion the means to retain the farm. He shook the reins and the trap rolled from the uneven yard out into the lane. Lizzie waved back excitedly at Jack, her eyes as bright as stars. To Edward this aspect of the arrangement was a bonus for he was convinced the child would give him much pleasure.

Throughout the bumpy journey Lizzie, seated between Edward and her mother and wrapped in a warm blanket, chattered excitedly, asking questions and pointing with child-like innocence at all she saw. This pleased him as it relieved him of the need to seek fresh topics on which to speak to Mrs Hardy. He was also delighted by the way Lizzie presumed that he knew the answers to all her queries, and so took great care to explain in a way that she would understand.

'Have you heard of Robin Hood?' he asked, as they crossed Loxley Chase. She shook her head, her large eyes turned to him enquiringly, awaiting his explanation. 'There was a man, many centuries ago who was supposed to have been born hereabouts, called Robin of Loxley. He was a wealthy man and refused to collect heavy taxes from the poor to give to the Sheriff. Because of this he was outlawed, sent away and became very angry. He started to steal from rich travellers and gave the money he'd taken to the poor people, or so the story goes. Perhaps he rode along this very road!'

'Why did they call him Robin Hood?' Lizzie asked wistfully.

'I believe it was because he and the other men with him wore green tunics with hoods fastened to them. The hoods protected them from the weather and shielded their faces so they would not be recognised.'

'Do you think he came back here?' she went on.

'Who knows? It is a long, long time ago. He may have hunted in this very valley, when it was filled with trees and wild animals. His friend, Little John, is buried at Hathersage in the same graveyard as my parents.'

Lizzie fell silent, her mind filled with vivid and wild imaginings of what might have been. She liked this man who told her stories, and showed her so many new and wonderful things.

Soon they were approaching Lipton Street and it was with some reluctance that he reined in and handed the pair down, again aware of eyes watching them from inside the houses, he smiled to himself wondering what they were making of it all. He then escorted Mrs Hardy to her house, promising to return later in the day once he had consulted his solicitor. He was eager to be away, for something had occurred to him on the journey which, the more he thought about it, the more feasible the idea appeared to be.

Having once stabled the horse and trap at the *Angel* he hurried along Bank Street to where Abe's solicitor, Mr Knight of Broadbents, had his office. He was light of foot now because he had virtually found a way round Abe's will, yet he had to be sure about what he was going to suggest for, once committed, there could be no going back.

Edward's footsteps rang out as he climbed the cold, stone stairway to Mr Knight's office. The room into which he was shown was austere and offered little comfort in spite of the fire burning in the grate, but Mr Knight rose to greet Edward warmly enough whilst at the same time dismissing his clerk.

'Ah! Mr Morton,' he said, shaking Edward's hand. 'What can I do for you?'

There seemed no point in beating about the bush, as it was sound advice Edward needed about the feasibility of his plan before he approached his own solicitor. 'Mr Knight,' he said, releasing the man's hand. 'I took your advice and placed an advertisement in the *Clarion* for a wife. To cut things short I have made acquaintance with a lady who may be willing to marry me if certain conditions regarding her future are assured.' He paused, expecting to see signs of amusement on the other man's face. However, there was only an understanding nod. 'In fact, we have agreed that she should be my housekeeper and live at the cottage for three months to allow ourselves to be sure of our commitment, whilst I remain at the farm. If, at the end of that time, we are in agreement then we shall marry. The lady in question knows all the facts and sees this as a business arrangement without emotional entanglement; however, she is willing to bear me a child. Her circumstances are very unfortunate and the proposition will be greatly to her advantage as well as mine.'

Mr Knight listened in silence, allowing Edward to get the matter off his chest before asking, 'You're sure that the lady in question is respectable? Don't you think under the circumstances it would be wise to let Mr Mills make some discreet inquiries into her background? Three months would allow ample time I think, for him to ascertain her suitability and she would be completely unaware of such an investigation.'

Edward thought for a moment, then agreed, and although he could see the wisdom in the suggestion he felt a strange sense of disloyalty towards Mrs Hardy in doing so. 'I know little of her position except that she is not without some education, and is a widow with a child of six years. She has, admittedly, become near destitute, and has struggled to survive after a recent illness. I wouldn't want her to feel that I don't trust her, yet on the other hand I think I would appreciate some help in this matter. However, there are a few other details which need to be resolved before I approach Mr Mills. What happens if we marry as laid down in the will and there is no issue? I may not even be capable of fathering a child! Do I then find myself saddled with a wife and step-child and no farm to call my own? Just how adamant was Abe in the matter if I did my utmost to fulfil the requirements; did he take into account these possibilities?'

After pondering for a moment, the solicitor agreed. 'I can see your dilemma. One cannot legislate for everything, and although Mr Bagshaw never thought of that point, I did. After all, a child is the all-important factor in the case.' He raised his eyes despairingly to the ceiling, 'I'm afraid things are never as straightforward as some people would like them to be'. Then with a sigh, he continued, 'I am forever sorting out complicated problems. I don't suppose,' he suggested, 'that you would fancy ensuring a pregnancy first, just to be on the safe side…it's a centuries old method.'

'No, I certainly would not!' Edward stated emphatically. 'I did wonder though, if a step-child would be considered eligible as my legal heir if I so willed it?'

Without answering immediately, Mr Knight sat deep in thought as if wrestling with some hidden problem, and when at last he spoke it was with some asperity. 'Has the Reverend Elliott been talking to you?' he asked, suspiciously.

'No!' Edward replied, a little startled by the man's attitude. 'I haven't spoken to him for some time. Besides, he would like the farm to go to the Parish, that I do know. Why, is there something else that I should know?'

'Only that as executors, and knowing our client's feelings and wishes, we do have the power in certain circumstances to authorise some changes to the will. The main desire was to see that your present relations receive no benefit from Mr Bagshaw's estate. It's no secret that your brother-in-law and nephews are involved with pugilism and cock-fighting, amongst other things. If what you propose takes place and there is no offspring then the step-child could inherit, but only if we consider the said child to be a suitable recipient. At least by marrying a woman with a child the farm would be yours, and the Parish would have no say unless you had no issue at all, or if we objected strongly. However, it would be most unwise for you to inform the lady of these facts as it would put you in a very weak position. It behoves you to produce an heir of your own lest the woman's child is unsuitable. Yes, the possibility is there but not guaranteed—I suppose the child is a boy?'

'Well, no! But a bright child nevertheless, one to whom I am already drawn. Does it change matters?'

'Not entirely, but females are hardly well suited to managing a farm, and not so respected by the labourers. They're physically weaker and therefore vulnerable to be taken advantage of. One that isn't is hardly likely to be genteel. It would seem to be an advantage to your cause if the lady had a boy, rather than a girl.'

This was not a theory to which Edward, from experience on the land, entirely subscribed but he had no intention of alienating the man by arguing. He had the answer for which he had come and resolved to keep his own council from now on. 'I appreciate your advice,' he said politely, revealing nothing further of his ideas. 'And I will instruct Mr Mills to make discreet enquiries about the lady for me.' With that he thanked Mr Knight for his time and left to make his way to his own solicitor where he explained all his plans in full.

The courtyard smelt strongly of sewage as Hannah hung her meagre washing out on the old rope which hung between her house and that opposite. There was little chance of the clothes drying in the damp morning air but she was determined that whatever she took to the farm would be clean. Shabby her belongings might be but never dirty.

Her fingers were sore from stitching, just as her hands were chapped from cleaning and washing in preparation for their departure. She had no desire to remain in Lipton Street any longer than necessary and she looked disparagingly around the yard at the broken window frames, rotting doors, and filthy paving. Certainly no one would condemn her for accepting Edward Morton's offer, rather they would ridicule her for being too proud if she refused. She thought then of the man himself and, whilst acknowledging him to be cold and strangely unfeeling, she had to confess that he appeared to be a very respectable gentleman in all other ways. However, on returning from consulting his solicitor as promised, he had spoken of their agreement with no more emotion than if he were acquiring an item of equipment for the farm, and this she found very disturbing.

She wondered if anything other than his obsession with the property stirred him to any great depth, and just wished she understood him a little. One moment he would be kind and considerate, the next reserved and remote almost to the point of rudeness. This discouraged her from expressing any joy or happiness at the move for fear that he would misinterpret her reason for doing so. She knew that she too must remain aloof from any emotional involvement in case Mr Morton began to resent his offer to her. Yet this was often difficult as there were moments when his kindness demanded a deeper gratitude, his behaviour to Lizzie being one such example. Before he left he had quite suddenly, as though embarrassed, handed her a further five guineas and instructed her to purchase good footwear and waterproof outer garments for herself and Lizzie, as the valley was cold and wet in winter. Had this been merely a practical gesture or was there within him somewhere a gentle consideration for others? If so, it appeared he had no intention of revealing the fact.

By carefully shopping around in the Norfolk Market Hall, Hannah made the money which he had given her go much further than perhaps Edward had imagined was possible, with the result that she was able to replace other items just as urgently needed. By working late into the evenings and using the light of several tallow candles she completed two simple homespun dresses, one for herself and one for Lizzie, in time for the journey back to Bradfield. The rest of the material she would make up during the long winter nights ahead. She had enjoyed having money to spend and taken pleasure in selecting her purchases instead of taking the cheapest goods on offer and, in making up the dresses, her spirits had risen even more.

The prospect of leaving Lipton Street was constantly on her mind, and her anticipation hard to contain until, by Thursday morning, it was difficult to ascertain who was most excited, Hannah or Lizzie as both ran to the window whenever there was an unfamiliar sound in the yard. Although she had informed no one of her impending departure she knew that her neighbours would already be speculating on the comings and goings of Mr Morton and Jack Gray—but she no longer cared what they thought.

Their meagre possessions were in a bundle by the door in readiness and Hannah made every effort to leave the place as clean and tidy as possible, but nothing could disguise the dilapidated state of the house. She had no furniture worth removing to the cottage and what bits she had possessed were already sold for a pittance to a man who dealt in such things. Whereas she was leaving with less than she had when she arrived, what she took she was proud of, and there was a degree of hope for the future. The contempt she felt for the other inhabitants of the court now turned to pity, but she knew that her disappearance would feed them with gossip for a while, then she would be forgotten.

However, Edward had not gone straight home after his last visit. Curiosity had taken him on one final visit to the Post Office to enquire if there had been any further response to his advertisement. It was therefore something of a shock, as well as a surprise, when the clerk handed him another letter which, from the pencilled date of arrival, had been awaiting collection for several weeks.

It was written on better quality paper than Mrs Hardy's had been but in a less practised hand. He opened it tentatively, aware of the attractive smell of perfume which greeted him and was completely oblivious of the presence of the clerk who would have taken no notice at all had not Edward suddenly exclaimed aloud. 'Well, I'll be damned!'

Aware now that the clerk was eyeing him with some curiosity, Edward quickly thrust the letter into his pocket and left the premises with a slightly reddened face. Once beyond the perimeter of the Post Office he paused and pondered on the contents of the envelope. Here now was another letter worth considering! If things were to be believed he had an offer worthy at least of further investigation if nothing else. The tone was lively, almost amusing, and it certainly implied a character of warmth and sophistication.

Without hesitation he purchased a sheet of paper and an envelope from a stationers in the Haymarket and sat in a quiet corner of the lending library to reply immediately in a business-like but cordial manner. It was only later after he had gone several miles on the journey home that the enormity of what he had done sank in. Suppose he were to find a more suitable liaison with this Miss Firth, what then would he do with Mrs Hardy and Lizzie? Could the woman sue him for breach of promise even at this stage? His impetuosity that afternoon appalled him, yet what a fool he had been to panic from the outset at Abe's conditions, when perhaps if he had taken his time he might have found someone with more to offer than Hannah Hardy. But wasn't a close relationship exactly what he had been trying to avoid all along, yet here he was for the first time in his life drawn by the fripperies and charm of a stranger who was already diverting his singularity of mind. Yes! He was indeed a fool, for the images conjured by the letter might yet turn out to be nothing more than a fantasy stemming from his overworked and overtired mind.

Darkness had fallen long before his departure from the town and the letter had distracted him, consequently he found the journey home both tedious and hazardous. He wasn't used to taking the trap out at night and now he was annoyed with himself for delaying his return. Perhaps his brain was addled. If he had taken too much wine or ale he would have understood himself more but not a drop had passed his lips all day.

'Oh, to hell with it—I must be out of my mind!' he bellowed, shaking the reins with such vigour that the horse nearly shied. He proceeded on his journey knowing full well that once again he was committed to return to the Post Office to collect another reply.

On reaching home he unharnessed the horse from the trap and stabled her, then, after entering the farmhouse, he took the letter from his pocket and re-examined it. Again the pleasant fragrance stirred his imagination and that, together with the buoyant tone of its contents, caused him to reflect on what he knew of Mrs Hardy. In her there seemed no liveliness of spirit, merely a dullness caused, no doubt, by acceptance of her lot. Her submissive compliance fitted in nicely with his plans; then suddenly he was struck by the complexity of it all and wondered where it would all end.

When Thursday finally arrived, both Hannah and Lizzie reached the farm full of expectation, and were greeted by Edward who appeared friendly enough, but Hannah sensed a preoccupation in his smile. However, she pushed this from her mind thinking it might be her imagination. Lizzie had no such reservations, she sprang immediately into his arms catching him off-guard and, for a moment, he seemed to relax once more.

During the three days prior to their arrival Edward had brooded, disturbed by inexplicable bouts of depression which had left him reluctant to greet Mrs Hardy with any enthusiasm or gladness of heart. A strange feeling of foreboding hung over him such as had not been there when the arrangements with her had been made. He now felt trapped, both by circumstances and his inability to throw off the dark mood which invaded him. It was little comfort to him to see that she had made considerable effort with her appearance, in fact she looked quite presentable. To her credit she was obviously quite skilled with a needle, even so, nothing could conceal the thinness of her body or take away the pale, drawn look from her face. He felt guilty at his inability to feel warm towards her, and also felt disloyal in not telling her about the letter he had received.

Her hand trembled as he handed her down from the trap, whether it was from the cold or nerves he couldn't tell, but he knew that he had no more desire to touch her now than when he had met her the first time.

Mrs Hardy soon settled in the cottage and within days it was as if she had always been there. She seemed compliant enough and willing to serve, perhaps too easily he thought, for surely no-one should accept their fate with such apparent resignation. Perhaps he was being unfair, for she might be feeling the strain of the ordeal every bit as much as he was; if so she hid it well beneath a mask of propriety. He could find no fault in either her manner or her actions. As a mother she was excellent, as a housekeeper a treasure, and in conversation polite, but the thought that one day he might cold-bloodedly share her bed gave him a sense of enormous unease. Yet she was behaving exactly as he had wanted in the partnership.

Hannah Hardy's presence at the farm did at least provide a companionship of sorts, although their conversation was not of an intimate kind, more that of employer and employee. She gave no cause for complaint and seemed to enjoy her work, whilst Lizzie in her childish way followed Edward and her mother about, trying to please both equally. He found the child's eagerness to please touching and endearing; and when she sensed instinctively that she was in his way, she would leave him alone and play quietly somewhere else. During moments when he knew that she was unaware of his observations, he would watch her play the little mother with a rather battered rag doll, which she took everywhere with her. It brought to mind the doll's house which he had found in the upstairs room and wondered what her reaction would be if he showed it to her. It would do no harm to let her use the house, providing she took care of it, for it held no sentimental memories for him and it would give her much pleasure.

'Mrs Hardy!' he said one afternoon, having made up his mind. 'I have something upstairs on which I would appreciate your opinion—would you follow me?' He turned to Lizzie and said gently but firmly, 'There is no need for you to follow, child. Your mother will call you if she wants you to come up.'

'Yes, Sir.' Lizzie agreed politely, happy to obey.

He took the bunch of keys from the desk drawer and led Mrs Hardy upstairs. 'I must confess that it gives me great pleasure to see Lizzie happy—I hope you have no regrets in bringing the child here?'

'I have not, Mr Morton. You have given us both something to live for. I fear that conditions in that house would have been too much to bear and might even have been the death of one, if not both of us, had we stayed there.' Hannah's voice rang with gratitude.

'I'm pleased to hear you say so,' Edward said, unlocking the door and leading her into the room. 'Now, look at that cabinet—is it not a fine piece of furniture?' There was a touch of mystery in his voice.

'Indeed!' she replied, amused by his playful manner, something he usually only displayed in front of Lizzie.

'Please, open the doors and tell me what you think!'

Hannah was a little hesitant as she took hold of one of the drop handles and twisted, pulling the door toward her. Then she gasped with surprise. 'Why, it's a doll's house—whose is it? What is it doing here?'

Edward laughed as he replied. 'I haven't the slightest notion whose it was or why it is here. I never knew of its existence until my employer died, and Abe had neither wife nor sisters. The cabinet was hidden amongst the old furniture and other rubbish, but it seems very old and rather intriguing. Do you think Lizzie could be trusted to play carefully with it?' Although she did not reply immediately, Edward knew that Mrs Hardy was just as fascinated with what she saw as he was so he waited patiently for her to speak.

It suddenly occurred to Hannah that beneath his composed exterior there still lurked a boyishness—though he would probably deny it existed. She bent forward, her work-worn hand involuntarily moving towards the tiny furniture. 'Oh! Mr Morton, I shall make sure she's gentle, and treats everything with respect—it is too fine to be spoilt.' She did not look up but spoke softly and with gratitude.

'Then call Lizzie,' he ordered a little roughly, concealing the momentary embarrassment her gratitude had on him.

Hannah rose smiling inwardly, knowing that for some reason he was not a man used to showing emotion. 'I'll go down and fetch her,' she said, and slipped out of the room.

When she returned with the unsuspecting child, Edward had regained his composure and was standing before the cabinet in the way he did when about to surprise Lizzie with something new. He beckoned the child to come to him and then, moving to one side, with a flourish of his hand indicated the closed doors of the cabinet. 'Close your eyes, Lizzie, while I open these doors, and look only when I tell you to.'

Lizzie obeyed, screwing her eye-lids together so tightly that her face crinkled and her mouth puckered.

Edward laughed softly, 'You look just like one of the cows, and not at all pretty,' he said and opened the doors. 'Now you can look.' She did so, and on realising what was inside, her eyes opened wider than ever. Stepping closer to the cupboard she peered in, more amazed at what she saw then delighted. She stood for several seconds, her eyes moving swiftly from one small room to another although she wasn't tall enough to see into the attic rooms. Then, in a very grown-up manner declared, 'It's very dusty!' She strove to peep into the top rooms and Edward fetched a chair on which she could stand without over-reaching.

Hannah was touched by this consideration towards her daughter, and although he was often tender to the child, to her he was polite and often distant. She was not aware that at that precise moment he was watching her intently. He was a little disappointed in Lizzie's reaction; Mrs Hardy's enthusiasm had matched his own, but perhaps it was not immediately obvious to a child that it was a toy. In fact it was hardly a plaything, more perhaps a whim of some wealthy lady and he wondered how Abe had acquired it. It never occurred to Edward that the child, having only a rag-doll to play with, would be in awe of the numerous tiny contents of the house.

'Don't you like it?' he asked Lizzie gently, concealing his dis-appointment. 'It's a doll's house, and needs to be cleaned and dusted just like a proper house. It's very delicate and is best looked after by tiny, careful fingers. Would you keep it clean for me?'

Lizzie nodded seriously, contemplating the contents. 'Are there no little people to live in it?' she asked wistfully.

At this remark Edward laughed out loud and bent to look more closely into the rooms. 'See, there is one, in the bed!' He pointed to a rather faded wooden face peering out from beneath the covers of a small four-poster bed.

'Ooh!' she exclaimed, almost falling from the chair in her excitement, 'Can I take it out of the bed?' Suddenly her total absorption in the figure became apparent and he realised with what seriousness she viewed the entire contents of the house. He knew that it would be lonely for the child on the farm throughout the winter months, until she had a chance to make friends, and although he loved to have her follow him about he could not always spare the time to answer her many questions. The cabinet-house would be an outlet for her creativity whilst at the same time encouraging her to be tidy.

'Would you like me to have it taken up to your cottage, Lizzie? Then you could look after it for me and, providing you are very careful, you can play with it.' What harm would it do? He had no use for it, and he knew Mrs Hardy well enough by now to believe that she would see things were handled gently.

At this Lizzie's eyes lit up with childlike joy. 'Please, Mr Edward—I won't spoil it,' she cried out gleefully. 'And you can come and play with it too.' Her answer pleased him, and he decided he would have two men move the cabinet to the cottage that very afternoon.

On the Friday of the week following the Hardy's arrival, Edward made his way into town once again, saying nothing before he left about his intentions except that he might stay there overnight. Just as he was leaving, Mrs Hardy approached him holding in her hand a linen cloth covering a packed lunch which she had prepared for him. This unexpected kindness served to increase the guilt he felt at the errand on which he was bound. Hannah and Lizzie had been at the farm a week now, during which time he had grown accustomed to the daily presence of the pair. Nevertheless, always at the back of his mind was the appointment he had made with the writer of the second letter.

'I thank you, Mrs Hardy,' he replied to the pale, upright woman who bade him farewell. 'Tell Lizzie that she can collect the eggs again just as she did with me yesterday, and you have two of them for your teas. Tell her to look after Bella for me as well!'

Chapter 3

December was not a good time of the year to be making the journey, Edward conceded, as he rode beneath the heavily laden sky towards Sheffield. In all his years at the farm he had not been in the habit of going to town often, but now this business with Abe had arisen, and here he was for the sixth time in three months, heading for the constricting atmosphere of the crowded town.

Judging by the sky it was quite possible that he could be cut off from the valley by snow if he delayed too long. However, he was sufficiently well-clad and well-equipped to stay overnight if the weather deteriorated, it was his intention to deal with the matter in hand immediately rather than postpone it. The farm was in Jack Gray's capable hands and everything had been left in order. His letter to Miss Firth had indicated his intention to meet her at the *Angel Inn*, a busy place where his visit was unlikely to cause comment, and where there was stabling for his horse if necessary. Unfortunately, he had suggested meeting at one in the afternoon, which might have been a mistake, judging by the sky. However, there were several other calls he could make whilst in town which would save time and trouble at a later date.

By mid-day he had completed his tasks and was in a nervous frame of mind, being unsure how he should greet Miss Firth, and also very conscious of the change for the worse in the weather. An inch of snow lay on the roof-tops and activity in the town was slowing down in preparation for a heavy fall of snow. At a quarter to one Edward seated himself as near to the entrance of the inn as possible to watch for her. However, only a few hardy patrons had ventured into the *Angel* and he was in some doubt as to whether the lady would even bother to show her face in view of the conditions.

Half an hour later he was about to give up his vigil, somewhat relieved at being let down, when suddenly the door opened and a cold draught announced the arrival of a small figure huddled beneath a snow-speckled cloak. Hesitating for a moment in case he was being too hasty, he watched as the hood of the cloak was thrown back. Normally he was a good judge of character but, for once, he was unable to make up his mind at what he saw. The small face was exquisite, spoilt perhaps by too much artificial colouring, but surrounded by an abundance of dark black hair set in a fashionable style. She looked cautiously round the room, the sparkling eyes missing nothing until finally they met Edward's as he sat quietly observing her. She smiled confidently. In both manner and style she was a complete contrast to Mrs Hardy.

He rose, 'Miss Firth?' he asked politely. At her nod he held out his hand, taking her soft, gloved fingers in his. They were surprisingly warm having obviously been kept beneath the cloak.

'Mr Morton?' she responded, inclining her head gracefully. 'I am Lydia Firth, and I am very pleased to meet you.'

'Let me take your cloak,' he offered, aware that the clear hazel eyes were studying him closely. As he took the garment and shook the snow briskly from it he was again struck by the same pleasant fragrance that had accompanied her letter. 'Please, do take a seat,' he said. 'I'll hang your cloak to dry and order some refreshments. Would a glass of mulled wine take away the chill?'

When he returned from ordering drinks for them both she had positioned herself nearer the fire and appeared completely relaxed as she watched him approach. He intended to be business-like, having placed his cards firmly on the table in the advertisement, but he was somewhat disarmed by her confident manner.

He opened the conversation, sensing that she intended him to do so. 'I appreciate your effort in meeting me in spite of the dreadful weather outside. Did you have far to come?'

She shook her head and smiled, 'Not far!' He realised that she had no intention of enlightening him further on that subject. Although the answer was direct, her smile showed that she meant no offence and he thought her wise to be cautious under the circumstances.

'Perhaps this is a strange way to meet,' he stated bluntly, watching her reaction. 'And you must wonder why I advertised as I did.' He felt the colour rise as if he were guilty of some crime or other.

She showed no embarrassment and, unless she was concealing her true feelings very cleverly, seemed to be genuinely interested in what he had to say. 'I may be wondering why you needed to go to such lengths considering that you are not an unattractive man, and seem also to be of some consequence,' she answered mischievously. At that moment the proprietor of the *Angel* approached with the wine and some refreshments, she fell silent, waiting until he had withdrawn before continuing. 'You may, of course, be wondering why I too should have had need to reply?'

Edward had a momentary feeling that she was playing a game with him. Why indeed had she replied? She was certainly a self-assured woman, and used no doubt to conversing with men, which was in itself a strange and forward thing, but then he was unused to the ways of townswomen. 'I'll be frank with you, Miss Firth—I had no intentions of marrying at all but now I find I have no choice if I am to inherit a certain legacy. I do not seek companionship or emotional entanglements, merely a business relationship. Does that shock you?'

'By no means! Indeed I am somewhat relieved to learn that you are not as strange as I had expected. You see I am an actress.' She saw his eyes widen, 'Now I have shocked you!' She laughed merrily, 'We actors are merely people doing a job of work you know!'

So that explained her directness and the slightly flamboyant manner which had so intrigued him! Was he shocked? He had no sense of moral indignation either way and confessed to finding her company pleasing, not vulgar as he would have expected from newspaper opinions—but what did she want with him? 'I must confess that the only knowledge I have of actresses comes from what I read in the papers, having never met one before' he said. 'My own lifestyle is of the country, and a far cry from the world of the theatre. What prompted you to reply?'

'Well, I am tired of travelling from one town to another and having no permanent roots. It is a precarious business and, since arriving in Sheffield at the start of winter with no other bookings in the foreseeable future, I decided that your advertisement was interesting and could be advantageous. Although I'm not sure that I could give up the stage indefinitely.' It was a statement of fact, even a suggestion of inevitability, a warning rather than a threat. At the moment of her confession he suddenly realised that she was more mature than he had at first thought.

He tried to guess her age but her make-up cleverly hid all tell-tale signs, and he was forced to ask outright. 'May I ask how old you are?' It was said with kindness and implied nothing more than a continuity of the theme on which they were talking.

She lowered her eye-lids coquettishly. 'Ah! That is a question I would normally refuse to answer but, under the circumstances, I may as well admit to being thirty-three.'

'Have you never married?' Edward ventured to ask, perhaps more abruptly than he'd intended.

The directness of the question caused her to hesitate and no amount of face-powder could conceal the flush of confusion on her face. She did not reply immediately and he was aware that he had momentarily caught her off guard. It had not been his intention to embarrass her, and he had been churlish, lulled into impropriety by her cordial bon-homie. He was inexperienced with women and had found it refreshing to talk to her so openly. 'That was rude of me,' he said apologetically. 'Please forgive me, I meant no harm. It is just that I would rather you be frank with me from the beginning.' He sighed inwardly fully expecting Miss Firth to desire the meeting to end there and then.

When at last she spoke it was in quiet tones, she did not raise her eyes but continued to toy with a glass on the table as though debating with her inner self. Her voice was hesitant. 'I may as well admit to my failing. I was not married in the true sense of the word, but as good as, for some long time to a comedian with whom I travelled. He eventually succumbed to a pair of eyes prettier than mine and promptly left me alone in a strange town. Since then I have avoided that sort of thing. Your offer suited me ideally but my background is obviously not conducive to your ideal plan.' She gathered the folds of her skirt in her hand as if intending to rise, her head bent low so that he could not see her face.

'No! Please, don't go!' he exclaimed, in an effort to restrain her. 'I admire your frankness, and think you very brave to admit your past. It is not for me to condemn anyone. I have never married, indeed I am not worldly in that respect, my present predicament was forced upon me, otherwise I would not have sought a liaison in this way. I offer not a romance but a business-like arrangement in which the lady would find herself financially rewarded, with security for life. All I ask in return is a child and the assurance that the mother bring me neither shame nor the attention of gossips.' It was difficult to assess her reaction to his statement, but at least she did not find him amusing nor did she seem affronted, and for that she had his gratitude. This made him feel strangely protective towards this small woman seated before him. Everything about her was petite, from the tiny hands to the small, pleasant mouth, and he had difficulty in imagining her soft voice carrying from the stage to an audience beyond.

Lydia Firth must have sensed his growing approval for suddenly she smiled gently, her eyes a little moist with appreciation. 'It would appear that we both have crosses to bear, but a woman alone in this cruel world receives little sympathy if she strays from the narrow path. I know from bitter experience!'

Edward felt more relaxed now, it was comforting to know that he was not the only one with problems, and if he could help her, then he would endeavour to do so. The tension had left her face and she appeared more relaxed. They chatted cheerfully for some time about this and that, as though they were of long acquaintance, until a chiming clock drew her attention. 'Oh, dear, it's getting late!' she exclaimed. 'I really must leave.'

'Perhaps we could meet again, as friends, to talk about matters when we both have had time to digest today's revelations—would that be possible?' he asked hopefully, rising. 'Now, while you think about it, I must see what it's like outside. If the weather is too bad I will stay here overnight, but I must get a carriage for you.' He went to the window and peered out. Some time after her arrival the snow had ceased to fall, having deposited no more than another inch. Seeing this, he excused himself and went to order a carriage and to consider his own position. Concluding that there was nothing to keep him in the town for the evening he decided to settle his bill and leave for home as soon as Miss Firth was safely on her way.

On his return he placed the almost dry cloak around Lydia's shoulders and was struck, almost intrigued, by her shortness of stature. He was convinced that she was small enough for him to carry her home himself if the need arose. They had been chatting amiably for several minutes whilst awaiting the carriage when Edward pressed her for an answer to his proposed second meeting. He had no idea where she lived as her letter had been addressed 'care of a friend', and once they parted that would be the end. He bent and whispered, 'How can I make contact with you? We will meet again, I hope?'

'We must!' she replied quickly. 'You may contact me at the *Surrey Theatre* in West Bar, or write care of my friend, Mrs Marshall. I shall not move on until I find fresh work. In the meantime, I will wash and iron for the cast, and fill in when there is sickness.' She gave him her hand. 'I too have enjoyed our meeting, and look forward to seeing you again when the snow has gone.'

As her carriage finally rolled away, Edward was at a loss to understand his feelings of reluctance to see her depart. Time however was running out if he were to attempt to ride back that night through the soft powdery snow. Fortunately the wind had dropped and it would be harder to travel the next day once the snow was compacted, or worse, frozen. Gathering up his bag and collecting Mattie from the stable he made his way slowly back, hoping that the snow was no deeper beyond the town boundary.

As always, the beauty of the snow-laden trees enchanted him, illuminated as they were by the bright moonlight, and his heart was lighter than it had been for some time. He had enjoyed the meeting with Lydia Firth, but was aware that her way of life was totally foreign to his own. Although he had Mrs Hardy's agreement to consider, he felt so at one with his surroundings that there seemed no urgent need to solve his problems as he trotted home.

Few travellers passed him by and it was as if everything in the valley slept, no sound disturbed the wonderful isolation. Yet, beneath the snow a world of wild things existed, no doubt waiting for an opportunity to stalk a meal whenever possible. He knew they were there, just as he knew they were listening to him, they were part of this land that he loved so much. By the time he reached the farm he was in a buoyant mood, even if tired and hungry, but the horse needed stabling as Jack had long since gone home. However, he could see that he had done his job well, the animals were safe within their stalls and were grazing contentedly at the hay, and Bella greeted him with a welcome bark.

Once inside the farmhouse, however, he came to the realisation that the large rooms were comfortless and unwelcoming, unlike those of the cottage. Just as the noise of his footsteps on the flagged floor rang as he paced up and down, so the tick of the clock disturbed his concentration when he rested in the chair. Conscious of the emptiness of the house, Edward found himself missing Abe more and more. It had been on quiet nights like this that they had chatted and sipped wine over a game of chess together, but now he felt out of place on his own in the rambling old building. At first he had enjoyed its spaciousness simply because it belonged to him, but as time passed he had begun to miss the cosiness of his former home. When, on long winter evenings, the wind swept down the valley from the moors and found its way through gaps in doors and windows, windows which Abe sadly had neglected so much, there was no joy in sitting after a hard day's work on his own.

It was no good, he was too tired to sleep and too disturbed to rest. Putting down his empty plate and, seizing his coat, he went out into the stillness of the night.

It was almost as bright as day now, a brilliant moon lit the snow-covered hills which stretched out to the horizon. He drew in a deep breath of sharp clear air, and let his eyes feast on the sight before him. Further down the valley, lights twinkled and plumes of smoke rose from several chimneys, the only reminders that he was not alone as he walked up the lane. Nor was he, for a set of paw-marks crossed the field leaving little holes in the snow. A fox perhaps, or a hare from the moors seeking food; only daylight would reveal which. Mrs Hardy too was awake, judging by the light shining through her unshuttered downstairs window. She had no doubt thought the conditions would have prevented him from returning tonight and had not bothered with her shutters as a result.

There she probably sat, quite happily settled in his former home, whilst he wandered about in the cold. Drawing level with the window he hesitated and, seeing no movement from within, wondered where she could be. Moving closer he looked in but there was no-one to be seen, although the light inside flickered considerably before the room suddenly went dark. This seemed rather strange and he wondered if there was anything amiss. After a few moments a light shone down from the upstairs window and he froze instantly, afraid of drawing attention to himself in case she thought him to be prying on her. As she closed the shutters and left him in darkness he breathed a sigh of relief.

Damn the woman! She had his cottage and now she had the power to make him feel guilty for no reason at all! There was something about her which he couldn't fathom and this irritated him. Perhaps it was her reserve? He knew nothing at all about her, and couldn't fault her in any way, yet he could no more marry her than he could refuse to see Lydia Firth again. At least she could make him laugh! For a while today he had relaxed in her company, had been able to share some of his fears and, at the same time, here was someone who understood his problems. She had coaxed from him in her vivacious teasing, things which he had never spoken of even to Abe. Try as he might he could not push from his mind the small, cheerful woman whom he hardly knew. Turning, he retraced his steps back to the lonely farmhouse.

The *Surrey Theatre* on West Bar was one of the most impressive theatres in which Lydia Firth had worked, with its museum and roof-top dancing when the weather was good. It had only one drawback, the audiences were not as meek and mild as befitted such elegant surroundings. Instead of quiet disapproval when a performance didn't live up to their expectations, there was raucous jeering and coarse gestures. Such exhibitionism rarely worried Lydia and she always played along good-naturedly, when she had a part that is. When Albert ran off with the saucy new addition to the company to which they belonged, she was left high and dry in this gloomy town. It had not been easy to find work in the six months since he abandoned her, she being only one half of their double act, but Tommy Youdan had offered work of a sort, waiting on at the bar. The rest of the cast had then moved on, leaving her in Mrs Marshall's lodgings, fearful for her future.

Lydia wasn't getting any younger and had little taste for menial domestic tasks, so without Albert she was nothing. She was unable, perhaps incapable of creating a solo act at her age; he'd taken her best years and then deserted her for Sophie Tyler. It wasn't Lydia's talent as his assistant that pleased the crowd but her good looks and vivacity, attributes, that were it would seem, easily replaced when the time was right. She should have seen the signs and got him to place a ring on her finger; little wonder he made sure she never got pregnant, unless he was only half the man she'd thought him to be. From now on she would have no scruples where survival was concerned; after all, in her profession, a booking was only good while it lasted. She would have to seek a more secure future the best way she could.

It had been whilst tidying up the theatre bar one day that she'd found the discarded newspaper in which Edward's advertisement had been published. At first glance it did no more than amuse her, then, as time passed, bringing little or no hope of moving on in the theatre circuit, she recalled the article. She knew only too well the reputation attached to an unmarried bar-maid, as well as the temptations being poor could bring. She had sifted frantically amongst the rubbish in the outhouse until she recovered the paper, and then promptly penned a letter which was carefully aimed at gaining the attention of a potential husband.

Several weeks later and much to her surprise, for she had given up all hope of receiving a reply, a letter arrived suggesting a meeting at the *Angel Inn*. After taking great pains to look attractive and yet respectable, she had gone, despite the bad weather, to meet Mr Morton. It had to be the greatest performance of her life, for her heart would never again be allowed to rule her head, but to her surprise she found the man to be modest and a quite presentable person. Within half an hour she had judged him to be honest, if a little naive, and decided it would be in her best interest to win his affections and, if possible, his name.

In the weeks that followed, Edward frequently took himself to town on one pretext or another and found himself succumbing to Lydia's charms. He told no-one of his business there but whatever drew him to Sheffield seemed to Mrs Hardy to be no bad thing. He was amiable, almost congenial, and she had begun to consider the contract made between them to be quite acceptable. Indeed, the prospect of further involvement at the end of the agreed trial period was not now quite such a daunting thing as it had first appeared.

He, on the other hand, was pushing the idea of marriage to her further and further to the back of his mind. With Lydia Firth he felt alive, aware of himself for the first time in his life. He had never been a concert-hall or theatre-going man, but with Lydia's persuasion he had gone to the *Surrey*, first to see a show and then, on several occasions, to meet her thespian friends in the spacious bar and saloon. They were a gay lot he had to admit, taking life more or less as it came, just as long as they could finish the night with a jar of ale or a tot of brandy. He would just get to know one set of her friends then they would move on to be replaced by another, but all accepted his visits cordially. It never seemed to bother anyone that Edward was both quiet and sober-minded; they had sufficient joviality between them to make up for what he lacked.

Their flamboyant tales of successes and failures amused him being, as they were, from a world far removed from his own, although he suspected many a story was exaggerated in order to enthral the listeners. Always Lydia stayed by his side, reassuring him that he was welcome. He was flattered by her attentions, uplifted by her gaiety and obviously falling in love with her. Each time he returned to the farm after being with her he was more aware than ever of the contrast between the two women in his life. Mrs Hardy was without doubt, in all respects, the more suitable, except that she was very reserved—and he didn't love her, whereas Lydia was impractical, totally unsuitable for farm life, yet it was she whom he loved. He was well aware that if he brought the latter out to live at the farm she would be stifled by boredom in his beautiful valley and would need taking to town in search of amusement.

From Lydia's actions and veiled hints, Edward was gradually being convinced that she would not refuse his offer of marriage and so, as the weeks passed, he wrestled with both his conscience and his desire. There seemed no reason why, providing Mrs Hardy was amply taken care of, she should be disappointed if he withdrew his offer of marriage. After all, it was security she sought in the long run, and he was in a position to give her that. Nothing was to be signed until the three months were up, then she could keep the cottage—and perhaps help Lydia in the house.

Having finally made his choice, he resolved to do two things. Firstly, to invite Lydia out to the farm as soon as the winter snows were gone and the spring was bringing new life to the countryside, and secondly, to inform Mrs Hardy of his change of heart.

As it happened, the weather did not improve and by the beginning of March, Edward was becoming impatient to put his plan into action. He was aware that Lydia seemed to be expecting a commitment from him, and delay could be dangerous, perhaps resulting in him losing her. He knew also that his agreement with Mrs Hardy was about to reach the point of no return. He felt he knew her well enough now, in a companionable way, for her to understand his feelings, and expected she would be quite relieved at his decision.

Almost seven moths had elapsed since Abe's accident, a quarter of the time in which Edward had to marry and produce an heir. In a short time his normally well-ordered life had been transformed and he was deeply torn between two worlds and two ideals: that of a sturdy, solid farmer with few real friends and little social life, and that of Lydia's carefree, extrovert one. The former no longer completely satisfied him, yet he knew the latter was a foreign world into which he did not and could never fit. With this realisation, and in spite of everything against it, he knew the future lay only in compromise, by releasing Mrs Hardy from her commitment, suitably compensated, and by bringing Lydia into his world. He intended to propose marriage on his next visit to town.

Chapter 4

riday the 11th of March, 1864, was a wet and windy day. The raging winds that had lashed the farmhouse recently had made his planned journey to town not only impractical but impossible; the need to remain and oversee the safety of the farm took priority over his own preference. The delay was unfortunate but it didn't lessen Edward's resolve, it merely made him impatient. Also, because there was nothing else he could do, he had to content himself with an eager anticipation of his next meeting with Lydia. In the meantime he must make every effort to win Mrs Hardy to his way of thinking, and so decided he would go to her cottage that very evening.

It had been some time since there had been such a prolonged run of bad weather and, after his evening meal, Edward felt an inexplicable sense of disquiet as the evening progressed. Even Bella was jumpy, and as a precaution he unchained her and shut her in the stable where she could move about instead of being cramped up in her kennel. He was too restless to relax, having told Mrs Hardy earlier that he would call to discuss a matter with her later in the evening when Lizzie was in bed. Finally, he donned his coat and went to check that all was well around the farm, then, finding nothing amiss, he set off towards the cottage.

The biting and gusting westerly March wind lashed directly into his face, slowing him down as he headed up the lane. Alarmingly, the wind had been gaining strength with each passing hour and now it was carrying rain. He hated the wind above everything else for it was unpredictable, finding weaknesses where there seemed to be none, but when combined with rain the two seemed bent on evil intent. The surface of the lane was running with water, and before he had gone fifty yards his boots were heavy with mud. It would have been more sensible to have remained indoors but he was determined to press on.

Suddenly, between gusts of wind, an unexpected sound from the road above caused him to lift his head and peer over the hedge—an act which nearly lost him his hat as the wind freshened again. The noise grew louder and he could see a pair of lights—surely no one in his right mind would be driving a carriage at this time of night, especially in these conditions? It was almost ten o'clock! He looked up the valley towards the dam and could see specks of light in the distance, moving to and fro, and he assumed that the hurrying vehicle carried an urgent message for someone working at the head of the dam. Had the carriage been travelling at such a speed away from the workings he might have been alarmed, for he'd seen them earlier that day on his walk to check on the flock up on the higher ground. Although he'd been surprised then how full the dam was, he felt no cause for alarm— it was such a massive structure. In fact he'd concluded that with the wind driving the waves against the head of the dam, throwing white sprays of water up into the air, any overspill would provide a remarkable spectacle as it cascaded over the top. Even now, as he walked to the cottage, thousands more gallons of water would be flowing into the dam from the countless streams above it. Earlier he'd both marvelled and shuddered at the sight of the vast sheet of turbulent water penned in by the enormously thick wall. The dramatic slapping of the waves against the embankment had been hypnotic to watch, as each fresh gust of wind seemed to increase the ferment against the stonework.

He arrived at the cottage, his arm aching and his sleeve wet as he fought to keep the hat on his head, and hammered on the solid oak door in hope that Mrs Hardy would make haste to let him in. As she slid back the bolt and opened the door the wind almost forced it from her grasp.

'Good Evening, Mrs Hardy!' he gasped, breathlessly, pushing through and heaving the door shut behind him. 'I was checking the farm because of the wind, are you alright up here?' He paused for a moment to recover his breath, removed the sodden hat and hung it on the latch from where it dripped, slowly forming a puddle on the flag floor. 'I think my things had better be left in the kitchen, they're so wet,' he exclaimed.

'Surely your business could have waited, for this is not a night for anyone to venture out,' she said, observing his clothes and muddy boots. 'And I doubt if there is anything much you could do even if something was wrong! The wind is frightening but all seems well enough here, these cottages were built to last.'

Edward had never seen her anything but neatly dressed before and he stared unwittingly as she stood before him, dressed for bed. 'Oh! I do apologise. It is rather late, I will go now that I know everything is alright,' he stammered lamely.

She too had forgotten in the bustle that she was unprepared for visitors and quickly drew the wrap tighter across her breast. In the soft shadows she looked younger than before, almost pretty in fact, as the loosened hair fell free about her face. He was at a loss for words yet he made no move to leave. It was a pity that he had to hurt her now, but he couldn't delay in telling her of his change of plans and, in furthering these, must make sure that she and Lizzie were provided for, no matter what happened.

'I thought because it was getting very late that the weather had prevented you from coming, and so decided to retire,' she explained and, sensing his reluctance to leave, did not press him. 'Can I offer you a warm drink before you tackle the journey back again?' she offered.

He nodded, grateful that she had overlooked his frank gaze, and removed his coat. 'I will remove my boots too,' he said, bending low and pulling hard. 'I'm afraid I have made a mess for you out there, Mrs Hardy,' he confessed, as he followed her into the cosy sitting room. 'You have made a comfortable home here,' he said looking around in quiet appreciation. 'Are you pleased that you came out into the valley?'

'I do not regret coming, but Lizzie has become a wild child in these past four months, and you encourage her. I'm afraid she is getting hard to handle.' It was a statement of fact rather than a criticism.

He laughed, 'Lizzie is learning to be herself, and developing an independence and freedom which you had to deny her, quite rightly, in that dreadful courtyard. You, too, must learn to relax! Here, life is hard but richer than in the town due to the closeness of the soil and the beauties of nature. Do you find it lonely here?'

Hannah Hardy sighed. 'The evenings are long and the constant wet weather frustrates me, but I was lonely before I came so I can accept it. I have good food and a better way of life so I am grateful. This is enough, Mr Morton.'

'You will find the valley to be very different when spring arrives, and eventually you too will learn to love each season for its own charms. You may even come to see why I could not give up the farm or the land without a fight.' His voice was intent as he expressed his passion for the valley, and he felt for the first time since her arrival that she might understand if not condone his decision. Perhaps in deciding to marry Lydia he no longer felt threatened by Mrs Hardy, and if she were to stay in the cottage they might as well be friends. 'And please—call me Edward' he said in a gentle voice. 'We need not be so formal.'

She blushed, 'I had not thought to do so until we were married,' she said apologetically. 'It will seem strange after so long, to call you...' she hesitated, 'Edward. I may forget and revert to calling you Mr Morton if I'm not careful, As you know, my name is Hannah. I prefer not to have it shortened.'

Relaxing, he settled back in the armchair and again looked fondly around the room. She had made her mark on his former home; how he preferred it to the farmhouse, and how well she had settled in. A sudden gust of wind rattled the shutters, taking them both by surprise. Hannah looked at him fearfully.

'It's only the wind, although it really is gusting strongly', Edward reassured her. 'It is often like this here, but you'll get used to it.' Then, as an afterthought, half to himself, he added, 'I feel sorry for the workmen up at the dam on a night like this.'

'You'd think they would have more sense than to work there in these conditions,' she replied, somewhat calmed by his assurance.

'Yes, it is a little strange, I hope there's no problem. I was never keen on having the dam there in the first place, no one was, but seeing it earlier today from the moors was an awesome sight. Still, the surveyors and engineers should know what they're doing.'

'At least now there will be plenty of fresh drinking water for the town,' Hannah replied, remembering the queues at the pumps, particularly in dry weather when the supply was low.

'It will certainly regulate supplies here too, but it has been an intrusion into the valley. Several farms have been demolished and the landscape scarred irreparably, and for five long years the peace has been broken by the constant traffic of navvies, wagon loads of building materials and sightseers.'

They chatted amicably for a while, drinking the warm gruel which Hannah had prepared earlier in the day. Hannah was a good cook, he admitted to himself. A surge of envy filled and saddened him; he would have preferred to stay in his old bedroom instead of trudging back to the farm. Hannah! A sober name he considered, watching as she still clutched modestly at the edge of her wrap. The country air had added a bloom to her once sallow features and in the short time since her arrival her painfully thin body, although still slender, had a roundness about it that was appealing. He did not want to return to his lonely surroundings, and so feigned drowsiness, watching her from beneath his lowered lashes.

Perhaps she had once upon a time been beautiful; of course he would never know if that were true but now, as she sat there unaware of his gaze, there was a modest girlishness about her which he liked. He fought off a sudden urge to touch her, to see if the reserve had gone forever. What was he thinking of! It was late and he must leave before his flight of fantasy became reality. He must be strong and honest with her and tell her his plans before she heard rumours from someone else and, in doing so, end up despising him. His heart was heavy with guilt.

Suddenly he was awake, catching her off guard. The wistful look in his eyes did not go undetected by Hannah and she was tempted to ask what ailed him. Their eyes met unavoidably, probing, yet revealing nothing, leaving each disturbed and confused.

'Hannah!' his voice was low, almost a whisper. 'I have something to confess. This arrangement we have—it isn't fair to either of us. I am releasing you from the contract.' The shock of his announcement seemed to stun her, and the colour drained from her face; he too could not go on. He forced the words from his lips, 'I am going to marry another!'

She stared at him for a moment, then her face became a mask through which angry eyes glared. 'Where shall Lizzie and I go?' She demanded angrily. 'You brought us here and now we cannot go back. I was willing to keep my part of the bargain!'

He heard a catch in her voice but the mask revealed nothing. She had retreated once more and he could not reach her. He spoke, more harshly than he intended, endeavouring to explain. 'I have found someone I love, and it is better that way. You and Lizzie may stay here in the cottage and help the future Mrs Morton. There is no thought of you having to leave.' She made him feel ashamed as though he had betrayed her. If he'd hurt her then he was sorry, yet he was angry too that she sat watching him in silent condemnation. Why didn't she speak? Didn't she realise how difficult it was for him? He could, if he was that sort of man, wash his hands of her for a mere settlement, but he wasn't that kind of person. He wanted to shake her, force her to lower her reserve, and tell her that she was an ungrateful wretch. He knew that he should leave but he wanted an answer from her first. 'Have you nothing to say! Aren't you grateful for what I have given you?' he demanded angrily.

'No!' she cried. 'I will not stay! I thank you for what you have done for us, but you have not bought me! I will find somewhere else to go.' Her eyes were proud and her voice filled with emotion. 'I had thought you to be a man of your word and now you discard me with no thought other than that of appeasement. I have survived before and will do so again.'

Edward was hurt and stunned by the strength of her outburst. She would survive, he could see that, but the fierceness of her determination alarmed him. What on earth could have happened in the past to provoke such bitterness in her? He realised that in his pre-occupation with Lydia he had paid little real attention to Hannah and mistakenly misjudged her inner strength. Why, after spending such a pleasant hour together had things gone so badly wrong? 'I think that I had better go,' he offered defensively. 'I would like the opportunity to talk to you further on the subject tomorrow, if I may?'

'There is nothing further to say. Lizzie will be heartbroken!'

Hastily pulling on his boots and coat, he hurried from the cottage, his face white but all anger had evaporated at the realisation that if Hannah went then Lizzie would also go. Lizzie had become the light of his life, following him everywhere, chatting merrily and asking the endless questions which innocent minds ask. It was Lydia he wanted but he needed Mrs Hardy on account of Lizzie! Tonight he had also recognised the same strength of spirit in the mother which the child had not yet learned to control. The visit had not gone well and although Mrs Hardy now knew of his plans, his heart was heavy with misgivings, and some guilt.

Beyond the turmoil of his thoughts he was gradually becoming aware of distant sounds and urgent, hurried cries penetrating the raging of the wind. He stopped and turned, puzzled. He could judge where the head of the dam was by the lights flickering here and there. Normally there was nobody near the dam at this hour and, although he knew they were behind in its construction, it didn't make sense for men to try to work on a night like this. There was something amiss, of that he was certain, he could feel it in the pit of his stomach.

He was remembering the power of the wind on the dam wall, and the tremendous increase in overspill earlier in the day, the hurrying carriage in the night, the lights and the urgent voices. It had to be the dam! If there was trouble up there then he would find out the measure of it for himself. Now he was running with the wind, heedless of his own safety, desperate to get to the farm and his horse. Collecting a storm lamp from the house, he saddled the already jittery mare and headed for the dam. Once he reached the road the going was easier, the surface having been prepared for the continuous stream of wagons with their heavy loads.

What he saw on arrival there did nothing to allay his fears, as anxious faces peered expectantly at him from the embankment.

'What's the matter?' Edward yelled to the nearest man, his voice striving against the wind.

'A crack in the outer wall!' came the cry.

'What? How bad is it—can I do anything to help?' Edward shouted, drawing nearer until he was practically shouting in the man's face.

'They're trying to raise the sluice-gates in the pipes and have been at it almost an hour now.' The man stopped to regain his breath. 'Once the pressure's off they say things will be alright.'

Edward waited apprehensively in the rain, wondering why the cursed gates wouldn't open properly in the first place. There was nothing he could do. The ground suddenly shook violently beneath his feet and he was deafened by the fearful noise of thousands of gallons of water surging through the air. He steadied himself, relieved that the gates had finally been raised and that the embankment was still intact. He then looked along the valley towards the village where lights still flickered in the farmhouses and cottages. He shuddered at the thought of what might have happened if the dam had burst.

The force of water surging through the pipes made a hideous sound, yet there seemed to be no lowering of the level of water trapped against the inner embankment—although of course there wouldn't be for some considerable time. He waited anxiously but soon realised that unless vast quantities of water were released quickly the embankment would surely be unable to withstand the strain any longer.

'It's not going to work!' Edward cried to several workmen who seemed mesmerised by the volume of water spouting down into the valley below. 'Something else will have to be done. 'Who's in charge?'

'They've gone to Sheffield to fetch Gunson, the engineer—they can't be much longer now. Though God alone knows what he can do!' the senior of the men replied. 'Someone's warned the villagers, and just as well!'

Edward turned sharply, 'Well, nobody bothered to warn me, and my farm's down there too.' He was worried now, he could see the wind whipping up the water against the bank-side with menacing force, and flooding over the dam wall. There was no let up in the rain either, as it continued to lash against everything in its path.

Suddenly a carriage arrived. 'It's Gunson! Thank God!' A voice cried out.

Jumping down, Gunson eyed the crack in the wall and was visibly disturbed. Judging by the look on his face in the lantern light, Edward decided not to take any chances. If the dam burst all hell would be let loose in the valley and everything he had worked for would be in line with the torrent of water! There was nothing he could do here, and Mrs Hardy and Lizzie were at the cottage, unaware that anything was wrong. Spurring Mattie, he rode back praying that the horse wouldn't stumble on the muddy road as he forced the pace. He was chilled and uncomfortable, his face chapped by the wind and rain, yet he dare not stop even to wipe his face. If Gunson's suggestion of blowing a gap in the wall of the by-wash didn't work, then a catastrophe might occur.

Dare he, once he had warned Mrs Hardy and got the pair of them to higher ground, go down and release some of his animals? He listened all the while for the blast that would further release pressure on the dam and decided that if it worked, then and only then, would he go back down to the farm.

He reined in sharply before the cottage, frantically yelling for Mrs Hardy as he did so and ran up the path. 'Come on! Come on!' he shouted impatiently as he hammered on the door.

Mrs Hardy opened the window, frightened by the commotion. 'Open the door as quickly as you can,' he shouted. 'The dam may give way any minute! Just get down here now!' Leaving the window swinging in the wind she ran down the stairs and wrenched back the bolts. 'Get some warm clothing on while I get Lizzie and some blankets,' he ordered. 'There's no time to lose. It may be a false alarm but I'm taking no chances.' He brushed past her, 'And fetch the storm lantern!' he called, climbing the stairs two at a time, then seized the sleeping child from her bed. Wrapping Lizzie tightly in the bedcovers he drew her closely to his chest and descended the narrow winding stairs quickly, but almost fell in his haste. By the time he reached the foot, Hannah was leaving the kitchen swathed in the cape she had snatched from the hook, and carrying her boots and several other garments over her arm.

'Roll them up and try to keep them as dry as you can,' he ordered, hurrying from the house towards Mattie, with Lizzie still in his arms. To his amazement he heard Bella bark close by and, on looking back, saw her silhouetted against the light from the open door. Somehow she must have got out of the stable and heard him calling to Mrs Hardy. Whistling for the dog to follow him, he soothed Lizzie and set her down on the ground for a moment as he turned to Hannah who had joined him. 'You must get up on Mattie and I'll pass Lizzie and the bundle to you.' He ran back to the door and slammed it so hard that the sound of the frame rattling rang out through the night.

Hannah allowed him to lift her up into the saddle. 'Where are we going?' she begged, fearfully.

'As high as we can. Now, take Lizzie and just hang on. I'll lead. There's no time to waste!' He was shouting as he led the horse quickly forward into the lane. Slowly in the dark, for a lantern would be useless in the blustery wind, they left the lane and made their way up the hillside with the rain beating against them and Hannah attempting to shield Lizzie with the bundle. It was not the easiest of routes but it was the quickest way he could think of to reach higher ground. Had there been sufficient time he would have taken a longer, easier way to where there was more shelter. Mattie stumbled constantly on the numerous scattered boulders, almost throwing Hannah from the saddle, but she clung on desperately. All the time Edward realised that the dog was up ahead, barking with short yaps as if encouraging them on. Of course, Bella was used to the rough ground, knew every path and stone as she brought the sheep up and down with the shepherd. 'Here Bella! That's my girl,' he cried out. 'Here now!' She came closer, enough for him to catch hold of her in the dark and tie his scarf round her neck. 'To the shed, Bella—go on gal!' he coaxed, gently.

The higher they climbed the more exposed to the elements they became and Edward looked around, trying to get his bearings. They had no light and without Bella they were lost, yet he believed that they were now well above the level of the embankment and not far from the lean-to which had been constructed for the animals to shelter in during the winter, and where Bella and old Ben took their break in bad weather.

By this time they were all chilled through and drenched, but Lizzie seemed undisturbed and merely moaned occasionally in her sleep in Hannah's aching arms, unaware of the threat so near at hand. Edward peered round, confident now that they were high enough to relax as he saw the bobbing lights below at the level of the dam. He had to find the shelter quickly and get Hannah out of the bitter cold, for she had left the cottage half-dressed beneath the cloak and her feet were clad only in socks and slippers. There had been insufficient time to pull on her boots as he dared not delay their departure, and he knew that she must now be cold and uncomfortable, to say the least.

Bella suddenly pulled on his scarf and barked excitedly. She had found the shelter and wanted to get inside without delay.

'Good girl, Bella! Good girl,' he said, soothingly, and once they reached the rough shed he released the scarf. Thank God the dog had escaped from the stable or they might never have found their way in the dark.

Gently he took the child from Hannah, and Lizzie moaned softly as he ducked beneath the entrance and placed her in the corner out of the wind and rain. He struggled for a few moments before locating the storm lantern which, fortunately, when he opened the shutter was still alight. The child had been well protected by the bundle but Hannah was shivering as he lifted her down from the horse, and she stumbled from the numbness in her limbs. Edward took a coat from the bundle and gently removed the wet cape from Hannah's shoulders. 'Here, let me put the coat around you or you will catch your death of cold,' he said kindly. 'We must also remove those wet socks and get the circulation going again in your feet. Sit down next to Lizzie. My eyes are becoming more accustomed to the poor light now but you must excuse me if I am a little clumsy.' He removed the cold wet socks from her feet and rubbed vigorously, causing her to wince, then put on her boots which she had valiantly clung to during the journey up the hillside. 'Now you must walk around and try to get warm. Come!' He seized her arm firmly and helped her towards the threshold. If there was any anger left in Mrs Hardy now over their earlier quarrel she was too numbed and bewildered to show it. 'Lizzie will come to no harm here with Bella to guard her,' he assured her. 'And I need to find out what's happening down there.'

Edward knew that if they walked close to the wall they would soon find a position where it would be possible to see over the valley, but when they reached the spot it was too dark to see more than the flickering lights from the embankment.

He sighed. 'I'm sorry, Mrs Hardy, maybe I was too hasty in dragging you both up here like this. It would seem to be a false alarm.'

For the first time since leaving the cottage Hannah spoke a few mumbled words, a shiver affected her voice. 'What made you think the dam was going to burst?'

'I went up there after I left you. There was such a commotion going on at the embankment that I could hear their shouting every time the wind dropped. I saw lights moving hastily about and had to go and see for myself just what was going on. It was an awesome sight as the waves raced across the blackness of the water and surged over the top. A long thin crack had appeared in the embankment, and I realised that if it should continue to widen the result could be catastrophic, but if it holds firm tonight, with that weakness, then surely it will survive forever. When I left, the men were laying explosives to blow a gap in the by-wash in an effort to release the pressure of the water, but so far I have heard nothing.'

'If only it were daylight!' Hannah lamented, shivering again violently. 'Do you think Lizzie is safe enough, and warm?'

'She will come to no harm with Bella and there is no other shelter to be had. The next farm is too far away and the route very difficult to risk at night from where we are, but the clouds are clearing a little which might be helpful.' She gasped in the chilling wind. 'Right now my worries are for you, not Lizzie. You are still very cold, but it is too dangerous for us to move about quickly enough to warm you up. The only solution is for me to protect you beneath my coat. That way the wind will strike me and not you. I don't mean to be familiar, but if we don't keep you warm the consequences could be quite bad.' He had expected her to protest, but instead she readily obeyed.

'I'm grateful,' she said. 'And I realise the dreadful situation you're in.'

'Thank you!' He replied, turning his back to the wind and, pulling her beneath the coat drew her tighter with his arms to provide greater protection, then peered again into the dark. 'I must watch' he said. 'But I feel so helpless up here.' He was conscious of her body trembling against his and for a fleeting moment wondered if she too was aware of their closeness. What on earth are they doing with those explosives? He wondered, and what was he doing up on the moors in this weather with Mrs Hardy in his arms? Everything seemed unreal. Hannah Hardy's back was soft against him and he unwittingly tightened his grip, drawing comfort from the contact.

Suddenly Hannah spoke up. 'But what about the other farms in the valley, and beyond?'

'Apparently the workmen warned the villagers, but nobody thought to warn me! Perhaps they thought the farm too high to be at risk, but I have seen the power of water in the past and fear its strength.' They stood in silence, each deep in their own thoughts until Edward said quietly. 'I'm sorry, but if I hadn't brought you to the farm in the first place you would not be facing these dangers now. I seem to have increased your miseries, not lessened them.'

'I am bewildered at the speed with which everything has happened, that is all. No two days seem alike any more.' Her voice was almost inaudible but he was sensitive enough to realise he had added to her problems, in many ways. Not least by telling her that he had found someone more suitable as a wife!

However, he had more worries right now. So far he had heard no explosion from the direction of the dam, and no sound of water breaking through the embankment. He began to wonder if he had been foolish in taking such a drastic step in leaving the farm. Even so, judging by the activity of the lanterns which bobbed about in the distance, there was obviously still some concern about the structure, otherwise the men would have returned to their beds!

The rain had eased now and the new moon fleetingly shone through the broken clouds, occasionally illuminating the hillside, allowing him to see further. However, the wind still persisted with its onslaught, lashing at his cape.

He was about to speak again when suddenly a frighteningly loud crack like thunder rent the air, followed only moments later by the terrible sound of water gushing and hissing with great force. 'My God!' He yelled, 'The dam must be giving way!' A further loud crash drowned out his voice. Then, in quick succession, a series of muffled explosions were just discernible through the awful noise, 'The charges! And not before time.' His voice was filled with relief. 'Perhaps they will do the trick.' Yet deep down in his heart he suspected it was already too late; the thunderous, crashing sounds from the valley below were not diminishing. He closed his eyes in spite of the fact that he needed to know what was happening, but he couldn't bear to look towards the dam.

The moon had disappeared again, leaving Edward and Hannah in the dark, clinging together out of fear and apprehension. He had no idea how long they stood there in terror, listening to the hideous sounds which came out of the blackness, nor did he realise that Hannah was crying softly to herself. Then, suddenly, there was a terrible, groaning roar, and he knew instantly that the whole embankment must have collapsed, sending a seething wave of destruction down the valley towards the village. There was no disguising the evil sound as the wall of water consumed all before it, tearing root and foundation alike from the ground, annihilating everything he loved.

Hannah was sobbing now and he became aware that he was unashamedly clinging to her. He lowered his head comfortingly against hers, his eyes filled with tears and his throat constricted with despair. There was nothing to be said, they were silent listeners to a disaster too horrible to contemplate, and even if he had spoken, the words would have been swallowed up in the terrible noise. They stood, it must have been for all of twenty minutes, numbed with disbelief, waiting for the rumbling and scouring to end. It was she who eventually spoke first, with an empty soulless voice. 'The water—it has to go somewhere, and the village lies directly in its path.' She shuddered, horrified at this thought. 'I don't want daylight to come—I don't want to see what has happened,' she sobbed hopelessly.

Edward's thoughts were dark and deep too, knowing to some extent the calamitous events which would be taking place even now.

'Please!' Hannah begged, tearfully. 'Take me back to Lizzie.'

Pulling himself together, he loosened his grip on her and gently led her back along the wall to the shelter where the child and dog lay huddled together, Lizzie asleep as if nothing were amiss, the dog watching her as if she were a young lamb. Edward was chilled and deeply shocked, and in the distance he could still hear eerie sounds from the valley below. He knew it would be stupid, and very dangerous, to go down in the dark to the unknown, to find out the true state of things. Dawn would bring only heartache, for he realised that people would have perished, and farms possibly been destroyed. They could all be homeless! His main thoughts now must be for their survival through the remainder of the night.

It was getting colder, midnight was long since passed, and he had known of men dying from exposure up on these hills on nights like this.

He attempted to lessen Hannah's fears, saying, 'We must conserve our energies and keep close together. It's going to be a long night, but at least we are sheltered from the wind and rain in here. There really is no alternative but to stay until dawn. Draw Lizzie to you and lie with your back against me while I rest against the wall. That way we can all try to get some sleep!'

Hannah obeyed without question, grateful simply to let Edward take charge, for he had the strength which she lacked. 'Do you think that once the water has passed out of the valley it will lose its power?' Her tone was hopeful. 'Surely by the time it reaches the town it will merely flood the rivers and roads? People will be upstairs in bed by this time, and safe from the rising water.'

'I don't know,' Edward confessed. 'It depends how much water has escaped but by the sound of it there's going to be an almighty torrent heading for the town.'

'You were right to bring us up here,' Hannah conceded quietly. 'You may have saved our lives.'

'I wish to God that I had been mistaken!' Edward said, sadly. 'Tomorrow we may all be without homes and work. Others may not even be as lucky as that, for the cruelty and power of water has to be seen to be believed. I know, I have crossed the sea many times and seen the terrible power it can have.'

'I'm truly worried for the village people, and just as concerned in case the farm may be damaged. I have come to enjoy living here.' Hannah confessed.

'It is all I have,' Edward sighed. 'Perhaps it was never intended to be mine.' His voice was bitter, and he stared out into the darkness, his thoughts dwelling on the possibilities of the morrow, thoughts too terrible to speak of. 'And I would have married just to keep it.' His voice trailed off but Hannah realised the true depths of his anger over the terms of Abe's legacy.

A strong feeling of resentment suddenly rose in her against the man who held her, and who had brought her out to the farm with such high hopes, only to cast her aside when it suited him. 'But now you have found someone else whom you want to marry!' She spoke sharply, her voice steady but it did not conceal her criticism of him.

He knew she was right to chide him and that knowledge only added to his despondency. 'I may have nothing left to offer her,' he replied irritably, aware that by morning he might not be so attractive a proposition for Lydia to consider.

Hannah was deeply annoyed by what he said, yet at the same time also knew the hopelessness of the situation. 'Surely, if she loves you enough it won't matter, and I shall be leaving the valley anyway?'

He was angry at her for reminding him of their earlier quarrel, as he had other things to occupy him now. However, the facts were there, and he lapsed into silence, praying for daylight to arrive. Whatever was revealed then would seal his fate with Lydia as, even if there was anything left to fight for, he knew she was hardly the type to roll up her sleeves and help. He had hoped to pamper her and, with the help of Mrs Hardy, allow her to live contentedly raising his child. Perhaps he'd been hoping for too much? But what was he thinking of, Lydia might at that very moment be in danger from the flood water! He groaned out loud without realising he had done so, whilst mentally trying to remember the course of the river. Although he had never been to where Lydia was lodging, he knew that it was not far from the bridge in Hillsborough, and might well be directly in the path of the flood!

Thinking the sound of his groan was over some inner conflict to do with the events of the evening, Hannah broke the silence. 'Things may not be as bad as you think, and I didn't intend to sound so spiteful—it's just that I am happy here and would be disappointed if I had to leave. Desperation brought us together, but if you can find happiness with the lady concerned I will not stand in your way.'

The cold was now beginning to bite into Edward's legs and back and he shifted uncomfortably. 'I must walk for a while to ease my muscles,' he said, easing her to one side and rising. 'Lean against the wall and try to sleep. I shall not be long.' With that he left the shelter and went back to where they had been earlier. There was nothing to be seen, however, even in the fleeting glimpses given by the moonlight, and as his stiffness had now eased he returned to find Hannah asleep. For this he was grateful, as now instead of speaking of his fears he could put all his mental effort into getting through the rest of the night.

It was Lizzie who woke him with her bewildered cry, dragging him from the shallow sleep into which he had drifted in spite of the cold, and his fears. Early morning mist clung to the hilltops, and for several minutes he hung between a waking disorientation and exhaustion. Suddenly recalling where he was, and why, he struggled to his feet. 'The world is not quite the same today,' he said, gently lifting her. 'Something dreadful may have happened to the farm. The water has escaped from the dam and washed things away.' He set her firmly on the ground, 'We came here in the dark and rain, so that we should be safe. And we are!' He reassured her, ruffling her hair lightly with his hand as Hannah slept on. 'Stay with your mother, Lizzie, we don't want her to be afraid when she wakes up in a strange place, do we? I'll be back very soon, so be a good girl—I am going to find Mattie.' Bella lay watching, one eyebrow raised expectantly, but remaining silent. 'Come, Bella,' he called quietly so as not to wake Hannah. The dog needed no second bidding, but got up and bounded after him.

'Please hurry and find Mattie,' Lizzie whispered anxiously.

Edward was filled with foreboding as he approached a vantage point on the valleyside, but nothing could have prepared him for what now confronted him. The broken edge of the dam lay like a sick dog from whose mouth spewed a trail of muddy vomit stretching towards and beyond the village. It was as if a huge scythe had swept down the valley, flattening everything before it and leaving scars too terrible to contemplate. This was no longer his valley. Gone were the green fields where only months before crops had grown and ripened. Now there lay a sea of ugly mud totally devoid of tree and bush. Huge boulders had gouged across the spurs of land and now lay scattered as if tossed carelessly about like a handful of pebbles. No feature remained unchanged, no wall stood standing and for a moment he was afraid to look towards the farm. When at last he did so, he was unable to see where the farmhouse had been as the whole valley had been so catastrophically altered, he turned away, his eyes closed and his throat tight with fearful anticipation, knowing that such devastation must have taken life as well as property.

He had to force himself to turn back and search the lower slopes for the cottage. There it was, grey and forlorn, just above the swathe of mud. There appeared to be little or no trace of the farmstead, it was as if it had been plucked from the earth without ever having existed at all. An eerie silence hung in the air and he noticed that no bird sang or chirped as if the creatures had been struck dumb by the horror of it all.

The raging deluge of the night had drastically changed things for Edward; although the land was still there, as was the cottage, had he the heart to begin all over again, especially if Lydia no longer wanted him? And what of the Hardys? It would be cruel to make them homeless now. His heart was heavy, both with anger and despair. Just what had been the point, he wondered, of his now futile battle to own the farm? Could he sell, or rent out the cottage, then go away to find new employment, make new friends elsewhere? What was the value of anything when in one night all could be obliterated by an act of nature, or man's incompetence? Who would care if he stayed or went? Each and everyone would be too busy putting to rights their own lives in the aftermath of this shocking disaster.

No! What was he thinking of? He was tired, overwhelmed by the events of the previous night and it was selfish of him to think that way when so many families relied on the farm for support. He must take upon himself the mantle of responsibility that Abe thought him capable of, and forget his own desires for the time being.

Unknown to Edward, Hannah was now awake, disturbed by the impatient Lizzie, and was observing his drooping shoulders from a distance. She was reluctant to impose upon his obvious distress, yet she needed to know how bad things were below. She gathered up their few damp belongings and waited patiently for some sign that he was ready to be disturbed. Mattie, on the other hand, after wandering all night complete with saddle, had no such scruples.

Edward was not aware of the horse until she breathed heavily over his shoulder, nudging him gently with her muzzle. He jumped, startled by her sudden appearance. 'Poor old thing!' he said comfortingly, rubbing her nose with his hand. 'And you've been in harness all night. I'm afraid we're both saddled in different ways, you and I.' He took the rein and led her back to the shelter where Hannah and the child waited.

'Is it bad?' Hannah asked, hardly daring to speak after seeing the distress on his face.

'A dreadful sight, a sickening sight. Half the valley has been swept away, taking the farm with it!'

'Oh! How terrible!' she cried, her face going white with shock.

'There is only one small consolation, the cottage seems to be alright, albeit on the edge of a field of mud and boulders. How much damage there is I can't imagine but at least it is somewhere to shelter. Until we actually get there I really won't know!'

She shook her head in anguish. 'I am so sorry!' she said softly, the depths of her sympathy apparent in her voice.

There was nothing to be said or done now but to go down and see what could be salvaged of their lives. 'Do you want to ride on Mattie with Lizzie, or walk?' he asked, wanting to get on with things.

'Walk, please, I'm cold and it will do me good.'

'Be prepared for a terrible sight, but try to sound cheerful for Lizzie's sake,' he whispered so that the child couldn't hear him. 'I was very lucky not to have been killed. Had I stayed in the farm I most certainly would have been, and it is obvious that a dreadful disaster has hit the villages in the lower valleys.

Slowly the little party edged their way down off the higher ground, saying very little as they went and, as if sensing the seriousness of things,

Lizzie refrained from her usual lively chatter. This was a relief to Edward for he was so cold and dispirited that he wished only to be alone and to sleep. It was Hannah who, once she had overcome the shock of seeing the damage, was determined to set about providing them all with a home, even if it was to be only for a short while.

Once down on the lower slopes Edward realised that some parts of the boundary walls had survived but these were half-buried by mud and debris. Similarly the staunch buttress walls of the farmhouse chimney stack remained standing, they must have blended in with the mud as he'd looked down from the hilltop earlier.

As the trio approached the cottage it became obvious that a surging wave of water must have lapped against the cottage boundary wall, leaving twigs and rubbish lodged between the stonework, before flooding through the gateway into the garden. Edward couldn't see any structural damage as he waded up the thickly muddied path, but was horrified on opening the door to see that the silt-laden water had seeped under it, covering the ground floor with a layer of stinking mud. Every piece of furniture was tide-marked, and the sodden rugs lay limp and buckled, shapeless and muddy on the stone-flagged floor.

Hannah's reaction was one of anger. She had been dismayed on the way down at the destruction she had seen but she was outraged to find her home had been invaded in such a way. 'Someone is to blame for not building the dam properly in the first place!' she raged, and would have begun sweeping out the mud immediately had Edward not stopped her.

'I don't doubt there will be an enquiry,' he replied, rather taken aback by the strength of her indignation. 'Then we may be able to lay the blame somewhere. Right now, though, we're all cold and hungry. Once we've changed our clothing and eaten we can tackle the mess. After all, we're lucky to find the cottage still standing. The first thing we must do is build a fire in the upstairs grate. There's plenty of wood stacked behind the cottage and that on the higher racks will still be dry. With a little oil we should soon have a fire going. You take Lizzie upstairs where it's clean, and I'll get the firewood.

Now was not the time to worry about the loss of the farm, but he couldn't help looking towards where the fine old house had been, and saw only a pile of mud-covered rubble. The force of the water had taken most of the stones away, leaving little to remind him of its former grace. There was no way of knowing if, beneath the shapeless heap, some items might be salvageable, or whether the contents of the cellar were crushed and submerged in dirty water. Certainly the animals were all gone, poor creatures, leaving him with only the sheep on the hillside, Mattie and Bella.

He was acutely aware of the fact that he ought to be down in the village doing what he could to help, yet first he must see that Hannah and Lizzie were provided for after their shocking ordeal. He would have preferred to leave them all and head straight down to Sheffield, to make sure that Lydia was safe and well, but he knew the thought to be a selfish one. Lydia just had to be alright he tried to convince himself, as he carried half a dozen of the driest logs back indoors to where Hannah waited, kettle in hand.

'Thank goodness there's some water in the storage jars,' she exclaimed. 'Though Heaven knows if the well still exists. We shall have to live upstairs for weeks until the place dries out sufficiently.'

If the foundations aren't ruined, he thought pessimistically as he struggled to light the fire. 'It will be dangerous to dry everything out too quickly—things will crack and distort if we do. It's going to take a lifetime to put the farm on its feet again—if I bother to re-build at all! The land can be cleared, but the buildings are all gone. I'm worse off now than I was when working for Abe. What monies he left won't last forever and I don't know if it's worth the effort to rebuild.'

'Of course it's worth it!' she replied indignantly. 'You're young enough to start again and at least you haven't lost everything. There are many people who live all their lives in conditions almost as bad as this, where every time there's a storm their homes are flooded, some even with sewage from the middens. Believe me, if you've never lived in those conditions then you don't know what existence in the poor part of town is like.'

Edward listened in amazement at Hannah's lengthy outburst. She was, he was beginning to discover, a woman of hidden depths, and whereas he previously thought her spiritless and compliant, he now began to realise the power and strength of her mind. He wasn't sure that he liked the change, but he had to admire her strength and courage at a time like this.

How different Lydia was to Hannah! She was mysterious, frivolous perhaps, yet she made him feel that there was more to live for than work. From the moment she'd entered the inn when they first met he had felt a desire to care for her, even spoil her, she was almost as childlike as Lizzie. With Mrs Hardy, however, there had always been something unfathomable and impersonal. Last night he had rejected her, hoping that their agreement was virtually at an end. Circumstances, however, had changed everything and now they were going to have to live together under the same roof, making it even more difficult for him to remove her if and when he married Lydia. It would be almost impossible.

Hannah took Lizzie upstairs to change, and returned to prepare breakfast for them all. She also brought down some dry clothing of his which she knew had been left in an old chest upstairs. There was little point in changing footwear however until the mud on the floor was got rid of.

After the meal Edward felt a little better and set about scraping as much mud as possible out of the cottage, so that Mrs Hardy could swill the floor with fresh water which he'd fetched from the well. At Hannah's insistence he then left to go to the village to see how his neighbours had fared the night before. It would depend very much on what he saw when he got there as to whether he ventured on to Sheffield, or not. He was no fool, he knew full well that it would have taken a miracle for the water to have passed on without causing untold damage and misery, but he hoped in his heart for the impossible to have happened.

The reality of the situation, however, was far worse than he had envisaged. Empsall Farm was half demolished and several houses had disappeared, as had the old mill. Even the bridge had been swept away when trees and debris piled against it and forced the great stone blocks to shift. Amidst the domestic flotsam and jetsam trapped against the fallen boulders he saw the protruding legs of a half-submerged animal, and with a shock realised that it could be one of his own.

Groups of numbed, bewildered villagers, some openly weeping, stood by their gates as he rode slowly into their midst, but he was powerless to alleviate their suffering. It would take years before the memory of this night's work was forgotten, if ever, and to some it would remain a permanent nightmare. Two men whom he recognised were digging amongst a pile of rubble that had been a cottage, he turned Mattie in their direction and rode up to them.

One man looked up, an expression of both surprise and relief appearing on his face. 'You're alright then!' he stated, rather than asked. 'It's a rum do and no mistake, Master Edward. I was coming up later on to see if you needed help. Someone had seen smoke coming from the cottage and presumed you were all alive at least. I just couldn't leave the work here at the moment.'

Edward shook his head despondently. 'You did right! But the farm itself has gone and there's very little left standing. The cottage escaped the worst but has been awash with water and mud. I came down as soon as I could leave. We spent the night up in the sheep shelter on the hilltop, and once we got down Mrs Hardy and her child were cold and in need of help before I could leave.' He turned, pointing to the huddled group of women. 'I can't seem to get much sense out of the womenfolk up there, something about a baby? Nobody seems to be able to talk without getting hysterical.'

'It's a bad business, Master Edward. Joseph Dawson's young 'un got washed away—plucked from its mother's arms and washed clean away. The wall of water must have been fifty foot high in places. A hideous sound it made—I never want to hear anything like it again as long as I live.'

Edward was at a loss as to what to say. He felt sickened by the tragedy, he hadn't even known the tailor's wife had given birth to the child, his mind had been on other things of late. 'Are there any more fatalities in the village?'

'Not human, but we've all lost animals. Hawke's Farm has completely disappeared. I'm sorry old Abe's place copped it—but at least you're safe and have the cottage. Some here have lost everything.'

'Have you heard if there's much damage further down towards Malin Bridge?' Edward asked, dreading the reply.

'Rumour has it that a family of ten was washed away whilst they slept in their beds. Things were made worse because the water built up again as it went through the narrows in the valley further down. The Water Board is going to have to answer for this, you mark my words.'

The voice of the other man then piped up angrily. 'Every time I hear a strange noise I think there's more water heading this way,' he shuddered violently at the mere thought of it.

'I wanted to go to Sheffield to find out if my friends are alright at Hillsborough. Do you think I'll get through?'

'They say it's left a trail of death and destruction for miles, we heard it from Tom Sharpe's lad who came up to see if his dad was alright. I guess if you keep to the high road you'll get part of the way. Some of the road has been washed out on part of the lower sections, so you'd best stay as high as you can.'

As Edward worked amongst the men he heard more evidence of the destruction, and realised that the whole business had taken a greater toll on him than he thought. It would be folly to go further, feeling as he did. He was weary and overtired, yet he had to know that Lydia was safe. By now the whole of the town would know the source of the flood, and if she were safe she would naturally be concerned for his welfare. He turned to one of the men working alongside him, one who was a regular worker on the farm. 'I'm going to risk getting through to Sheffield. Get someone to let Mrs Hardy know where I've gone, and see if you can find Jack Gray and tell him I shall still need him at the farm. His job is still safe, for a while anyway. He's to call up tomorrow—you come as well!'

'Right oh! And good luck!'

He and Mattie took the high road which was above the water-damage level but both he and the horse were weary. From his high vantage point the full impact of the flood lay before him. Having broken through the embankment, the wall of thundering, foaming water had swathed through the lower part of Bradfield and gone through the next valley which was much narrower; then it had surged out, razing to the ground every house, mill and tree which stood in its path. Who would have imagined that three miles down stream there would have been so much destruction and carnage? If anything, structural damage here seemed far worse. He swallowed hard and shook his head in disbelief, trying to blot out the vivid impression of what it must have been like to be trapped in the path of the raging torrent, and to have been in a house swept away without warning. The water here had gathered momentum instead of slowing down, sweeping away all before it. People had slept unsuspectingly, no warning having reached that far down the lower valleys in time. Through Bradfield, Damflask, Little Matlock and Malin Bridge it must have gone, then into the outlying townships, killing, maiming and destroying everything in its path.

Edward could not go on. His head throbbed and his body ached. If he went further he would be unable to make the return journey, and somehow the spirit to continue had left him. He was incapable of facing any more destruction. Indeed just what was there left to offer Lydia? He had the responsibility and expense of rebuilding the farm in order to make a living, and from the look of expectancy on the faces of the men who worked for him it was his duty to do so. He might as well forget marriage to Lydia and throw himself back on the mercy of Mrs Hardy.

His strength was going and it was as much as he could do to remain in the saddle, so he turned poor bedraggled Mattie and let her lead him faithfully back through the village until they came to a halt before the cottage gate. To his relief Mrs Hardy saw him from the upstairs window and came down immediately.

'Mrs Hardy!' he called out weakly, as he dismounted and struggled to remove the saddle from Matties back. 'Can you put Mattie into the back field, please? I must rest, I fear I am overtired.' He swayed, his face clearly showing signs of exhaustion, and walked unsteadily, carrying the saddle with him towards the door.

'It's all so dreadful,' Edward said gloomily. 'Did someone come up to tell you where I'd gone?'

'Yes,' Hannah nodded. 'And I've heard of so many terrible things that have happened today, that I was almost unable to work for thinking about it.'

'It is even worse than you can imagine, Mrs Hardy.' Weariness was reflected in his voice.

'You go upstairs where it's warm,' Hannah urged. 'I'll bring you something hot to drink. Don't worry, I'll see to the horse!' With that she took the reins gingerly in both hands and led the docile animal around the back of the cottage, thankful that Mattie's spirit to resist had long since disappeared. Hannah was weary herself. After Edward had cleared the well of all the stones, mud and branches lodged in it, he made a path through by which she could more easily fetch fresh water back to the cottage. She'd hauled bucket after bucket of water inside, swilling out the residue of stubborn mud, until her arms ached from the unaccustomed and prolonged exercise. Nevertheless, she was slowly seeing the surface of the flagstones reappear from beneath the silt deposit.

There'd been an air of unreality about everything as she monotonously pushed the broom backwards and forwards across the floor, but she was no worse off than when living in Lipton Street. Jack Gray called with Edward Morton's message and told her about the damage in the village. It had not been easy, waiting for Edward's return and not knowing where she stood in his life, or how they would be affected by all the upheaval. She was also painfully aware that not half a mile away, people she had begun to know grieved and suffered in the aftermath of the flood.

Over the past few years her main concern had been that of survival, working where she could, often for a pittance in exchange for a home, and without much opportunity for pleasure. Mrs Green had given her a chance but death soon put paid to that, and so in Edward she'd seen the opportunity to hold her head high again. Last night his news had sent her world crashing down around her once more, and here she was today, toiling as though nothing mattered but the removal of mud!

She had been at the window looking out at the hills on the far side of the valley when Edward returned. Her eyes had been directed above the mud level and the destruction, and she knew that in years to come trees would grow again in the devastation below. Men's memories would dim and fade, just as she would one day return to the earth and no one would know that she had ever existed. She had made no mark on the world, other than by ensuring life went on in having Lizzie, nor would she now by the look of things, as when Edward married she would have to move on yet again. Like Edward, she too needed to sleep, but hers was a sleep of a different kind, the sleep which only the oppressed and weary crave.

After tending to Mattie she climbed wearily up the stairs with a mug of hot tea for Edward, aware that there was only one bed in the cottage, and that he would probably be in it.

Edward Morton lay asleep in the large oak bed, his boots and leggings carelessly discarded on the floor beside his jacket. Obviously he had no need of the tea and was totally unaware that curled up very close beside him was a child who, without inhibitions, sought comfort so trustingly. He looked older than his thirty years, drawn with fatigue, and Hannah covered the sleeping pair with the quilt and let them sleep. There was no escape from her own tiredness however, so she dragged an old armchair from the spare room into the bedroom, lowered herself into it and sank into instant oblivion.

When Edward finally woke it was quite dark in the room; only the embers of the fire glowed and flickered, casting shadows on the walls. He had no idea what time it was, nor did he care, but he was conscious of a source of warmth by his side and that it moved when he did. He turned and found Lizzie there, then sleep claimed his weary mind once more.

Chapter 5

The audience at the Surrey had been a small one for a Friday night, due no doubt to the inclement weather. As a result Lydia had little desire to leave the theatre for the wet and very windy streets. She was tired of returning to the rented room in Mrs Marshall's lodging house in Hillsborough, and bored with staring at the four drab walls of her bedroom. With Albert gone she sometimes chose to remain behind after the performance when her fellow artists drowned their sorrows in the basement of the theatre, playing cards and drinking.

On this fateful night in March they had again all preferred to sit in the cellar amongst the clutter of dusty costumes and discarded stage props, rather than go home. They were a carefree lot and cared little if the owner, Mr Youdan, returned to evict them as their antics became wilder with the emptying of the bottles. Lydia understood them well, and enjoyed the company of the small groups of thespians who came and went on the never-ending circuit of theatrical venues. She'd given up all hope of ever finding anyone to partner her again on the stage, in fact, if truth be known, she was finished in their world, having little talent of her own except her looks. As time passed since Albert's departure, her greatest fear was that Tommy Youdan would find her a burden on his wages bill and send her on her way.

'Give us a song, Arnie!' a large, rounded man called out. 'Come on then, who's for a song?'

'You'll attract the attention of the Bobbies and get us thrown out!' cried Willy the contortionist. 'Just keep your voice down! It's too late to go home now—old Mrs Wright'll have locked the door already.' He sidled up to Lydia, obviously hoping she would keep him warm for the night. 'Come on, love,' he said cheekily as she pulled away. 'Aw come on, it'll be a miserable night without a bit of comfort, and Albert's not coming back you know,' he wheedled.

She pushed him away again none too gently. 'Get off, Willy! And don't be a chump, you've got a wife and family somewhere. Albert may have gone but that doesn't mean I'm looking for anyone else, you old clown!' He wasn't actually drunk but the audience had been a bad one. In the middle of his interlude act, members of the audience had thrown orange peel at a group of youths who wouldn't desist from smoking, instead of retiring to the corridor, consequently uproar broke out in the auditorium. This did nothing to smooth his already hurt pride; the poor fellow was past his best and used to cat-calls, so now he was, as usual, simply drowning his sorrows in whisky.

'Bugger the Bobbies!' Fat Larry shouted out suddenly, before breaking into song. 'I knew a fat lady…' he paused for breath, 'as fat as a pig,' his voice petered out at the lack of response.

'It's a lousy town this one, anyway!' Willy complained pathetically, before slumping into a corner of the basement, seeming not to have taken any offence at Lydia's rejection.

'Oh, shut it, you two!' The 'straight' man Fred snapped in frustration. 'You're nothing but drunken slobs! Some of us are trying to play cards. Why don't you go home if you don't like it? After tomorrow you can do what you like when you get to Leeds. We've got to earn a living in this place for another week yet.'

Lydia had seen and heard it all before. The nerves, the boredom, the drinking after the shows. Poor audiences and cat-calls were all in a day's work and how sick she was of it all. She didn't know why she'd stuck it all these years, and especially now with Albert gone, she didn't fit in any more. It was time she got out of the business, but unfortunately she wasn't suited for anything more than domestic employment, and that she hated! She was working on it though; Edward Morton was the best thing to have happened to her for a good long time and he seemed quite happy with her company. She knew that if she played her cards right it wouldn't be long before he asked her to marry him. Besides, she was growing to like the tall, quiet man. She was an actress, the rest should be easy, and she would be secure for the rest of her life.

She looked around. The grubby, smelly dressing room was a depressing sight! The clock on the dresser showed just twenty minutes after midnight, and she'd had enough of sitting idly about. Her companions were a hopeless lot, forever on the move, meeting each other only when bookings coincided. The more successful ones would eventually end up running beer-houses or lodging places, the rest would find a trade willing to take them, or they would end their days in the workhouse, unless they died in harness treading the boards.

She was in no mood to stay cooped up in the basement. If she left now the streets would be deserted, and what's more, as she was a long term lodger in Mrs Marshall's house, she had a key.

Taking advantage of the uproar between Fat Larry and Willy, she slipped out of the door, put on her cloak and climbed the stairs to let herself out of the theatre into the dark and drizzle of the night. It was a long but fairly straight road to the house at Hillsborough and she quickly passed from one gas-light to another, well aware that she was foolish to be out alone so late. It was wet and windy, also strangely noisy. For several minutes she made her way along the street, puzzled as to what the low murmur meant, it seemed to be increasing with every passing moment. She stopped, listened, and became frightened by the now heavy rumbling ahead.

The sound was rapidly getting louder and closer, adding panic to her fear, and she turned instinctively to flee back along the road, stumbling on the uneven paving stones and catching the toes of her shoes in the hem of her skirt. A hideous crashing and cracking seemed to follow her and she half expected the earth beneath to open and engulf her. The ground shook violently and the roar seemed to deafen and embrace her. She screamed hysterically and ran blindly up to the doors of the theatre, but they were either locked or jammed and would not open. She beat frantically upon the heavy wooden panel. 'Larry! Willy!' she screamed, striking hard with her fists. 'Open up! Please, open up!' She shuddered, terrified, half anticipating being seized by some unknown monster.

Something horrible was approaching. 'Oh God! Please let me in!' she pleaded, her spine tingling and she half fell against the door in fear. Instead of abating, the turbulent sounds about her reached a peak and she hammered wildly again on the door. Certain sounds were familiar now, masonry falling, wood splintering and creaking, then the discernible sound of water smashing itself against immovable objects.

Perhaps Willy or Fat Larry were too drunk to hear her. She thumped again and again, increasing the pain in her already bruised fists. 'Open up! Open up!' She could even hear the echo of her knocking as it rang along the corridor inside.

The door was flung open at last and Fat Larry, white-faced and trembling, stared at her. 'Lydia! What the devil's going on out there?' he yelled against the noise, 'Is there an earthquake or something?'

Saying nothing she forced her way past the shaking man. 'Shut the door!' she cried, pushing hard against it with her slender frame. 'I don't know what it is,' she sobbed, once the door was finally slammed shut. 'Everything is collapsing and I can hear water threshing about in the streets below.' She gasped for breath, her eyes wide with fear. 'It sounds as though it's coming from the direction of the river.'

In the basement the lounging figures had risen quickly at Lydia's hysterical banging, then as the roar penetrated the walls they stared in bewilderment at each other. They could see from Lydia's stricken face that whatever was happening outside was of dreadful proportions, but in her state she could explain no more. The intensity of the noise was abating somewhat but it could be discerned from the vibrations that destruction was still taking place. They, at least, seemed to have escaped whatever cataclysm had occurred.

'She thinks it's water!' Fat Larry cried, having followed Lydia into the room once he'd locked the outer door. 'It sounds as though the world is crumbling. What shall we do?' His voice was shaky and his mind confused by a combination of whisky and fear.

The basement in which they were gathered was dry enough and the walls almost impenetrable, but for how long? 'Should we go out and look around?' Willy suggested feebly, having no real intention of going himself.

'No!' Larry stated firmly, 'Not until there is dead silence outside. You can tell that it's not over yet.'

Lydia sat down heavily on an old props basket, and leaned back miserably against the doors of a cupboard, staring ahead at the freshly painted flats standing against the wall opposite. Normally the smell of new paint on canvas filled her with excitement, but not tonight. Ironically they were for the new show starting on Monday and depicted scenes of the town itself. The nearest, of Lady's Bridge and the River Don, was of a peaceful scene which lay not a quarter of a mile from the theatre. The scene bore no resemblance to the imagined horrors outside which had frightened her so much. She was determined not to venture out again unless the walls around her showed signs of collapsing first. Only in broad daylight, when it would be possible to see what had truly happened would she go through the outer door again. Sitting there, miserable and despondent, she began to cry softly to herself. What was she doing there with this strange collection of people and theatrical baggage, which moved from town to town with neither roots nor homely comforts? If Edward Morton asked her to marry him she would obey him dutifully forever, or at least play the part to the best of her ability.

Silence fell on the inmates of the room, each now quiet with their own thoughts, and sobered by the occasional sounds from beyond their sanctuary; each one afraid of the unknown, and only too aware of their own inadequacies and failures. Had an audience witnessed the plight of these poor performers, they could have been forgiven for thinking that they were watching one of Tommy Youdan's spine-chilling melodramas.

Lydia fared no better in her quest for sleep than did Edward or Hannah, who sheltered that night high on the cold exposed hillside above Bradfield. She was, in spite of the safety of the theatre, still haunted by the sounds which had driven her in panic back within its walls, and disturbed also by recurring memories of her past life. When she closed her eyes she could not sleep for her deep feelings of despair and failure. She desperately sought escape into oblivion, just as Edward had done to ease his aching limbs after his exertions on the hillside.

When dawn finally revealed to the shocked citizens of Sheffield the immense devastation around them, it brought with it misery and dumb disbelief. With their humble dwellings gone or damaged beyond repair, and many workplaces ruined, it was clear that the disaster had taken a huge toll of human life. Broken bodies lay twisted and unrecognisable, half buried in deep stinking mud. Pitiful objects and evidence of individual tragedies protruded here and there. A wicker cot, empty of life, a mangled pair of spectacles or a broken chair. Worst of all were glimpses of limbs, even torsos, lying half submerged in the filth.

As shaken men made their way to factories, unsure if they would find themselves still employed, the small group of players plucked up sufficient courage to venture out from their shelter. Pale faced and curious they emerged into the dank, foul-smelling air, yet there was no sign of damage near the theatre!

'Did we have too much to drink do you think?' Willy asked, puzzled.

'Perhaps there are demons in the bottle after all! Or Lydia's powerful imagination frightened us half out of our wits!' Larry offered, as he stopped a grim-faced man who walked past as if in a trance. 'Has there been an accident?' he asked casually, fearing the man would think his question foolish.

Slowly the man answered, his voice trembling with emotion. 'There's been a flood! It's swept away everything in its path. I've never seen anything like it!' He walked on as if having spoken without knowing it.

'He was crying!' Willy exclaimed. 'It can't be that bad, where would sufficient water come from to do such a thing?'

The bewildered group walked along the road, turning into Workhouse Lane which led down to the River Don from West Bar.

'Good God!' Larry cried in a strangled voice, his eyes focusing on the distant bridge, as they approached Bridge Street. The whole area was now covered in a sea of mud and debris. Halting in unison they stared numbly for several minutes, Lydia clutching Larry's arm. All were so shocked by the scene that for once they made no sound.

Crowds were gathering as the light improved, and Lydia stood mutely amongst them on the fringes of the mud, unable to really absorb the dreadful implications of the scene. All around, men and women wept openly, the women huddled beneath shawls, mute, peering into the ruins as their menfolk endeavoured to rescue any meagre belongings they could from the mire.

It was Willy who finally broke the silence, his usual lively manner surprisingly calm and quiet, all traces of his alcoholic spree of the night before having disappeared in the cold morning air. 'Thank God Lydia was on the higher road last night, and that we stayed put! I pity the poor sods who got caught in the water's path.' Fat Larry nodded meekly. His head ached and his mind was spinning from the night before. The sight of the sea of mud before him became too much and he retched convulsively onto the ground near the hedge against which they stood. Willy ignored Larry's discomfort and continued, 'We must let our people know that we're safe.

When they read about it all in the newspapers tomorrow they'll think the worst. We should go back to the higher road away from the mud and damage, and take Lydia back to Mrs Marshall's.'

The party heeded his suggestion and walked up the side street towards the hospital, peering nervously down each road which fell away to the river below, as they went. It was obvious that their fanciful imaginations of the night had not been a product of their drinking bout, but for which they would have left earlier and some likely have perished on their normal route home.

Rumours of the cause of the flood began to circulate, whispers and accusations were rife, but one theory began to emerge which grew as the time passed. It was no swollen river or flash flood, they were certain of that!

'No volume of water that great can have come from anywhere other than a bursting dam. No river can build up so quickly or cause so much damage, and the mill dams don't hold that much water!' This comment was from a man whose attire was that of a well-educated person, his appearance adding credence to his statement.

'Tis the new Bradfield Dam!' a youth exclaimed. 'I heard it just now from a man who got it from a writer on the *Independent*. He says there are dozens of bodies washed down river, and homes and factories ruined from Bradfield right through to the Wicker!'

The gentleman turned sharply to answer the youth. 'Careful now, you'll cause panic by spreading rumours. There's misery enough without adding to it. Exaggeration only makes things worse.'

The lad pouted, his face flushed with annoyance, 'T'aint a lie, mister. I've come from Crookes and from the hill you can see the damage all along the valley. If there aren't hundreds of deaths it'll be a bloody miracle!'

'Poor devils!' Larry exclaimed, his face still pale after his recent vomiting bout. He saw that Lydia was staring intently at the young man, her eyes strangely wild.

She touched the youth's arm, 'Please, do you know if there's much damage in Bradfield?' she begged, remembering Edward telling her that his farm lay near the embankment of the new dam.

Pleased with all the attention he was receiving, the youth nodded boastfully. 'I've heard it tell that there's nobody left alive up there, and all the lower farms have gone.' He revelled in the stir he was causing amongst the gathering crowd, and gave no thought to the heartache he was creating.

Larry felt Lydia's hold on his arm slacken and he caught her quickly before she fell to the ground in a daze. 'Now look what you've done, you stupid fool!' he shouted angrily, well aware that the youth thought his performance enjoyable. 'You should be bloody well ashamed of yourself!'

With Willy's help he managed to sit Lydia on a low wall, her face ashen and her eyes closed. 'Mrs Marshall's house will be flooded, I think, if nothing worse. Let's get her to my place until we can find out for sure how the land lies. She'll be alright after a good sleep. Don't forget she was out in all that disturbance last night—no wonder she's about done in!'

Together they slowly walked Lydia with linked arms supporting her to Larry's lodgings, and let her sleep soundly on his bed, after explaining the circumstances to his landlady.

'Didn't that Morton fellow come from Bradfield way, Willy?' Larry asked suddenly, realising why Lydia had been so overcome at the boy's terrible news. 'That's what it is! Poor Lydia, life's not been very good to her, and as for Albert you'd have thought she'd have more sense than to get mixed up with him in the first place. Yes, I bet she'd got designs on that fellow from Bradfield.' With these thoughts in mind they went back to see the extent of the damage in town.

Chapter 6

*W*hen *Edward finally awoke* he was bemused to find Lizzie curled up by his side. How long she had been there was a complete mystery to him. He eased her gently away and attempted to rise but as he did so the room began to spin giddily before his eyes and he fell back heavily on the bed, narrowly missing the child. Lizzie stirred, and it was only then that he noticed Hannah Hardy sitting, or sleeping in the chair by the fire. She had been oblivious to his awakening, but on hearing Lizzie whimper, she jumped to her feet and came to his aid.

'You're exhausted!' she exclaimed softly, so as not to disturb Lizzie. 'It's dark outside and there is nothing much that can be done until daylight. You would be better off resting and trying to eat something nourishing before you sleep again. I have some gruel simmering on the stove downstairs which I'll fetch. You will soon feel your strength returning once you have eaten.'

He was struck by the kindly but firm tone in her voice, one which she usually kept for her daughter. 'I'm much obliged to you as I do feel weak,' he admitted. 'But what time is it—how long have I slept?'

'It was late afternoon when you returned in a state of collapse, and now it is almost ten o'clock. Please don't attempt to rise without my help, I will be as quick as I can.' With that she hurried from the room leaving Edward resting against the pillow.

On returning with the gruel she found him sitting up in bed, a rueful smile upon his face. She placed the tray across his lap and turned away saying, 'I must put a couple of logs on the fire before it goes out.'

'Thank you,' Edward said, 'I am most grateful for your help. I'm afraid there's such a lot of work to do that I cannot afford to be ill. I just hope this weakness is due to tiredness and nothing else.'

'I'm sure things will work themselves out!' Hannah said, reassuringly. 'Whilst you were gone I lit fires in every room and I've almost got the floors clean again. I think we will be able to manage well enough in a day or two.'

'You're right of course, but it won't be easy,' he agreed, and again the rueful smile appeared on his face. 'Things have turned out rather strangely have they not, Mrs Hardy?' She looked at him quizzically, and murmured agreement. He made to rise, 'You must let me take the chair and you sleep in the bed,' he said, but his head spun and his legs refused to take his weight.

'You stay where you are,' Hannah ordered. 'You need the rest more than I—you have the farm to run. Tomorrow we can sort out the other bedroom, until then you must rest!' Hannah was adamant, he realised.

Edward could do nothing other than obey as he was too weak even to stand. However, his mind was restless, so he finished the gruel in silence then proceeded to draw Hannah into conversation. 'Things are in great disarray down in the village, and I dread to think after what I've heard and seen, what it must be like in the town itself. I suppose you heard something of this when they brought the message?'

Hannah took the tray and nodded thoughtfully. 'It really is hard to believe that only two days ago there were signs of spring in the fields, and hope for the future. That such devastation could happen overnight is both frightening and sobering. It's as if we are mere straws to be blown about or destroyed by whims of nature'. Her voice was distant as though speaking to herself more than to Edward. 'No matter how hard one tries in life, it is so difficult to throw off the mantle of misfortune once it has taken hold of you. Maybe my arrival has brought misfortune with it?'

'It appeared before you came, and started with Abe's death! However, you are very profound Mrs Hardy.' He was amazed how much her sentiments mirrored his own. 'In this case, however, it is not so much an act of nature but more probably a result of man's incompetence.' After a pause he continued, 'I'll tell you something in confidence. Whenever I go up on the moors and look over the valley I feel as though I exist purely in the soul. I forget myself entirely and wonder how a God could take care of so many people in need at once, without favour. Yet as I found today, it would seem there is always someone whose fate it is to be forgotten. I feel that I am merely an observer up there, and it is only when I stub my toe and trip on some stone, that I am reminded of my mortality. Out here one has time to think more deeply, to realise that everything has a permanence, unlike we humans. It takes a momentous happening to change a tiny part of nature and yet only a small thing can make us lose our grip on reality. In a few years when the trees have grown again, and the valley has covered her scars with a green mantle, even we will forget most of the horror. Following generations will think that what they see has always been so.'

At this she responded quickly. 'Well in that case, don't you see that you can't give in but must rebuild, not only the farm but your life as well. It would be a shame, I feel, for you not to make the most of what you have. When you have nothing, then a little is all important, but when you have so much, to abandon it is wicked. I have watched you often when you were unaware of it, and have seen the pride and love you have for this place. If you were to give it up you would find yourself forever seeking solace elsewhere. Any town is a dreadful place in which to live after having this, and you would shrivel and die inside.' Hannah was flushed with the strength of her feelings, her eyes alight with conviction, and she was completely oblivious to the fact that she had no right to offer her opinions on his future. She must suddenly have become aware of this because she abruptly turned away, embarrassed, and said no more.

'You must have been very miserable and unhappy there, Mrs Hardy.' Edward said, kindly and with sympathy. 'It must have taken a lot of courage for you to write to a complete stranger, offering yourself as a wife?'

Her colour deepened and she replied defensively. 'Not so much courage as desperation! It isn't easy to bring up a child alone without help and I was almost at my wits end. My poor mother would have called me shameless had she ever found out, but fortunately she is dead!'

'I'm sure that had she been alive your problem would not have arisen in the first place,' he replied. 'Your courage makes me almost ashamed of myself for thinking of giving up. I admire your strength of purpose for that's what it was, and it carried you through. No! I shall not give up without a fight; having to accept Abe's challenge was not easy, so perhaps it has taken this one last straw to make me appreciate the chances I've been given.' He paused, astounded by his own sudden acceptance of things, and added, 'I'm pleased that you understand at least a small part of my feelings. You see I'm not the calculating man you must have thought me to be.' He made one last attempt to leave the bed but his strength had not returned.

'Do you want me to remove Lizzie, so that you can rest more easily?' she offered, setting down the tray to which she had clung throughout their discussion.

He shook his head. 'There is no need, besides, where would you put her? I just wish that I could get up and assist you in assembling the other bed, but I can't.' He looked towards the tray, 'That was very welcome—thank you!' Then out of curiosity he asked, 'Does Lizzie always sleep in here with you?'

'It is a habit we have acquired through circumstance and for economy's sake,' she admitted off-handedly.

Frugal to the last, he thought, and probably as well, he would need the other room himself from now on. Then, remembering that he had lost all of his personal possessions that had been transferred to the farm, he asked. 'Would you be kind enough to look in the chest in the spare room, please, and see if there are any more discarded clothes of mine still there? Everything I own at the moment is either wet or thick with mud from helping down in the village. It's probably just as well I didn't get to Sheffield dressed as I was.'

As Edward attempted to tidy himself up, he glanced down fondly at the sleeping child whose trust in him moved him deeply. He must see that she never, ever wanted for the necessities in life; he would provide for her as a reward for the pleasure and companionship she gave him.

Hannah found him several garments and remarked, 'You're fortunate, I think these will save the day until you can get some more, and in the morning I will wash and dry the others'. She spread the garments out on the bed where he could see them in the light of the lamp. 'They're rather shabby, I'm afraid.'

He sighed with relief, 'At least I have these left. Perhaps you would be kind enough to air them for me? Of late I've had enough dampness to last a lifetime.'

For a while he watched her busying herself about the room as if she were Mistress of the house, as indeed he'd promised her she would be. It would be impossible now to find her any alternative accommodation, either here or in the town, with so many properties destroyed. The longer she stayed on helping him the harder it would be to send her away, and she would take Lizzie with her. He resolved under the circumstances to make the most of things, and concentrate on their shared adversity.

'Mrs Hardy,' he said hesitatingly. 'It's Sunday tomorrow, and I think we should go to St Nicholas' Church in the village as a mark of respect for the families who are suffering. We may be able to offer some help. Will you accompany me?' A look of consternation crossed Hannah's face at this suggestion, and she did not answer immediately. 'Are you against religion?' he asked, puzzled by her lack of response. 'I must confess that I never go unless circumstances force me to. I merely intend to show my sympathy and respects to those who grieve.'

'You leave me no choice,' she agreed with some reluctance. 'It is little enough to ask of me when others have suffered so much.'

'You are a strange lady, Mrs Hardy. I do not insist upon you coming with me, although I would appreciate your company. The idea of sitting alone in that tomb of a place at this time does not appeal to me, but perhaps we should thank God that we are safe.'

'No! I will come,' was her short reply.

Edward was taken aback by her abruptness. Obviously, and with some justification, Mrs Hardy's resentment over his disclosures the previous evening had not lessened with the trauma of the night, and he realised he would need to take great care in his assumption as to their future relationship. He was suddenly embarrassed, knowing how out of his depth he was in dealing with women, so attempted as best he could to continue the conversation in a more conciliatory fashion.

'Thank you! It is strange, I know that I can trust and depend on you, yet I know so little about you. Am I right that you have no time for religion? Usually it has a greater draw for women than for men—is that not so?' She seemed reluctant to be drawn into further discussion on the matter and her silence intrigued him, she was certainly a woman of mystery. He was therefore taken aback when suddenly she asked a question.

91

'Do you think it advisable for me to stay here under the same roof with you, in such a small house? People will gossip, especially if we attend Church together!'

Ah, was this the real reason for her hesitation, he asked himself? 'I'm afraid it is something I'd not considered,' he responded quietly.

'It is something which must be considered!' Her voice was prudish now. 'How will you explain my presence to your intended, and the villagers? There is also another matter which I wish to raise—I hadn't intended doing so until things had sorted themselves a little, but as you are sufficiently awake and intent on drawing me out, I will raise it now. As you intend to marry, and this is your only home at the moment, when do you expect me to leave? I must know as soon as possible.'

The question shook him, and he felt threatened once more by circumstances beyond his control. She had every right to know where she stood, but he could hardly tell her of his doubts about Lydia's reaction to his sudden loss of property. However, if she left, and Lydia refused him, he would be back in the same position as he was six months before! He did not, could not ever love her as he did Lydia.

So many conflicting issues raced through his mind that he was incapable of rational thought, yet she waited patiently for him to speak. She had already accepted his rejection of the agreement; to give her fresh hope now, then reject her later would be both wicked and unkind. She had proved that she had the spirit to survive, but the question was, could he survive alone? A feeling of guilt and shame overcame him in acknowledging that he was using her for his own ends, but he was also becoming impatient to see order restored to his own life.

Hannah watched with bitter disappointment as he struggled with the turmoil of his thoughts, which were so apparent on his face. Was she to lose everything he had promised? Was she to be thrown back into the degradation of the town slums? She was becoming angry to think that there had been moments when she'd greatly admired Edward's cool command of matters, and other times when his dilemma had found sympathy in her heart. Had she not, from the outset, deliberately forbidden her emotions to become involved in their agreement, she would by now be beside herself with unhappiness. There had been those odd moments when she could quite easily have lowered her guard, but her past life had been a hard and bitter school to learn in. Fortunately she had learned her lesson well.

Edward was bitter and resented the fact that he was unable to control his own destiny. With the farm to re-build, workers to pay and an imminent fight on his hands with the Water Board for compensation, for he held them responsible for the damage caused by the breach, there was no room for sentiment. Everything weighed heavily in Hannah Hardy's favour and nothing in Lydia's, except for the stirrings of his affections. In that respect he had managed well enough so far in his life without such needs, surely he could suppress them again under the banner of necessity.

Blanking out all emotion he cleared his throat and spoke, his face now a mask revealing nothing; his voice however was strained, a fact which did not go unnoticed by Hannah who listened in shocked bewilderment.

'Anyone can see,' he began, 'that I have little to offer now except hard work. The future will depend as much on luck as it will on sacrifice, and I don't know where I stand financially. There are families who depend on the farm for support and who may now be desperately worried. It is up to me to do what I can to help, even to re-build the farm if that is feasible.' He paused, aware that what he was about to ask was almost an insult. 'I would, therefore, be obliged if you could consider the comments I made on Friday night to be a mistake, and accept my apologies for the harsh way in which I conducted myself. Sadly, the plain truth is that you need security for yourself and Lizzie, whilst I need to fulfil Abe's conditions. Do you think us companionable enough to return to our original agreement? We are both sensible in respect to each others independence and although we would be married I should move into the farm as soon as it can be re-built. Will you consider this under the light of our new-found situation?'

This dramatic and sudden turn of events stunned Hannah far more than she dared admit as she strove to control the many conflicting thoughts which ran through her head. Initially she heard his cold suggestion with relief, but this was quickly followed by a growing anger at his arrogant insensitivity to her feelings. Not only was he using her as a means to an end but in doing so he was carelessly and heartlessly casting aside the woman he was supposed to be in love with! How could he? However, if that were the case then she certainly need not feel guilty at seizing the opportunity which fate had placed to her advantage. Neither did she consider her gain to be the other woman's great loss, for the farm and Edward's wealth were non-existent at this time, and his love was obviously a very shallow thing. If, as a result of his action, he ended up with a cold, unloving wife then surely it was no more than he deserved. She must consider her own needs and those of Lizzie to be of greater importance. They were merely returning to the original reason for meeting in the first place.

He was aware that she refused to meet his eyes, thus concealing any glimmer of reaction or emotion at the proposal. Whatever her decision was, he knew that it would be after careful deliberation, as was his, and that it would be final.

'I am willing,' she said slowly and with restraint,' to revert to our original agreement. However, I am not willing to wait until the farm is re-built to marry you. If we are to share this house in the meantime then I insist on having a ring upon my finger, if only for Lizzie's sake. Tomorrow I will prepare the other bedroom for you, but you must make up your mind! I am willing to work hard in order to see the farm flourish again, but only if I am to all intents and purposes Mistress of it!' She stood determinedly before him, intent on extracting a promise from him, or else she would leave in spite of her lack of prospects.

'And would you still be willing to have a child?' She nodded in agreement, although he sensed rather than saw resignation in her manner.

'Then so be it Mrs Hardy, you have my promise. As soon as is decent, considering the tragic events of the past few days, we shall be married.' He was saddened to think that he had cornered her into submission this way, for she was an honest, vulnerable woman and he was not without admiration for her many good qualities. To try and lighten the atmosphere he added, 'I thank you again for all the hard work you have done today. You deserve far better than life has given you.' He was strangely overwhelmed by his admission and knew that to say more in this vein was beyond his emotional capabilities. Instead he wished her 'Good Night', and tried to get to sleep. With a heavy heart and a sense of guilt this was almost impossible, he lay there with his eyes closed, his mind a jumble of thoughts and questions as to what the future might bring, until, mercifully, sleep did eventually come.

News of the collapse of the Dale Dyke Dam in the valley above Bradfield spread rapidly through the town of Sheffield, and those who couldn't bring themselves to accept such a possibility set off to see if such a calamity could indeed be true. Some went with ghoulish curiosity on an excursion of pure self-indulgence, whilst others were driven by the dreadful knowledge that relatives and friend's homes had been in the path of the overwhelming flood water.

They thronged the roads, many going out as far as the collapsed embankment in their search for satisfaction, having little or no respect for the suffering of the bereaved and despairing.

It wasn't long before reporters arrived in the town from the outside world to record the incident, including one or two with cumbersome photographic equipment. Enterprising tradesmen seized the opportunity to set up stalls on the roads leading up to the disaster areas, not to feed the newly-made homeless but to extract money from, and to entertain, the gathering sightseers. Sadly, this was not a diversion appreciated solely by the working classes; carriages of all kinds trundled through the mud and rubble-strewn surfaces in order to get a better view of the catastrophe. Well-dressed ladies simpered and shook their heads in horror at what they saw, but none left until they had seen sufficient to be able to retell all to neighbours and friends over the weeks which followed. A few with consciences did set about raising funds to alleviate the suffering which they saw, but not many.

Fortunately, of these public-spirited people, those who were sufficiently moved put pressure on the powers-that-be to move quickly in organising relief, but the dead were beyond help. For those thousands of people whose homes had been invaded with stinking, sewage-laden mud, every contribution was a godsend.

Whilst many of the public, from the outset, laid the blame squarely on the Water Board, proving it and obtaining compensation, was to be a long and tiresome thing.

Meanwhile there were mouths to feed, the homeless to rehouse and bodies to find, identify and bury.

Edward was awakened on Sunday morning first by the sound of carriages, then by the noise of people talking, and excited, scampering children.

He rose, feeling better for his deep sleep and with a strong determination to get on with putting the farm to rights. He looked through the open window towards the broken embankment and saw in the distance, several tiny human figures already standing on the crumbled banks which flanked the gap of the ruined dam, and saw more making their way towards it. He accepted, with dismay, that there would be little peace in the valley until the public had taken its fill of excitement and finally left, taking any sympathy they might have had for the victims with them.

Hannah, on the other hand, had risen early, allowing him to sleep on in the hope that the rest would renew his strength. She had witnessed the early arrival of the first visitors to the valley, and merely pitied them their ignorant search for distraction. She had lived amongst the poor long enough to know that the harsh monotony of their lives was broken only by troubles and happenings such as these. Many would have walked miles with merely a crust of bread for sustenance, whilst others would have brought a picnic and eaten it there amongst the destruction. All would have then returned home, tired but temporarily diverted from their humdrum existence. For her, however, there was work to do, especially now that she was reassured and could remain in her home.

By using the cottage as a base, Edward would be able to take stock of what had survived. He had Mattie, Bella, and the flock of sheep which grazed up on the high ground, although some of the ewes were dangerously near to lambing and he might have lost one or two lambs during the past forty-eight hours through neglect. He would bring in men from the village to provide extra help, for his own workers had enough problems of their own. This would leave him free to go to town first thing Monday morning for supplies and, whilst there, ask Mr Grayson to lodge his claim for compensation with the Water Board. Fortunately Abe had been a shrewd man with his money and had invested it wisely, failing in just one venture, that of a railway expansion scheme a few years back. Some time earlier Mr Knight had allowed Edward to see the books for the farm, and what he had seen indicated that there would be sufficient funds available to make a start in re-building, and to pay for help. Providing the money drawn was spent on the farm there should be no objection from Abe's solicitor over its use.

He wouldn't tell Mrs Hardy of his plan to find Lydia whilst there, his aim being solely to make sure that she was safe and to tell her gently that he had no option now but to keep his word to Hannah after all. His heart was heavy at the prospect of telling her this, just as it was at the possibility, heaven forbid, that she might have been killed or hurt in the flood. He had to pass the *Surrey Theatre* on his way into town and would make that his first call, although he doubted if she would be there so early in the day.

True to his better nature he took Mrs Hardy and Lizzie to church on Sunday, a sombre occasion which gave him little pleasure but did allow him to judge the mood and needs of the villagers. In the end he decided that his part would be best played in offering paid work to some of the sufferers, whilst at the same time getting the farm working again.

He took the Parish Clerk to one side. 'There's extra work up at my place,' he offered, 'to anyone who wants it; just pass the word around if you would? I'll pay well for a good day's work, on a temporary basis, but make sure the needy are told first!'

'Why, that's good to hear!' the Clerk replied. 'I'm sorry about the farm; you seem to have lost as much property as anyone and the men were wondering if you would want to re-build, or give up.'

Edward stiffened a little, wondering if the man had got wind of Abe's intention from his superior. 'Abe left more than just the fabric of the farm,' he quickly assured the man, 'and I've no intention of giving up. I intend to fight the Water Board for compensation,' he said firmly. 'We must all do that!'

The man nodded, 'I agree entirely.'

'One more thing,' Edward said, 'I need to see the Vicar but perhaps it would be better done during the week. It hardly seems a good time to tell him, but Mrs Hardy has agreed to become my wife, and we would like the ceremony to take place as soon as possible.'

'Well I never!' the man exclaimed in surprise. 'I never thought we'd see you in church as a bridegroom. Congratulations! That will give the villagers something cheerful to occupy their minds rather than this sad business. It's been such a dreadful time for everyone.'

'I'd be obliged if you'd keep it to yourself for a while,' Edward stated, hopefully, 'until I've seen the Vicar.'

'Well, it will surprise a few, but good luck—and thank you for putting work out to the men. They need something to hope for right now. When do you want them sending up?'

'First light Tuesday morning—by the old gate near the cottage, with any pick axes and shovels they can muster. Mine went in the flood.'

With his tasks in the village done, Edward returned to the cottage chatting in a companionable manner all the way with Mrs Hardy, then afterwards he set about checking on the welfare of the sheep up on the hillside. He found most of the ewes in a satisfactory condition, two having sturdy new offspring happily suckling away, whilst one showed signs of having given birth but was without a lamb. On looking around he found a new-born but lifeless carcass; it was a pity, and a loss, but was to be expected under the circumstances. Hopefully, once things settled down he could get a full-time shepherd to tend the flock for him. In his early days on the farm, he had been fortunate in that Abe had let him run a few sheep of his own amongst the flock; this of course had given him a greater incentive to watch over them than he otherwise might have done.

Later on in the day he viewed what was left of the old farm, its yard and the buildings more closely. His worst fears were confirmed for, if anything of use still remained, it lay beneath a sea of mud; everything else had been lost forever. It soon became apparent that he might as well start again from scratch, building on new foundations and using the stones that were left scattered around. It was fortunate that his crops were planted on land near Storrs, untouched by the water, and they would ripen in the summer.

During the evening he sat deep in thought, his mind seeking ideas which would help bring his plans to fruition. Mrs Hardy sat sewing by the light of the lantern, aware that during his long periods of silence he had not forgotten her presence, in fact she was quite pleased that he occasionally asked for her opinion. Perhaps, after all, between them they could build a future for Lizzie?

Early next morning Edward set off for Sheffield and the nearer he got to the outskirts of the town the deeper became his dismay at what he saw. It was now three days since the flood and although many men were back at work, there were still a great many people sightseeing all along the six-mile trail of destruction, from the town right up into the valley. He found it hard to accept that so much damage could have been done over such a great distance, yet the evidence was there to be seen. Mills and buildings had completely disappeared, while rows of houses had been ripped apart, exposing what was left of their meagre furniture on the upper storeys. Bed frames hung precariously from broken floors waiting to tumble to the ground at the slightest movement. Edward had heard from a reliable source, the death toll was almost two hundred, with more bodies being washed down the River Don as far as Rotherham, some even beyond that. His problems were small in comparison. Whole families were destroyed, mothers and children had been torn from each other's arms, drowned before loved one's eyes; but there were miracles too. A floating cradle with its contents safe, a child asleep on the top of a wardrobe unaware that the water had receded leaving him safe and alive. Now there remained the task of clearing away the pollution before disease and sickness took a further toll on the population.

Edward approached the theatre with foreboding. Yes, he was informed, Lydia was safe, although she had been ill. Even the Saturday performance had gone ahead, following which the cast had moved to Leeds. No, no one had seen Lydia since Saturday, Mrs Marshall's house had been damaged but there had been no loss of life, but if he cared to come back on the morrow they might be able to tell him if Lydia had left any messages. Sorry, they said, the show must go on and they were having trouble with the scenery for that evening's performance. It was the best they could do for him and they were too busy to talk any longer. Not that they could help him much anyway, and with these hurried comments he had to be satisfied.

At least she was safe. Maybe it was better if she had in fact gone with her friends, after all he had nothing to offer. His own future was now mapped out so that to face her with the truth would have been painful for them both. He would miss the feeling of warmth which she had brought into his austere life and, although it would not be easy, he must discipline his thoughts and emotions and make the best of things.

He spent the rest of the morning buying and ordering replacement tools and necessities required to make a start on re-building the farm. He purchased several items of new clothing and toiletries which he left at the *Angel* before going to see both his own and Abe's solicitors with whom he had made appointments earlier in the day. The news that he was about to put Abe's wishes into practice would, hopefully, induce the release of sufficient monies with which to pay for the day's purchases and the men's labour during the next few weeks.

Mr Knight was pleased to see Edward alive and well, and greeted him with a smile. 'When my clerk told me of your visit earlier today I was most relieved, as from various newspaper reports and rumours over the weekend I hadn't known just what to expect. Whereas some stories have been greatly exaggerated, in others ill-informed comment has minimised real tragedies and the truth. I have seen parts of Neepsend and the Wicker for myself and have been appalled by the destruction. Apparently the Wicker was a deep raging torrent which destroyed most of the contents of every shop.'

'Then you cannot conceive what has taken place up the valley!' Edward responded. 'It is catastrophic, and no figment of anyone's imagination. To have been there and heard the hideous sounds in the dark, then in daylight to see such desolation makes me shiver, even now. The farm has gone, except for part of the wall in which the chimney stands, and part of the barn. The cottage remains although some of the furnishings may be ruined by the mud and water which got in. At least I have a home, and the flock is safe up on the hillside, but the ewes are about to lamb and need shelter. I've lost all my personal belongings except for my horse, so I urgently need money for building materials and wages, as well as for clothing. I also need to find out where I stand in claiming compensation from the Water Board. I presume that as trustees of the estate you will undertake that, and Mr Grayson will obviously represent me? There is so much to do out in the valley that I can't spare any time in town, besides you are better equipped to fight them than I am, and will, I am sure, get better results.'

'I had better come out to see for myself just what we should claim for,' Mr Knight stated, solemnly. 'There's no doubt that there will be compensation made, but how much remains to be seen, and how long it will take is another matter. However, there are funds available from the estate for the upkeep of the farm, so if you will have all the bills sent direct to me, providing they are reasonable, I shall see that they are paid.

'That's a great relief,' Edward sighed. 'I've already offered work to the villagers in order to start re-building the barn, and I'm sure Abe would have been pleased about that. I may re-site other buildings as appropriate. But I have also agreed to marry Mrs Hardy in the very near future—that would probably have pleased him too.' Edward could not refrain from adding a little sarcasm to his voice.

Mr Knight ignored this, choosing instead to take a positive view on the matter. 'Well!' he said cheerfully. 'Let's look on the bright side—everything you do now will be of personal benefit, and your work will be for yourself and no one else. I'm pleased you have finally come to terms with things and hope that happiness will ensue. At least by bringing a child to the marriage we have almost fulfilled Abe's wishes. I have done some investigation and am satisfied that there are no obstacles to hinder the course of the affair. Now, it would seem that there are quite a few matters to be discussed in detail before I come out to view the damage, so we had better get on with things straight away.'

Edward's visit to his own solicitor, Mr Grayson, took very little time and so he set out for home in the early part of the afternoon.

Passing the theatre on his way he made one more effort to obtain news of Lydia. However, there was none, so he left knowing that in spite of his resolve to banish her from his mind forever, he never could. He left a note saying how relieved he was to hear she was safe, and wished her success in Leeds. Then he continued his journey home in a sombre mood, unsure how he would be able to fill the void Lydia's going had created.

At first light on Tuesday morning Edward waited by the old gate at the top of the lane leading down to the farm. A couple of men were already approaching with their own tools, whilst others were winding their way along the road behind, heading in his direction. It was a relief to see them and he recognised several as seasonal workers who would have come to the farm later in the summer anyway. All were seeking an opportunity to earn extra money after the long, harsh, winter; many were just pleased to be returning to the farm.

Jack Gray was the first to arrive, accompanied by his lad Tom. His brother John trudged along some way behind, on his own as usual. Edward gathered the men around him; there were nine in all and each known to be reliable and hard-working. 'Right men, thank you for coming,' he began, looking them over approvingly. 'These are difficult times for us all and I'm sorry that the tragedy has hit some of you very hard, but there is money to be earned here, for a while at least, providing you work well enough. The first thing I need is for you to build a shelter to house the new tools which are arriving tomorrow, and then a shed for lambing. I will also need a stable-cum-cow shed. I don't mind how many hours you work, you'll be compensated well enough, however, it is important to get the shelter built as soon as possible. Give your names to Jack Gray here, he will supervise whilst I take a good look at the fields. The stone walls have been scattered everywhere, but if you can find the foundations of the old barn beneath the mud then build on those. I may have some of the other new buildings erected nearer the cottage when I have had time to think about it. You'll have to gather up many of the stones from the old farmhouse for the new buildings. Leave the dressed stones until later, I'll be using them to build another house.'

He led the gang down the lane, set them to work then left them in Jack's charge before setting out to inspect the flock. He was quite confident the men would work until they dropped if necessary. Abe had earned their respect and, over the years, he had slowly relinquished more and more responsibility to Edward. With it had come that same respect; they knew they could expect a fair deal in exchange for a fair day's work from him too.

He found nothing amiss with the flock which grazed contentedly on the lush spring grass, ignorant of the troubles in the valley below. With Bella's help he rounded up the more heavily pregnant ewes, then herded them down into the field at the back of the cottage where he could keep an eye on them until the shelter was ready, hopefully by nightfall.

The exercise and fresh air did Edward good and he found, for the first time in several days, a degree of optimism for the future. He vowed, when he had the time, to bring Lizzie up onto the hills now that the weather was improving; he was sure that she would enjoy the freedom as much as he did.

When he eventually returned home it was to the smell of freshly-baked bread, reminding him that he had eaten nothing at all before starting out that morning.

Hannah Hardy looked up as he entered the kitchen. 'Did you find the flock alright?' she asked, drawing a hot tray from the oven. 'At least the morning is bright, and you look less drawn than you did. I'm glad of that!'

'Yes!' he agreed. 'Thankfully, there were no problems and the exercise has done me a power of good. You should get some fresh air yourself, Mrs Hardy.'

She smiled. Edward had not seen her smile quite so readily before and he was grateful, for this lessened the tensions which had lingered since their last deep conversation on personal matters. 'I will,' she replied. 'I think I'll take a walk with Lizzie after dinner to see if I can be of help. I thought to take a little fresh bread; it might be appreciated by someone who has suffered over the weekend. Do you think it would be welcome?' She seemed to want his approval.

'I'm sure it would, and it will give you an opportunity to meet some of the villagers whom you haven't already met. Since your arrival the weather has been so bad it has given you little opportunity to mix with them.' It was a kind gesture on her part and he had to admit that he greatly admired the way she had worked to clean up the place without any sign of resentment. 'I should thank you for the way you have buckled to and cleaned up the mess. In doing so you have relieved me of the responsibility and allowed me to put my mind to the recovery of the farm. It cannot have been easy for you, especially when you believed me to be going back on my word. I will remember that, and you will not find me ungrateful.'

She looked at him with candid eyes. 'When everything you have is threatened there is nothing to do other than get on with what you can. You gave me the chance to regain my strength, and for that I am grateful, for I fear I would not have survived the winter in that damp, unhealthy house in town.'

'Then our arrangement is a good one!' he exclaimed, sincerely. 'We shall all benefit from it and will have the opportunity to work to build a future for Lizzie. I shall treat her as my own—I am very fond of her, you know. Where is she, by the way, I haven't seen her all morning?'

'She went with Jack to watch the men working. He said he would keep an eye on her and bring her back if she got in the way, but that was an hour ago so all must be well. He says she can go and play with his children when the weather has improved.'

'Jack's a good man,' Edward agreed then, as he appeared to be deep in thought, Hannah let him be.

'I've been thinking,' he said at last. 'If you don't mind I'll walk with you to the village this afternoon, that way I can introduce you to Jack's wife and whilst I'm there I can see the Minister about the wedding. You haven't changed your mind, I hope?'

'No,' she said quietly, 'I have not.' No, she hadn't changed her mind but the whole business was beginning to fill her with foreboding. Supposing she was incapable of pleasing him? It was a strange situation, they had not touched each other, never offered a word of affection, nor could she bring herself to call him Edward. She shivered inwardly at these thoughts, trusting that they did not reflect in her face.

'Then that's what we shall do—immediately we have eaten.' There was a positive tone in his voice. 'The brighter weather would seem to be an omen for us, don't you think?'

Hannah nodded her agreement. He was a difficult man to understand and this cheerful enthusiasm was hard to reconcile with the cold, serious outlook he often had. The mood sat oddly on him, although it pleased her greatly, but he was a complex man, and almost a stranger sitting at the table. He could be both caring and thoughtful, yet she knew that he had deeper, darker moods which often caused furrows on his brow.

'You prepare lunch—I'll go and fetch Lizzie back!' With that he left her to bustle about, deeply absorbed in thought as she got things ready.

He ate heartily of the meal which Hannah had placed before him and watched her unobtrusively between snatches of conversation with Lizzie. She would make a fine housewife but he wished he could talk to her without feeling that there was a barrier between them that would never go away. It had been easy to talk to Lydia and, at first, when he had been at a loss for words she had unconsciously filled the gap with her joyful chatter, drawing him out. She had become quite breathless in her enthusiasm, so that in the short time they had known each other he had become less restrained. However, of this strangely reserved woman who was going to be his wife he knew nothing that wasn't formal, or impersonal. Perhaps the fault was his, he was happy enough in serious discussion with a male contemporary, but he'd never mixed much in large groups of people, or indeed with any women.

Once the wedding arrangements had been made to his satisfaction, Edward left Hannah in the village and walked back to the cottage alone. He was relieved to have the details settled and felt somewhat reluctant to start work again. However, daylight hours were precious at this time of year and were not to be wasted. It was a pity, for it was the first time since Hannah's arrival that he had the cottage completely to himself, yet it felt strangely empty without her and Lizzie. Prior to the flood she had made only a few changes about the place, but the necessity of drying out and clearing up had resulted in a complete re-organisation, very much in her favour. He didn't really mind; after all, when so much had gone, he was grateful for what little was left of the past, no matter where it was placed.

He was resigned to his fate now and had to confess that the walk to the village had been a pleasurable one. She had allowed him to carry the basket of freshly-baked bread whilst she held Lizzie's hand, and any stranger observing them would have been forgiven for thinking them to be a happy family.

He was about to return to the men who were working on the construction of the shelter, when he heard the sound of carriage wheels in the lane outside. Thinking it might be full of sightseers who had mistakenly taken the wrong track, Edward remained indoors, determined not to be drawn into answering their many questions. He was, therefore, surprised to hear a knock on the door, and to find a burly figure standing in the open doorway. He did not see the figure sitting in the carriage by the gate because the stranger at the door immediately engaged him in conversation.

'Does Mr Morton live here, Sir?' the man asked politely. 'Only there doesn't seem to be another house for some distance, and I was directed this way.'

'Why, yes!' Edward replied, wondering who the stranger could be. 'I'm Morton—what can I do for you?'

The man turned, indicating with his hand to the carriage, 'I've got a lady asking for you—shall I hand her down?'

Edward's eyes followed the gesture; he stared for several seconds before he recognised with disbelief, the woman in question. 'Lydia!' He called out with a strangled cry, his face draining of colour. 'What are you doing here?'

'Oh, Edward,' she sobbed in a childlike voice. 'You're safe!' A tear rolled down her cheek and he moved towards her, a look of shocked amazement showing plainly on his face. She made no effort to accept the driver's hand to get down, instead she watched Edward with tearful eyes.

'But I called at the theatre yesterday, didn't they tell you? They led me to believe that you had gone to Leeds with the others.'

'I have been ill since Saturday,' she lamented, distressed by the misunderstanding, 'and haven't been to the theatre at all. Today is the first time I've been out of the house since Larry took me to his lodging, Mrs Marshall's house where I live was flooded with three feet of water.' She was obviously shaken and Edward's heart went out to the diminutive figure which sat so forlornly in the carriage. He held out his hand to help her alight, relieved to know that she had not gone away, yet totally bewildered at seeing her there before him. The driver stood back patiently, then walked discreetly to the front of the vehicle and tended to the horse which was becoming restless through waiting.

Lydia trembled at his touch and he noted how subdued she was, in spite of the gaiety of her dress and her careful make-up. 'You shouldn't have come all this way when you're not well.' The reproof was gently said, but he could see that she took it to heart, and he added, 'If only you had sent me a message I would have come into town to see you.'

'But I didn't know if you were alive or not, or who could tell me! I am much better now, but just a little weak. I have been so worried for I knew you lived here in the valley and nobody could tell me anything.' She allowed him to lead her into the cottage where she sank gratefully into the chair which he provided for her.

'I'm afraid the room is a little damp and is sparsely furnished as, with the water coming in, we have moved some things upstairs. Seating himself, he continued. 'You should not have come,' he admonished. 'It's a long and rough journey, especially with the roads broken up as they are.' Once again he realised that she didn't appreciate that it was purely his concern for her that made him say this.

'Are you sorry that I came?' Her eyes were moist and her voice soft. 'I couldn't rest without knowing whether you still lived!'

'I'm not sorry!' Edward stammered, huskily. 'Of course I'm happy to see you otherwise I would not have called at the theatre to enquire after you. But you look so frail and I would be unhappy if you became ill again through coming to find me.' He struggled to find words of re-assurance which wouldn't betray the true depth of his feelings for her, and in so doing give her false hope. He wanted to take her in his arms and comfort her yet, if he did, she would surely know the joy he felt at seeing her, then all would be lost. Instead he told her, not unkindly, that he was well, and prayed inwardly that Mrs Hardy would not return from the village for some time. To be confronted by both women at once would have been more than he could have endured.

'If you had been dead,' she said, 'then I would have gone to Leeds with the others. I would have had no reason to stay, although there would have been little future for me there either!'

'This is not the farm; that was almost washed away!' he said suddenly, playing for time whilst he endeavoured to get his thoughts into some kind of order. It was all too late, she was not part of the plan now. What was the point of explaining, it would only bring misery to them both? He couldn't meet her gaze either, the sight of her reminded him just how fragile she was and, as she sat in the pale green silk gown with those flamboyant feathers in her bonnet, he knew that life in the valley was not for her. It would take a stronger woman than she to survive the ravages of this valley's winters, nor could he put that frail body through the act of childbirth. He wanted to stroke her hair gently with his fingers and kiss her furrowed brow to show her that he did care, but he mustn't. Only by sending her away as quickly as possible could he defuse the situation and enable himself to keep the commitment which he had made to Mrs Hardy.

Suppressing the emotional conflict which raged within him, he adopted the cool manner which Hannah Hardy so often found disturbing, and told her the truth. 'Lydia, I really thought that you had gone away for good! With that, and because I am forced, on account of the disaster, to move into this small house with my housekeeper and her daughter I am in no position to ask for your hand in marriage. I cannot send this lady and her child away after what they have gone through and all she has done to help me. I have nothing left to offer a bride now, and rather than compromise Mrs Hardy I have asked her to marry me. It is not a love match, nor will it ever be, but I must marry if I am to keep the farm. I cannot go back on my word at this stage as the Parish Clerk has the banns ready for reading on Sunday.' He was well aware of the bluntness of his words, as a result of which he would lose Lydia forever, and he hated himself for his selfishness. 'If only I had known earlier that you had remained in Sheffield!' he added lamely.

To his surprise Lydia did not weep, instead her spirits returned and she sprang from the chair, her voice raised in anger. 'So! Now you can keep your precious farm, and I need not have worried about you! You have survived far better than I had hoped!' He made to stay her by catching her arm but she would have none of it. 'I wish you well,' she shouted. 'After all, your inheritance is of prime importance, but the price you pay for it may be your downfall!' She pushed her way past him and ran down the path.

'I made you no promises!' he cried wildly after her. 'I believed that I had nothing left to offer you, and that you'd gone away!'

She was in no mood to listen and climbed unaided into the carriage, much to the astonishment of the driver who hastened to her aid. 'I wish to return to town immediately,' she ordered, deliberately ignoring Edward's pleas and refusing to glance his way.

He stood back and watched her go, his heart saddened, and he was ashamed of causing her so much distress. It was all too late! He had nothing left to offer, neither love nor chattels, and only the latter could he eventually give to Hannah Hardy. Neither of the women would ever really understand the dilemma in which he found himself, one which he would never have chosen or thrust upon anyone else. Never before had he felt such anguish as he did at this moment, or the desperate need to comfort anyone as he did Lydia. Her damaged pride would recover, of that he was sure, but as she had been hurt too often in the past he feared that she might succumb to the ways of her thespian friends. Life in the theatre was hard, that he knew, and Lydia was vulnerable to flattery. Her need of affection and comfort were her weakness, he had not been blind on that score. However, he had witnessed a subtle change in her since their first meeting and could take some credit for that. Now, though, he had to let her go rather than face the consequences of deserting Mrs Hardy, and there would be no one other than himself to blame if anything happened to her.

Once out of sight of the cottage, Lydia's anger subsided, as did the defiance which caused her to shout at Edward; only tears remained as she contemplated the future. She was alone again with no permanent home or friends, other than those which passed as ships in the night. Where could she go, what would she do? The only thoughts which had occupied her over the past few days of her sickness had been to wonder if Edward lived or not. His name had not appeared on any published list of fatalities and she had hoped against hope that she would find him well. Her fears were allayed when, in the village, she was informed that Master Morton was alive and uninjured, but living in the cottage as the farm had been destroyed. From that moment her spirits had risen considerably, only to be dashed by the news that he had betrayed their friendship and her affections in order to retain the farm.

'Please stop.' she called out, brokenly. 'I wish to get down and be alone for a while.'

The driver did so without question, hiding his curiosity behind a bland expression. After all it was a pleasant afternoon and the lady was paying quite handsomely for his services. He lowered the step and helped her down, 'I'll walk the horse on a little way if you don't mind, Miss,' he said tactfully. Lydia nodded, saying nothing in case she betrayed the tears which she fought to hold back.

Lydia looked around and could see that for all the damage done to the valley, it had once been beautiful. She had crossed such valleys and moorlands on her travels with Albert in the past, and realised that but for the flood this could have been her home. She could also see why Edward preferred living here, rather than being amongst the smells and grime of a busy town. She wondered where the farmhouse had been, and acknowledged that what she had seen on the outward journey had emotionally upset her, so that when she finally saw Edward she was not her usual self. Had she been, she might have been in a better position to make him change his mind.

The mantle of winter still hung over the hedgerows where, in spite of the gentle spring warmth, few trees showed signs of leafing. So, after taking several deep breaths of clear air, she allowed her eyes, now wiped dry of tears, to gaze freely over the rural scene. There was a sense of peace and belonging which soothed the hurt which she felt, such feelings seem to have been denied her all her life and she envied Edward his passion for the place. No doubt, under similar circumstances, she too would fight to keep that which she loved so much. Did she really love Edward Morton or was she merely desperate to make something of her nomadic life? What had she achieved in thirty-three years that was worth fighting for? The flood had taken away the one chance she had of finding out.

She stirred; it was time to leave and return to a life blighted by uncertainty and loneliness. With a heavy heart she walked, head down, staring at the mud which clung stubbornly to her small leather boots, until she caught up with the carriage.

Pulling Lizzie to the side of the road, Hannah allowed the approaching carriage to pass by, wondering as she did so what could have brought the finely-dressed woman within, to the valley. 'What a handsome dress she wore, Lizzie!' Hannah commented admiringly, once the road was clear again. 'And such beautifully coloured hair. I wonder who she is and where she has been?'

On reaching home Hannah found Edward about to leave. He gave no indication of having had a visitor and said little, but Hannah sensed a change in him. Gone was the relaxed companion of less than an hour ago, instead his dark brows were furrowed and forbidding. Common-sense told her that it was best to leave him alone to brood, yet she was both bewildered and frightened by this sudden transformation, as she could see no reason for it.

It was only on entering the sitting-room that a strange, pleasant fragrance disturbed her, and her suspicions were aroused. Only ten minutes earlier the passing carriage had left in its wake that self-same perfume. And what was this on the floor by the chair? With great restraint she left the small pair of soft kid gloves where they had fallen, for Edward to find. So, there had been a visitor in her absence, and judging by his bad mood something of great importance had transpired which displeased him.

Hannah recalled the handsome figure in the carriage she had seen earlier, and knew instinctively that this was the woman whom Edward preferred to her. Only circumstances had given Hannah the edge on her rival, and it was fortunate that the whole village now knew of their impending marriage. At least Edward Morton was a man of honour, and hardly likely to make a spectacle of himself at this stage by backing out. However, she would feel safer once she had become Mrs Morton!

Nothing was said about the visit; the gloves were discreetly removed, Hannah knew not where, and she knew that it was prudent to let the incident pass rather than risk Edward's anger at being quizzed. But somehow this incident did more than alarm her, it left her feeling empty and a little forlorn.

In the days preceding the wedding Edward immersed himself completely in the re-building of the shed and barn down by the ruined farm. The arrival of a wagon-load of supplies from Sheffield removed some of the problems from his mind, and he worked unstintingly from dawn till dusk alongside the labourers, as the buildings grew from the scattered stones. The work was gruelling, yet the result of each day's labour encouraged him and strengthened his determination. By the time he had eaten his supper and tended the lambs each evening it was time for bed. His sleep, fortunately, was undisturbed when he found a shepherd whose skills resulted in only two lambs being left motherless. Lizzie had been most alarmed when she found him putting one of these into the oven by the fire, and the other in a box near the grate.

She watched with large, disbelieving eyes until Edward called her gently to him. 'Come and see, they haven't got a mother to keep them warm so I put them here instead. The fire keeps the oven warm but not too hot, unless I make it so by opening the damper, like this.' He closed it again promptly before the heat became too much for the lambs. 'Do you think you could keep an eye on this one and see that he doesn't cry too much?' He lifted the lamb out of the box and placed it gently on her knee as she sat on the small scorched stool watching him.

'What happens if he cries?' she asked in alarm, her face set in the serious little way he had come to know.

'Then we must feed him with milk. John gave him some earlier but you can help next feeding time.' He watched her hold the tiny creature gently in her arms and realised that, although he did not love Mrs Hardy, he was certainly under the spell of her enchanting child. He knew also that if he wasn't careful he was in danger of allowing her to twist him round her little finger.

Clearing the ground on which the farmhouse had stood for nearly two hundred years proved a great deal easier than expected, as little of the original remained standing. There was simply no point in trying to re-build it to its former glory, instead, Edward decided that his best interest would be served by extending the cottage to include another bedroom and sitting room. In addition he would have several out-buildings and a stable built adjacent to this extension so that he could run the farm from the enlarged home. The barn and sheds now under construction around the old cobbled yard would stay and a small cottage be erected for the use of the shepherd and his family. As a result of this plan Mrs Hardy and Lizzie would be housed separately but under the same roof; thus no-one would know of their strange method of co-habiting.

As expected he found nothing of value recoverable from amongst the debris, except the stonework, for all the furniture had either been swept away to be smashed to pieces against walls and tree trunks, or crushed by falling masonry during the first moments of the impact of the water. The cellars had been partially filled with collapsing floor beams, flagstones and other debris, excep where the two foot thick walls were close enough to support falling items. Slowly the water in the cellars seeped out down the hillside and there emerged from the deep bed of silt several intriguing shapes which needed investigation. However, these proved to be nothing more than broken tools not worth the effort needed to extract them from the mud.

Edward had only given the cellars a cursory glance after Abe's death, mainly because the weather had been sufficiently cold to allow him to keep his food at ground level in the larder. He had no time to mess with the improbable, knowing that everything would either be ruined or rusting, and as time passed he merely added more debris to the pile.

The day very soon arrived when, in order to obtain the legal right to his legacy he had to take Hannah as his wife and, to the villagers gathered on that sunny afternoon in the Church of St Nicholas in the Parish of Bradfield, he appeared to be as nervous as any other bridegroom who promised to cherish his bride forever. Neither of them however, had the happy thoughts and aspirations one would normally expect at such a time.

His mind had, in fact, been far away. The memory of green silk and feathers which represented Lydia Firth haunted him still, just as the memory of the fiery spirit she had shown at her disappointment in him left him full of misery. She had flounced into the carriage with a disdain that almost broke his heart. Those delicate hands, the tiny frame of her body, both would have been a joy to hold, yet he believed they would soon have been wearied and calloused by the work which lay ahead.

Now he had a wife, and she had not disgraced him in appearance as they walked up the steep road to the village church, with the chattering Lizzie by their side. Certainly he had been pleased with the effort Mrs Hardy had put into making a new gown, one of simple fashion yet well-made, cream in colour and trimmed with the lace he had fetched back from town on his last visit. Entwined in her well-brushed hair were several spring flowers, and she held a posy of pussy-willow, mixed with primroses which grew wild on the undisturbed bank behind the cottage. On seeing her thus, her face calm and sober, yet touched by a slight flush of country colour, he knew that at least she would never bring shame on him. Her face was beginning to lose the peaky look which made her appear so thin; occasionally a smile hovered pleasantly on her lips when someone greeted them, but he could not tell what was in her mind. Perhaps one day he would come to admire her and possibly enjoy a mutual pleasure from working with her, more than that was beyond expectation. At least he would not be disappointed by having anticipated too much.

If the day had not been marred by their individual emotional conflicts, it would have been a magnificent one. Warm springtime weather accompanied the small crowd of well-wishers and excited children, all cheering the newly-weds as they left through the arched doorway to look out across at the green hills in the distance.

The wedding came as a brief but welcome respite to the villagers in the aftermath of the previous week's disaster, and they urged Edward to take his bride in hand and kiss her. There was a momentary pause, which the folk put down to shyness, when those hitherto unfamiliar lips touched, and

Edward had been surprised at the softness of Hannah's mouth as she yielded to the crowd's delighted urging. He released her and was aware of the heightening colour of her cheeks which brought fresh cheers from the watching villagers. Taking her arm he guided her towards the road which led back home.

Once away from prying eyes they dropped all pretence and walked in nervous silence, having left Lizzie happily playing with Jack's children, where she would spend the night. Hannah was at a loss as to what to say as she walked by the side of her new husband, she knew so little about him. He was tall and straight, a proud man, however today there was an air of unreality in his behaviour and she sensed that the situation both embarrassed and unnerved him.

They approached the cottage onto which Edward had already started to build the extensions, and entered the cool dark rooms. She shivered, believing the chill to be due to leaving the warmth of the sun, and then busied herself about the kitchen, putting away the small gifts pressed upon them by the village women. Such kindness from those who had so little, she thought. A small stone jar of jam, probably made the previous autumn, a couple of eggs, a small simnel cake and a besom made of local twigs with which to sweep the floor; all but the latter she had placed in the basket specially woven for her by one old lady. Her heart was warmed by these simple gestures, and she was happy in the knowledge that at last she would have a settled home. Never again would she have to submit, out of necessity, to the whims or fancies of demanding old ladies who could hire and fire her at will. She was mistress of her own house, the wife of Edward Morton. A lump rose in her throat and she glanced hesitatingly at him.

If only he would speak instead of sitting, staring at the fire as though the end of the world was nigh. Was he thinking, as she was now, of the one act yet unfulfilled that would seal their agreement? She trembled, almost dropping the stone jar which she held. Had he noticed her nervous state? She was unable to break the silence which seemed to deepen and grow more ominous with each passing moment. Suddenly Edward rose, muttered something unintelligible and stumbled from the room. At that Hannah sank slowly into the chair from which he had risen and cried quietly to herself.

When finally he returned the sun had gone down and had seemingly taken with it the dark mood which had possessed him. He thanked her graciously for the meal which she placed before him. 'I was very rude to take off like that,' he said, humbly. 'Please forgive me. The day has been an emotional one, and a strange one.' His voice betrayed none of the nervousness which caused him to flee earlier, and he seemed more at peace with himself. His tone became almost gentle, 'I didn't say this before, but you looked well and behaved fittingly for a farmer's wife, and I thank you for that.'

She smiled shyly. 'The day was a good one, and the people so kind, even the sun shone upon us. I'm happy that you were not displeased with me.'

The answer she gave took him by surprise and he swallowed hard, unsure of what she expected of him next. It was a strange situation to be in because the intimate side of their agreement had been avoided by both of them, and had not been discussed in depth, ever. No doubt most men in his position would have taken advantage of the situation but he was more ill-at-ease at the prospect of going to bed with her than she would ever know. He toyed absentmindedly with the food on his plate, contemplating how to tell her that, as Lizzie was now in a position to inherit, she was excused the need of going to bed with him at all. Once he had decided to marry Lydia he had not contemplated children with Hannah again, until his tiredness and anxiety after the flood made him change his plans. Lizzie had been his salvation, but the softening tone in Hannah's voice and the words of encouragement shook him; how could he tell her that he didn't need a child now that Lizzie was his step-daughter?

He was loath to broach the subject and had anyway planned to postpone the expected consummation indefinitely, in the hopes that she might find the delay acceptable in the circumstances. At this instance, with Lydia still on his mind, he had no desire to go to bed with Hannah Hardy; he liked her well enough but could not approach her in a physical way.

It was she who hesitatingly raised the matter, her face averted from his gaze, and her voice barely audible. 'If you would give me notice of when you intend to retire, I would very much like time to prepare myself before you come up.' Then, without waiting for the answer, she hurriedly left and ran up the stone stairs where, once inside the room, she lay on the bed and buried her face in the pillow in distress. She groaned inwardly at the very thought of what she had said. How could she have acted so wantonly? By now he must have a very low opinion of her.

Edward was stunned! He had just about been ready to explain everything, when she had confronted him first, then, as if terrified of him she had fled his presence! Having lost his appetite, he pushed the half-empty plate to one side and nervously listened for sounds of movement from the room above.

Upstairs beneath the covers of the old bed, Hannah lay in some trepidation, aghast at the situation she was now in. She closed her eyes to help blot out the enormity of what she had said to Edward, knowing it had only been because of his inability to cope with the strain of their predicament. But she'd panicked, and spoken out before he could sink once more into a dark mood. During his absence earlier, when he'd probably been up on the moor, it had disturbed her to think that he was possibly upset over losing the woman he really loved. Obviously due to their present circumstances, he had chosen her instead and was having difficulty in coming to terms with his decision. In desperation she'd clumsily tried to put them both out of their misery.

Since arriving at the farm on that first day, and knowing why he needed to marry her, she had never quite known how to act or respond to him. She had closed her mind to everything except finding her security as Mrs Morton. If only he had shown some genuine personal need of her, instead he'd appeared as Master of the farm and totally remote. He was an unpredictable man, as the night up on the hill had proved when they had held each other in mutual need and comfort against fear, and the cold. He had been protective and yet as vulnerable as she, but everything was spoilt because of his love for this woman whose name she didn't even know.

Thank God, tomorrow all would be over! Unless of course she didn't conceive, or never conceived; would it go on forever? She was far from experienced in that sort of thing, in fact she wasn't even Mrs Hardy, but Miss Hardy! A brief unfortunate incident in her younger days had left her alone with Lizzie and disowned by her father, forced into a world far harsher than she could ever have imagined. Since that time she had kept herself to herself and was not now prepared for what lay ahead. In this state of misery sleep finally claimed her.

Edward entered the room not knowing what to expect; only the cold sweat on his brow and the slight shake of his hand betrayed his inner anxiety. 'Mrs Hardy?' he whispered kindly, realising that she might be asleep. 'Are you alright?' He ventured a little nearer. There was no answer and moving closer he watched for several seconds, then became aware that she had been crying. He touched her shoulder gently with one hand. 'Mrs Hardy—what's the matter?'

She woke with such apparent distress on her face that he started, mortified. 'What on earth is it?' he asked, his voice genuinely full of concern. 'Surely you're not frightened of me, are you?' He was hurt; this was the one thing he'd never considered, the possibility that she might not want him to touch her. He'd presumed that having been married before she knew what to expect.

The unexpectedly gentle touch of his hand and the real concern in his voice only added to her distress. In vain she tried to stem the flow of tears which for years had lain deep within her, but to no avail, and she sobbed uncontrollably.

He waited patiently, helpless to find words of consolation because he was now equally distressed at not knowing the real cause of her tears, but suspecting the worst. 'Hannah!' he begged, using her first name to calm her. 'Don't take on so, let me help you, if I can. Nothing can be so bad that talking about it to me wouldn't help.'

'I'm sorry!' she sobbed, rubbing her eyes. 'I have no right to refuse you.'

'What!' he cried in disbelief. 'I wouldn't—I couldn't force myself upon you!' His face was as white as chalk. 'Please! Listen to me. I'm not a cruel man—and things have gone far enough; this is a wicked business and I wish now that I had ignored Abe's demands and never attempted to fulfil them.' She appeared to calm down a little at his words, although she would not look at him. He reached out gently and took her hands in his in an effort to comfort her. 'Listen, I'm not used to the company of women and, as I told you once before, I had never intended to marry. I'm just as bewildered and nervous as you—at least you have had a husband, whereas I...' He stopped, conscious of his inadequacy. Then a thought entered his head, one which he should perhaps have considered long ago. 'Maybe I've been so preoccupied with my own problems that I've been blind to yours. We have never discussed Mr Hardy—was his loss so hard to bear that you can't even talk about it?' He looked keenly at her now, 'Or do you wish that he was here now, instead of me?' A look of embarrassed confusion appeared on her face and she attempted in vain to free her hands from his. 'No! It is important!' he insisted, maintaining his hold. 'You are now my wife and I am responsible for you as such. I shall not move until I know the truth, so in turn you must learn to trust me. I never asked you to love me, only to be loyal.' Her head was still bowed, her eyes shielded from his close scrutiny and he tightened his grip, determined she should answer him with honesty.

Hannah knew that she must speak out, her prolonged silence was only adding to their pain and confusion. How could she tell him the truth about her past, she had deceived him and he had every right to be very angry with her. His grip slackened, although he had no intention of letting her hands go, instead he held them encouragingly, almost tenderly.

'I have lied to you,' she blurted out suddenly, plucking up courage, and her hands began to shake nervously in his. 'I had no husband, I am unmarried. I should have told you the truth, but we needed a home.' She let the tears flow, no longer caring what he thought of her, and too weary to battle on.

Edward was not entirely surprised by this disclosure and, as her shoulders sank in despair, she reminded him of Lizzie, who in moments of chastisement looked exactly as Hannah did now. 'It doesn't matter that much!' he said, trying to comfort her. 'It is something my solicitor suspected but could not prove, and something which I found hard to believe.'

'It was easier to keep quiet than risk everything by confessing,' she admitted tearfully. 'Once my past is known I am shunned by better class employers, but as a widow I am accepted. I did it for Lizzie's sake.'

'I know that times have been hard for you, though I didn't realise why, but you have done your best! Lizzie is a beautiful child and I shall see that neither of you ever want again.' He was afraid that she might misunderstand his motives or he would have drawn her close and held her like a child. Instead he squeezed her hand comfortingly, 'You'll feel better after a good night's sleep,' he said, rising from the edge of the bed. 'We'll talk about everything tomorrow. Just remember that you are safe now, and that no one else need ever know your secret but me.'

'Thank you,' she whispered softly. 'I am more afraid of myself than I am of you. I have kept myself to myself in case anyone discovered the truth and that was hard, being without friends. I didn't deserve your kindness, and you trusted me. I am only sorry that I have taken the place of the woman you really wanted to marry.'

Lines of sadness marked Edward's face, signs not missed by Hannah. He hadn't wanted to think of Lydia tonight, and the mention of her only confused things more. He sat back on the bed with a sigh, and shook his head. 'Lydia is in the past, it is we who have to resolve our difficulties if we wish to find peace of mind.' After a few moments of quiet contemplation he decided that as Hannah had confessed so frankly, he might as well draw out of her the rest of her story. 'Don't distress yourself, but may I ask, what of Lizzie's father—did he not know of your plight?'

Hannah's reply was subdued, resigned. 'He is nothing to us. I worked in a large house when I was younger, as a companion to a widowed lady, and foolishly imagined myself to be in love with one of her sons. He flattered me at first, then before long he wanted to come into my bed.' She paused, ashamed to go on.

'Go on—it is nothing new,' Edward assured her gently.

'I was in awe of him, and if I had refused him he would have used some pretext or other to have me dismissed from the house. I would not have been able to find work in the district, or go anywhere without references…'

'And if, by complying, you got pregnant you would have to move anyway! Isn't that the way it always works? Did he not give you any means of support?' Edward spoke quietly, without condemnation or reproval.

She was grateful to be able to speak, at last, to someone who, although not approving her actions, seemed to understand a little of the nightmare she had been through. 'I was paid to go away and hide my shame. The money seemed sufficient at the time, but without work and with a child on the way the money soon ran out. I've worked hard ever since, wherever and whenever I could. It wasn't easy, as no one wants a woman with a child in tow, or the responsibility of taking care of her and a child if she becomes ill.'

'Yes,' he agreed, 'that must have been a frightening situation to be in. We all appear to be victims of life in one way or another! Perhaps we were never intended to lead lives free from hardship and pain, although I am sure we are often tried to the limit and, as a result, betray our inner, better natures. However, because we cannot put to rights that which is already done, we must, you and I and Lizzie, endeavour to rebuild our lives, and the farm. I am still willing to do that, if you are?'

She hadn't thought of Edward as a compassionate man and wondered whether his solitary lifestyle had been the result of some past disappointment; she dared not ask, but hoped that one day he would speak frankly to her as she had to him. He was, however, a good man who deserved respect, and if he had ideas which were not always easy to understand, then so be it.

Edward felt a growing sympathy for the sad figure by his side, and it was only now when the truth was out that he began to appreciate fully the restraints which Hannah had placed upon herself. The self-imposed mask of propriety which she had erected was her means of defence and because of it she had survived. Had it not been for their mutual needs she would have remained an outcast without hope, until sickness finally broke down her barrier of defence and all would have been lost. He recognised the sheer desperation which led her to answer his advertisement in the first place, and in doing so acknowledged that he had been a poor sort of a man to use her as a means to solving his own problems. Nor had it ended there, he had twice changed his mind where her welfare was concerned and not once had he really tried to find out what her inner thoughts and feelings were.

'I shall not touch you, Hannah,' he said, kindly, as if to a child. 'Lizzie is my step-daughter now and can inherit the farm, so you don't have to bear me a child, and I shall sleep in the other room. Lizzie can stay in your bed until the cottage is enlarged, and when that happens there will be sufficient room for all of us to live our lives without hindrance.' She appeared calmer now and he wasn't sure whether to leave or indeed what to do next.

She was encouraged by this and lifted her head; her eyes, although moist from the tears which she had shed, were brighter and full of gratitude. 'I am truly grateful for your understanding. When I agreed to our arrangement it was as if we were speaking of a time in the far distant future, something almost unreal. I thought I would adapt when the time came and didn't think too much about the details. As it turned out things changed rapidly, forcing us together with no emotional ties. What we were proposing to do was so cold that it served to remind me of the deed which brought about my downfall in the first place. I have no feeling of revulsion for you, I just haven't allowed myself to think of you in that way, it was more a feeling of shame with myself. I must be a very weak person to give in whenever life pulls me down.'

'No!' Edward responded emphatically. 'You have a strength of character which is to be admired. Most women in your position would have given up long ago. I'm proud to call you Mrs Morton, and hope that in time we may come to laugh with affection at what we have done today.'

Edward rose the following morning relaxed and relieved that he now understood Hannah a little better. She'd tossed and turned for a long time after he had gone to his own room, that much he knew, until sleep had finally overtaken her.

He wasn't sure how she would behave in the light of what had transpired, and even less sure what his own reaction would be. He was somewhat surprised therefore, to find her downstairs before him, neatly dressed and with not one wisp of hair out of place. How different she'd looked last night with loose dishevelled hair and tear-stained cheeks. It was strange that, apart from the night of the flood, he'd never seen her anything but tidy, calm, and fully in control of herself.

'Good morning!' he said brightly, before crossing the room to where he kept his boots. Then, looking enquiringly and directly at her before attempting to pull them on he asked, 'Did you sleep well?'

She smiled diffidently. 'Eventually,' she answered quietly as she rose to fetch the long-handled shoehorn which he used when pulling on his boots. 'And thank you for your understanding and kindness last night. I had hoped never to tell you about myself, but I realise that it was silly and unfair of me to deceive you so.' She passed him the shoehorn to save him getting up, her eyes lowered.

He took the horn, touched by the gesture. 'There is no need for you ever to hang your head in shame again. That chapter of your life is closed forever, and we shall not refer to it again unless you wish to.' He pulled on the boots and sat back. 'Now let's have breakfast, there is work to be done!'

With a tremor in her voice she said, 'I shall not forget your kindness.' Then she filled the plate before him with food.

He chose to leave the matter there even though he would have liked to have known more of her life, but it could wait until she felt more like confiding in him. 'I'm going to clear some of the ditches today,' he informed her. 'It will help the drainage to return to normal. If anyone needs me I shall be working on my own down towards the bottom field. The last of the lambs have arrived and Joseph has everything under control there. The rest of the men know what to do.' Edward ate on, aware of her quiet presence across the room. This time it was a more comfortable silence, and one which he was loath to break.

'What will you do today?' he ventured to ask, although he knew she would have to fetch Lizzie back from the village at some time.

'Well, I have to fetch Lizzie back. I do hope she enjoyed playing with the children, she has never been away from me for a whole night before! It will be good for her to have some friends out here in the valley.'

Edward agreed. 'Tell her that one day, when we've got through this period of re-building, I'll teach her to ride a horse. Do you think she would like that?'

'I'm sure she would,' Hannah replied. 'But if you tell her now you'll never hear the end of it. I'd leave it for a while until you're ready to teach her.'

'Perhaps you're right!' he nodded. At that he made to leave the kitchen but paused a little self-consciously, 'I admire your courage, and I promise that your secret will always be safe with me.' With that he quickly left the room.

An expression of pleased surprise appeared on Hannah's face at the remark, and she realised that he was embarrassed at his outburst. Perhaps things might yet turn out well for them all in the end.

It was probably a little early for Edward to be up and about on the morning after his wedding, but he felt the need to be alone; to think and deliberate on the dramatic change in his relationship with Hannah. No doubt people who saw him would ponder momentarily as to why he was working so early today of all days, but in the main most were still pre-occupied in putting some sense of order back into their own disrupted lives.

He felt strangely light-hearted, even humming the occasional tune to himself—something he hadn't done for a long while, and in this mood was quite oblivious to anything beyond his immediate surroundings. He was coming to the conclusion that in spite of the anxieties of the past few weeks, and the truths which had emerged the previous night, he was finding Hannah's company quite congenial. He was engrossed in these musings, and so unaware of the passing of time, that he never saw the youth observing him as he worked.

'Uncle Edward? Is that you?' The enquiring voice came over the drystone wall, catching Edward by surprise.

He started, as much at the familiarity of the question as the unexpected arrival of the young man now peering at him. He lowered his foot from the spade with which he was clearing the ditch, and, leaning it against the wall, looked keenly at the youth as he did so. 'I might be,' he replied carefully, 'and who might you be?'

'I'm Peter Martin, your sister Betty's son!'

Edward, who had not quite recovered from the sudden intrusion into his thoughts, gazed at him intently. It must have been all of three years since he had set eyes on any of his young nephews, and was certainly long enough for him to fail to recognise one now. The older ones, he recalled, were a rough lot like their father, but this one seemed polite enough. 'And what brings you this way? My sister's not ill, is she?'

'No, Uncle. I was in the neighbourhood and thought to pay my respects. I'm on my way to Stocksbridge and although we got your message after the flood to say that you were alright, Mother wanted me to see how bad things were. I have always meant to call before now, but never seemed to make it.'

'Oh!' muttered Edward. 'Well, here I am! You're the youngest I take it, and I see you're more like your mother than you are your father.' He was cautious, aware that Peter wasn't the only one being weighed up, yet he sensed no guile in the boy. What he saw didn't displease him, the youth seemed friendly enough, certainly less arrogant than his brothers, and better looking too! Yet there was a fineness in the features which sat ill on a country lad, Edward judged, then felt ashamed of his unkind thoughts. In order to placate his conscience he heard himself saying, 'Why not call into the farm when you've finished your business? I shall be finished here by tea-time and will write a note for you to take home to your mother.'

'I should like that,' the youth agreed quickly, 'but I won't be back until tomorrow and then I can't stay long. As you know it's a fair distance from here, but I'll call in.'

'Good! Can you be here for dinner at one? My wife will tell you where I am if you arrive early.' The youth agreed with a nod. 'See you tomorrow then!' Edward said, and picked up the spade to resume his task, raising his head every so often to watch the figure as it disappeared along the lane.

Perhaps, at least, this one was of a different calibre to the rest of the family? Strange that their paths had not crossed in recent years, especially as, when business took Edward past his sister's place, he hadn't actually ignored their existence. He'd not been inside her home for years, instead he'd simply sent a neighbour in to fetch Betty out, rather than risk any confrontation with his disagreeable brother-in-law. It was a sad state of affairs which created a barrier between his sister and himself. They still greeted each other with affection, but as time passed they had less in common to discuss, and he always left her with a feeling of sadness. It hadn't been his intention to abandon Betty to her lot, but he received no pleasure from the barrage of insults heaped upon him by her husband if they met, and he knew that, once he'd departed, Betty suffered at the hand of Henry Martin because of their meeting.

Edward was curious as to the reason for his nephew's visit to Stocksbridge, but no doubt the lad would tell him on his return. As far as he knew, his sister had had no trouble with this her youngest boy, and he quite looked forward to finding out from Peter how things were with Betty. He would write a letter that very evening to her and apologise for having taken a wife without informing her that he had done so.

When Hannah heard of Peter's impending visit she was exceedingly pleased, and Edward realised that this was the first real visitor she had received since coming to the valley. It was a small enough incident but seemed to give her pleasure, and for this Edward was grateful, as he knew that country life could be lonely for anyone not used to it. Admittedly he himself was reluctant to mix too freely with the inhabitants of the village, but he knew that he ought to provide Hannah with an occasional social distraction. Perhaps a trip to market now and then would do them all good. That, together with the occasional visit to a fair or circus if only for Lizzie's sake. Strange how, once his visits to town to meet Lydia and her friends ceased, he felt no further desire to return, and was content to revert to his previous way of life.

Lizzie, having enjoyed her stay with Jack Gray's family, was nevertheless more than happy to return home, and awaited the visit of the stranger with interest.

By lunchtime the following day Peter arrived as expected, and was met in the lane by Edward returning from the moors where he'd been checking on the state of the flock.

'So, you've made it then!' he greeted Peter, and fell in step with the long-legged youth. 'My wife will be pleased that you're here in time. You've certainly picked a warm day for walking so far—I suppose you'll be ready for something to drink before we eat?'

'Yes please, Uncle! I would appreciate that but before we go inside I'd like to see what happened to the farm. It seems unbelievable that it's gone. I vaguely recall the cobbled yard but it's the cottage I remember most.'

'Come on then,' said Edward, leading him down the lane, 'We've just got time to look before dinner. I didn't think you'd be able to remember the farm, it's years since you came. There's not much left to see, and although we've built a new stable and a shed in the past couple of weeks, I have no intention of re-building the farmhouse. Instead, I will build a workman's cottage on the site and extend my cottage. We've made a start as you will see later. Much of what I finally do will depend on how much compensation we get from the Water Board.'

'Mother says you are lucky to be alive, and I can see what she means.' Peter looked around, unable to recall the finer details of the vanished house. 'Mother didn't tell me you were married.'

'No, Peter. It was all rather sudden, as a result of the flood you might say—so you'll have to tell your mother all about it when you go home. I've written her a letter, so don't let me forget to give it to you before you go.'

They retraced their footsteps and entered the cottage where Hannah waited patiently, having been informed by Lizzie that Edward had met the stranger and taken him down the lane.

Once Peter was introduced, the four sat comfortably chatting together around the well-scrubbed table and Hannah asked what had taken Peter over to Stocksbridge.

'Well, you see, I need work and was told of a farmer over that way who urgently needed an extra man, so I thought it worth giving it a try.'

'Why so far away from home?' Edward enquired, a little puzzled. 'Surely there's work around Bamford?'

'I want to get away from the family, Uncle Edward. I'm fed up with being treated like a lackey at home. Because I'm the youngest I get put on, and they treat me as though I'm a bit soft in the head.'

'You don't give me that impression,' Hannah responded in a kindly tone. 'What makes you think that?'

'I'm not at all like the others. I like to read books when I can but they resent me doing so, and if I read in a quiet corner it irritates them. I do a fair day's work but I'm not as robust as they are. Perhaps if I retaliated more it would help, but that's just not my way. They say I'm a dreamer, and in that they are probably right.'

'You can't be that weak,' Edward rejoined. 'It's a long hard trek from Stocksbridge to here, and you've still got a long way to go.'

'I don't mind the walking, Sir, and I like the freedom up on the moors.'

'You'd better be careful, the moors are private property, and old Wentworth's man can be keen with his gun when he wants to be. I lease land up there for the sheep so he knows me. He doesn't take kindly to strangers wandering about, so stick to the main tracks then you won't get lost, and head for the *Strines Inn* in case the mist comes down suddenly. You're not familiar enough with the terrain hereabouts to take risks.'

'I don't suppose I'll be back in the area often, but I'll watch my step in future,' Peter promised, grateful for the advice.

'Did you get the job?' Hannah asked, as she offered him another helping of rabbit broth.

'No!' the youth replied, dejectedly. 'But then there was only a slim chance of me getting it anyway. I suppose I could go to Sheffield and look for something there, although frankly I don't think I'd like town work, nor do I want to work locally in the cotton or wire mills.'

Edward shook his head. Well, I'm afraid if you've not served an apprenticeship you'll end up with nothing more than a labouring job, and fear it would be the death of you, after farming. Why can't you find work on one of the farms nearer home?'

'I've got ambitions, Uncle Edward!' The boy spoke out with youthful confidence. I don't want to spend my life shut away on a farm, working each day from dawn till dusk until I'm old and grey. I want to see the world before I die, see some of the things I've read about and go to places full of life! Mother says I'm just like you were, in some ways.'

Edward recoiled inwardly with surprise. What had his sister been saying he wondered? He caught Hannah's enquiring look and thought he saw a fleeting sign of amusement there. At least the boy had spirit. Edward took a keener look at his nephew; he looked nothing like himself as a youth, they had the same eyes maybe, now he came to think about it, and plenty of confidence, but that was all. 'Oh, your mother said that did she,' he said, with a wry smile. 'And what exactly was I like?' He was now slightly amused by the conversation and sought to egg the lad on a bit.

'Mother said you were always restless, always talking about going away. You did, didn't you, before you came here?'

'Does your mother often talk about me then?' Edward's curiosity was aroused. 'I thought your father disliked anything to do with me!'

Peter shook his head. 'She only talks to me about you when the others aren't there. They wouldn't be interested anyway. Mother's very proud of you and thinks I should take you as an example to follow, but I don't want to be a farmer.'

'Nor did I, Peter. I suppose she told you that I went to Sheffield and worked for a farrier with the horses at the Barracks? I certainly learned a lot there amongst the so-called gentlemen officers, and from ordinary soldiers. Some were a rough, drinking lot but I suppose it opened my eyes to the ways of the world.'

'You went to the Crimean War, didn't you? Mother hasn't told me the details but she said that you had been to sea several times.' Peter's eyes flashed with the usual enthusiasm of inexperienced youth. 'That's something I'd like to do.'

'Not as I did, in war-time, I hope. There was nothing glamorous about me going to sea. I was merely taking horses out to the soldiers who did the fighting. We gathered thousands of the poor creatures from farms all over the country and shipped them out for the Army to use, only to see them cut to ribbons along with the men. I'll never forgive that happening. My worst experience was a raging storm as we crossed over to Varna on the Black Sea. Once the animals were safely delivered to the cavalry we came back to port and caught another ship home, then when we got back we rounded up more horses to ship out again.'

Peter interrupted, his face flushed with excitement. 'I think perhaps I might do the same—join the Army I mean. It's a chance to travel and get away from it all!'

'A soldier inevitably goes to war, my lad! That was half the trouble with the Crimean War. There had been peace for nearly forty years and the Generals had lost the art of battle. The whole affair was badly organised, and ill-managed. I saw at first hand how confusion in forwarding and distributing supplies caused great deprivation, and how slovenly soldiers put their lives at risk through carelessness. It was enough for me to see the state of the wounded who'd been fighting. Poor devils, they were bleeding and dying not just of their wounds but of cholera, dysentery and lack of proper medical attention. I've seen things that would put you off being a soldier forever!' Edward now had a sad, reflective look on his face.

Lizzie sat in silence through all this, her spoon suspended above her dish and her eyes darting from Edward's face to Peter's, and back again, totally absorbed in their lively exchange of words. Edward, realising that she was far too young to hear such dreadful descriptions of war, brought the conversation to an abrupt conclusion. 'I think we've said enough on that matter, and Lizzie here shouldn't be listening to stories of war.' At that Lizzie perked up and began to eat once more. Then, for her sake, he added, 'but I did see Queen Victoria once, she came in a carriage from Farnborough to Aldershot.'

Lizzie got excited. 'Did she wave to you?' she asked with childlike exuberance.

Edward laughed out loud, 'Not at me—to the crowd. But I waved to her.'

It was left to Hannah to embark on a lighter topic of conversation, which pleased Edward who was left to finish his meal in a less stressful manner. He actually enjoyed the company of his young nephew, even though his dinner was almost cold as a result of their discussion. He was, therefore, rather disappointed when after dinner Peter announced that he'd stayed longer than intended, and must leave immediately if he was to be home before dark.

'I hope you'll not let it be too long before you call in again, the door will always be open to you.' Edward said warmly, and handed over the letter which he had written the previous night. 'Here, take this to your mother, and don't forget to give it to her. I know young people, when they have their minds on too many things at once they usually forget something.'

Peter made a special point of thanking Hannah for the trouble she had taken on his behalf, and bent to shake hands with Lizzie in a playful farewell before leaving, thus winning her heart forever. His behaviour did not go unnoticed by Edward, who watched them with deep satisfaction. He must tell Betty in his next letter that she should be proud of her youngest son.

Once the youth had gone, Edward sat deep in thought, remembering the close relationship he had once had with his sister. She and Abe had been the only people privileged to know his inner thoughts, the only ones he had ever felt he could trust implicitly not to let him down.

'What a pleasant young man Peter is!' Hannah remarked, breaking into his thoughts. 'Couldn't we find him work ourselves?'

Edward frowned pensively, 'I don't think it advisable, Hannah. We don't really know much about him, and the will was made as it was because Abe didn't want my sister's family involved here. The trustees would hardly approve of my hiring Peter, particularly as so little time has elapsed since Abe's death. If they wouldn't adapt the will to make things easier for me then they're not likely to accept that idea. I agree with you, Peter brings a breath of fresh air with him but he needs to find his own way in life, as I did.

Besides, I'm bound to employ local men, those who have served the farm well in the past, and sadly, because of the flood, once the extension is finished we won't need as many full-time workers. Only when we harvest the fields up towards Storrs will I need to take on casual workers. As there is a shortage of work locally it would be unacceptable to bring in a stranger at this time.'

'That's a shame! But then perhaps farming is not the answer for him. However, I would like to know how he goes on.'

Edward was surprised by Hannah's concern for someone who was little more than a stranger to both of them. 'So would I,' he agreed, then, after a moment added, 'I would like you to meet his mother, my sister, one day. I'm afraid she's to be pitied for having married a man who is an idle bully. He's been in trouble no-end of times, especially for associating with the pugilists. The *Bell Hagg Inn* was raided when a fight broke out and, as usual, he was involved. Peter would seem to be the pick of the bunch, taking after his mother, whilst the other boys are more like their father.' He looked cautiously at Hannah, unsure whether to express his thoughts out loud. 'I really don't think she would have married him if he hadn't got her in the family way.' He sighed, wondering if he should have said what he had, but the truth would no doubt have come out sooner or later.

Hannah seemed not to take the statement personally. 'It's little wonder the boy wants to get away. Can't we do anything—have you no contacts?' she pleaded.

'I'll give it some thought,' Edward promised. 'I've never been one to mix socially here in the valley, certainly not sufficiently to ask favours, but leave it with me. Now I must go, I've wasted enough time today, I must get on.'

On returning home later, Edward stretched out leisurely in his chair, as usual. It had been an interesting but tiring day, and strangely he had no desire to do anything other than read. After several pages his concentration faltered, partly due to the distance of the lamp from his chair, and he fell to pondering on the happenings of the past few weeks. So much had changed, and here he was now with a wife and step-daughter in his small cottage which would soon be turned into a farmhouse. He was pleasantly contented over the whole affair, conceding that he had enjoyed the family atmosphere with his nephew earlier. He closed his eyes, allowing the feeling of peace to flow over him, and fell asleep.

By now Hannah was used to his habit of appearing to be asleep and knew full well that when he thought her preoccupied he would raise his eyelids and watch her. At first it was disconcerting for her to be so closely observed but once she realised that he meant nothing by this, she relaxed. This time she realised, after several minutes, that for once he was actually asleep, and took the opportunity of studying him in turn without fear of detection or embarrassment. It was hard now for her to accept that the man resting so peacefully before her had once filled her with fear and trepidation. His reaction on discovering her past had been in complete contrast to her expectations, and revealed a generosity of spirit and tolerance which she had not anticipated. Then, with Peter's visit had come the added knowledge that there was so much about Edward that was both interesting and unusual, so much so that she'd sat earlier, like Lizzie, absorbed in the exchanges between the two men.

In slumber he appeared vulnerable; his hand hung awkwardly over the arm of the chair and would eventually have gone numb. Hannah gently lifted the hand and placed it slowly on his lap without waking him. She removed the book which was in danger of falling from his knee, placing it on the table beside him before returning to her chair.

On waking from a deep heavy sleep, he noticed that the book had been removed from his lap and wondered why he'd not been aware of Hannah's movement. There she sat in the lamplight apparently serenely contented. He gradually found himself watching her as she painstakingly stitched together the multitude of coloured hexagonal pieces of material needed to form a quilt. He admired the tenacity in her which never seemed to fail, even in the most trying situation. She was still very much a mystery to him in many ways, but this no longer disturbed him because he knew now that there was neither guile nor cunning in her make-up, just the habit of concealing her inner self from the world.

Suddenly, sensing his gaze upon her, she raised her head and smiled warmly, 'You've slept soundly for an hour, you must have been exhausted'. He returned the smile and agreed, then, retrieving the book, settled down happily to resume his reading.

Almost a week went by during which time Edward received confirmation that he was to get a quick and suitable compensation for the farmhouse, livestock and farming implements lost in the flood. He was lucky and would not be out of pocket as the farm had not been his to begin with, so that, by adding to the cottage instead of re-building he was actually increasing his own estate. Sadly, this was not so for many of the other poor victims, as no amount of compensation would make up for, or remove, the memory and trauma of the catastrophe. Yes, he was indeed fortunate, as two hundred and thirty-eight lives had been lost and their grieving families were, in many cases, still homeless, or endeavouring to prove their claims valid. The generosity of both rich and poor alike throughout the nation had touched him deeply, but he couldn't help thinking that the distribution of monies sometimes seemed unfair. He'd heard of a sugar refiner in town receiving just over half the value claimed, whilst a poor woman with nothing in life received a mere 2/6d for the loss of a child! So much for the value of human life! He had been able to rely on a good solicitor to fight for him, whereas some were going to have to wait months for a settlement.

He and Hannah were discussing these matters one evening when a knock on the door took them both by surprise. Usually, unless there was trouble with an animal, it was a rare occasion for anyone to call on him so late, and Edward anxiously went to the door.

'Peter!' he exclaimed with astonishment, on realising that the uniformed man standing before him was his nephew. 'What on earth are you doing in uniform, and arriving so late in the day? Come on in!'

Hannah came hurrying forward, and pleased as she was to see him standing there, was even more surprised at his attire. 'What have you done?' she cried, half admonishing, half out of concern for the boy.

'I would think it obvious!' Edward remarked dryly, not at all enamoured by the actions of his nephew, who he had not realised was so anxious to get away from home. 'I hope you know what you have done!'

Seeing his uncle's reaction Peter flushed with indignation. 'I think so— in fact I'm looking forward to making a new life for myself!'

'If that's what he wants, Edward,' Hannah said, in an effort to calm things down, 'then who are we to discourage him? Perhaps this is his opportunity to escape a life for which he wasn't cut out.' Her encouragement brought a look of grateful relief to the youth's face, and won for Hannah his lasting affection.

Acknowledging that he was beaten in his efforts to counsel his nephew, Edward relaxed into a more amiable frame of mind. 'I see I am out-numbered. I just hope you haven't done something you'll regret.' He led Peter through into the sitting-room and poured him a glass of wine from a bottle which he had opened earlier. 'Now, you know that you're always welcome here, but why so late in the day, there's nothing wrong is there?'

'No, it just took me far longer to walk here than I anticipated. I had hoped to get a lift on a cart, but I wanted you to know that I'd taken steps to do something with my life. It will be easier now for me to call and visit since I am living at the Barracks, that is until I'm sent away on duty.'

'Here, give me your jacket and take this wine. It's a long walk, I know, having done it many times myself. What have you enlisted as?' he asked, his interest growing.

'I'm in the 8th Foot, and when I've done my basic training I hope to become a clerk in the Quarter Master Department.' There was no disguising the pride in his manner, something which Edward recognised as a quality needed for a man who chose the Army for an occupation.

Trying not to be too encouraging, Edward pointed out the obvious. 'You'll still be expected to go on active service should there be a campaign, or war, you know. This might be a peaceful period but who knows what lies around the corner!'

'That I accept—I'm not a coward!'

'I know that, Peter, but brave men still get killed!'

Peter brushed aside his uncle's remarks good naturedly, and changed the subject. 'I would have been here earlier but the road is still a mess after the flood, particularly in the dark. By the time I reached Malin Bridge I could imagine how terrifying it must have been that night, and to have lived through the deluge. It's hard to credit that huge grinding wheels were totally removed from their mountings, and that other buildings disappeared completely! At the Barracks, in the married quarters, a Paymaster-Sergeant lost two of his children that night. A three-foot-thick wall gave way on the river side of the perimeter, flooding the lower married quarters to ceiling level. The Paymaster got out with his wife and one child after breaking open a door to escape the rising water, but when he went back to fetch the other two children, the door had been forced closed again by the pressure. Once the water had subsided a Colonel and another man went in and released the water, but it was too late to save the children.'

'Poor dears,' Hannah sighed. 'It doesn't bear thinking about, you know Edward could have been killed in the farmhouse, if he hadn't come here to discuss something with me.'

'Thank God he did! Until I went into Sheffield a few days ago on my way to the Barracks, I really had no proper idea of the true scale of the impact beyond this valley. I never imagined the force to have increased as it went down river. When I left here previously I climbed over the hill to Bolsterstone, and saw very little from that vantage point.'

'Of course,' Edward said. 'This time you would have gone in on the Hathersage Road to get to Sheffield and the Barracks. It was the junction at Malin Bridge which took a great deal of the impact.'

'Yes, it must have been a dreadful sight,' Peter agreed. Then he turned to Hannah and asked, 'Have you been to Sheffield yet?'

She shook her head, sadly. 'No, but Edward plans to take me shortly so that we can replace things lost that night. I must admit that it is one aspect of the outing which fills me with dread.' She shivered at the thought, then realising just how late it was, asked, 'Do you have to go back tonight? We could make a makeshift bed in here if you would like to stay?'

'That's very kind of you. I had hoped that you would let me stay as I don't have to be back until dinner-time tomorrow.'

'By all means, do stay,' Edward said, although he was worried lest Peter found out about his and Hannah's strange sleeping arrangements. 'You can bed down in here; we've only got two rooms upstairs until the building is finished, and Lizzie is already asleep.'

'I wouldn't want you to disturb her; in any case I'm used to roughing it at home, and of course I have to share quarters at the Barracks, so I reckon I can put up with anything. The thought of having this room to myself, just for one night, is a luxury.'

'It's just as well you're used to making do, Peter, because we haven't much spare bedding at the moment, but you're welcome to share what we have,' Hannah warned him. She was quite excited at the prospect of going to town to purchase the many things they needed, especially as she had never before been in possession of money that was not destined either to pay her debts, or be meted out with extreme care as she had with Edward's gift before she came to the valley.

'Now, what did your mother say about my getting married?' Edward enquired. 'Was she surprised at the suddenness of it?'

'Hardly sudden!' Peter laughed. 'She said that it was about time, after being a bachelor all these years. Of course she was surprised to have no previous hint of your intentions, but wishes you well and regrets she doesn't know how to write a letter to you. I read out the one you wrote to her, it pleased her very much.'

Edward sighed with resignation at the fact that his sister had never mastered the arts of reading and writing, she missed so much by not being able to do so. 'At least you have acquired the skill to read; how did you manage to achieve that in such surroundings?' he asked.

'There's an old man down the lane from the house who reads and answers letters for those who can't do so for themselves. I have often helped him with his garden and, in return, he taught me, first to tell the time of day, then to read and write. I'm the only one at home who can do more than sign my name. That's why the others mock me. It used to bother me in the beginning, but now I pity them their narrowness of mind, for they will never be able to explore the finer things in life.' This said, he asked after Lizzie's welfare, and told them of some of the things which had influenced him most over the years.

Later, after supper, Hannah made a bed of sorts for him in the sitting-room, she was glad that the weather was mild, for in spite of there being a fire it had little effect on the draughts which blew under and around the doors in the cottage.

Three months had passed since Edward and Hannah's marriage, and the extension to the cottage was nearing completion. In all that time Edward had slept, as promised, in the smaller of the two bedrooms, the rest of the cottage they shared amicably, awaiting the time when there would be more space in which to move about. No longer would they be compelled to share the cosy little sitting-room or climb the same narrow stairway to their respective bedrooms. Edward was now in a position to offer Hannah the privacy which he had always intended she should have, and it was obvious that unless the new rooms were to remain empty, they had to be furnished. Edward therefore proposed that they should go to town and purchase several pieces of furniture and rugs at the earliest opportunity.

Although Hannah was excited at the prospect, she was aware that this was a step towards her withdrawal from the companionship which she had come to enjoy with Edward. She found this to be strangely disturbing but came to the conclusion that it was the result of yet another change coming in her life. Lizzie, however, thought it was a great adventure to ride in the cart which Edward had hired from the village blacksmith, her legs wrapped carefully in a blanket to save them from chafing on the sides. Unfortunately the vehicle had seen better days and Edward vowed that he would buy a gig for the farm as soon as he was able to do so.

They had set off early in the morning with Hannah and Lizzie in the back, soon convinced that they would be bruised and battered by the time the journey was over. This was only the second time Hannah had left the valley since the disaster, but sobering evidence still remained of the flattened mills, broken walls and destroyed bridges. In places, trees still held pathetic reminders in their branches of household goods swept away, some perhaps torn from their owner's hands and which, so far, had been missed by the hordes of souvenir hunters who had visited the valleys.

By the time the party reached Sheffield, Hannah's eager anticipation was almost too much to bear. Edward pulled into the yard at the *Angel Inn* where he left their conveyance in the safe hands of the ostler. He had no personal desire to shop, to him it was a necessary inconvenience which kept him from more important work. Hannah on the other hand had no such scruples; she dragged him excitedly from store to store, comparing prices and carefully examining anything which caught her eye.

To Edward's relief she was as selective and keen-eyed as she was prudent, and it was quite some time before even the smallest purchase was made. He was rather touched by her concern for his likes and dislikes, even though he'd stated how much she could spend, and that the furniture was to be her choice. It took them all morning to view every furniture-maker from Market Place, through Fargate and Pinstone Street, and half way down South Street, before Hannah dragged him back to Cocking's in Watson's Walk to purchase the sofa and a matching chair with which she'd fallen in love.

So, having helped select, in addition to the sofa, a chest of drawers, a single bed, a side-table, a rug and finally a second-hand but well preserved sideboard, Edward at last considered it safe to leave Hannah to buy the smaller items herself. They eventually arranged to meet later by the

Crimean Monument at Moor Head, and after collecting some of the purchases left in various shops, he sank wearily onto a bench-seat at the *Angel*. Breathing a sigh of relief he refreshed himself with a glass of ale and a sandwich in preparation for the journey which lay ahead.

When finally they arrived back at the farm with the over-filled cart, Lizzie was fast asleep, and it took Edward some time to remove the many smaller packages and bundles which Hannah had bought. The furniture and larger items were to be fetched by two of the men with a sturdy hired wagon the following day. As he contemplated the array of parcels he wondered why it was that a woman needed so much more with which to exist than did a bachelor. He hoped he would not have to repeat the day's exercise on a regular basis, pleasant though this had been.

As they sat later in the evening amongst the clutter of their purchases, Edward began to acknowledge that he no longer looked forward to the thought of Hannah removing herself to the new sitting-room, thus leaving him alone. He also had to admit that he enjoyed her company far more than he'd ever imagined possible.

Since the night of their wedding Hannah's trust in him had manifested itself in many ways, revealing her softer nature, and as a result he found his admiration and appreciation of her increasing with each passing day. As spring had passed into summer, so her features had filled out, eradicating all signs of the emaciated, pale face he had first observed which was replaced now by a much more healthy complexion. He admitted that she could never be classed as a woman of outstanding beauty, yet she was becoming serenely handsome, and livelier of spirit. It was clear that his sympathetic reaction to her confession had convinced her that he was no monster, and had removed the barrier which Hannah had of necessity built around herself. She wasn't capricious, in fact rather the opposite, and the longer they conversed the more he found her thoughts to be compatible with his own. Her interest and understanding of subjects usually found dull by other women both pleased and surprised him.

He was greeted each morning by her welcoming smile, which never failed to appear even when he knew she was troubled by something or other. No longer did he stay up on the moors for hours on end, for he quite missed her company and, as he drew near the cottage, his steps would quicken in anticipation of their spending a leisurely evening together. He was now dreading the day when she would perhaps out of choice decide to retire to the new sitting-room instead of being with him.

He still knew little about her past but refrained from probing, in the hope that one day she would feel sufficiently at ease to confide more in him. She appeared to be content, yet never said whether she was happy with their arrangement. He would have liked to think so, and began to wonder if their present strange relationship might eventually become untenable. The more they laughed together and shared the close confines due to lack of room, the more he realised that she was becoming part of the fabric of his life. There were occasions when he mused on how, on the night of the flood, he had held her protectively against his body, totally unaware of anything but the catastrophe taking place in the valley below. They had clung together in the dark for warmth without being conscious of their physical proximity; had he done so he would have thought himself being disloyal to Lydia. Lydia, who had been like a beautiful moth, so delicate and in need of protection. Yet he wasn't in love with Hannah, not as he had been with Lydia. The feelings he had for Hannah were very different, but often, seeing her in the soft light of the lamp he had wanted her to remove the combs which held her hair so primly in place, and allow it to cascade loosely about her shoulders. He was curious too! How much more attractive might she be if the severe neckline of her dress was left undone a little, revealing more of her delicate skin? On odd occasions, when he realised she had become aware of his gaze, he had dropped his eyes, or made suitable comments on the events of the day.

Hannah, however, was not unaware of Edward's watchfulness though she would never admit that she took pleasure in this knowledge. She knew that if he realised this he would become embarrassed. She was beginning to see just how unworldly he was where woman were concerned, for he sat there thinking her too busy to notice his interest in her.

Her observations of him were much more subtle, or so she thought!

As they sat surrounded by their purchases, neither letting the other know that they contemplated the forthcoming separation with some regret, they lifted their heads in unison. Their eyes met and something strangely warm passed between them.

Hannah had never thought to like the man who so coldly asked her to become his wife, yet, with the passing of time she found it hard to refrain from sometimes touching his hand reassuringly, or from placing her hand encouragingly on the shoulder of his leather jerkin which he wore when cleaning the barrel of his shotgun. What, she wondered, had caused him to become such a reserved, withdrawn man? Beneath the hard exterior she now knew lay a gentle, unassuming person who was perhaps more vulnerable than any man she had ever met. She wondered how she could ever have mistakenly thought him incapable of human feeling. The evidence, however subtle, had been there from the outset, when he'd sent her the sovereign and in his kindness to her child.

Hannah knew that although Edward would never admit it, he was, with his defences lowered, a lonely man. Once the sturdy reticence was relaxed he evinced all the normal emotions caused by pain and joy. She had seen it in his drooping shoulders the morning after the flood when he had looked down into the valley; seen his heartfelt sympathy for the stricken villagers, and the pain on his face when he thought her to be repulsed by him on the night of their wedding. In his unguarded moments she had witnessed tenderness and laughter in his eyes, and a quiet hesitancy due to his lack of knowledge of womanly things. To the outside world he was master of himself, but she knew differently. She also knew that to reveal her knowledge would be to destroy his trust in her forever.

Such was the state of their existence that the completion of the additional rooms was bound to change everything which had gone before. Unknown to each other, Edward and Hannah found themselves thinking hard about these changes, changes which would set the pattern of their lives for the future.

Lizzie was, however, happy with her lot for she loved both of them and now had several friends in the area with whom to play. She also had Peter who was becoming a regular visitor to the house and could easily be cajoled into reading to her. She would sit spellbound at his feet on a small stool, as he sometimes invented stories to please her. Some stories he would repeat over and over and if, through tiredness, he missed out a little she would remind him of his omission.

The evening drew to a close, and with some reluctance Edward rose from his chair, tidied away his own belongings, and made to leave the room. He wasn't sure why, but he was no longer tired, nor did he wish to climb the stairs to the emptiness of his bedroom.

Sensing his hesitancy Hannah remarked, with a smile. 'I hope we didn't spend too much today. I'm sure when the wagon arrives and everything is placed to advantage we'll find that nothing was bought which wasn't needed.'

Edward nodded, and replied wistfully, 'No doubt I will get used to the changes, but it will seem strange to have the old place so altered.'

She hadn't missed the sad note in his voice, and realised with a pang that her joy was in complete contrast to his regret at the situation now forced upon him. In a softer tone she merely responded, 'Things won't be as bad as all that, and the plans you have for the farm seem to be coming along very well.'

'Yes, they do, don't they?' he said, brightening a little. 'And with more rooms we shall have almost doubled the size of the cottage. In fact, I must confess that I found the farmhouse too roomy for one man; somehow Abe must have liked hearing his own footsteps rattling around the place, whereas I did not!'

That he felt this way did not surprise Hannah and she felt sorry for him standing there, obviously not wanting to leave, yet unable to say more. He must have realised that she was watching him closely, for he suddenly said, 'I wish you good night then,' and went to bed.

The following evening he returned early from the fields, having seen Joseph and John returning earlier in the afternoon with the wagon-load of furniture. He was curious to see what there was to show for the large amount of money he had laid out. Yet again the living-room showed signs of rearrangement; some things had been removed while other unfamiliar items had appeared in their place. He didn't mind, it was only furniture and not so important that it mattered to him, and at least the result was pleasing to the eye. However, the door to Hannah's new sitting-room was firmly closed and he presumed from the noise within that she was already happy with the situation. An unexpected pang of sadness struck him when he realised that this was to be the way of things from now on, so he went rather despondently to his bedroom and changed from his dusty outdoor garments with less enthusiasm than he had done of late.

Hannah had no idea that Edward would be at all offended by her preoccupation with the new sitting-room and came out, closing the door behind her, intending to surprise him with it later. She noted that he seemed rather quiet throughout tea but put it down to his exertions during the long hot day. Nevertheless, she was disappointed by his lack of interest in the effort she had made on behalf of them both. Was it, she wondered, that he disapproved of the amount of money which she had spent? She had taken great care to be prudent with it and had returned a goodly sum.

She did not go to her own room once Lizzie had gone to bed, but sat as usual with Edward. As the evening progressed she sensed in him a growing air of detachment and the feeling of warmth which had begun to develop between them was no longer there. She was bewildered and disappointed by this, yet refrained from raising the matter in the hope that it was just a temporary mood on his part. Perhaps he had expected her to retire immediately to her new part of the house, thus leaving him alone in his? After an uncomfortable hour or so, he rose and made to leave the room. Not once had he shown any interest in what she had done and his present indifference hurt her deeply. He was almost at the door when Hannah, unable to contain herself sprang from the chair and ran past him, barring his way.

This unexpected action stunned him, and he stood motionless only inches away from her, speechless at her uncharacteristic move.

'Don't go!' she implored, with more feeling than she realised. 'What have I done? It is as if we are strangers again!' He remained silent, watching her as if in a trance. 'We were getting on so well—please, Edward, what have I done?'

'Nothing!' he muttered, still amazed at her outburst. 'Nothing. You have done nothing wrong, what makes you think you have?'

'Because in spite of the fire in the room there is a chill in the atmosphere which frightens me. You are so distant. It is as if you don't even see me, just as it was when I first came here. I believed things had changed, and there were even times when I thought you'd accepted our new situation, indeed almost enjoyed my being here.'

'But I do!' he protested. He was angry now with himself for having brought this about, and seeing how deeply disturbed she was, said, 'What do you want of me? I confess I don't understand at all.'

'No, you don't!' she cried accusingly, a touch of anger entering her voice. 'Not at all!' She drew her head upright, her eyes defiant and she was filled with a spirit that he had not seen before.

He sensed that she would have struck him had she not feared his reaction. 'Stop it!' he cried, angrily. 'What on earth has come over you?' This was so unlike the placid woman he had grown accustomed to that he was deeply disturbed by the change in her.

Suddenly she was aware of a strange look in his eyes and her angry frustration subsided immediately, leaving her bewildered and ashamed of her outburst. She flushed with embarrassment. 'I'm sorry,' she stammered. 'The excitement of the past two days must have made me edgy. I should not have spoken as I did. I was just disappointed,' she admitted, 'that you seemed to show no interest in what I have done today.'

It was true, Edward confessed to himself, he had been inconsiderate, and so concerned with his own comfort that he had paid no attention to Hannah's needs. He had seen the closed door as a barrier, excluding him from her life, and hadn't liked it.

'No,' Edward sighed. 'You have done nothing wrong, it is I who should be ashamed of myself. You have worked hard and I presumed that now we were to go our separate ways within the house.' In her anger she had stepped closer and he could feel her warm breath on his face; he flushed with embarrassment, aware that for some strange reason he wanted desperately to make peace with her.

Seeing the forlorn look on his face Hannah became deeply moved. Instinctively she wanted to comfort him in some way, but she did not dare. To touch him would have added even more strain to their already fragile relationship, yet that was what she felt drawn to do. If at that moment he had held out a hand or moved towards her she would have clung to him, instead she tried to explain. 'I was looking forward to showing you what I had done with the furniture, hoping that you would come and sit in there with me sometimes, as I did with you tonight. Perhaps I've behaved like a child in wanting to surprise you, I have no desire to sit alone every evening.'

'I provided you with what I promised, your own accommodation,' he said, lamely. 'What more do you want of me?' He looked suddenly very weary, as if unable to understand her deep sense of disappointment. His eyes betrayed a struggle of inner conflict, one she was not party to.

'You have been solemn and quiet all evening, as if you wished me gone already; I wondered if I should have left you alone and stayed in the other room?'

'No!' he cried, with unexpected fervour. 'I enjoy your company. I thought that was what you wanted, to end the close relationship we have created. I never dreamed that I would ever find myself in need of company, yet I cannot now go back to living my life alone. You have brought this cottage to life, and I am happy with that.' He'd never admitted, even to himself that he'd changed so much, but to have told Hannah was almost an act of betrayal of his former beliefs. Just what did he want? Simply, at that moment, to be alone to think, and try to understand why he felt so miserable and moody.

It was painfully obvious that his outburst was quite unplanned, and revealed more to her of his feelings than was intended. She also realised that for him to have spoken out so freely was a sign of his deep disturbance and unhappiness with the situation, just as she herself felt.

'It's late,' she whispered softly. 'Tomorrow, in the daylight, I will show you what has been done.' Then, without quite knowing why she touched his face tenderly with her fingers before leaving him alone with his thoughts.

He remained standing, unable to move. Without thinking, perhaps on an impulse, she had affected him more deeply than she could ever have imagined. He had wanted to prevent her going, yet he had no idea what to say to her, he only knew that if she had stayed he would have clasped her to him. In that simple act of tenderness she had unleashed a depth of feeling which had previously been unknown to him. Slowly he lowered himself into a chair and looked around with sadness, too disturbed to go to bed. Hannah had arrived unwanted in his life, adversity had thrown them together, and by rising above it from the ruins of the flood, together they had unknowingly bound themselves to each other forever. It was he, not she, who had caused the conflict by refusing to acknowledge that her presence was good for him, that he needed her not just as a companion but as a man needs a woman. By many acts of kindness on her part she had given proof of her integrity, but in touching him so gently he had seen an affection which was unknown to him. Only an idiot would fail to see that she was worth a dozen of poor Lydia, and he had not thought of that lady for weeks now. He had in plain truth dreaded the thought that his peaceful evenings with Hannah would end, and so had shut his mind against the inevitable until it had been too late. Slowly and unintentionally, she had worn away his independence, leaving a vulnerability which he had always feared. He had seen a spirit awaken in Hannah, transforming her as if she had risen from an inner sleep and he had been too blind to see it. He trembled slightly at his inadequacies and his inexperience, and wondered what would happen now, as nothing could be the same again.

With these newly awakened feelings on his mind, Edward prepared for bed, his movements almost mechanical as he secured the fire and barred the door before climbing the stairs to his bedroom. A thin shaft of light shone under Hannah's bedroom door, but he heard nothing. Would she, on rising at dawn, be embarrassed by what she had done or was he reading too much in the gesture? He sighed, got into bed and lay there unable to sleep, his mind far too alert, his emotions in a tangle with the constant reminder of her touch. Then the thought came to him—did he want there to be more in the incident? After all, she had shed tears on the night of their marriage and they had never mentioned anything so personal again.

Hannah shivered beneath the bedcovers, not with fear this time but with a well-nigh irrepressible desire to go to Edward. She knew he wasn't asleep because his bed squeaked as he continually tossed and turned, something he rarely did. She had been wrong to leave him so suddenly, and he had seemed so unhappy, but in touching his face she had feared she might have gone too far. Her one dread was that in the morning he would rise before her and disappear up onto the moors without waiting to speak to her. She would then spend the day in trepidation at the thought of the coming evening. Suddenly she remembered that Peter was to visit them the following evening and there would be no opportunity to talk to each other alone. To leave the matter unfinished would bring nothing but misery, besides she was so restless that she was afraid of disturbing Lizzie. There was nothing for it, she would have to approach him and find out where they stood.

Edward heard the creak of Hannah's bedroom door opening, and saw a shaft of light appear under the door of his own room. It could have been Lizzie who sometimes woke and came through to him, but tonight he felt in no mood to deal with the child. He half hoped, half sensed it might be Hannah, but it was most unlikely. There was a gentle tapping on his door, something which the wandering Lizzie never did. He sat upright with some optimism and called out for her to enter. As the door opened he saw Hannah framed in the light of the lamp in the doorway, and was glad that she had come.

She crossed the room, hoping that the shadows cast by the lamp hid her face, and said softly, 'I can't sleep.' She felt foolish and vulnerable standing there clutching her shawl, waiting for some indication that he didn't mind her coming to him.

'Neither can I.' he said, trying to read her expression in the dim flickering light. She was obviously nervous and he felt that perhaps he should have gone to her, indeed he would have done so but for Lizzie.

'Can we talk, Edward?' There was a tremble in her voice now which caused a rush of tenderness in Edward. 'Too much has happened for us to quarrel and I know that you are far from happy. Peter is coming tomorrow so we will not be able to discuss anything in private, and I could not bear to have you angry with me all day.'

'Come here,' he said gently, and as she moved forward with the lamp her eyes met his questioningly. 'I have lain here this past hour thinking of nothing else,' he admitted. 'I was unable to come to you because of Lizzie being there, yet I needed to talk to you, to know what you were thinking.' His voice was kindly, and he beckoned her to come nearer. He watched her draw the shawl close around her with one hand as she moved towards him, and noted how small she looked in her white gown.

Hannah now stood merely a yard from him, aware that, in spite of the shawl, her body was trembling beneath the flimsy cotton nightdress which she wore, yet she was far from cold. She remained standing as if awaiting some command from him and he rose from the bed, took the lamp from her shaking hand and placed it on the chest by the bed.

She felt naked without the lamp in her hand and, as the light outlined Edward's powerful form, she knew that if he were to touch her at that moment she would have neither strength nor the desire to resist him.

Seeing her standing thus, defenceless and trusting, he made no move to touch her, instead he looked directly into her eyes as if to reassure himself that the attraction he saw there was not something of his imagination. He saw only shyness and gentleness in the reflected glow of the lamp, and remembered with pleasure the feeling he had experienced earlier as her fingers touched his cheek. Hesitatingly, he held out both hands to take hers which now seemed lost without the presence of the lamp. They were soft and warm and trembled in his, but Hannah made no attempt to withdraw them. He knew that, in spite of himself, he had come to love this quiet, determined woman who stood before him with such nervousness.

Hannah flushed shyly as he clasped her hands firmly between his own, and said softly, 'Was it wrong of me to have come to you?'

'No,' he said, huskily, and drew her slowly towards him, as if frightened that she would back away. 'I have been a fool,' he whispered, pulling her into his arms, 'not to have realised why I was so miserable.' She was soft, her cheek against his like cool silk, and her hair caressingly comforting. He remembered holding her once before, up on the hillside, and shivered at the thought of that long dreadful night. They had clung together then out of a mutual desire for comfort, but now it was a need of a different kind which moved them. He had treated her abominably since her arrival in the valley, and as if to obliterate his bad behaviour, he protectively pressed her fiercely against him. She gasped, and Edward loosened his hold, thinking that he had imposed himself upon her, but to his relief she made no move to withdraw from his arms, or to shy away from him. The passionate embrace which stemmed from his own guilt now became a tender clasp of endearment.

Hannah was surprised by Edward's sudden, overwhelming demonstration of affection, but found she could hardly breathe! By that one spontaneous act she knew that she had been right to come to him, for he was obviously not as worldly as she'd imagined him to be. Her understanding of him was growing, and it was in such unguarded moments as these that she saw beneath his unpredictable reserve a shy, compassionate being as equally capable of suffering as was she. He held her gently now in contrast, as if afraid of hurting her, and she again placed her cheek tenderly against his, reassuringly, all the while aware that through the thin nightgown her body yearned to be closer to him.

Edward thrilled at her response and, cupping her head in his hands with infinite gentleness kissed her forehead. No words passed their lips in those intimate moments of pleasure, and when he released her he was overjoyed by the expression of love in her eyes. With his hand he brushed the stray wisps of hair from her face; never, in the remotest corner of his mind had he ever imagined her holding such an attraction for him. Suddenly the light of the lamp seemed to engulf them in a warm glow, drawing them closer in spirit and, before he realised it, his lips were seeking hers with desperate longing. It was not the embrace of wild, uncontrollable passion but one of a precious wakening of love. It was as if, at last, they had reached the end of a long wearisome journey, and found a sweet homecoming.

Chapter 8

Ten Years On (1875)

*E*dward *stood on top of a well-weathered gritstone rock,* looking at the purple haze in the distance, and breathed deeply of the sweet smell of heather which drifted on the balmy evening breeze. The high moors were at their best at this time of year; the pink and orange sunset adding a backdrop unlike anything that man could devise. The summer had been a glorious one, leaving his skin deeply bronzed and his mind relaxed; only the thought of tomorrow's meeting disturbed the completeness of his contentment.

In spite of the passage of time he could still be considered a good-looking man. However, on closer inspection his face displayed signs of approaching middle-age. No longer was his unruly hair tied back in the old way, but was shorter and flecked with grey, adding dignity to his already impressive appearance.

Ten years had passed since Abe's death and in that time the cottage had become the centre point of the farm, which prospered. By destroying the original farmhouse, the flood had taken away some of Edward's bitterness, and his marriage to Hannah had both mellowed and changed him. Although he regretted the destruction of the old building in an historical sense, he had never come to terms with living in the draughty, cavernous old place. The present farm was of his own making, and to some extent only a minor part of the legacy; the cottage and the immediate land on which it stood being his after Abe's death anyway. Life had gone on peacefully in so many ways; the scars in the valley had slowly healed and another Dale Dyke Dam was almost completed in a safer position.

Life with Hannah had been remarkably happy and contented; their companionable co-existence had developed into a tender and enduring love affair, marred only by the fact that they had remained childless. Edward threw himself whole-heartedly into re-building the farm and being a good father to Lizzie. He'd very quickly forgotten Lydia's existence, and was only reminded of it once when, fourteen days after the first anniversary of the flood, in the middle of the night, the *Surrey Theatre* at West Bar burned down. There were no deaths, no casualties, even the animals in the menagerie were saved, and Lydia was long since gone, but it shook him. The irony was that the theatre was presenting a performance of 'The Great Fire of London' that week, obviously with such realism that, at two o'clock in the morning, fire broke out and destroyed Tommy Youdan's celebrated theatre and casino, thus closing a chapter of Edward's life completely.

He grew to worship Hannah, who tolerated his occasional moods and in return Edward treated her with gentleness and kindness. This most agreeable situation lasted almost eight years until she died quite suddenly from Low Fever, leaving Edward distraught and lonely. Life was made bearable only by Lizzie's dependence upon him, with the result that he spoiled her dreadfully.

Once the initial shock of her mother's death was over, Lizzie had turned even more to Edward, becoming his companion everywhere they went, until they were almost inseparable. Oh, how she had teased him, tormented and adored him, and he her, but his dependence on her company had increased until in the end he'd considered it wiser to send her away to school when she was sixteen. There were tears of resentment as she threatened never to return if he sent her away, but she was growing wild alone with him on the farm, and he'd taught her all he could. She needed to be instructed in more refined, ladylike ways of which he was ignorant. Although the decision had been a right and proper one, in making it he was left in a void which was difficult to fill.

At first he visited her regularly at Worksop, but each visit caused nothing but distress for them both, and the memory of her tear-stained face haunted him for weeks afterwards. In the end he stopped going, making excuses for his absence, but knowing full well that she did not accept the reasons he gave. For his part he buried himself in work, consoled only by the knowledge that it was for her welfare and a better future, and hoped that in the end she would forgive him. They frequently exchanged letters, but hers always pleaded to be allowed to come home. He kept them all in an old chest which he'd bought after the flood, together with a photograph for which she'd sat so patiently in order that he should receive it as a gift on his birthday. It was a sombre face which stared out at him from the silver frame, reminding him so much of Hannah that he couldn't bear to look constantly at it. She had a fine pair of resolute eyes and would be a handsome woman one day, he could see that, and wondered what on earth he could offer her once she returned to the valley.

Country life was simple, with few diversions to occupy a lively young mind, and the winters were long, sometimes too long and bleak even for him, especially now that he was alone.

His evenings were quiet and would be a poor substitute for those she spent with her young friends and described so vividly in her letters. It made him wonder if she would return for a short while only and then leave him when boredom and the harshness of the weather threatened to confine her to the farm. It was this prospect which made him so anxious, for she was the only close family he had, apart from Peter, and he was always away with his regiment these days.

He shook his head. He was being foolish he tried to tell himself, for this was her home, as she reminded him in every letter. Once the wind had teased those immaculate curls of hers, and her cheeks became tinged with colour, she would be his own Lizzie once more.

The long shadows cast by the setting sun were slowly disappearing, and Edward knew that it was time to return to the farm. In spite of the mellowing influence of nature which surrounded him he was again filled with apprehension as he contemplated Lizzie's arrival on the morrow. Her impending return filled him with both joy and dread as he wondered what one year away from him had done to her. Would she find it in her heart to forgive him his banishment of her? It had not been easy to send her away, but under the circumstances he had considered it necessary.

He marvelled as the glorious colours of the evening sky sank slowly towards the horizon, and his spirits rose. Only when those same hues began to blend with the dark of nightfall, and the air became cooler, did his misgivings return. She was no longer a child but a young woman, and a stranger at that! In childhood there had been no barriers, in girlhood as they sat in a silent room their minds had become as one, but was the gulf created by their separation too wide to bridge? Was this then, to be his punishment for sending her away? He would just have to be patient, for Hannah's sake, and see how things worked out.

The train from Worksop was delayed for over half an hour, and this increased the nervousness which caused Edward to tap impatiently with his foot on the platform. Come on, come on, he urged to himself. He was tired of hanging around aimlessly at the station.

He watched with some irritation as a harassed mother endeavoured to control, with little success, the two boys who persistently ran giggling around her luggage. Then, much to everyone's relief, a distant sound heralded the approach of the train.

'It's here!' the woman cried with relief. 'Now, do be still,' she admonished, 'or we shall become separated and all the coaches will be full.'

Edward looked fleetingly at each carriage as it passed, until finally, and with a shuddering jolt, the train came to a halt under the glass canopy covering the platform. Where was she? He'd almost given up looking when, from behind, an excited cry caused him to spin round. 'Lizzie!' he cried in amazement, hardly recognising the splendidly attired young woman who spontaneously flung her arms round his neck and kissed his cheek. 'Lizzie!' he remonstrated, his face flushed with embarrassment at the unaccustomed public show of affection. 'People are staring at us!'

She drew back unperturbed by his obvious discomfort and laughed, playfully. 'Are you angry and tired of waiting for me?' she asked. 'It's not my fault that the train is so late, you know.'

'It's nothing to do with that, Lizzie!' he replied sternly. 'Just that you should restrain your exuberance in public! Now, where are your belongings? We must get them to the trap. Have you forgotten that we have a long way to go?'

Instead of arguing Lizzie looked along the platform and then led him to a pile of boxes and a trunk which the porter had earlier been instructed to lift down for her.

'How on earth do you imagine I'm going to put all that into such a small trap?' Edward exclaimed in dismay. 'What on earth do they all contain?'

'Books, and clothing, and a present for you!' she quipped, ignoring completely the frown of disapproval on his face. 'I have so much to show you when we get home.' She bent and picked up two of the lighter boxes, whilst Edward called to another porter to bring a cart with which to transfer the luggage to where the horse and trap waited in the capable hands of a young boy.

With Lizzie's numerous possessions safely installed, they both squeezed into the small space which was left for them in the trap and followed several other carriages past the elegant, newly-built Victoria Hotel, down the long wide drive away from the station.

Once their journey was underway and the traffic had thinned out, Edward realised that his welcome had not been a warm one. 'I'm sorry for my irritation back there,' he apologised. 'I'm not a patient man, Lizzie, and coming to town amongst all this hustle and bustle doesn't suit me very well. But I'm pleased to have you back home, although I must say that in spite of looking very pretty you are hardly dressed for life on the farm. I do hope you have some sensible garments packed in those boxes. I sent enough money, which I hope wasn't wasted on fripperies.'

'I have been very careful, I can assure you!' she answered confidently. 'But I was not leaving Worksop dressed like a farmer's wife! I thought you would be proud to see me looking like a lady.'

Edward was quite disturbed by her pert reply. This was not the Lizzie he remembered and he fervently hoped that the time spent away hadn't spoilt her good nature. If it had it would be a great shame for she had been a pleasant child, and would never have answered in such a vein in the past. Nor was he inclined to suffer such defiant behaviour now. 'I'm afraid you're going to find life in the valley a great contrast to the past year, Lizzie,' he said firmly. 'And I have no time for waste or foolishness!'

'Then why did you send me away?' she demanded, sulkily. 'I didn't want to go, and you stopped coming to see me!' She sounded more like a wounded child than the woman she was endeavouring to portray. 'I know it was a long way to come, but I thought you loved me!'

He softened his voice, and sighed. 'I did Lizzie! I still do, but every time I came to see you, you wanted to return home with me. You had to learn how to become a young lady! I couldn't teach you that, or to sew, or any of the gentle ways of life. It wasn't right for there to be just you and me on the farm, together. You needed more if you were to make the most of your life, and to make a good marriage.'

'Who says I want to get married?' Lizzie retorted, sharply.

Edward was tired of the conversation which seemed to be leading towards a confrontation of some kind. 'Thank you for the letters,' he said, trying to change the subject. 'I enjoyed reading them and have kept them all.' He was at a loss as how to deal with her. By sending her away he'd sought merely to do what was best for a young girl of sixteen, and had never meant to hurt her as apparently he had.

'Now, tell me truthfully, Lizzie,' he quizzed, kindly. 'Was the time away so dull and monotonous that you would rather have stayed at home with me, than experience exciting new things? I would have been very selfish indeed not to send you away. You have an enquiring mind. Don't you see, that to keep you sheltered from the world would have been wrong. I was left alone here, while you were learning about life.'

'You may have meant well, but to send me away from everything and everybody I knew and loved was very cruel.' Lizzie remonstrated

'For that I am truly sorry!' he conceded, knowing her accusation to be true. 'But didn't you enjoy yourself just one little bit?' He asked teasingly, and waited for her response which she seemed determined to withhold, keeping him in suspense before answering. He glanced sideways, catching her off-guard and she flushed with mischievous embarrassment at being caught out, and in consequence they both burst spontaneously into laughter. 'That's more like my old Lizzie,' Edward laughed. 'Now can we be friends again, and drive home in peace?'

She nodded, tucked the rug firmly around their knees, slipped her arm through his as she had always done and chatted away happily as though nothing had changed.

However, Lizzie herself had greatly changed, and it was a very thoughtful and subdued young woman who roamed the familiar and ancient pathways around Bradfield Dale in the late summer of 1875. At first the joy of seeing old familiar sights pleased her and it seemed as though she had never been away, yet somehow things were not the same. A strange restlessness was growing within her and she realised that she no longer enjoyed being alone.

This was brought to her very sharply on one of her walks when, from a distance, she observed the harvesters in the fields. Edward's new reaping machine was working efficiently whilst several youths and girls followed behind, quickly binding up the sheaves of corn as they fell to the ground. Lizzie recognised one or two young women who had been her friends at the small village school. They worked with such easy vigour, seemingly content with their lot, but Edward had forbidden Lizzie to work amongst them, considering that it was beneath her now to toil in the dust and heat of the day.

Where, she wondered sadly, did she fit into this rich and ancient agricultural pattern of life? As a child she had been happy working with such willingness at harvest time, but the memories of those halcyon days were remote now. Edward's attempt to give her the best he could, now meant that she no longer fitted completely into the valley life she once knew.

In the weeks that followed her return she tried hard to adapt to the long hours of solitude, however, her perception of the future was vague and time hung heavily on her hands.

Edward observed her carefully, painfully noting the subtle changes and wondered for the first time if he had been foolish to open her mind to the wider world. What was he to do with her now?

After Hannah's death he had been compelled to hire someone to clean, cook and to watch over Lizzie, and as a result there had been a long line of women who had kept house for him, all returning to the village each night when their work was done. Mrs Fox had been with him the longest, starting immediately after Lizzie's departure for Worksop. She was so competent and well-organised that she left no task undone which otherwise might have kept Lizzie occupied. Edward was well aware that Mrs Fox liked to rule all she surveyed and that she saw the return of Lizzie as a threat, yet the girl needed to learn to take responsibility if she was to eventually inherit the farm. Since her return, because of his preoccupation with harvesting, he had neglected her and he knew that it was time to right the wrong before it was too late.

Gradually the outward signs of Lizzie's inner restlessness increased, and the lively creature who had virtually pounced upon him at the railway station was now no more than a mere shadow of her former self.

On returning home one evening and finding her in low spirits, Edward decided to tackle the problem—although he was at a loss for a solution. 'Have you no book to read, or needlework to do?' he asked, joining her by the fire.

'I find too much reading bad for me!' she replied, solemnly. 'Since my return I have read several of your books but these only unsettle me. I cannot hide in the adventures of others, and needlework or mending I find dull. There is not really enough work for me, as Mrs Fox is so diligent, and to interfere with her routine would upset rather than please her.'

'Why not invite a friend to stay with you for while?' he suggested hopefully, aware that this would only provide a short term distraction; nevertheless it would give him time to think of a better idea.

'I'm not sure,' she replied, contemplating the matter at length.

'Didn't you make friends at Worksop, one of whom might enjoy staying here for a while?'

'The problem, unfortunately, is a more complicated one. Before you sent me away I knew nothing other than that which I learned from you, and the village school. Now I am no longer content simply to amuse myself, or do housework. I need to employ my mind as well as my body and the valley offers little relief to my frustration.' There, at last she had been able to speak her mind, and she felt somewhat better for having done so.

Edward was shocked and disappointed to realise that the schooling he had provided for her had seemingly driven a wedge between them. He was also disturbed by her apparent lack of interest in the farm. 'Have you no love for the valley, or the farm? This land will be yours one day—surely you haven't forgotten that? In order to run the farm when I am gone you must first learn to manage it.' She eyed him sadly, as if being scolded. 'You are very young,' he said, comfortingly. 'In time you will realise how fortunate you are to be the recipient of Abe's legacy. Your mother made a great sacrifice to ensure that your future was a good one.' Immediately the words left his lips he knew that he had almost betrayed Hannah's trust in him. Oh how he wished that Hannah were alive at this moment, to comfort and help them both.

Lizzie eyed him keenly. 'In what way did mother make a sacrifice for me—I thought she was happy here and that you loved each other.'

He thought carefully, wondering what he could say to defuse the situation without lying or hurting her. She was too young to understand what had happened between Hannah and himself, and he mustn't risk distressing her further at this time. He merely said, 'Your mother found life hard out here at first, but she came knowing that you would be happier here than in the run-down part of town you came from, and yes, we loved each other very much! I don't mean to be hard but there's not much you can do out here, Lizzie. You wouldn't want to go into service like the other girls in the village have done, it's nothing but slavery; besides, in your position it is neither necessary nor acceptable.'

'Then what am I supposed to do other than marry? Why did you have me educated beyond my expectations? I know that I'm not bright enough to aspire to being a teacher, nor do I want to be a governess. Besides, I don't like children enough to work with them. What am I to do?' The dilemma in which she found herself was mirrored in her eyes, and Edward felt a pang of despair, acknowledging that her deep misery was half his own doing.

'Oh, Lizzie!' he cried, anxiously. 'The clock cannot be turned back now, and times are changing! One day, in the future, there may be the chance for women to achieve greater independence and fulfilment but that time has not yet arrived. It is a great pity, but you have to realise that many a man is stuck in a menial job without any expectation of doing anything other than provide inadequately for his family. For them, too, there is no escape, nor will there be. Perhaps some day things will improve, meanwhile one has to learn to suppress impractical ideas in order to find peace of mind.'

'How did you do it? You have the intelligence of a man educated beyond this valley and yet you seem happy with your lot!'

Edward smiled ruefully, 'I'm not educated Lizzie. What I know I have learned through reading, and by listening to Abe, my former employer. I am only content because the hills and moorlands hold me in a tight bond, without them I lose all sense of reality. When I go to town I am so disturbed that I can't wait to return here.' How could he explain his lack of desire for adventure without appearing dull and set in his ways? 'I'm not happy away from the land; my fulfilment comes in seeing the crops grow and the animals which I rear in good health.'

'I do envy your contentment, but I just see the years ahead to be empty and hopeless,' she said despairingly.

'Oh, come now, one day you will marry and have children to comfort you!'

'No! No!' she cried vehemently. 'Once I am content I may marry, but until then I must find something that will satisfy me—that will exercise my mind and give me a feeling of excitement.' She was near to tears of frustration now, and Edward was overwhelmed with pity for her youthful aspirations.

'You are still young, and restless, child. Be patient, do as I suggest and invite a friend here to stay for a while, you may think differently then.'

She knew that he was unable to properly understand her feelings, much as he tried, so there was no point in making them both miserable by continuing with the discussion. She leaned across and fondly placed her hand on his arm. 'I'll try, really I will. You've been a good father to me and I will try to make you proud of me!'

Edward was touched by her demonstration of affection, but knew that he must assure her that he was trying to understand. 'I'm already proud of you, Lizzie,' he told her firmly. 'I'm just sorry that by sending you away you have become so unhappy. Unfortunately, you would have grown up and changed sooner or later, and which of us can know whether things would have been better or worse than they are now?'

Much to Edward's delight, and as if offering a solution to their present problems, Peter made a sudden and unexpected visit to the farm. It was good to have both young people around him again; he knew of nothing else which would have provided a finer distraction for Lizzie at this time.

Peter had become a frequent visitor over the intervening years since Hannah's death, calling as and when his duties permitted. Edward was both proud and fond of his nephew who was now twenty-seven and had done well for himself in the army. Four years earlier he had bought himself, with

Edward's help, a commission and transferred to another regiment further afield. However, a short time after he had settled to life in his new depot at Aldershot, he volunteered to serve on the coast of West Africa, helping to suppress the unruly Ashanti tribe there. On the surface this appeared to be a small skirmish, the latest weapons of war being used against the black man's primitive fighting methods. There were many in the Government who would have been only too pleased to see British interests pushed off the coast of Africa altogether without any regret, but the skirmish had not been as easy as at first anticipated. The gloomy jungle conditions bred disease to which the soldiers very quickly succumbed. Peter had gone with reinforcements who were sent to overcome and subdue the Ashanti chief, King Kofi Kari-Kari. The death toll had been low but, out of 400 wounded men, Peter had been one of the few fortunate enough to recover well. Had his flesh wound not been promptly treated he would probably have lost his arm, thus ending his military career.

His unexpected visit to the farm, following so closely after Lizzie's return, threw Mrs Fox, who was not used to having her domain invaded by lively and untidy young people, into a state of anxiety. Nevertheless, the moment of his arrival heralded the disappearance of Lizzie's lethargy, and relieved Edward of his worries about her for the time being.

'Lizzie! Is that you?' Peter had cried, on seeing his cousin for the first time in eighteen months. 'Where has my wild tormentor gone?'

With wide excited eyes, Lizzie hugged him in much the same way as she had done Edward at the station on her return, only this time she blushed profusely afterwards. Peter merely laughed, then proceeded to enlighten Edward with the news of his journey. Later, as they sat around the table catching up on events which had occurred since they had last met, she listened with enthralled attention.

'I've come with some good news, Uncle,' Peter announced. 'You remember me writing to tell you about my being rather taken with a nurse who tended me after my wounding in Africa? Well, I've asked her to become my wife. Now what do you think of that?'

Lizzie clasped her hands together with delight. 'What's she like? What's her name? How did you receive your wound?' Lizzie demanded, one question following another in quick succession.

'Hold on, Lizzie,' Edward remonstrated. 'Let Peter speak, for goodness sake!' Then, addressing his nephew, he said, 'Well done! I'm as proud of you as I would be of my own son! Well done!' His tone was fatherly and sincere, and Peter accepted the praise with pleasure.

Lizzie's excitement at the news had abated a little, but her curiosity was not diminished by Edward's rebuke. 'Tell me how you met,' she demanded. 'And her name!'

Peter smiled at her persistence. 'Well, first her name is Clara. You would like her, Lizzie, for she has a sense of humour equal to mine. She is almost as tall as Uncle Edward, and is a very handsome woman. On the journey back from Africa she was the nurse accompanying the injured men classed "fit to travel". I was amazed at her ability to stay calm despite the conditions at sea, and no matter how trying the behaviour of the men, she coped with it all. Once back in England I made sure that our paths crossed again, with the result that she found my company to her liking. There, does that answer your questions?'

'When do you propose to get married?' Edward enquired. 'Are we likely to meet the lady before the day?'

'I had hoped to bring her with me this time but it wasn't possible, and because the wedding is to be in the spring I may not be able to return here before then. However, I wanted to tell you about the marriage myself and not trust the news to a letter.'

'I appreciate that,' Edward replied, approvingly. 'You know this house is yours whenever you come and I look forward to welcoming your bride as soon as you wish to bring her.' He slowly pushed his chair back from the table and rose. 'Now, if you'll excuse me I shall go to bed, I have to make an early start tomorrow and unfortunately have made arrangements to go to Sheffield in the afternoon.'

Taking a watch from his inside pocket, Peter glanced at it and, much to Lizzie's disappointment, announced, 'Goodness, I hadn't realised how quickly the time has passed. I think I too shall retire as it has been a long day. Perhaps tomorrow, Uncle, you will show me what changes you have made since my last visit? Also, I wonder, could I borrow a horse so as to visit mother who, I understand, has not been too well of late?'

'By all means, help yourself,' Edward replied. 'Give my love to your mother and I'll find a few eatables for you to take her.'

When they woke the following morning a blanket of grey mist hung over the surrounding hilltops, leaving the valley below damp and gloomy. As Peter had already been out early with Edward and then gone to his mother's, Lizzie made use of the time by writing a letter to Peter's intended, expressing her pleasure at the match and hoping that they would meet in the near future. That done she became restless as she waited for Peter to return so that, by the time he did, she was in low spirits again. Unfortunately, she'd turned down her father's offer to take her to town, in the hopes that Peter's company would be more entertaining. Peter sensed her mood, having learned earlier from Edward that she was far from happy, but he was at a loss as to how he could ease the situation in the short time he intended to stay with them. Nor was he in a mood to meander around the farm when he could be doing something useful. 'The mist has lifted, Lizzie,' he declared.

'Shall we walk to the village? Edward's horse has a loose shoe—I was going to tell him when he got back but we may as well take the horse to the blacksmith ourselves, especially as we've nothing else to do.'

By the time they returned and put the horse back in the stable, Edward was back from town where he'd been to select a new gun and cartridge maker to replace his ancient shotgun which had a badly worn barrel. There had been a dog roaming the area worrying the sheep for several weeks and, so far, no one had managed to shoot it. Edward was determined that none of his sheep would be taken.

Peter examined the gun carefully, casting an experienced eye over the quality of the workmanship. 'Not bad!' he said, feeling the balance and testing the trigger action.

'Nor should it be, not at the price I paid for it.' Edward rejoined. 'We'll try it tomorrow if you like?'

Having agreed to this, Peter continued with his inspection. 'It's a bit modern for your needs don't you think?' he asked as he then examined the new cartridges.

'Oh, I thought a breech-loading gun would hold its value rather more than a muzzle-loader,' Edward replied nonchalantly.

'I'd like to take Lizzie out riding tomorrow if the weather is fit,' Peter suggested suddenly. 'You don't mind do you Uncle?' He wanted to get Lizzie away from the farm so that he could find out what ailed her. He'd tried to do so during the walk to the village but she had been too busy questioning him about Clara.

'Oh, how splendid!' Lizzie exclaimed, her face lighting up immediately with enthusiasm and wondering why she hadn't thought of riding before; but then it would have meant riding alone. 'You don't mind do you?' she asked, turning to Edward with bright eyes.

Edward was delighted to see Lizzie alive with expectation; perhaps by riding and returning to her old ways she would feel closer to the valley again. 'You know where everything is, just help yourselves! But take care of her, Peter, she's not ridden for a year or more now, not that one forgets how to ride but the horses are young and frisky—Mattie's too old now to be taken alongside one of the newer mounts.'

An hour later the two riders paced themselves out at a swift exhilarating gallop along the Old Mortimer Road towards Strines. The old familiar feel of fresh, cool wind on Lizzie's face, for it was a pleasant autumn day, filled her with excitement. She had taken so much for granted in the past, but once away from the valley she had sorely missed its many simple pleasures, ones which had meant nothing to her new companions. 'Wait for me!' she called out breathlessly, as Peter pressed on ahead at greater speed while she endeavoured to catch up with him. The road through the plantation was straight even if it was rugged and churned, but it gave Peter the edge on Lizzie who was only too aware by now that she hadn't been in the saddle for some time.

'Come on, slow coach,' he called back, even more convinced that it had been a good decision to come out onto the hills, where the ride was helping to satisfy his continuing need of physical activity—army life suited him well in this respect, with its never-ending challenges. Reluctantly he pulled on the reins to slow the horse, which appeared to be enjoying the pace every bit as much as he was. 'You're very much out of practice, Lizzie,' he called. 'How long is it since you came up here?'

'When we were together last! But don't forget I've been away from horses for more than a year now,' she panted, drawing up alongside him.

'Yes, I know that,' he conceded. 'I'm surprised, though, that you've not been out riding, you've been back several weeks now?'

Wincing at the truth of his remark, she responded, 'I should have done, I suppose, but I had no desire to ride by myself, I'm afraid I've been a bit of a misery. You see I find life so tedious after living in Worksop.' Her voice was flat, and just a little self-pitying.

'Hasn't Uncle Edward been out with you?' Peter persisted.

'He's been too busy with harvesting—I suppose he doesn't really know what to do with me now that I'm older.'

'This isn't like you, Lizzie, you're usually so full of life,' he said, somewhat puzzled by her response. 'In which case I'm glad I thought of riding today, we'll soon rid you of those depressing thoughts. Come on, keep up the pace or I will ride ahead and wait for you at the *Strines Inn*. I'm ready for some ale.'

Not to be out-done, and with no desire to be left behind, Lizzie spurred the lively young stallion on, joining Peter on the steep, downward slope which led to the bridge where several moorland streams converged to form a boggy inlet to Strines reservoir. Once having climbed out of the narrow gully they headed towards the inn, where they intended refreshing themselves before going on.

'We'll go back a different way,' Peter said, as they dismounted. 'Do you think you're up to crossing the fields past Sugworth?'

In spite of her aching limbs Lizzie nodded, determined not to let him see her discomfort, then held the reins of both horses while Peter fetched their drinks. 'That's better,' he said, as he supped at his mug of ale, and Lizzie laughed as the froth caught on his well-groomed moustache. 'What do you think of my whiskers, then?' he asked, as he wiped the foam away with his hand. 'Don't you think they suit me very well?'

Lizzie eyed his facial hair with some distaste. 'They make you look too old,' she stated, unkindly. 'I'm not at all enamoured by men with whiskers!' Much to her surprise and amazement Peter roared with laughter.

'I'd not be an Army man without,' he teased. 'I'd be a laughing stock, that I would.'

Lizzie knew little about men and was beginning to realise that Peter was no longer her playful cousin of the past. She supposed that he was handsome in spite of the whiskers, but he had a brash air of self-confidence which sometimes made him almost a stranger to her. She'd never really noticed just how tall he was; now he seemed taller than she remembered, his long lean limbs showing off his clothes to their best. She preferred him as he had been before, clean-shaven and roguish.

They left the inn and made their way to a point from which they could see over the Strines reservoir and the hills surrounding Bradfield Dale. By now the sun had broken completely through the misty layer of cloud which often hung over the moorlands at that time of year, and the autumn tints of bracken and rowan, contrasting with the blue-grey water of the dam, created a delightful picture.

'By God, it's a beautiful sight!' Peter exclaimed. 'I miss all this sometimes, even now. One day when I'm old and grey I intend to return hereabouts and get a place where I can breed horses for the Army.'

Lizzie gazed at all before her. Yes, it was indeed a wonderful spectacle at this time. However, when the bleak winds and rains of winter came, the isolation in the farmhouses was almost unbearable. She envied Peter his strength of purpose, whilst at the same time conceding that she herself had no plans and no dreams, except those which, as a woman, she perhaps should not have.

'I have a dream too,' she said timidly, as if expecting to be ridiculed. She hesitated, reluctant to go on.

'Well, come on then, out with it!' Peter sensed her embarrassment and attempted to draw her out, knowing that she was obviously no longer the young, carefree girl he knew of old. 'What dream can be so wild that you can't share it with me?' he added with brotherly affection.

Plucking up courage Lizzie spoke in a low voice, 'I want to travel, Peter! I can't stay in the valley all my life. When I hear you speak of far away places and wonderful sights I want to see them for myself. Is that so wrong of me?'

'No,' he replied thoughtfully. 'It isn't wrong, but it is maybe impractical. Can't Edward take you to London or something? He certainly wouldn't allow you to travel alone, besides where would you go, who would you go with if Uncle can't leave the farm? Have you thought of what you would do? It would take a vast amount of money, and with that money you would be vulnerable to all sorts of unscrupulous people. The world is full of villains.' He paused, seeing the tears behind her lowered lashes, and softened his voice. 'Lizzie, life is good for you here, better than for most people, and travelling is not as pleasurable as you think. Edward has protected you too much, the majority of people can think only of work for which they receive insufficient money to support their families. No, Edward would not allow it, of that I'm sure! Perhaps the fault is mine and I am guilty of painting too pretty a picture of my adventures.'

She seemed to ignore his self-recrimination and said with some resentment. 'Yet he sent me to Worksop, when I didn't want to go!'

'For your own good!' Peter added hastily, in an effort to calm the situation.

'But there is something deep within me crying out for excitement, and the need to create something worthwhile,' she cried, longingly. 'What am I to do?'

Peter was silent for a moment, not knowing how to comfort her. 'Have you told Edward any of this?' he asked, stirred by her strength of feeling. 'I'm not unaware that life can be frustrating for a woman, especially one who has been educated. My Clara is a nurse; she is a very modern woman yet even she is constrained by old-fashioned prejudices and ideas. You should meet her—perhaps talking to her would help you. Do you think Edward would allow you to visit us in Aldershot? Now that might be a good idea!'

Her eyes lit up, 'Oh, do you think so?' she cried. 'Do you really think he would let me come so soon after returning home from school? I did try to explain how I feel but he merely thinks I'm unsettled and that when I get used to being here again I will be happy.'

'I think it would be a little selfish of him to refuse, besides it may just help you to come to terms with your situation.' By now they had reached a lane leading down to a small farm. 'Shall we go down here, and cross the field towards Sugworth Hall? That would shorten our journey somewhat.'

'Yes,' she agreed readily, feeling in a lighter frame of mind, and followed him closely until they had gone beyond the farm to where the rugged contours of the land prevented further serious conversation. Suddenly Peter sat upright in his saddle. 'Come on,' he shouted excitedly, gathering speed. 'Let's jump the stream!' He immediately raced towards a small stream which wound its way down a gully on the hillside.

'No!' she cried out, but it was too late. She watched, half expecting him to fall as the horse stumbled on the muddy slope of the far bank, almost throwing him from the saddle, but he righted himself and stood waiting for her with a wide grin on his face.

'That was dangerous and foolish!' Lizzie shouted, her voice filled with annoyance. 'You could have lamed the horse, then Father would have been very angry!'

He laughed at her reproof. 'So it's not my health that worries you then, just the horse and Uncle Edward's temper!' There was no smile on Lizzie's face and he realised how disturbed she was by his playful act. 'Yes,' he conceded. 'It was a little foolhardy of me, but when you've done the things I have in my life, one more risk just gives an added spice to living. It's no good being a soldier if you're not prepared to take chances.'

'That's not the point,' Lizzie retorted. 'Father can't afford to lose a horse, besides that's a good animal and I wouldn't like to see him hurt.'

Peter nodded, and replied apologetically, 'Alright, I'm sorry, I should have known better. One day you'll know the thrill of a real challenge and the satisfaction achievement can bring. Now, shall we get on?'

That I should get the chance would be a miracle, she thought to herself. Before long she found herself forgiving Peter and enjoying the ride, the old feeling of quiet companionship with him returning as they headed home. The fresh breeze had blown her fair hair back from her face into a wild tangle and, with the exertion of the long ride, she had to admit to feeling rather tired from the unaccustomed exercise. If only she could go with Peter to Aldershot, then she might find out for herself just what it would take to achieve a sense of purpose in her life!

It was almost dark when the pair finally returned to the farm, and mist once more concealed the valley from the outside world. Edward strode out to meet them. 'Where have you been?' he demanded, barely concealing his anxiety. He knew he was being foolish but couldn't help himself. He'd not expected them to be away all afternoon and had spent the last hour wondering if there had been some sort of accident which prevented their return. He knew Lizzie would be feeling the effects of the long ride and had seen the mist gathering for some time prior to their arrival. He bit back further comments knowing that his concern might be construed as un-welcome interference, nevertheless, he was none too pleased with Peter's apparent lack of regard for Lizzie's welfare.

'We didn't realise how long it would take us to make a full circle of the dams,' Peter declared as he dismounted, and handed Lizzie down from her horse. 'I'm sorry if you were worried, but you should know I wouldn't put Lizzie in harm's way.'

Edward said nothing, instead he took the reins and made to lead the horses towards the stables.

'I'll do that!' Peter said a little sharply, somewhat annoyed by his attitude. 'It's the least I can do!'

At that Edward handed him the reins, muttered something to himself and went into the house, leaving Lizzie to limp up the path behind him, her limbs aching and her head heavy with tiredness.

It was quite some time later that evening before the atmosphere in the house mellowed and the trio began to enjoy each other's company again.

Lizzie, feeling the need to placate Edward's fears, had been careful not to say anything to upset him, yet she was on tenter-hooks waiting to tell him how much she would like to go to Aldershot.

'It seems a long time since the day I first sat at this table with you and Hannah,' Peter mused reflectively, his annoyance with Edward having completely disappeared. 'That was the day that changed my life—I found my goal in life so to speak, thanks to the pair of you.'

'That was almost eleven years ago,' Edward spoke wistfully, thinking of the happier years before Hannah's death. 'So you have no regrets over the path you chose? Do you think your life would have taken a different course if you hadn't called here then? Your decision was so sudden that we often wondered if you would come to think it was too hastily made.'

Peter laughed heartily, 'You need have no worries in that direction, Uncle; it was the best thing I could have done. Everything good that has happened to me since then stems from that decision.'

'I'm pleased about that. Hannah would have agreed had she been here today.' Edward's face had taken on a look of sadness and he lowered his eyes to hide the emptiness he felt. He still missed her, but when he was completely alone the desolation was bearable, only because he felt she wasn't too far away; it was when he was with young people that he felt a little out of place.

Without realising this, Lizzie intervened, much to Edward's relief. 'I remember sitting there that day listening to you telling Peter about the Army and what you had done during the war, Father!'

'But you must only have been six or seven then!' Edward said in amazement.

'Perhaps so, but I could imagine the sea and all the horses, it made me wonder if I too would ever see such things.'

Edward shook his head, 'I never realised that you had understood so much, Lizzie. Is that where your dreams of freedom stem from? I'm afraid you would not have enjoyed what I encountered on those journeys.'

'No, not the war, but to see important places and events, and to describe them in a diary would please me.' Lizzie spoke as if confiding her innermost thoughts without knowing it.

Peter's eyes met Edward's across the table in mutual astonishment. 'I had no idea that a young child could be so influenced,' Edward said in wonderment.

Peter grasped the reality of the situation far more quickly than Edward, and spoke out in an effort to play down any illusions Lizzie might have created from their shared experiences. 'If you want to know about foreign lands and exciting lives, Lizzie, then listen carefully and you may learn enough for you to see that this beautiful valley, which may seem too quiet, is a haven compared to many places. You heard your father's story but do you remember him telling us of lives being destroyed or lost in dreadful conditions in faraway countries? Of incompetence and deprivation? Now I'll tell you of my experiences.

'I have been robbed on my journeys, beaten on account of the uniform I wear, and frustrated many times when the Army's ways were not mine and, especially since having been at peace for so long, we are sometimes ill-prepared for skirmishes or insurrections.' He paused for a moment, then continued. 'You would think that by now slavery of the black man was over and done with, wouldn't you? To all intents and purposes to the British it is, but we, and the rest of the so-called civilised world, taught black men to capture men, women and children of rival tribes, then sell them to us as workers and slaves. However, once our Government had been prevailed upon to stamp out slave-trading, it meant that one tribe in West Africa, the war-like Ashanti, lost a source of income.'

'You mean the black men sold each other?' Lizzie declared, horrified.

'Yes, because we paid them to do so,' Peter explained, patiently. 'Then, you see, in order to protect their income, the Ashanti over-ran another tribe, the Fanti people who were friendly to us. They then advanced to within twelve miles of our headquarters at Cape Coast Castle. Their chief, Kofi Kari-Kari, we called him 'King Coffee'. Lizzie laughed. 'He coveted the port at Elmina which the Europeans had held for 300 years, he saw it as an ideal trading post from which to sell slaves and was therefore determined to take it. Over the past fifty years his tribe have often attacked our settlements which we got in a treaty with the Dutch, and the last time he did so we decided that enough was enough, he must be taught a lesson. On that occasion he actually reached Elmina where our Marines, West Indian and other colonial troops were. Fighting took place and fortunately we won the battle in the town, our main weapon being nature itself, for the invaders suffered much from disease.'

'But if conditions were so bad, why did we want to stay there if we no longer traded in slaves?' Lizzie asked, somewhat puzzled at the logic of fighting for something useless.

'Gold!' Edward interrupted. 'Peter didn't say that the Ashanti had gold, which was of more than a passing interest to us.'

'That's true,' Peter conceded. 'But after hundreds of years the use of the ports for trade was also of great importance to us. This is where my regiment came in. Sir Garnet Wolseley went out in advance to prepare plans for the arrival in the Colony of our 2,400 white troops, but we soldiers were delayed until nearly Christmas due to bad weather. We finally got there and had to reach Kumasi, Kari-Kari's capital, and return by the end of February '74, before the rainy season began and the rivers flooded. When Wolseley arrived on the coast, he found that of 130 Englishmen then ashore, only 22 were fit for duty. It was a known fact that for every extra day the war extended beyond February there would be more deaths from sickness, fever and the appalling humidity. My regiment arrived unprepared for what was to face us,' he said, glumly. Then, after a pause, he continued, 'We started out on the 6th January, '74, but access to the enemy was much more difficult than we'd expected. Between the coastal ports and the Ashanti lands lies a dense, insect-ridden jungle through which we had to pass. It took us twenty-nine days of hard fighting in the oven-like gloom of the jungle, and two pitched battles before we reached Kumasi. We lost sixteen officers and men and four hundred of us were wounded, but by the time we got there the King had fled and was still refusing to agree terms with us. So, according to plan, we destroyed his great palace, burned his capital and marched back to the coast and safety.'

'But you were wounded,' Lizzie pointed out, very softly.

Peter looked down at his arm. 'Oh, it was merely a cut. However, in spite of taking care to protect the wound, by the time I arrived back at Headquarters infection had set in. I was lucky not to have lost my arm, or even my life. As we made our way back though, messengers bearing gold from the King caught up with us, and our proposed treaty was handed to them. A month later the King signed it and thereby renounced his claim over our territories, promised free trade and pledged to end the practice of human sacrifice. He also had to pay us 50,000 ounces of gold by instalments.'

'My view is that the story won't end there,' Edward said ruefully. 'By all accounts they are a bloodthirsty lot, and hardly likely to change their ways of thinking after hundreds of years. I can see there being trouble again before long.'

'Just so long as I don't have to go back there; it was my own fault for volunteering to go in the first place,' Peter said emphatically. 'It's a sobering thought that any form of greed can, at any time, change men into animals and diminish their respect for other people's beliefs and practices.' Peter subconsciously rubbed the wounded part of his arm, as if his thoughts were still in the heat of the skirmishes. 'But then I have a small souvenir myself,' he said proudly. 'When we sacked the Palace I managed to snatch a small piece of gold jewellery—the decoration work on it is extremely fine. I intend to give it to Clara when we marry.'

'May I see it?' asked Lizzie.

'When you get back with me!' Peter replied. No sooner had he uttered the words than he encountered a sharp enquiring look from Edward, and he realised that he had spoken carelessly.

Edward immediately sensed that there was more behind the slip of Peter's tongue than he knew, and looked long and hard at Lizzie, his eyes demanding an explanation. A sheepish look appeared on Lizzie's face and Edward knew he was right to be suspicious. 'Now then, what's going on?' he demanded.

Sadly, she was now faced with telling her father about Peter's invitation straight out, rather than leading up to the disclosure in a more casual way.

'It's my fault, Uncle,' Peter butted in. 'On the spur of the moment I suggested it might be pleasant if Lizzie came back with me to Aldershot, to meet Clara. I really thought it might help her to sort herself out a little.'

'We intended to ask if I might go for a few weeks, but you were so angry when we returned from the ride that I thought it better to wait a while.' Lizzie looked at him with sorrowful eyes, pleading with such earnestness that he was at a loss to find any sensible reason to forbid her. 'I would be staying with Clara,' she explained as if it were all agreed.

'I suppose there is no reason why I should object,' Edward said, resigning himself to the matter. 'Providing Peter can convince me that you will be chaperoned in a manner befitting a daughter of mine.' His voice lacked conviction, and Lizzie was fully aware that if he'd been able to find a strong enough reason to refuse, he would certainly have done so.

Knowing this she tried to reassure him without allowing him any opportunity to change his mind. 'It means that I can meet Clara, and I will only stay a short while, I promise.'

Edward sat back feeling numbed by the speed with which events had once more interfered with his life. He was far from pleased and really didn't want her to go away again so soon after her return. Intuition told him that this was a move full of temptations, and one which could result in her leaving forever.

'You have my word, Uncle. Lizzie will be protected at all times and will be kept from anything which might have a bad influence on her.' Peter's manner was positive and Edward appreciated just why his nephew had done so well in the Army; however he wasn't sure that it was to his liking at this point in time.

'And when, pray, do you intend leaving?' Edward felt moved to ask.

Peter chose to ignore the begrudging tone in his uncle's voice. 'I have to return the day after tomorrow. If Lizzie went with me it would be a more sensible arrangement than having to make plans by letter, and it would also mean that Lizzie need not travel alone. If I return then I will have time to see Lizzie settled with Clara before I resume duties at the weekend.'

To Lizzie, going away was her one chance to experience a much wider world than the one offered here in the valley, yet she felt a pang of sadness at her father's all too obvious disappointment in her decision to leave him again. 'I'll make it up to you, truly, and I promise to return before Christmas,' she pleaded.

Christmas! Edward hated Christmas, it was a time in the middle of winter when winds roared and snow and ice abounded. For a farmer even the smallest of jobs became difficult, and it was a time when families withdrew into their own secluded world, leaving him alone and missing Hannah. His spirits fell. What comfort could he offer Lizzie in their isolation when, no doubt, Peter and Clara could offer so much more?

'I cannot deny you this opportunity, Lizzie,' he said in a quiet voice. 'Your mother would not have wanted me to do so—but I hope you will spare a thought for me on occasion.' There was such sadness in his manner that his answer struck at Lizzie's heart.

She smiled, kindly, 'Oh, Father, you cannot know how much fondness I have for you. Of course I shall think of you, and will return a happier person, I am convinced of that.'

Chapter 9

With *Peter and Lizzie gone,* Edward settled down to work, but there was little joy in his heart as he looked around at all he owned. Several days had passed since their departure but so far he'd received no letter from either of them and the thought of the many long, lonely years ahead far from cheered him. For the first time in his life he saw only the monotonous routine of work stretching before him.

Had Abe also reached such a point in his life, and been persuaded by experience to ensure that Edward escaped a similar destiny? Edward felt suddenly very weary; how he envied Peter his brash confidence. So much had changed in the world in such a short time that, for once, the isolation of the valley seemed suffocating.

Lizzie, on the other hand, with her spirits renewed intended enjoying every precious moment of her visit to Aldershot. No sooner had Peter handed her down from the train than every other person they met either saluted him or shook him warmly by the hand. As they waited for a cabby to notice them waiting, she was in awe of the immense respect in which he was obviously held by passers-by, although she knew his position as an Officer deserved no less. She was delighted to be in his company and with the attention showered upon her by the bevy of gallant young officers also waiting for transport. Indeed, by the time their hansom cab arrived before Clara's front door, Lizzie was in a state of delightful euphoria.

Peter was bemused by the flushed, excited Lizzie beside him; she was indeed on the way to becoming her old self again.

Edward wondered why there had been no communication from Lizzie. He shook his head and reminded himself that young people could be most inconsiderate of other's feelings when their own happiness was at stake. However, nearly a week passed before a letter finally arrived, and the shortness of its content confirmed his low opinion of youth.

Dear Father,

Please forgive me for taking so long to write to you. We arrived safely at a very busy time, but I won't bore you with such small details. Needless to say, I am very happy here. Clara was quite a surprise to me, although I'm sure you would approve of her. I have seen and done so many things and, as Peter keeps his promise to take me everywhere, I'm not sure that Clara isn't a weeny bit jealous of me.

This can't be a long letter or it would mean my missing the next post, but I will write again soon. I hope you are managing quite well without me. Peter sends his good wishes to you.

Your fondest Lizzie.

He was to wait yet another week before the second letter arrived.

My Dear Father,

I cannot believe that I have been away for two whole weeks now and I'm still not bored! As Clara is so busy at work, Peter makes a point of escorting me everywhere, dancing, riding and even to the Theatre. Clara says that I will return home even more worn out than when I arrived, can you believe that? Clara and I go walking round the shops when she has time, but I think she only does it to amuse me, and because Peter wishes it. I feel that Peter and she aren't really suited to each other, yet I wouldn't say anything of course. Peter sends his best wishes, and we hope you are well.

Please write when you can.

Your fondest Lizzie.

For some inexplicable reason Edward was disconcerted by this second letter, and although there was no single factor on which to base his unease he read it more than once in an effort to reassure himself that all was well. It was only with the arrival of the following that he became more than concerned by Lizzie's view of things.

Dear Father,

I am writing again, very quickly, because Peter is too busy to take me out at the moment. Clara seems displeased with me, I think she finds me a little lazy, but I'm not, it's just that she is so terribly fussy about things. Peter says she really ought to laugh a little more. When Peter is with me I think he is very happy, more so than when he is with Clara. He really is very handsome, you know, and such a catch, she should appreciate him more. When we walk out together all the ladies look with secret admiration at him.

159

When are you going to write to me again, I have only had a
short note from you, and one letter—are you displeased with me?
I have to finish writing now, I wish to look my best for when
Peter arrives. We are to stay in tonight and play cards.
Hoping you are still well.

Yours, Lizzie.

Edward was becoming worried over Lizzie's obsession with Peter, and had
to remind himself that it was probably only her romantic imagination at
work; Peter was quite capable of warding off any advances from a slip of a
girl. He wrote back urging her to be more circumspect in her behaviour and
to consider returning home before the winter weather became severe. She
replied thus:

My Dear, Dear Father,

Why do you sound so angry in your letter? I will not thank you
for writing if you are unkind to me. I am very happy here and I
know that I promised to return home by Christmas, and I will, I
promise, but Christmas here does sound as if it will be a
wonderful, exciting time.

You say in your letter that I am to respect Clara's wishes as
she is kind enough to let me stay with her. I really do try you
know, but she is set against Peter taking me out so much, I really
do think her to be jealous. They are always arguing and I am
beginning to wonder if Peter loves her at all, he seems so much
happier with me.

You must remember to keep warm, for the winds will be biting in
the valley soon. Please write a kinder letter, when you have time.

Yours, Lizzie.

There seemed to be an artificiality in Lizzie's letters which had not been in
any sent from Worksop, and he suspected that the freedom she was now
experiencing was far from beneficial. She must be urged to return
immediately before more harm was done. He wrote telling her in no
uncertain terms that he would not allow her to stay until Christmas. Her
reply angered him greatly.

Dear Father,

I am hurt by your letter, and I do not thank you for it. Peter
says he cannot understand your attitude, and that you sound

160

*more like Clara every day. I have decided that I would like to
stay here and that if you don't agree then I will find some kind of
work in a shop locally.*

*I think it better if I don't live with Clara any more and Peter is
to find me lodgings with a lady in the town. Peter will pay for my
lodgings and says you need have no worries for he will take care
of me. He is such a fine man and constantly fends off any
admirers I have because he says they aren't good enough for me.
Secretly I think he wants to keep me for himself.*

*How bored you must be with nothing to do but work. Please
don't let us make each other unhappy any more. You would like
my hair now, I have it in the latest fashion and I really do believe
it makes me look quite beautiful.*

Your Lizzie.

To Edward this latest epistle was the last straw, and in spite of the
inconvenience it would cause he resolved to travel to Aldershot as soon as
possible and bring her back, whether she liked it or not. He was both
annoyed and hurt to think of the change in Lizzie, yet he wasn't fool enough
to ignore the fact that things had been going wrong for weeks prior to her
departure. What he would say and do on arrival at Aldershot was still to be
decided and he dreaded the confrontation which lay ahead. He was about to
start work the following day when he received yet another letter from
Lizzie.

Dear Father,

*You say I am to come home as soon as possible, but I am to
move on Thursday next and plan not to come home until after
Christmas. I am very happy here and yet you wish to spoil it all,
but when I tell you the news you may be much happier than
before. I really think that Peter and I are in love, so that he is
hardly likely to marry Clara now. What would you think if your
two favourite people were to marry. We could look after you
when you are too old to look after yourself.*

*I think when you read this news you will not be so angry with
me. It will all work out in the end and you are not to worry. I
miss you very much, please write soon for I want to know that
you are happy for me.*

*Please don't tell Peter what I have told you as I think he is
very worried about Clara at the moment.*

Your Lizzie.

This news so angered Edward that he immediately made plans to get an early train to London the next morning.

Accordingly, soon after dawn he saddled Mattie, and, accompanied by one of his labourers, rode as far as Malin Bridge. Here, having despatched the lad back to the farm with both horses, he boarded a horse-drawn omnibus to town. Being angry and in no mood to converse with anyone unnecessarily he sat in silence until alighting in town where he immediately headed with all haste towards the station.

Once aboard the train and settled in his seat, Edward felt compelled to consider what his words should be when he came face to face with Lizzie. He knew from previous experience that to confront her head on would be a grave mistake and merely cause her to close her mind to reason. He felt that the fault was completely his as, since Hannah's death, he had allowed Lizzie the freedom very much denied other young people of her age, and in plain truth he had spoilt her. He also found it hard to believe Peter capable of such ungrateful and cadish behaviour, preferring to think that it was Lizzie's over-active imagination at work.

If he was wrong in this assumption however, then he was faced with an even bigger problem than at first realised. Lizzie could not marry Peter without revoking Abe's will! Whereas she was not a blood relative, it was Peter's family that had caused the problem in the first place and all his efforts to comply with the legacy would have been to no avail.

What was the point of it all? He sighed deeply, drawing a perturbed look from the elderly lady seated opposite. He smiled reassuringly at her, nodded, then returned to his own private thoughts. He wasn't sure that he liked the picture that was forming in his mind regarding Lizzie or Peter, or that he trusted himself to judge the young man's motives completely. Surely after all these years he knew him well enough to believe him incapable of deliberate contrivance? Had he deliberately set his sights on Lizzie? No, it was impossible for no one knew about the will, not even Lizzie. Perhaps he was letting his imagination run away with him—once Lizzie was home, things would calm down again. Or would they? He could not see into the future but he knew if he wasn't careful there was a serious risk of destroying the only family he had.

Arriving at Aldershot Station late in the afternoon, Edward was surprised to find little he could recognise around him. He stood under the canopy of the station building and tried to get his bearings. Nothing was familiar enough to suggest the direction he should take, so there was no choice but to seek help by instructing a cab driver to take him to Clara's address. As it turned out, he could quite easily have walked the short distance by crossing the footbridge and taking a path through the fields to his destination. However, it was raining and walking would have made his boots muddy. He was relieved to find Clara's house situated in a relatively open area with trees along the unsurfaced road. Only the north side of this was developed and, as the cab pulled up in front of the railings of Nightingale Villa, Edward's curiosity was aroused, he wondered what Clara would be like.

'I'm not sure if there will be anyone at home,' he explained to the driver. 'Can you wait until I find out?' Opening the gate he walked the short distance to the front door where he pulled the bell and waited patiently for someone to answer his call. He felt a little strange, unsure of himself and conscious of his country clothing. He was also at a disadvantage in that he had no idea what Clara's surname was! He was, therefore, somewhat embarrassed when the door opened and a fine-looking woman of about twenty-five years of age looked questioningly at him across the threshold.

He cleared his throat and spoke hesitatingly, 'I do apologise but I'm looking for a young lady whom I only know by the name of Clara! I believe this to be her address?'

The young woman observed him keenly and asked, 'Whom shall I say is calling?'

'I'm afraid I have no card,' he explained. 'I'm Edward Morton, and have travelled from Sheffield in search of my daughter, Lizzie, who is staying with Miss Clara. I may not be known to the lady of the house but if I could have a word with her I think she will realise who I am.'

Much to his surprise a smile broke out on the face before him and a hand reached out to greet him. 'I'm Clara Burton,' she said brightly. 'Do come in. I've heard much about you from Peter and am very pleased to make your acquaintance.'

Edward took the outstretched hand and was surprised by the firmness of her grip. He immediately warmed to Clara, whilst being intrigued by her forthright welcome. 'I must pay off the cab first,' he said, placing his bag on the step. He returned a few moments later to find Clara holding the bag and waiting to show him into the house.

'I'm afraid my maid is out,' she said, as if explaining why she herself had answered the door. 'She is walking with Lizzie at the moment. Did Peter or Lizzie know that you were coming? If they did it was very remiss of them not to have told me about it!'

'No! They didn't know,' Edward replied hastily. 'It was a quick decision on my part to come, for I need to discuss something with Lizzie. Do you think she will be long?'

'I don't think so now that it is raining again. Lizzie gets a little bored sometimes, especially when both Peter and I are at work. Peter, of course, doesn't live here but he is expected this evening. I suggested that Mary Ann, my maid, took Lizzie shopping with her this afternoon.' By now they had reached a commodious sitting room, 'Do take a seat,' Clara said, removing a book from the chair on which she had obviously been sitting when he rang.

'You're very kind,' replied Edward, who had noted the title of the book. 'I see you read Thomas Hardy! I find his work a little gloomy sometimes, not at all the thing to read in the country in the depths of winter. I'm not one for whittling at wood or the likes, after a long day's work.' he smiled. 'I'm an avid reader myself and am afraid Lizzie must find very little inspiration in my company, particularly now that she's getting older.'

Clara laughed in agreement. 'She's quite lively, I must admit. I fear she finds even my ways very restricting, but nursing makes one have a tidy, orderly mind.'

Edward half expected Clara to be antagonistic towards Lizzie, judging by what he had read in her recent letters, but there were no signs of animosity in the amiable young woman before him. 'I do hope Lizzie has not been too much of a handful,' he said, cautiously. 'It was a little unfair to have her thrust upon you without warning.'

'No, it is rather pleasant to have a companion in the house. It's a large place for one person but I am fortunate in having inherited it from my late parents in the first place.' She paused, suddenly remembering that he'd had a long journey. 'I'm sure you would enjoy a cup of tea, am I right?'

'That would be most welcome, providing it's not too much trouble. Then I must find lodgings for the night. Perhaps I could return this evening when I've settled in, when Peter is here?'

'I'll give it some thought, but first a drink!' She left the room and Edward glanced inquisitively around in an effort to understand the character of the owner. If this was a town house, he thought, then it certainly was a most comfortable one, and was well cared for. It pleased him to see a glass-fronted bookcase almost full of books, and he rose to read the titles of some of the volumes. He was surprised by the number of medical volumes, so much so that he failed to hear Clara's returning footsteps.

'My father was a surgeon,' she explained, as if anticipating his curiosity. 'He was an Army Doctor. Perhaps you didn't expect a woman to own such books, and although I do read them sometimes, mostly I enjoy *Notes on Nursing* by Florence Nightingale.'

Edward was a little embarrassed to be caught peering into the bookcase. 'I should not have let my curiosity get the better of me,' he apologised.

Clara smiled, 'Please, think nothing of it. Books are there to be read, and you're very welcome. Now, do have some tea before it goes cold. Would you like some cake or a scone?'

As he drank his tea, Edward realised that it had been several hours since he'd eaten and he was grateful for the refreshment. 'I didn't appreciate just how thirsty I was,' he admitted, and took another scone from the plate at her invitation. 'Thank you,' he said. 'I did wrap a few sandwiches to eat on the train but they disappeared some time ago; this will keep me going until I find an inn. Is there a suitable one nearby which you can recommend?'

'There are several, but I feel you would be happier staying here with Lizzie and me. It's not as if you're a stranger and there's a small bedroom in the attic which you are most welcome to use.'

Edward started to protest. 'It would be an imposition, especially after Lizzie descended on you without warning as well.'

'No, I insist!' Clara stated firmly. 'It's settled, you're to stay here with us.'

'That is very good of you,' Edward said, accepting the offer without further hesitation. 'It would have been no hardship for me to go to an inn; however, I must admit that it will save me a lot of bother, and will be most helpful in the circumstances.' He was in fact more than grateful not to have to go out again seeking accommodation, although he was loath to prevail upon Clara's obvious kindness by asking her to provide something more substantial in the way of refreshment.

As if anticipating his needs Clara quickly intervened. 'You will be more than welcome to join us for supper,' she offered obligingly.

'I thank you kindly,' Edward replied, somewhat relieved. He was more than impressed with Peter's choice of a future wife, but he was still mindful of the reason for his visit here. He sat back into the chair and said, 'I understand that you are to be married to Peter soon, am I right?' He was hoping that this would bring a moment which might shed some light on how things were between the pair of them in the wake of Lizzie's last disturbing letter.

A frown appeared momentarily upon Clara's face, but this was quickly replaced by a pensive smile. 'We had intended to marry in the spring, however, as things stand we will probably delay the marriage a while.'

Edward was tempted to ask the reason for the delay but good manners prevailed and he held his tongue. He wondered if the frown had been an indication that there was some sort of trouble between the three of them but there seemed no point in speculating unnecessarily, so he changed the subject slightly, hoping this might prove more fruitful in the end.

'How is Lizzie?' he asked, 'Does she behave herself, or does she disgrace me?'

'She certainly has an active mind,' Clara smiled knowingly. 'I do hope Peter hasn't exposed her to a way of life which she will find hard to leave behind. There is so much going on in a garrison town that one forgets how much quieter other places must be.'

Edward's brow was furrowed, 'I fear that I have allowed Lizzie too much freedom in the past. After her mother died I was all she had, and, being a child who could amuse herself, I allowed her to roam unhindered. However, in the end I was compelled to send her away to school before she became too wild. Sometimes she was nearly unmanageable! She resented going, but what could I do, being a man alone in a quiet valley with a restless child on my hands?'

'It was probably the best thing to do,' Clara nodded in agreement. 'Yet many men remarry very quickly simply in order to find a mother for their children. Would that not have been easier in the circumstances?'

Edward was taken aback by Clara's forthright question. He shook his head as he answered, 'I'm afraid that I'm a solitary man and don't mix easily. That I married at all is quite surprising, and a long story, but I was very happy with Lizzie's mother and accepted Lizzie as my own right from the beginning.'

'You mean that Lizzie is not your daughter?' Clara asked in amazement.

'Well, no! Didn't you realise that? I presumed Peter had told you that Lizzie is my step-daughter!'

Clara seemed to sympathise, her eyes becoming very understanding. Then she asked, 'Have you no other children?'

'Unfortunately not, and I presume never will have. I suppose that is why I gave Lizzie so much freedom. She is all I have, apart from Peter who is more a friend than nephew, but he has his own life to lead.'

'You have been very good to Peter, that I know,' Clara said, thoughtfully. Then, after a moment she spoke with deliberation, 'I am beginning to understand Lizzie a little better now that I know her story, and see why she clings to Peter so much.'

Here Edward saw an opening and sought to turn the conversation to his own advantage. 'I do hope she isn't too demanding of you both?' he queried. 'I know only too well how exasperating she can be at times, but she is a good child at heart. Lately, since her return home she has been restless and appears not to know what she wants. I was beginning to despair about her until Peter came to visit, and took her under his wing.' A door opened somewhere beyond the room interrupting his train of thought. He looked questioningly at Clara, 'Are you expecting someone?'

'That will be Lizzie and Mary Ann,' she replied, her head tilted, listening for conversation. 'I'm sure she will be very pleased as well as surprised to see you here. In here, Lizzie!' She called without rising from her chair.

A moment later the living room door opened and Lizzie entered with a flounce. 'I really do think that people should be more careful!' she said angrily, looking straight at Clara. 'Just look at this dress, splashed by mud from the wheels of a carriage! It's raining heavily again and I'm all wet!' Turning her head she suddenly became aware that Clara was not alone. With a start she recognised the figure at the other end of the room. 'Father!' she cried. 'What are you doing here?' then she flushed, as if caught out in some act of mischief.

'I came to make sure you weren't up to anything you shouldn't be!' Edward replied sternly, not at all happy with her aggressive behaviour on entering the room. He now saw Clara eyeing him strangely and asked Lizzie, 'Aren't you pleased to see me?'

Lizzie smiled, almost sheepishly. 'Of course I am! But why are you here, I wrote to you only a few days ago; surely you didn't leave the farm in answer to my last letter?' There was more implied by the question he knew, but he had no intention of allowing Clara to become suspicious of the fact.

He thought quickly. He had no desire to hurt Clara in any way, especially if Lizzie was being led astray by her overactive imagination. It would, therefore, be better for him to appear merely to be taking a fatherly interest in his daughter. 'Can't I come to see for myself what holds you here? You write to me in your letters of the wonderful time you are having and I simply thought I should take a break before the bad weather sets in, and make my acquaintance with Clara.'

To Lizzie this was an obvious lie. She knew Edward well enough to realise that he would never leave the farm without good reason, especially at this time of year. She could also tell from the firm lines around his mouth that he was far from pleased with her, and recognised too a warning in his eyes telling her to be discreet. Summoning up courage she sought to smooth things over by crossing the room and kissing him affectionately on the cheek. 'I'm sorry, I've not given you a very warm welcome,' she said, with a note of contrition in her voice. But I never expected to see you sitting there.'

Obviously not, thought Edward, who was grateful that she had at least heeded his warning by seeking to make their meeting appear as normal as possible—once the initial shock at seeing him had past. 'Clara has kindly offered me a room here, Lizzie, isn't that good of her?' He turned to Clara, smiling, 'And I have accepted.' Turning to Lizzie he said casually, although he knew that she would take his words to have a deeper meaning. 'Yes, Lizzie, I got your letters including the one that came yesterday morning. I see that you seem to be settling in here, but you know you can't stay forever!'

'You haven't come to take me home have you?' Lizzie cried in alarm, aware that if he wanted to take her back at that instant she could do nothing to prevent him.

'We'll see, we'll see! But I do need to talk to you urgently on a matter connected with the farm. It is a subject which will be of little interest to Clara, so in a quiet moment together I will speak to you of it.' Lizzie raised her brows nervously, wondering how to interpret Edward's message, suspecting it contained a threat of some kind.

Peter's welcome, when he arrived, contrasted greatly with that of Lizzie's, being warm and cordial, and once supper had been eaten the group proceeded to play a modest, yet enjoyable, game of cards.

'How long will you stay?' Peter enquired as he shuffled the pack. 'Unfortunately I'm tied up during the day but I could spare sufficient time to show you around the Barracks. You might be interested in the newer weapons we have there.'

'I had planned to stay a couple of days,' Edward replied thoughtfully. 'Although I could stretch it to three I suppose. If that is acceptable to you, Clara?' He looked enquiringly at her. 'I admit I'm most intrigued at what I have seen so far, and would particularly like to go to the Royal Library if there is time to do so.' He had to admit to himself that the evening had been a pleasant change, and one more night would do no harm.

Clara nodded in agreement, 'Another day here or there makes no difference. Stay as long as you wish.'

'Good!' said Peter, as he dealt the cards. 'Then we could even go to the Theatre tomorrow night if Clara is in agreement. It's merely a music hall show, not at all sophisticated but it's usually well attended—how about it?' He looked around at his companions and seeing signs of approval, nodded with satisfaction. 'We'll make it tomorrow night then!'

Edward noted with relief that Lizzie had her feelings well under control and, allowing for the odd silly slip, she handled the cards far better than he did, probably as a result of her stay in Worksop. He himself was not an expert with cards and it had been several years since he'd last played. It was however, a pleasurable way to pass the time and gave him an opportunity to observe each of his companions at some length. There was no outward sign of any strife between Lizzie and Clara, or Clara and Peter, who, to give him credit, appeared to treat both women equally. This congenial atmosphere both puzzled and relieved him as, ever since the arrival of Lizzie's letter, he had dreaded facing a situation that was fraught with problems.

'Well!' Declared Peter, at the end of the game. 'I'm afraid I have to go now in order to be in Barracks on time. Clara will tell you where to come tomorrow, Uncle, and if you can make it for two o'clock that would be most convenient.'

The party broke up and Clara left the room with Peter, leaving Edward and Lizzie alone for a while. Lizzie looked uncomfortable and, for once, was tongue-tied. Taking this opportunity Edward confronted Lizzie directly, 'I want a word with you, young lady, when we are alone.' His voice was firm and his intentions clear, and Lizzie lowered her eyes rather than face him. 'I want to know exactly what is going on, and what game you think you're playing. You're wise enough to know that I have a farm to run and can't afford to leave it at the drop of a hat.' He heard the front door close and they waited for Clara to re-enter the room. He rose, stretching his legs after the long session sitting at the table, whilst at the same time drawing Clara's gaze from Lizzie's flushed countenance. 'If you don't mind, I would like to

168

retire,' he apologised. 'I've had a very long day and it would be a pity to spoil a pleasant evening by falling asleep down here.'

Clara smiled warmly, 'I'm afraid I too have to retire as I have to be up and away to the hospital early in the morning. I'm quite sure Lizzie knows her way around Aldershot sufficiently well by now to be able to show you the town tomorrow, and take you to the Barracks.' She held out her hand, 'It has been a pleasure getting to know you.'

Edward clasped her hand warmly, 'I thank you for your hospitality, the evening has been most enjoyable, and I would not have appreciated going out at this time in order to spend the night at some dreadful inn. Now, I must make some recompense for the trouble I've caused. Please let tomorrow night's visit to the Theatre be my way of thanking you.'

Clara laughed as she withdrew her hand. 'As you wish,' she conceded. 'I shall look forward to the evening with great anticipation. Lizzie, please make sure all the lights are extinguished before you both retire.' So saying, she bade them both 'Good night' and left.

'Peter is a lucky man to have Clara, Lizzie. Remember that!' he said when Clara had gone, and he watched Lizzie turn off the gas lights as though she had done it all her life. He marvelled at the ease and convenience of this form of lighting, and sighed knowing it would be years, if ever, before gas lighting reached the valley.

On reaching the small room which Clara had shown him earlier, Edward quickly undressed and sank gratefully onto the soft feather bed where he immediately fell into a deep slumber.

If Edward's tiredness caused him to fall asleep straight away, it was in complete contrast to the state of mind of the other two occupants of the house who, for diverse reasons, lay waiting a long time for sleep to claim them.

Clara was overtired through rising very early that morning and from the hard work she had done at the hospital. She was also puzzled by the strange relationship between Edward and Lizzie, for she sensed that all was not well there. Lizzie, on the other hand, felt that her father's visit heralded the end of her stay in Aldershot, and she feared his wrath, wishing she'd been more circumspect in her correspondence with him.

As a consequence of their inability to sleep, both women woke next morning feeling less than rested, and rather reluctant to leave their respective beds.

Edward, however, was up and about as was his habit, long before either of them and was downstairs reading one of Clara's books when she came scurrying down to see to her guests. He noted the tired look in her eyes and thought it a pity that she was compelled to spend the day at the hospital before going to the theatre that night. He would have enjoyed discussing certain of her books whilst walking together in some pleasant spot, but he knew they both had important tasks to perform before evening arrived. However, he did not delay her with idle chatter as she was so obviously in a hurry, and was sorry when she eventually left the house.

Nearly an hour later, a very subdued Lizzie finally descended the stairs to face her already impatient father who was not used to idling his time when important matters were waiting.

When Lizzie finally settled down to plan the morning's activities with him, Edward thought it best to clear the air immediately by challenging her directly. 'Now what is all this which you write about concerning Peter?' he demanded, looking straight at her so that she could not avoid his eyes. 'Peter and Clara seem happy enough, and she is the most understanding of people, can't you see that? Is it your fanciful imagination or has Peter been indiscreet? If he has I will never forgive him.' He waited, watching the varying emotions playing on her young face. In previous times he would have sympathised with her, but she had never before angered him so much by her apparent foolishness. If Hannah were alive now, she would have known what to do, whereas he simply had no idea of the workings of the mind of a young girl. All he could do was speak out in his own clumsy but well-meaning way.

'Peter has been a gentleman!' Lizzie said, defensively, her eyes tearful and with a catch in her voice. 'But I know he loves me, every bit as much as he does Clara!'

'Has he said as much, then?' There was a sharpness in Edward's question, and his face was grim.

Lizzie flushed, 'Not in so many words, but we are so close! I want him to love me—you wouldn't mind that would you?' The words tumbled from her lips without caution. 'You are fond of Peter, and if he and Clara were unhappy together then what is to prevent him marrying me?' She watched him, her eyes pleading for his understanding.

Edward sighed, and was silent for a moment. 'Lizzie, you cannot marry Peter—it is impossible! There is more at stake than you realise.'

Lizzie turned defiantly, her tears seeming to evaporate with her indignation. 'I will marry him, I will, you wait and see!' She made to leave the room but Edward caught her by the sleeve of her dress.

'He isn't yours to take, Madam!' He cried, his angry voice ringing round the room. 'You will ruin everything, everything I have worked for!' Never before in his life had he been so consumed with rage that he raised his voice to another human being. 'I should have smacked you long ago,' he said fiercely before his anger subsided and a feeling of despair crept over him.

Stunned at first by his outburst, Lizzie stopped and stared at him, then on seeing the look of pain in his eyes she ran from the room and went upstairs out of the way. Once in her room she threw herself sobbing onto the bed with a mixture of pique and resentment. Never before had he spoken to her in such a manner! It was unreasonable of him to forbid her to love Peter, just as it was wrong to accuse her of spoiling everything! How was she doing that? If Peter and Clara were unhappy together then he would be better off without her. She was sure Peter loved her and not Clara, yet he'd never actually confessed to such feelings for her. It made her even more miserable to think it might only be her imagination after all! These thoughts brought her to the sober realisation that if he did not love her, and her father challenged him about it, then everyone would think her a ridiculous child! She must leave the house before that happened! Leaping from the bed she grabbed her small trunk and hurriedly threw her belongings inside, but how could she lift it downstairs by herself, without anyone knowing? Where would she go? Tears of anger and frustration ran down her face and in this defeated state she decided to leave the house quietly so that she could seek Peter out and confess that she might have compromised him in her father's eyes.

Edward meanwhile paced the room, unsure what to do next. He could hear Lizzie moving about in her bedroom above and presumed she was in a fit of temper. What was he going to do with her? Once again he felt himself the victim of Abe's will. From the grave he still had the power to ruin his life, to make him do and say things which were normally foreign to him. Abe's intention had been to prevent his sister's family getting their hands on the farm, and if Lizzie married Peter then all was lost, and his own desperate measures would have been wasted. In befriending his nephew he never dreamed that such a liaison might occur. In fact he had always felt guilty that in spite of Peter's good character and hard work, he could not inherit that which an uncle might have normally bequeathed to a favourite nephew. Such had been his strength of feeling on the matter that just prior to the act of Parliament abolishing the purchase of commissions, he'd helped Peter to buy a commission and even given him a small allowance. He felt betrayed by both of them, yet if Lizzie was to be believed it was more an affair in her mind than in Peter's. He had to get her away from Aldershot and back to the farm as soon as possible; they would go first thing in the morning.

Suddenly realising that the noise from above had ceased he listened intently and then heard a soft muffled sound in the hallway. Suspecting that it was Lizzie he strode quickly from the room and found her already at the front door.

For Lizzie it was too late. Edward intervened and ordered her, none too lightly, back into the sitting-room where he made her sit in a chair. 'Where did you think you were going?' he demanded, determined to make her see sense.

Lizzie hung her head and refused to meet his eyes. 'I was going to find Peter,' she said lamely, her voice barely audible. 'I was going to tell him about the trouble I'd caused and to ask him to forgive me.'

Edward looked at her bent head with compassion, hating to see her spirit so broken. What was he to do? His voice, when finally he found words to express himself, was kindly and encouraging. 'Lizzie, if this is all in your head about Peter then listen. Come back with me tomorrow to the farm, and I'll say nothing about this to Peter or Clara. But if half of it is Peter's doing then I shall forbid him from ever coming to the farm again.'

'But why?' she pleaded. 'Why is it so wrong of me to love him? He has done nothing wrong.'

'No!' Edward agreed with a deep sigh. 'No, he hasn't, but he is your cousin—therefore you can't marry!'

'But it is not against the law!' Lizzie butted in defiantly, 'I know someone in Worksop who married her cousin—besides, Peter is not truly my cousin at all.'

Her knowledge was sound, Edward was forced to admit very reluctantly to himself, moreover there was now a look of determination in Lizzie's eyes which he knew from past experience would not be easy to dispel. He felt obliged to offer some explanation if she was to be pacified. 'What you don't understand' he said gently, 'is that if you were to marry him, then the farm cannot be yours when I die. Abe, who left the farm to me, made a condition that none of my sister's family were to inherit it. I had no say in the matter and, at that time, hardly knew Peter myself. I have no other family, certainly no children, so that on my death the farm will automatically go to the Parish if you marry him.' He had no intention of enlightening her further and watched anxiously, trying to assess her reaction to this news.

Instead of the indignation which he expected to follow his explanation, a perplexed look appeared on Lizzie's face. Finally she spoke, haltingly, almost as though his words made little sense. 'If Abe didn't know Peter, then why would he not want him to have the farm?'

With a very heavy heart Edward sought to explain. 'You see, my sister married a worthless man, Peter's father, and all the boys of the marriage were cast in the same mould as him, but Peter it seems has turned out to be a better man than all the others put together. I can quite understand why Abe felt as he did at the time, he wasn't to know that there would be one good son amongst the brothers, or that I would necessarily choose him as my heir.'

Lizzie was still perplexed and spoke hesitatingly, 'Then what did he hope would happen when you died if you had no children of your own?'

At this Edward became alarmed. He had no desire to lie to her yet, on the other hand, he could hardly tell her the truth. He thought for a long moment, aware that she was waiting for an answer, until finally, and avoiding her gaze he said, 'It would still go to the Parish. I decided I didn't want that and so I did what Abe suggested I should do, and got married. Otherwise I was merely working the farm for other people. I did marry, and as my step-child you will inherit the farm—but not if you marry Peter!'

As if all was lost, Lizzie wistfully replied, 'I had this lovely dream that Peter would leave the Army and that we could all work together on the farm.'

'No, Lizzie, that would only bring disaster, and I would lose the farm. Besides, Peter isn't a farmer at all—he enjoys adventure too much. Perhaps when his days of travelling are over he may settle down, but at the moment he is too young to give up the life he loves.' Edward gazed fondly at Lizzie, pleased that at last she was listening sensibly to him. 'I know it must be difficult for you to understand the ways of adults, especially when the things they do have such far-reaching effects on other people. When I heard Abe's will I was devastated to realise that all I had worked for was in danger of being taken away from me unless I married.' He had said too much! Lizzie looked at him strangely and he knew that she was about to question him further.

'I don't understand?' she said, haltingly. 'Do you mean that Abe said you must marry? How could he even think to make such a demand?'

Everything suddenly came flooding back to him, the shock of Abe's death, his horror at the demands of the will and the total disintegration of his way of life in the months that followed. His tormented emotions must have been all too apparent on his face, for she paled and cried, 'Oh, Father, what's the matter, are you ill?'

'Child, child!' he cried out in anguish, without realising it. 'It is too painful for me to relate and you could not possibly understand my motives in doing what I did. In the end it all worked out well, and your mother and I, and you, were wonderfully happy. But had I known at the time the trouble my befriending Peter would cause, I would never have encouraged him to visit us so frequently.' He was trembling now, the depths of his anger at Abe rearing itself up once more after lying dormant for so many years. He sat there, emotionally and physically spent, wanting only to be alone now to calm his spirit. He was so far from the comfort of his valley, his one source of strength.

'What did you do that was so bad?' Lizzie whispered, disturbed and afraid of what she saw on his face, and the despondent droop of his shoulders. He had always been so strong and determined, now he seemed lost and vulnerable.

Edward strove to find a way of explaining his feelings without burdening her young mind with facts that would perhaps make her despise him. With a note of resignation in his voice he finally spoke, 'I'm not a bad man, Lizzie. All I ever wanted in life was the freedom to work the farm and roam my beloved moors. One day I was happy and contented, and I had a friend and employer with whom I shared my way of life, the next he was killed in an accident and my whole way of life was dramatically and totally changed. I'd never sought to hurt anybody, or anything, nor to have something which I hadn't earned with toil and sweat, then suddenly everything was to be taken from me unless I obeyed Abe's dreadful wishes. The farm was all-important to Abe! He must also have been a lonely man, never having had a wife or family, and he sought to make sure that I did not follow in his footsteps, by demanding that I should marry. If I did not, I lost the farm.' Edward said no more, praying that enough had been said already, for Hannah's sake.

'Did you love my mother?' Lizzie asked wistfully. 'Is that why we came to the farm in the first place?'

'I came to love your mother very much, and she me—I believe. At first we agreed to marry because she had been ill and you were both living in poverty, and yes, I wanted to keep the farm. It was a very sensible arrangement, then, after the flood, we learned to love each other. Now she is gone and I am alone without her!' He swallowed hard, his voice betraying the sadness he felt, and she noticed his hand trembled on his knee.

'And because of this I cannot marry Peter!' It was a statement of fact yet there was a ring of resentment in her voice.

'Do you think,' Edward said softly, 'that Peter's kindness to you has been misinterpreted? I have seen no sign to make me think he intends more than true friendship and cousinly affection. You were miserable and sought distraction, Peter tried to assist in relieving the boredom. Don't make him regret his kindness, or embarrass him, otherwise things will never be quite the same again between us all.' Lizzie looked helplessly at him, unsure and bewildered what to think. 'You have given Clara a hard time, Lizzie,' he went on, 'but she realises that you are young. For all our sakes make peace with her then come home with me.'

Lizzie's head hung dejectedly. They were a sorrowful pair. In former times she would have readily come to him for comfort but, as it was, the time spent away from each other had driven them apart. All he could do now was to share her unhappiness. For her the years ahead would bring their rewarding compensations, time would heal and memories fade, but in comparison his future was set. There was nothing to look forward to but uneventful hard work. One day Lizzie would marry and perhaps move away from home, a prospect he'd never seriously considered until now. If only she had been a boy whom he could have trained and instructed in the work of farming, or that he and Hannah had produced children of their own. This now could never be and, as a result, he would end up exactly as Abe had been, alone.

'Come, child!' he cried finally, trying to hide his own fears. 'We're a couple of lost souls at this moment. I have to go to meet Peter—and shall say nothing of our conversation. He will merely think you are homesick and want, quite naturally, to be at home. Tonight we will go to the Theatre, put on a brave face and try to enjoy ourselves.'

Lizzie nodded gloomily, accepting that it would probably be better to return home rather than risk humiliation and the sorrow of constantly being in Peter's company, knowing that he might discover her foolish adoration of him.

Edward was not entirely satisfied, and asked, 'One thing still puzzles me, why did Peter offer to find you your own accommodation here, and encourage you to stay?'

'I told him I wanted to stay and find work, but that I thought myself a burden on Clara. Peter said he knew someone who needed a companion for his daughters whilst he and his wife served in India; I would receive an allowance and free accommodation. Now, apparently, the daughters are to go to India with their parents after all and my services are no longer required.'

Edward received the news with relief. India was not a good place for English women, and Lizzie might have been tempted to go there with the girls. The Indian climate dried out their skins, whilst many also found army life tedious, it could also be unsafe with the occasional uprisings. Had Lizzie become a companion he could quite see her taking the opportunity to follow Peter there. Not wanting her to see his relief he merely nodded and said, 'I see. Well, you will eventually find something to interest yourself, and it will be up to us to discover what would please you when we return home.'

When Peter greeted Edward at the main entrance to Willems Barracks, Edward was pleased to have his mind diverted from his problems. After introducing him to his fellow officers, Peter proceeded to show him the more interesting parts of the Barracks. Eventually he took Edward to his quarters where he proudly produced several souvenirs of the Ashanti campaign. The gruesome twenty inch bayonet, with its sharp edge on one side and saw edge on the other for hacking a passage through undergrowth, seemed to have pride of place for Peter, beside his medal. The latter Edward examined with interest.

'Were you as close to the fighting as the embossed figures suggest on the back?' Edward asked, looking hard at the scene of hand-to-hand fighting, with the twisted figures, jungle growth and general carnage so much in evidence.

'Near enough!' Peter replied. 'We followed up at the rear—the heat and humidity was almost as bad as the actual fighting. Sometimes a white clammy mist would engulf us, almost entombing the men in the dense undergrowth as we waited, knowing that all the time the Ashanti were not far away.'

'That must have been eerie, even frightening!' Edward shivered at the thought.

Peter laughed, 'It made the back of my neck crawl at the time, I can tell you. The absolute silence was strange, almost as if the birds and animals waited, watching, knowing that all hell was about to break out. Then through the mist we saw them come!'

'You like the life though, don't you!' Edward stated, watching his nephew closely. 'Do you intend to stay in the Army while ever you can?'

'Without a doubt! In fact I wouldn't mind a spell in India, given the chance. One can grow old in this place without ever seeing real active service. There are some who have been content to stay the length of their service here—but that's not for me.'

'How would Clara take to the idea of India?'

Peter thought for a moment, 'Has Clara said anything?'

'Well, no!' Edward replied. 'It's just that you are about to be married and they say that English women don't wear too well out there, and are restricted by the culture and customs of the country.'

'Clara has doubts about India certainly, but it would be no fun for me to leave a wife back here, not with the activities that go on there amongst the Officer class.'

Edward let the question of India drop and announced that he and Lizzie were to return home the following day. If Peter had any strong feelings against Lizzie's return he concealed it well enough to set Edward's mind at rest regarding him. He spent an amicable afternoon with Peter, his tour culminating in a visit to the Prince Consort's Library which was filled with hundreds of books collected from the hospitals and recreation huts of the Crimea. The two men then separated in order to refresh themselves and prepare for the evening at the theatre.

As the small party entered the theatre later that evening, Edward felt conscious of his attire, which, although presentable enough, was rather conspicuous when observed amidst the smart dress uniforms of the young officers around him. It seemed also that on the arm of each man rested the hand of an equally resplendent young woman. Ah, to be so young and confident, he thought wistfully. Except for the brief period when Lydia entered his life, such activities had always been remote to him.

Peter took their outer garments to the cloakroom whilst Edward went to pay for the evening's entertainment. Although it was a chilly evening the party had chosen to walk the short distance through the streets to the theatre, rather than hail a cab. This had pleased Edward and, in particular, Clara, who sought to rid herself of the day-long smell of disinfectant at the hospital.

As Edward left the pay-desk he accidentally knocked into a lady by his side. He wasn't usually a clumsy man but he had misjudged the movement of the diminutive figure and almost sent her reeling into other patrons entering the foyer. For one heart-stopping moment he half expected Lydia to right herself and stand before him, so similar were they in stature and appearance.

'I do apologise,' he murmured quickly. 'It was very clumsy of me.' He was flustered by the thoughts which had entered his mind over the incident. It certainly wasn't Lydia but the shock of thinking that it might be caused the blood to drain from his face. He quickly composed himself, ensured that the lady was unharmed, then hurriedly joined his own party where they waited at the entrance to the small auditorium.

In a moment of privacy both Clara and Peter had remarked that something was sadly amiss with Lizzie. Now, on seeing Edward's pale, drawn face after such a trivial incident, Clara was filled with alarm. She needed no nursing experience to realise that Edward was deeply disturbed by something other than his slight mishap, and she resolved to keep an eye on him throughout the evening.

At first she was seated next to Peter but she contrived to change places with Lizzie on the pretext that, being the taller, it would be better if she sat behind the lady with the rather large hat, thus taking the seat next to Edward. Lizzie of course needed no persuading to move next to Peter and was somewhat mollified by his close proximity.

Although Edward laughed at the repartee between the two principals on stage, Clara sensed that he was preoccupied, so much so that, on one occasion when he failed to laugh with the audience, she glanced his way. The sight of his unhappy face immediately killed her own laughter and from that moment she spent the duration of the first half of the show worrying about him.

Edward was unaware of Clara's concern and sat there longing to be back in his own domain amongst the animals, those sane creatures who demanded nothing more than food and protection. The human animal he decided, exhausted the emotions far too much! He certainly had no strong feelings left regarding Lydia; it was simply that the strange moment in the foyer, coming so closely after his talk with Lizzie had recalled for him the heartache of the distant past. It had reminded him too of Hannah, of his initial misuse of her, and the knowledge that, as a result, he would feel remorse for those actions to the grave.

Clara was relieved when the curtain finally fell and she sought to lighten Edward's mood by directing her conversation to him in preference to Lizzie and Peter, who were engaged in light-hearted banter of their own. Peter suddenly offered to fetch them all a glass of wine, and he and Lizzie set off to find the bar, while Clara and Edward remained seated. This kindness on Clara's part was not lost on Edward who was grateful to be drawn out of himself, and before long he began to relax, forgetting his troubles completely. By the end of the evening he was almost sorry that he'd informed everyone of his intention to return home so soon. He was in no doubt that meeting Clara was the best thing that could have happened to Peter, and seeing Lizzie in a happier frame of mind convinced him that he was right; she would in time forget her infatuation and marry someone hopefully more suitable to his plans.

They walked back to Clara's house through poorly lit streets, reassured of their safety by the presence of an occasional military patrol which walked the town with their flickering lanterns, peering into the gloom for would-be trouble makers.

Once Peter had left the house to return to his quarters, Edward and Clara fell, much to Lizzie's despair, to discussing the merits of the writings of Thomas Hardy. At this she promptly retired to her bed.

'Would you care for a glass of wine?' Clara asked after Lizzie had gone. 'I'm afraid I'm much too awake to retire now. Fortunately I'm on a later duty tomorrow, so I will be able to please myself what I do in the morning.'

'A glass would be very pleasant, thank you!' Edward accepted, happy to be able to carry on with their discussion. 'I have always found Hardy to be a strange writer,' he confessed, 'rather sombre in fact, although they say his latest novel, *Far From the Madding Crowd*, is by far the best. Is that your opinion?'

'It has its moments of tragedy,' Clara agreed, handing him a glass and looking towards the bookcase where the novel was. 'As a farmer you would no doubt appreciate the husbandry in it, but whilst enjoying it, I do wish his characters could find a little happiness. So often it is as if he is exorcising some cruel streak in himself.'

Edward laughed. 'Is it that bad then? He certainly makes a meal of men's weaknesses and I suppose his work is much truer to life than one would expect in a novel. I prefer Dickens, who wrote about what he observed. He was part historian and part reformer in his own way, whereas Hardy seems to delight in creating characters aiming for self-destruction.'

'I actually prefer George Eliot myself,' Clara responded. 'But one needs to keep up with these newer writers. Do you find it difficult to obtain the latest literature, being as far from the town as you are?'

'We're not so far away from the town, but I dislike the crowded, noisy streets, and it's so dirty!' he sighed. 'Perhaps for Lizzie's sake I should take her there more often than I do. But what could I find there to satisfy a young girl?'

Clara smiled. 'I would rather like to see this valley of yours which Peter tells me so much about. I'm not a country person myself but I often long for peace and solitude, a place where nothing happens to stir one's tranquillity. Here there is always marching, noise and comings and goings.'

Edward chuckled to himself at her rather naive remark, for he knew that enough went on behind closed doors even in his remote part of the land, to sometimes disturb the peace she aspired to. He wondered also with some amusement, what Thomas Hardy would have made of his and Hannah's story. 'There are scandals enough even in the valley,' he said, trying to conceal a smile.

Clara, although oblivious to his inner amusement, saw a hint of it in his eyes and was deeply intrigued as to what prompted this extremely sober man to come to life. She too laughed inwardly, then wondered if she'd had one glass of wine too many. 'Believe me, there are all sorts of carryings on in a town of this sort,' she admitted, returning his smile. 'One gets used to it and is no longer surprised when something new happens.'

'You must see extremes of both gaiety and sorrow, and as a nurse you must often be disturbed by what you see. I was in Aldershot in '53 and '54, but there's not much I can remember now of the original town. I'm simply amazed at the changes that have taken place here. The first time I came there seemed to be a vast number of canvas tents and wooden huts, virtually growing out of the heather and gorse of the heathlands and fields. There was dust everywhere caused by the never-ending stream of heavy horse-drawn wagons and carts, and these were usually piled high with timber and yellow bricks to build the present barracks. There was hardly a tree in sight, but now the spaciousness of the layout, in spite of the extent of the development, beggars belief! The tree-lined roads and avenues, especially with the chestnut trees, look as though they have always been here!'

'It does seem hard to credit, doesn't it?' Clara responded with interest. 'But in which regiment did you serve? I don't remember you saying?'

'I wasn't in the Army. As a boy I used to help gather up horses for shipment from Portsmouth to the Crimea, but on my last voyage I became so ill that I was despatched home and lost my job as a result. I returned to Sheffield, where of course I had to find employment, and fortunately I was offered work on the farm that is now mine. It's a long story, however, so I won't bore you with what has transpired over the years.'

'My father was a surgeon in the Crimea,' she exclaimed. 'Who knows, you may have even sailed on the same ship together!'

'Possibly! I made several voyages, but I doubt if your father would have noticed a mere stableboy. The experience, however, was one which I have no desire to repeat. What happened to your father?'

There was a sad look on Clara's face as she told him of her father's death in India. 'Cholera is always prevalent in hot climates, especially where sanitation is poor. Obviously, as a surgeon, he was exposed to all manner of diseases, and in one outbreak he too succumbed. My mother and I returned to this house which Father had purchased before leaving Aldershot, then mother died a couple of years ago and is buried here in the town. I rented out the house whilst I trained at St Thomas' Hospital in London, and I am, I believe, very fortunate to be as independent as I am. Now Peter wishes to serve in India, but I have no intention of ever again setting foot in the land where my poor father lies,' she said resolutely.

'Where then does that leave you and Peter? He could be in India for years!' He paused, aware that he had no right to ask such questions but he felt sorry for her and had merely been responding to her forthright comment. He apologised, asking, 'Perhaps it is impolite of me to put such a question to you?'

She shook her head. 'It is of no consequence, and I have no one else to discuss the matter with. You may as well know that I have told him emphatically that I shall not accompany him, even if it means our not marrying.' She seemed suddenly to regret having confided in him, for she said, 'I hope you will not tell Peter of this conversation, I'm afraid he is far from pleased at my decision.'

Edward shook his head sympathetically. 'My nephew is still young and adventurous, however I do not blame you for refusing to go, I'm told the conditions there can be appalling.'

Clara studied Edward appraisingly. 'For a man who lives in isolation you are well informed about many things. How does one acquire such knowledge in remote area such as yours?'

Edward smiled, not at all offended by her curiosity. 'I had a well-educated employer who became my friend and mentor, and it was he who instilled in me the desire to increase my knowledge. I read a great deal throughout the long winter evenings, and of course have newspapers brought out to the village on a regular basis. It is I who isolate myself, not the village that is so isolated. We are certainly small in number and out in the wilds, but the Parish is one of the largest in the county and all the administration is done from Bradfield.'

Considering his remarks for a moment, Clara then commented, 'I do not condemn you for enjoying your own company more than that of others, except that it seems a pity for Lizzie's sake. Aldershot is not a place of great culture or interest and I would not like to see her wasted here in such an artificial environment.'

'Then what am I to do if I am to satisfy her needs?' pleaded Edward hoping that, as a woman, Clara could solve the problem.

'Alas,' she replied, 'I am powerless to advise you, other than to suggest that by some means or other you must take her out into society so that she can adjust her life before it is too late. Is it possible that she could train in nursing? She has been with me to the hospital here and has shown great interest in the work we do. The pity of it is that if only we lived nearer to each other I could have done something to help. Believe me, she behaves no differently to many other young women of her age, be assured of that.'

This statement warmed Edward's heart, filling him with hope, and he noted again the compassion in her voice as she addressed him. Her fine, grey, intelligent eyes met his, and she smiled encouragingly.

Before he could reply, she added softly, 'Isolation is not a good thing for anyone, you know. Perhaps you yourself fear the closeness of others, thinking that in some way they will impinge on your precious, private feelings. It is never good to bottle up one's finer emotions, and I have observed in the bravest, that the release of their emotions gives comfort of a kind. Lizzie is immature, so tell her that you care for her as much as when she was a child—it may help.'

If you only knew a few of the heartaches which we both hide thought Edward. He sighed without realising it, a sigh so deep that Clara pitied him. He marvelled at the wisdom of one so young and knew that as a nurse she must be capable of giving great comfort to those unfortunates in her care. Without knowing why, he found himself saying, 'I would that I could show you the beauty of my valley. You have the power to understand and would receive great solace from that fine, proud landscape.' He knew that his eyes were moist and turned his head so that she wouldn't see how moved he was.

They sat for a while, enjoying their quiet companionship until the clock chimed, breaking the silence of the room. 'How thoughtless of me!' he exclaimed, suddenly. 'It's one o'clock in the morning and you must be exhausted. Do forgive me!' He rose from the chair and continued. 'I have poured out my problems and you have done me the kindness of listening. I envy Peter his choice of bride—had I been a younger man,' he said with a smile on his face, 'I would challenge my nephew for your affections.' His voice, although full of humour was nevertheless sincere, and his eyes twinkled kindly at her.

Clara laughed playfully. 'I think we have both had a glass of wine too many—however, I accept your compliments with gratitude.'

Edward hesitated in the doorway before leaving the room and was loath to leave her pleasant company but, it was late, so, as she awaited his departure, he said, 'I intend to make an early start tomorrow with Lizzie, as you know, and hope to catch a train to London as soon as possible. I must therefore express my thanks now, as I am most grateful for the way you have tolerated my step-daughter, and I will strive to take heed of your suggestions regarding her welfare. I'm afraid I have occupied a great deal of your time in the past few days, and I shall certainly miss our discussions. I hope that Peter will bring you to stay with us, perhaps in the spring, which unfortunately comes a little later to the hills of the North. You would enjoy the lambing season, even though it is one of the busiest times of the year. Not that it would matter, you would still be welcome.'

'I shall look forward to it very much,' Clara declared a little hesitantly, almost as though she wasn't sure of what the future held. 'It would indeed be sad for us not to meet again.' At that Edward bade her goodnight and went thoughtfully to bed.

The following morning he rose early and set off for the station to find a hansom cab which he required should call at the house for nine o'clock to deliver him and Lizzie back to the station for 9.30.

Edward had few belongings to pack, whilst Lizzie on the other hand had so much that when Edward returned he found Clara sitting on Lizzie's trunk trying to force it shut. Promptly at 9 am the cab arrived, and it was with a twinge of regret that he lifted the trunk down the stairs to the front door. Lizzie was quiet and withdrawn, not sullen as he'd expected her to be, and he squeezed her hand kindly. 'We'll stop in London tonight, how about that? Would you like to see St Paul's and London Bridge?'

In spite of herself, Lizzie's eyes brightened, and he vowed to heed Clara's words of wisdom before it was too late. He looked at Clara, who smiled approvingly, and he shook her hand warmly, hoping their paths would indeed cross again. With some reluctance he climbed into the cab and waved goodbye.

Alighting at the station, Edward called a porter to assist with the trunk and heard Lizzie give a little gasp of pleasure, as Peter came briskly out of the station entrance to meet them.

'Good morning, both of you! I've just been able to snatch a few minutes to see you off—I wasn't sure last night if I could be free at this time.' So saying, he escorted them to the platform and when their train came in quickly saw them comfortably settled.

As the train slowly departed Peter blew Lizzie a quick kiss, and Edward commented as he saw her bravely brush a tear from her eye. 'He'll always be your cousin, Lizzie, no matter what!' With that they waved back at Peter until he could no longer be seen from the train.

At Waterloo Station Edward enquired at the booking office for reasonable lodgings, and an obliging cab-driver soon delivered them to a small but clean-looking house not far from the river. Lizzie was keen to take a closer look at the Thames, and it wasn't long before they were able to leave their lodgings and join the bustle of carts and wagons on the manure-strewn street outside. Traffic was heavy and the pavements crowded at this time, and Edward drew little pleasure from this and the cold December weather. The river, when they reached it, lay half concealed by a blanket of mist, and they shivered, drawing their coats closer around their bodies. Lizzie had never seen a river of such great proportions before, and she was surprised by the sight of so many boats, barges and lighters, and surprised even more by the filthiness of the water itself.

'Not a pleasant stretch of water!' Edward declared. 'Interesting maybe, but verging on the disgusting.'

They watched the comings and goings of the many different vessels, all making their way in and out of the numerous jetties, loading and unloading a wide variety of cargo. Compared with the clear, dancing rivers of Bradfield and Loxley this murky waterway appeared evil in the patchy mist that lay on it.

Eventually, tiring of the activity on the river, they wound their way towards St Paul's Cathedral, climbed the steps and entered the church where they stood in amazement at the vast splendour of it all. Neither had ever been in a building such as this, and the hollow ringing of their footsteps disturbed the peace within the hallowed sanctuary. Once their appetite for its quiet solemnity was satisfied, and to satisfy Lizzie's curiosity, they left and walked on to Ludgate and Chancery Lane which Edward had read of in Dickens' novels. They then went to Covent Garden which, to their disappointment, was almost deserted due to the lateness of the day. So, eventually tiring of the many new sights which had met their eyes, they found an eating house where they sank gratefully onto chairs, and allowed the warmth from a blazing fire to creep into their chilled bones.

'That's better,' Edward said, once he'd eaten, and looking through the small panes of the window noticed how dark it had become outside. 'It's almost dark, and I think it would be safer if we took a cab back to the house.'

By the time they arrived at their lodgings Edward was appalled to see how the fog, which earlier had been only a mist, was beginning to thicken and envelop everything around them. When he woke next morning he couldn't even see the buildings across the road from his window. There would be no point in their staying in London in these conditions, so later, and with great difficulty, he eventually found a cab to make the hazardous journey through the fog to the station. He marvelled at the skill shown by the driver, who assured him that such weather was a common occurrence in the capital, and that if one did not succumb to chest complaints then a living still had to be earned in spite of the conditions.

Lizzie was greatly disappointed not to have seen more of London, but admitted that she found the fog almost frightening. She blew her nose as they waited on the platform for the train to arrive and couldn't believe how soiled her handkerchief was as a result.

'Next year, Lizzie, in the summer, I'll bring you back so that we can see the parks and the Palace,' Edward promised. He was as disappointed as Lizzie not to have seen the many other places about which he'd only read in the past. He coughed, the dampness and acrid smell irritating his nose and throat. 'To think that people live here all their lives, in a place where fog is a persistent nuisance. I thought Sheffield was bad enough but this atmosphere is indeed a killer. I shall not be sorry to return home and get some fresh air into my lungs. We're very fortunate living where we do, just imagine the dirt which the prevailing winds carry north-eastwards from Sheffield towards Rotherham.'

Nodding in agreement, Lizzie pressed her lips together, trying not to speak for fear of inhaling the dirt. It was a great pity that the weather had shortened her first visit to London, but she hoped they would indeed return and had every intention of keeping her father to his promise.

All trains were delayed due to the fog, and it was with considerable relief that eventually they climbed into their carriage and secured good seats. The journey had hardly begun when the sound of a muffled explosion disturbed them, and the train immediately began to shudder and jolt violently, before finally screeching to a halt throwing some of the passengers forward and onto the laps of those opposite.

When the noise and confusion had abated, and realising that the worst had passed, Edward dragged himself to his feet and reached out for Lizzie, lifting her gently back onto her seat. He was anxious and feared that she might have been injured in some way. However, although dishevelled and white-faced, Lizzie appeared unharmed. Once reassured of this, Edward went to the window and peered out into the dense fog, but was unable to see anything further along the line beyond the next carriage. He turned nervously to one of the men who shared the carriage with them, and who had risen from the floor at the same time as himself.

'Do you think that anyone has been killed?' he questioned, although he doubted that the man would know any more than he did.

'It's not a crash,' the man replied with authority, 'certainly not with this train. I travel this route quite often and am able to recognise certain happenings. There was a muffled explosion you may recall, just before we started to pull up. That was a detonator put on the line by a guard to warn our driver that there is a problem ahead, perhaps there is another train delayed on our line. All we can do is sit and wait. Now, close that window to keep us warm and shut out the fog.'

'Does this happen often?' Edward asked, sitting down beside Lizzie and noting how drawn she looked. She reminded him of Hannah as he'd seen her on their first meeting, so long ago, in Lipton Street. 'Are you sure you're alright?' he asked quietly and with such tenderness in his voice that she promptly burst into tears and threw herself into his arms, sobbing like a child.

'Oh, Lizzie,' he cried, holding her against himself to protect her, not just from the shock of the incident but because he knew that much more lay beneath it all. When Hannah died, Lizzie had said little, although it was obvious she pined for her mother, and she had never shed a tear in his presence. The evidence had been there however, when she'd appeared from some corner or another, with streaks down her cheeks. She'd transferred her devotion to him completely afterwards, staying close to him, holding his hand, and had even taken to climbing into his bed in the middle of the night. It had been this habit which had been hardest to break and was the main cause of him sending her away to school. She was, after all, becoming a young woman and beyond his knowledge and understanding. Oh, how he too missed Hannah! 'Don't be afraid to cry, Lizzie!' he whispered, his voice full of emotion. Hannah had changed his life so that he could no longer be independent of other human beings. He stifled his own emotions, aware that their travelling companions were watching them, partly from bewilderment and partly from embarrassment at the open display of affection confronting them. Edward forced himself to get a grip on his thoughts and sought to explain.

'My daughter,' he said, speaking across the carriage, 'is shocked and has suffered much of late, I'm afraid she is a little overwhelmed.'

'Ah, that is a great pity!' the man opposite replied, relieved to be able to resume a normal sitting position, for he'd twisted round to stare into the gloom out of good manners, yet seen nothing outside but fog.

Edward repeated his earlier question, 'Does this happen often?'

'I'm afraid it does, in these conditions,' the man replied.

'Should we go out and see if there is anything we can do?'

'No! That would be extremely dangerous!' The man's voice was emphatic. 'Any trouble will be much further up the line, and we were warned to stop before we could approach it. A man once stepped out of a carriage in the fog and fell from a parapet to his death. He was, of course, on a viaduct and not a station platform.'

At this Lizzie sobbed again and clung even more to Edward for comfort. Strangely enough Edward was relieved by her desperate need of him. Her renewed trust was lessening the barrier which had grown between them.

He left his arm round her shoulder and chatted amicably with the other passengers, then suddenly realised that Lizzie was asleep. After what seemed an eternity the train shuddered forward slowly and resumed its way along the track. By the time Lizzie stirred the outskirts of London were left far behind and the sky could be seen clearly through the window of the carriage. For the remaining hours of the journey they talked companionably while watching endless rows of leafless skeleton-like trees and tiny hamlets pass by. In the early evening, tired and shaken by the long journey, they finally arrived back in Sheffield; there now remained the journey out to Bradfield! If, at this point, Lizzie had not had her fill of travelling, Edward certainly had. He threw all prudence to the wind and directed a cab to take them to the *Angel*, where he booked a pair of rooms. Desperate though he was to get home, he refused to travel any further.

The day had been a wearying one for Lizzie, who was by now exhausted from the long and tedious journey. So, after having eaten one of the inns' long celebrated beefsteak dinners, she left Edward and went to her room. Reflecting on the strange events of the past few days, she began to remove her clothing and stared in disbelief and annoyance at her white under garments which were now almost grey from the effect of the fog.

Although she was loath to admit it, she was quite looking forward to rising early the following morning, as her father had planned, in order to reach home as soon as possible. With Christmas only three weeks away, life in the village was always more enjoyable, even magical at this time of year, then spring would follow and winter would be once more forgotten. With these thoughts she quickly fell into a deep, contented sleep.

Chapter 10

Christmas came and went very quickly and Edward had little opportunity to venture far from the valley due to the inclement weather. This didn't worry Lizzie too much as she had taken to writing a daily journal which she illustrated with drawings, and she also wrote regularly to Peter and Clara. As their replies came Edward marvelled at Lizzie's fortitude in the aftermath of her great disappointment, and this he put down to youthful resilience.

He happily read the letters that arrived, enjoying Peter's dry sense of humour, although he never read those Lizzie wrote to him. In fact he quite looked forward to Clara's with her clear positive thoughts, and was almost tempted to reply to these personally, but thought better of it and sent messages via Lizzie instead. He could hardly take up correspondence with his nephew's future bride.

One morning, towards the end of February, Lizzie found him gloomily staring out of the sitting-room window. At first he seemed unaware of her presence, then instinctively he felt that he was being observed and, in turning, realised that she was watching him.

'Is there something wrong?' she asked, glancing at the note in his hand.

Edward let the letter fall onto the window ledge with resignation, 'My sister is seriously ill and may not have long to live.' There was a note of despair in his voice.

Lizzie could see that this news had hit him hard. 'Oh, I am sorry,' she said, comfortingly. 'Will you go to see her before it's too late?' She had only ever met her aunt Betty once or twice, although she had been told of her poor situation by both Edward and Peter, but what she remembered of her brought to mind a rather down-trodden little body.

'I must,' Edward replied. 'Though what my reception will be like I hate to think. At least one of my nephews has had the decency to inform me of her condition before it's too late.'

'Would you like me to come with you?' Lizzie asked, feeling powerless to offer anything more constructive to ease the pain.

'No,' Edward shook his head. 'It's best I go alone. You can help me more by looking after things here. It will only take me an hour and a half to ride over there, and if I go now I can be back before dark.'

'Will you be alright?' Lizzie asked, her face full of concern. 'It's a long way there and back.'

'I know,' he said sadly, 'that's why I intend to go alone, then I can ride harder.'

Saddling a horse, Edward set off, praying that the respite in the weather would hold until his return.

To Lizzie there was more than a pang of sadness at Edward's news for she knew that Peter was very fond of his mother, in spite of his long absences. He was her one pride, and in this she took her joy by allowing him to live a life far more fulfilling than it would have been if he'd remained permanently at her side.

The roads and ancient tracks on which Edward travelled crossed some of the finest countryside on the borders of the two counties of Yorkshire and Derbyshire. Wild moorland, the magnificent crags of Stanage Edge and the fertile green valleys were places which, under normal circumstances, would have caused him to stop and gaze in awe, places where time itself seemed to stand still. Today, however, his thoughts were scattered in many diverse directions, and memories of his childhood came flooding back. He and Betty had been close then, so close that in the end as they got older he resented her following him wherever he went, particularly when he needed to be alone. She'd been a bit like Lizzie in her attachment to him, but he would have defended her with his life. Then one day she had allowed herself to be flattered and eventually debauched by the man she had to marry.

Edward felt bitter as he approached the stone cottage in Bamford where she had existed in poverty for so long. He went up to the door and knocked. His brother-in-law opened the door, 'You'd best go up,' he muttered absent-mindedly, for once in his life forgetting to sneer at Edward. He looked drawn and subdued, older in countenance than Edward had ever seen him. Perhaps only now, when it was almost too late, did he realise the value of the good woman who lay dying in his bed.

Entering the bedroom, Edward saw his sister's small ashen face on the pillow, and realised that she was too ill to greet him. Betty could do no more than raise a hand a fraction from the bed and beckon him to her. Edward recognised two of his nephews who were also in the room, and acknowledged them with a nod, then took Betty's hand tenderly in his own and squeezed it gently. At this a weak smile touched her lips and she tried to speak to him. He bent his head and listened intently. In a low, barely audible voice he heard her say, 'Take care of Peter, for my sake!'

'You know I will,' he answered with a choked voice. 'Have no worries about that.' He stayed for an hour, exchanging few words with the other occupants of the room, simply keeping a silent vigil beside his sister's bed, until he knew he must leave if he were to travel home safely. He bent and kissed Betty gently on her forehead, and whispered, 'Good night'.

'Let me know when she's gone,' he asked quietly, knowing that he would never see Betty again, as she would probably be dead before the night was through.

As he left the cottage, his brother-in-law followed and Edward sighed inwardly, anticipating his usual caustic and harsh words. 'Thank you for coming,' the man said, gruffly. 'It was what she wanted.'

'Have you let Peter know?' Edward asked, relieved at this change of attitude.

'The Parson sent a telegraph message to him yesterday, but it'll be too late.'

Edward nodded, sadly. 'Don't bury her until he gets here—at least do that for her sake.'

During the twenty-four hours that followed Edward waited anxiously for news of Betty, and presumed rather sadly that she had died without anyone informing him of the fact. He acknowledged that in order to bring him a message someone would have to travel a considerable journey on foot, not a task any of his nephews would willingly undertake on his behalf.

'If I hear nothing today,' he vowed to Lizzie, 'I will go in the morning and satisfy myself on the matter. I suppose it is possible that she could have rallied a little, although I know that's unlikely.' He didn't know quite what to think! If Betty was in pain and things were only getting worse then she would be better off leaving them, but whilst she lived there was hope, of a sort.

He had just closed the barn doors prior to returning to the house when Bella began to bark loudly. It was dusk and Edward could neither hear nor see anything unusual, yet the dog continued to give the alarm. 'Do be quiet, Bella!' he shouted, straining his ears above the racket. It wasn't long before he heard a carriage coming down the lane, and saw its lanterns flickering as the wheels hit pot-holes in the rough stony surface. Strange, he thought, for anyone to come visiting at this hour, and it was not a carriage he recognised as it halted before the house gate.

Edward hurried forward and then saw Peter alighting a little stiffly, in the gloom. 'Peter!' he called out in surprise, then remembered that his nephew had come in response to the news of his mother's condition. 'Have you seen your mother?' Edward asked anxiously. 'What news have you?'

'None, Uncle, not yet! I aim to go first thing in the morning. It was too late to go home directly as I have Clara with me and we would have had nowhere to sleep. I couldn't take her to stay there!' He turned to help Clara climb down from the carriage. 'You have no news then?' he called back to Edward.

'Not since yesterday, I'm afraid. I was thinking of going over tomorrow, but now we can go together,' Edward replied, observing Clara with a feeling of pleasure and moving forward to greet her.

Meanwhile the driver had lifted down a valise and a small travelling trunk, then called out to Peter, 'I'd be much obliged if you'd square up with me, Sir! Then I can head back to town whilst there is still a little light left.'

'Why, of course!' Peter replied, leaving Clara in Edward's capable hands. 'What do I owe you?'

Clara's smile was sincere and friendly but held a hint of tiredness which was not lost on Edward. 'You must have had a very tedious journey, my dear. Let's get you into the house where it is warm,' he said, leading her along the path towards the door which suddenly opened and threw a shaft of light in their direction, making all around even darker. It was Lizzie who, hearing voices outside, had come to investigate. 'We have visitors, Lizzie,' he called. 'It's Peter and Clara.'

For a moment Lizzie stood looking at Clara in disbelief, then with a broad smile on her face, hugged her in genuine friendliness before peering further in search of Peter.

Having paid off the driver, Peter waited as the carriage swung round in the yard for its return journey, then picked up the valise intending to collect the trunk later. At that moment Lizzie ran down the path with youthful enthusiasm and threw her arms around him. Peter, to his credit, laughed playfully at her simple gesture and almost dropped the bag, then teasingly led her to the house, his arm still around her waist. Seeing this Edward immediately read more into the situation than was intended, due mainly to the joy which radiated from Lizzie's face, and he glanced towards Clara. If she saw anything untoward she concealed it well, although as the evening wore on Edward sensed a coolness between the couple that had not been there in Aldershot.

Since his visit to Clara's house, Edward had thought long and hard and, in spite of the constant exchange of letters, he knew that something was amiss, so he never expected to ever welcome Clara into his home. Once they had eaten and she'd rested, and in order to give her a little exercise after many hours of physical inactivity, he showed her round the house, explaining the extent of the alterations he'd made after the flood. It pleased him to hear her favourable comments and he looked forward to revealing to her the wonders of his beloved valley, if time and weather permitted.

At first light next morning Edward and Peter left the farm, intending to reach his sister's home as soon as possible. It was a bright, crisp morning but, where water had settled into ruts in the road, ice had formed, making the journey both hazardous and lengthy. Peter, as a younger man, was inclined to ride swiftly without fear, whilst Edward, ever cautious, was less willing to rush. One bad slip on the ice and the horse could fall, causing all manner of injury and problems. 'You go ahead,' Edward suggested at one point. 'You can warn them that I am on my way.'

'No, I'll stay with you, at least until we reach the more populated areas,' Peter insisted, although he found the slower pace irksome.

Their journey took much longer than Edward's previous one, however, they reached the house safely and Edward then hesitated. 'You go in Peter, she's your mother. I'll wait until someone fetches me.'

Peter nodded gravely, handed his reins to his uncle and went to the door not knowing what to expect. He knocked lightly so as not to disturb his mother and entered the house, noting as he did the abnormal stillness about the place. He called out softly to attract someone's attention just as his brother Bill appeared at the head of the stairs. There was little love lost between the two; it was the woman who lay dying that bound them together, and once she was gone Peter knew there would be nothing left to draw him back again.

'Is mother still alive,' he asked quietly. 'Or am I too late?'

Bill muttered something which Peter missed, then he said in a louder voice, 'She's still with us, just. Once she knew we'd sent for you she seemed calmer, that's probably what's keeping her alive.' Peter sensed a touch of resentment in his brother's voice but sought no trouble. He wanted to see his mother before it was too late and then would leave the house for good.

After a while, Edward, who was waiting patiently outside, stamped his feet on the frosty ground to warm up and wondered what to do. If he was not going to be invited into the house he might as well go to the local inn where he could wait in comfort. However, if he did no one would know where he was! He looked at his pocket watch and decided to wait five more minutes before riding off, in the hopes that Peter would remember him, in spite of his distress.

He'd no sooner replaced the watch than the door opened to reveal his brother-in-law who, with an unusually sober face, came up to him and with a sigh of resignation said, 'You'd best come in, I think she's only been hanging on to see Peter.'

To this Edward replied, amicably, 'I'm just pleased that he's arrived in time. Yes, I will come in out of the cold if you don't mind.' Tying up the horses he followed the man into the rather shabby living room which, to Betty's credit, even though untidy was clean in spite of the fact that she'd been ill for some time.

'I suppose you could do with a hot drink,' his brother-in-law said flatly, getting an old jam pot from a shelf in which to give Edward some tea. 'I don't know where her best cup is,' he said, indicating the ceiling above which his wife lay in bed. 'You'll have to take it as it comes.'

'How long has Betty been ill?' Edward asked, accepting the stone jar of tea whilst at the same time endeavouring to make conversation with a man whom he'd never liked.

'On and off for a couple of months now. The Doctor says it's stomach cancer and you know what that means.' Edward nodded sadly. 'We've never got on you and I,' the man said suddenly. 'Nor do I expect we ever will, but for her sake I'll not be mean at this time. You've done well by Peter, even if you've encouraged him in his fancy ways.'

'You can justly be proud of him, he'll never want in life, he's not the type. I only helped because I recognised in him something worth encouraging—he achieved the rest by himself.'

The door opened slowly and Peter entered. 'Mother's gone,' he announced with a tremble in his voice. 'It's all over.' He looked sadly round the room seeing not the present, but only the memories of a tender, caring mother. He took a seat without saying more, for words were meaningless when his loss was so great.

Edward's heart sank too, at the news. In his present surroundings he could neither give nor take comfort as he would have had he been alone with Peter. Each man mourned Betty's passing in his own way without knowing the depths of the other's feelings, but Edward took comfort in seeing tears in his brother-in-law's eyes. Yes, he thought, when the nights are long and you are alone, then you will realise just what you have lost in my sister. It was Peter he pitied most because Betty had been the lad's only champion in that unruly household.

The door opened once more as the Parson, followed by Peter's brothers, entered the room. 'Someone will have to tell our Nat,' one of them said, and Edward remembered that there was one brother missing. After offering words of comfort, the churchman agreed to the burial taking place the following afternoon, thus allowing Edward and Peter to arrive with Lizzie and Clara in the trap. The journey would take considerably longer with them and would be far from comfortable.

At last, taking leave of the assembled group, the two men slowly made their way home, sometimes riding in silence, at others discussing the fragility of mankind, but at all times aware of a deep sense of loss.

To Clara the visit to the farm was both exciting and unexpected. Her heart had gone out to Peter when he'd informed her that his mother was dying and consequently when he'd asked her to accompany him on his journey she felt compelled to do so. Her absence from the hospital would result in others having to work that much harder, she knew, but she was a hard worker and rarely took time off, so she didn't feel too bad about it. Once on the journey, she found herself looking forward to seeing Lizzie and Edward again, and to seeing the valley which they had all spoken of with such affection.

She was not disappointed at what she saw, for, as Lizzie pointed out, the weather was uncommonly fine for the time of year, thus the valley proved a sight to behold. Edward had warned her that spring arrived much later in the north, even so she was surprised by the sharpness of the air compared with that of the south. To see bare and thorny bushes glistening with frost in the bright sunlight made her shiver, albeit with a feeling of pleasure at nature's artistry.

The valley was indeed all that they'd told her it would be, the stillness like balm to the soul. Clara drew Hannah's old chair up to the bedroom window, and for some long time she looked out from that same window that had given Hannah her first glimpse of the hills. It was strangely peaceful in the room and for some reason she did not feel really alone as she waited for the men to return. At one point she felt the need to reach out as though to touch something, someone. Nothing happened, there was no one there, yet she did not feel foolish at what she'd wanted to do. Something stirred within her and she then found herself gently touching the neatly-sewn quilt on the bed. It was so beautifully done, so patiently sewn by someone whom she felt drawn to in spirit. It was Hannah's quilt.

When finally she saw Edward and Peter coming home, Clara did not immediately rise from the chair for fear of breaking the spell of contentment around her. However, she was drained by what she had experienced in the room and was moved almost to tears.

On rising the following morning, Edward found the weather to be appalling, and far worse than he'd known in late February for years. It was as if heaven itself was shedding tears for Betty, and obvious that the funeral party would be both wet and miserable long before they reached Bamford. There was nothing else to be done other than to hire a covered carriage and driver from the local blacksmith, set off, and then find shelter at the *Angler's Inn* when they got there. Edward was bitterly disappointed that the rainfall continued so relentlessly, thus increasing the sadness and gloom within the carriage. He supposed this was more appropriate under the circumstances, but it would have been such a pleasure to point out to Clara the outstanding beauty of the area. Instead she might assume that he lived amongst the dreariest of landscapes. He pitied their poor driver who drove them along the muddy tracks, almost hidden beneath his waterproof cape and apron for protection against the rain.

Finally, and much to everyone's relief they reached the village and drew up before the inn, where they hoped a warm fire and a friendly landlord would welcome them.

Not only did they find the inn open, but a considerable number of men were gathered inside, presumably because the weather prevented them from working in the fields. Having made sure that his companions were comfortable, Peter felt obliged to go to his home where his father would no doubt be expecting him.

Edward stayed with the ladies and as they enjoyed a very welcome cooked meal he explained sorrowfully, 'I'm afraid we have a further two miles to go. Betty is to be buried in Hathersage with my mother and father, where there is room in the grave.' As he spoke he noticed a man in his early thirties watching them with considerable interest. There was something familiar about his attitude which mildly irritated Edward, and he took a dislike to the man, even though he didn't know why.

Continuing his meal, Edward took no further notice of the inquisitive stranger and carried on eating and talking as if there was nothing untoward. Much to his surprise and annoyance however, the man came forward and addressed him in an almost insolent manner.

'You don't know me, do you?' the man said, amused by Edward's obvious irritation at his rudeness.

'No!' Edward replied bluntly. 'Should I?'

'One would think so be'in as 'ow I'm Peter's brother!'

At that Edward bristled, and was annoyed with himself for not realising where he'd seen the fellow before. 'I thought you'd be back at home with your father, instead of drinking in here.' He was in turn being rude, but he couldn't help himself. 'I suppose you must be Nathan?'

'That I am,' came the fellow's arrogant reply, then he turned directly to Lizzie and Clara, anticipating an introduction to the pair. This Edward did with great reluctance, having heard of the man's womanising reputation in the past, and before he knew it Nathan was addressing himself to them both.

Edward was well aware of Clara's gaze on him and realised that she would not know why he was both blunt and annoyed with his nephew. Not wanting her to see him in a bad light he suppressed his intense dislike of the man and tried to keep a civil tongue. Betty had suffered much at the hands of this son, so much so that Edward had avoided all contact with him in the past. Admittedly he was a handsome fellow, although coarse, and with little regard for the feelings of others.

Nathan took Clara's hand. 'So you're to marry Peter, are you?' he said, acknowledging her with a nod, before turning his attention to Lizzie. 'Ah, little cousin Lizzie. It's a pity uncle Edward's kept you hidden for so long.' Lizzie blushed as he held her hand over long.

Edward seethed inwardly. This was the day of his sister's funeral and here was her son almost flirting with a stranger. There was nothing he could do about it; the sooner the funeral was over and he could get home the better, as would be his temper and peace of mind.

Several minutes later, after making a few banal comments, Nat left to join his friends, thereafter he seemed to be eyeing Lizzie with great interest. It was, therefore, a relief to the three of them when the time came to leave the inn and proceed to Betty's house, where Edward was pleased to see that her sons had at least hired a suitable carriage for the immediate family. The money however, would have been better spent during Betty's lifetime making things easier for her, he thought, rather than now when it was too late. He could quite understand Abe's viewpoint regarding the legacy, but wondered also what Clara's assessment had been of her future brother-in-law. Perhaps, knowing Peter, she would now understand just why he had brought her to Edward's farm to stay rather than to his family home.

Fortunately during the journey to the graveyard, which was on the hillside, and throughout the committal, there was no call for social conversation amongst the mourners, other than brief introductions. Only later, on their return to Bamford, was it impossible to avoid such contact. Indeed Peter could hardly refuse to go into the house and, because he had travelled inside the carriage with Edward and the ladies instead of on horseback, they were unable to return to Bradfield ahead of him. To sit outside the house waiting for Peter would have been both cold and uncomfortable, so Edward, Clara and Lizzie were, after all, obliged to go inside and join the other mourners. The older villagers stood or sat on the fringes whilst the younger men-folk supped ale as though Betty were still sleeping upstairs. This behaviour was not to Edward's liking but there was nothing he could do that would change the established pattern of these events.

Peter, sensing Edward's discomfort and being also somewhat embarrassed for Clara and Lizzie, came up to Edward and said quietly, 'I won't be long. Give me ten minutes then I'll make the state of the weather as our excuse, and we'll leave. I'm taking a drink out to the driver, poor fellow, but fortunately he can shelter in the carriage.'

Having little choice but to wait, Edward felt he ought to say a few words of condolence to his brother-in-law, and so left the two ladies talking to each other. No sooner had he left their side than Nathan moved closer to them.

'I'm sorry about your mother,' Clara said sympathetically. 'I wish that I had met her.'

He seemed of a more sober disposition than he had earlier and replied, 'She was a good sort, our mother! You'd have liked her, lass. You too,' he said, directly at Lizzie. If his manner at the inn had been a direct result of Edward's irritation, it would explain why he was now attempting to appear in a more gracious light to the ladies. 'I hope we'll meet again, once young Peter and you are wed. When is that to be, then?' His question was almost offensive.

Clara flushed slightly, taken aback by his ill-mannered attitude. 'We haven't decided,' she stated lamely, suddenly wishing that Edward would hurry back.

Apparently without noticing Clara's discomfort, he turned his attention to Lizzie, appraising her rather boldly as he said, 'No wonder Peter preferred to stay with Uncle Edward instead of us, he's certainly got an eye for a pretty face.'

She knew that he was being over-familiar. But why? She hadn't given him any reason to be so forward, nor did she even like him. Her face reflected her thoughts as she was too inexperienced to disguise them, the result being that Nathan, who enjoyed nothing more than a challenge, was determined to continue with his teasing.

He bent his head and spoke softly so that only she could hear him, 'I may come riding over your way next week. You watch out for me!'

Lizzie shrank back in dismay, not realising that he spoke in jest, and her face paled when she thought what her father would do if this objectionable man came to the farm seeking her. After his warning to her about the family, he would think she had encouraged him! She wished he would go away and turned with wide, staring eyes to Clara, who was now in conversation with an elderly gentleman seated next to her.

Across the room, Peter, who had been attempting to extract himself from a lengthy discussion, saw the look on Lizzie's face and immediately suspected that his brother had been up to his old tricks again. 'You must excuse me but I hadn't realised the time,' he explained hastily, caring little whether the man understood or not. 'We must go now if we're to get back to Bradfield safely before nightfall.'

What followed next left Clara quite shaken and bewildered. Having seen the frightened look on Lizzie's face, she was about to ask what the matter was when Peter suddenly appeared, his face as black as thunder. Having heard Edward's account of the previous incident at the inn he was in no mood for games. 'I want a word with you,' he snarled at Nathan, whilst at the same time indicating that he wished him to move somewhere private.

Although unable to hear the short but heated exchange between the two brothers, it was obvious to Clara and Lizzie from the way they finally parted, that there was no love lost between them. It came as no surprise to others also, as funerals were noted for either uniting bereaved families or sometimes driving a permanent wedge between the survivors.

In this case Edward had half expected trouble of a sort, so when it arose he was not over concerned, except that he'd not expected Peter to be involved. However, knowing him as he did, Edward decided to extricate the four of them before things got worse. Turning to Peter's father, he said, 'I'm sorry, but we must go. I have to return the carriage before nightfall.' He then went and grasped Peter firmly by the arm, saying, 'We'd better get a move on. Get Clara and Lizzie while I tell the driver we're leaving.'

Once settled in the carriage, Edward realised that there was far more to the altercation than he'd realised. Peter sat glumly in his corner whilst Clara and Lizzie were both pale-faced and apparently troubled. Edward was disturbed by the atmosphere and it wasn't long before he felt obliged to say so. 'I don't know what's going on here,' he said, 'but it's a fine state of affairs when we all end up so edgy and miserable—what on earth's the matter?'

Clara spoke up a little reluctantly, 'It has all been a little too much,' she murmured sadly, her mild statement seeming to have broader implications. Edward realised that she had been very quiet throughout the day, and had put it down to the fact that she was merely a by-stander in the events of the past few hours. Now, looking keenly at her he saw a deeper conflict within, and knew that to enquire further at this moment would only embarrass her. Later on, should an opportunity arise, he would endeavour to have a quiet word with her in a way that would not suggest interference on his part. He could only admit to himself that today's association with his in-laws had seriously and adversely affected them all. He decided to bide his time, and contemplated the landscape through the carriage window. This allowed his companions the freedom to think their own thoughts, whilst reducing the risk of words being spoken which might later be regretted.

As Edward entered his own comfortable home after such a depressing day, he acknowledged that he had, after all, been fortunate in falling in with Abe in the first place. He could so easily have returned sick and jobless from the Crimea, only to face poverty. Instead, the farrier had put in a good word for him to Abe's friend the parish clerk, and this no doubt helped. He dreaded to think what life would have been like had he gone to live with Betty and her family, working in the cotton mill at Bamford or labouring on some farm nearby.

'Right!' he said, once they were all inside removing their outer garments. 'Now I think we need a glass of good wine to brighten up our spirits.'

'I'll agree to that,' Peter exclaimed, suddenly springing to life. 'It's been a hell of a day.' He took the glass from Edward, raised it and said, 'To two lovely ladies who've suffered much today on our behalf!'

'Hear! Hear!' Edward agreed. 'Let's put the whole business behind us, have something to eat, and once I've checked with Jack that all's well with the farm, we can play cards or just simply relax by the fire.'

As the evening wore on both Clara and Lizzie regained their usual composure, and as a result the room became a cosy haven from the cold wind which howled outside. 'Now you are seeing for yourself what winter in the valley can be like,' Edward said, speaking mainly to Clara. 'It isn't always damp and windy though, tomorrow could be as bright as today has been wet. What a shame that so far you have been prevented from seeing the splendour which I described to you in Aldershot.'

Clara smiled reassuringly, 'You were pre-occupied yesterday and may not have realised that I saw some of its beauty in the frosty sunlight.'

'So you did,' Edward agreed. 'I'm afraid that so much has happened this week it had slipped my mind. Let's pray for fair weather tomorrow so we can take a walk. Or do you ride?'

She shook her head, 'No, I'm afraid not, but if anyone else wishes to do so I will be quite happy to stroll down to the village and back by myself.'

'I wouldn't hear of it,' Edward replied firmly. 'We shall all walk together if the weather permits.' He had no intention or desire to ride thereby leaving Clara by herself. He saw a look of disappointment flit across Lizzie's face but, as Peter agreed to walk also, she accepted the decision with good grace. Up to this point there had been little evidence of her previous infatuation with Peter; perhaps her spontaneous greeting on his arrival was a little over-enthusiastic, and maybe she had felt genuine disappointment at not being able to go for a ride. Nevertheless, Edward resolved to watch her carefully to ensure things did not get out of control.

He was quite looking forward to their walk, even if it meant him rising earlier than normal to organise the work needed on the farm that day. Before long he would be alone again with Lizzie, and their old way of life would resume, so he must enjoy company while he had it.

As if nature was on his side the morning broke clear and bright, although the air was quite chilly, so in a light-hearted frame of mind Edward finished most of his tasks before the others were even up and about. They were no doubt taking this opportunity to have a lie-in, thus allowing him also to wash and change ready to go out. When Mrs Fox arrived to start her work about the house she was quite surprised to find Edward reading at the kitchen table, taking things easy instead of being his usual busy self.

'Good morning, Mrs Fox,' he greeted her cheerfully. 'And it's a lovely bright one at that.'

'It is indeed, Mr Morton, certainly there are signs of spring in the air.' She eyed him keenly, quietly wondering why he seemed in such a good humour. Had he not buried his sister just the day before? She had never quite understood her employer; however, he paid her wages and it was not her place to question him.

Edward sensed her puzzlement at his change of routine and explained. 'My visitors are still here, Mrs Fox, and I would be grateful if you could prepare a late breakfast for four when they get up. We're walking to the village afterwards to show Miss Burton what a pleasant spot it is here. I believe it's Sale day at the *Plough* today, am I right?'

She nodded, 'Most certainly—not that there'll be much to excite a lady of quality there.'

Edward smiled, shaking his head. 'Nor me I expect, but she might like to see our village life, such as it is.' He felt quite eager to get started, and was relieved when Peter finally descended the stairs, followed a few minutes later by Clara and Lizzie. Together they ate a leisurely and wholesome breakfast served by Mrs Fox, who was quite put out at the extra work, but was careful to hide her feelings.

'Mrs Fox,' Edward said, as the party was about to depart on their walk, 'I wonder, could I impose on you to stay a little longer today so that you can prepare an early evening supper for us? Do you have any other commitments to prevent it? If not I would be most grateful for your help.'

She thought for a moment, knowing full well that she had little in particular to draw her home, but felt if she appeared too eager he might make a habit of asking favours of her. 'It depends how late I need to stay,' she replied finally, as though she was needed elsewhere later in the evening.

'If we ate at six-thirty would that suit you? I'll see you don't lose out by helping here, a little something extra at the weekend, say. Of course I'll see that John drives you home too. How does that sound?'

This was exactly what Mrs Fox wanted to hear and she readily agreed to stay, just as long as she could be away for seven-thirty.

Pleased with her response, Edward said, 'Right everyone, shall we make a start?' He then turned to Lizzie, 'Make sure that Clara has something warm and sensible to wear in the cold, just in case the weather turns nasty.'

Although it was very muddy underfoot, and care had to be taken as they walked along the lane, the bright crisp air was a tonic after the dampness of the previous day. When they arrived at the *Plough* the auction was already in progress, and Edward led the party through the archway into the yard at the back. He viewed the collection of old ploughshares, scythes and farm implements nonchalantly, and watched as Peter inspected an ancient but still usable saddle which he'd spotted amongst the better items. It was Lizzie who saw beneath a pegged rug, together with a few other household items, a portable writing box in need of a good polish. She whispered to Edward that she would very much like to have it.

He bent casually to examine the box which he pulled out from beneath the rug, noticing that apart from having one hinge missing it could be made quite presentable. He pushed it back without saying anything and waited until this particular lot was offered for sale, hoping not to pay a great deal for it. He was quite right in his assumption that few people thereabouts could afford such unnecessary pieces, and for a few shillings he acquired the box, the rug and an assortment of junk he didn't need—or want. 'Now I'm compelled to send a man down with the trap to collect it all,' he complained good-humouredly, shaking his head. He was quite unused to such spontaneous actions and began to wonder what he was doing there instead of working on the farm. He glanced up from his purchases and caught Clara watching him with a look of amusement on her face, and he smiled back wondering what she was thinking.

Having arranged for the items to be collected later in the day, the four walked towards the Parish Church of St Nicholas, which, located as it was on a commandingly high position overlooking the valley, gave Clara a different perspective of the area. Much to Edward's dismay she insisted on entering the fifteenth-century building, which held so many memories of Hannah, but he followed reluctantly. The interior had been altered considerably after her death, the galleries had been removed and the whitewashed walls stripped down to natural stone, but overall it still disturbed him.

It was impossible for him to remain sad for long though, with the other three chatting away and exploring the church for its original Norman remains. He endeavoured to answer their many questions with the result that by the time they left he was quite calm, relieved even to have seen the church on such a happy occasion, rather than a sad one.

Without thinking, Lizzie led them to Hannah's grave where, for a moment, Edward reflected on the past. He wasn't one for visiting graveyards, believing that when the soul had departed from the body, merely an empty framework was left behind. He could talk to Hannah just as well up on the moors as he could here.

Strangely, in the presence of the others, his feeling of emptiness over his loss was not as great as usual, and he was quite happy to stand there with the warmth of the sun on him. After a minute or two, it was decided that as the weather was continuing in their favour they would extend their walk until the ladies felt they'd had enough exercise for the day.

The higher they climbed the more magnificent the surrounding landscape appeared to Clara, and Edward felt his prayers were answered as the sun's rays grew stronger, enhancing the view. Taking her arm he helped her over the larger obstacles in their path, quietly envying Peter his luck in finding such a pleasant and enquiring companion. He watched Clara when finally they stood looking out over the moors, her hand shading her eyes as she looked around in all directions. He swallowed hard at the thought that tomorrow, or certainly soon after, they would be going back to Aldershot and he would be alone with Lizzie once more. He suddenly noticed that Clara's inadequately light boots were caked in mud, and the hem of her skirt was splattered too.

'Your boots may be ruined now by our dragging you further than first intended,' he said, apologetically. 'I'm afraid I've been carried away once more with my enthusiasm—and look at your gown!'

At this Clara looked down and said simply, 'It's of no consequence, my pleasure in walking far outweighs any damage which may have been done.' A lapwing suddenly soared above them and she watched the bird closely. 'You are indeed fortunate to be part of all this.' She moved her hand in a sweeping gesture, encompassing all she saw, and Peter nodded in agreement.

Clara's approval pleased Edward enormously, and as he watched Peter assist her back down the slope he pondered on the unusual relationship which the pair seemed to have. Neither was over-affectionate, perhaps Peter took after him and was slow to show his feelings in public, yet their whole affair seemed to lack the sparkle of a couple in love. The more he watched them together the more strange he found things and, although he hated to admit it, he found some satisfaction in the apparent lack of affection between them.

'You'll find that the fresh air and exercise will have made you feel tired,' Edward explained to Clara as they entered the farmhouse. 'Why not rest a while? I have work to do and no doubt Peter would like to borrow a horse and ride?'

'Indeed I would,' Peter answered enthusiastically. 'You don't mind do you, Clara?' he asked.

'No, not at all, and I think I'll heed Edward's suggestion, otherwise I shall probably spend the evening half asleep.'

Peter lost no time in leaving the house to find a mount, and Lizzie would have followed him had she been suitably dressed. However, she seemed to accept that Peter intended riding alone, so retired to the sitting room to sew.

The writing desk and other items arrived at the farm after being collected by Jack's son, John, who'd been despatched the minute Edward arrived back from the walk. John was told to help himself to anything he might find useful, then to scrap the rest. Edward took the desk and examined it to see what repairs would be needed. Some of the baize lining was stained and worn but no doubt Lizzie could reline it herself. Once polished, the rosewood would soon shine again and another hinge could be bought on his next trip to town. One ink bottle was missing, and a small silver box lay in the bottom of the desk inscribed, 'Accept this trifle from a friend whose love for thee will never end!' A touching verse, he mused, and before leaving to get on with his work he placed it with the ink bottles on a shelf until the desk was repaired. He was quite looking forward to the evening and was grateful that Mrs Fox had agreed to stay and help.

Later, as they neared the end of their supper, Edward enquired of Clara, 'What do you think of my valley, then? Even in winter her starkness is beautiful, and in spring she comes to life with breathtaking new growth.' He paused for breath. 'You must excuse me,' he said, realising that he'd given her little opportunity to reply. 'I get carried away with enthusiasm.'

Clara smiled across at him, 'I sense that 'she', the valley, pleases you as much as a pretty woman might please other men.' She suddenly blushed at her analogy, and lowered her eyes from his gaze, but not before he saw the look of warmth there.

Peter laughed heartily. 'You do amaze me sometimes Clara, with your outspoken opinions. Whatever Uncle Edward will think, I don't know.' He was unaware of the confusion Clara's remark had caused her, and simply carried on. 'Now, however, you can see for yourself how the region inspires poets and writers alike. The hills, moors and river valleys hereabout fill men with a passion that never lessens, even when fog and blizzard obscures them.'

'You know that Jane Austen and Charlotte Brontë took inspiration from Derbyshire, don't you?' Lizzie broke in, encouraged by Clara's directness.

'I had never really considered it before,' Clara confessed, having recovered a little of her composure by this time. 'I've read their books, of course, but never gave a thought to their setting.'

'It's a pity that yesterday was so sad', Edward remarked. 'Otherwise I might have told you something about the village of Hathersage where my sister has been laid to rest. Miss Brontë visited the village many years ago, and reputedly based part of *Jane Eyre* there. There are many things to be seen which give credence to this and she certainly stayed at the vicarage for a few weeks. What a shame we couldn't look around while we were there to see some of the places which obviously inspired her.'

'I would have liked that!' Clara exclaimed, her enthusiasm matching Edward's, and a glance of deep understanding passed between them. This unexpected rapport made her fall silent and she lowered her eyes once more, then slowly she finished off what remained on her plate.

'Even I didn't know that!' Peter said, seemingly unaware of the intimate glance which had thrown both Clara and Edward momentarily off balance.

'What?' Edward asked, his mind far from the subject of the conversation. 'I'm sorry Peter, for a moment I was pre-occupied. What did you say?'

'I said,' Peter reiterated, a little puzzled by his uncle's lack of attention, 'that even I didn't know about Hathersage being the setting for part of *Jane Eyre*.

Edward got a grip on himself, and replied, 'No, you left the area when you were seventeen, but I was only away for two years, and the history of the villages has always been an interest of mine.' He knew that his face must have reflected something of his inner confusion when Peter spoke again.

'Is everything alright? You seemed to have something on your mind a few moments ago.'

'Nothing to worry you,' Edward reassured him, whilst not daring to look in Clara's direction in case their eyes met again. He wanted to study her without her knowing it, to be able to accept truthfully that what he felt was merely a friendly attraction towards her, but he was a poor liar even to himself, and he knew that slowly, over the past couple of days, Clara had become far more to him than this. He felt his own colour deepening and glanced involuntarily in her direction, seeing in her eyes a look of both warm affection and bemusement.

Fortunately, the others seemed oblivious to all of this, and Peter suddenly made a suggestion which took their interest in a very safe direction. 'Now, why don't you two ladies go to town shopping tomorrow? Do you think someone could take them as far as the omnibus, uncle?' he asked. 'You see, I would like to ride over and just make sure my father is alright before we go back. Would you have any objections to that?'

Seeing both Clara's and Lizzie's eyes brighten at the suggestion Edward quickly agreed. In fact he was rather relieved at the thought of being alone for a while. 'An excellent idea,' he said. 'John can take them to Malin Bridge, then meet the omnibus again later in the day.'

For the duration of the evening, Edward was careful not to be left completely alone with Clara, and at a suitable time feigned tiredness so that he could retire to bed, leaving the young people alone.

True to his word, the first thing Edward did on leaving the house next morning was to arrange matters for Clara's and Lizzie's expedition. He had already left a message on the kitchen table saying that he had work to do down in the fields, and was gone before the others were up. Clara was a little disappointed at this but accepted it to be part of farm-life, and it was only when Lizzie made some comment about him seeming a little strange the night before, that she wondered if he'd deliberately absented himself.

John soon arrived to take them to Malin Bridge and it wasn't long before they set off. The day was dull, yet warmer than the preceding one, but the spirit within the trap was light-hearted and happy.

Once aboard the horse-drawn omnibus, Clara settled down to viewing the homes and buildings which she'd only glimpsed from the cab's window on her arrival three days earlier. When they arrived at Hillsborough, several more passengers boarded the 'bus, causing the occupants who were already seated to squeeze together. 'It's a good job the fashion for hoops has passed,' she said. 'It must have been a curse for the proprietors as they would not have been able to carry quite as many passengers.' She smoothed out her crumpled skirt and, wriggling as the bustle of her dress pressed against the side of the 'bus and added, 'Nor is it very comfortable sitting like this. Fortunately, as you know, I rarely need to use an omnibus in Aldershot—and for that I'm grateful.'

As the horses slowed on the incline beside the turreted barracks, Lizzie said, turning to look behind them, 'That's where Peter first joined the Army. I remember him doing so when I was a child of seven.'

Clara turned too. 'It's almost a miniature Windsor Castle,' she said, her interest deepening as they passed the main entrance.

Lizzie was surprised. 'Have you seen Windsor Castle?' she asked.

'Yes, I have,' Clara replied. 'When I was training to be a nurse in London I made a point of visiting many of our famous buildings and places of interest, and found Windsor on the river to be one of the nicest places I've seen.

'When we were returning from Aldershot,' Lizzie declared wistfully, 'we stopped in London but the weather was so foul that we saw very little there. Perhaps one day I'll get the chance to see more!'

'I'm certain you will,' Clara assured her. 'I'm so glad that Edward took the opportunity to show you something of the City.' She was pleased that he had taken heed of her advice when in Aldershot, and she settled back contentedly into the seat as the yellow sandstone barracks receded into the distance. They had travelled another half mile towards town, when they stopped opposite a large elegant Georgian building on the other side of the road, sited amidst a large landscaped area. 'What's that impressive place?' she enquired, peering past the other passengers.

'That's the Infirmary,' Lizzie replied. Then remembering that Clara was a nurse went on. 'It's quite old now but was purpose built, I believe, as a hospital.'

'That's wonderful,' Clara exclaimed approvingly. 'Our old cottage hospital in Aldershot will not give service for much longer. There is constant talk about building a new one, but only time will tell when it will happen,' then Clara paused. The 'bus had started off again now and was entering the older part of the town where she became aware of a much grimier atmosphere. The roads and streets were narrowing and becoming thronged with the bustle of carts and wagons. 'I hadn't realised what a large place Sheffield is!' she remarked. 'Compared to home it is vast.'

Lizzie pointed to the number of shabby little theatres and music halls which dominated the area around West Bar. 'For some reason or other they seem to catch fire very easily,' she complained, as if despairing at the carelessness of human beings.

'It's probably because they use burning lime and gas to illuminate the stage, and where there are flames and curtains you can expect fire,' was Clara's observant answer.

'You know so much,' Lizzie said with admiration, and Clara smiled, accepting her innocent comment as a compliment.

When they eventually reached the market place, both women alighted with a feeling of relief. 'Where shall we start?' Clara asked. 'You know the town, and I would like to see everything which you think might be of interest.'

'I'm afraid I don't know Sheffield all that well,' Lizzie replied. 'I came shopping with Mother occasionally but that was long ago, and Father comes in so rarely nowadays.' She led Clara to the edge of the crowded walkway, saying, 'What I have told you on the journey here is simply what my father has explained to me during our visits. I remember the Market Hall, High Street and Fargate which leads right along and down the Moor, but I don't recall going off the main thoroughfare.' She turned. 'That's the new Norfolk Market Hall,' she said, pointing to a large and imposing structure further down the street.

'Then we shall explore that first, you and I, and afterwards we shall have a cup of tea and a cake.'

Together they entered the spacious hall with its large iron and glass roof. 'This is a lovely airy place to shop, Lizzie,' Clara stated as she stood by the handsome Italian-style fountain in the middle. 'It reminds me a little of the Crystal Palace.'

Laughing at Clara's praises for the Market, Lizzie shook her head. 'Nothing about it ever inspired me before,' she said, beginning to appreciate the companionship which Clara was now providing. It took them almost an hour to look at every stall before they left to find somewhere to eat in the Haymarket.

'Where shall we go next?' Clara asked as she sipped her tea. 'I would so much like to take home some new materials and trimmings to made a gown for summer.'

'I recall mother going into a large emporium in Fargate, it may still be there.'

Victoria Buildings in Fargate was more than a shop, in fact R. & G. Gray's establishment sold everything that a lady of quality might need in the way of fabrics and haberdashery for her home, and would ensure she was clad in the latest of fashion. Curtaining displays and quilts hung from the high rafters, bonnets plain and fancy were displayed amongst laces and tulle, even mourning clothing of every description was on offer.

'This is wonderful,' Clara cried, clapping her hands in delight. 'I have never seen such an array of goods in any shop outside of London. Lizzie, I don't understand why you wish to leave this area at all; what I see of the town is very favourable.' She went to a counter on which lay a paisley shawl in pretty colours. 'I'll have a look at that if you don't mind,' she said to a smartly-dressed assistant. Having examined the shawl for quality and weight she smiled and said, 'I'll take it please, and do you have any wool for berlin work?' She turned to Lizzie. 'Would you like me to show you how to do berlin work, like the tapestry you saw at home?'

By this time Lizzie was quite overwhelmed by Clara's enthusiasm and was thoroughly enjoying the outing. 'I would really appreciate that,' she answered warmly. 'I liked the fire screen which you did very much.'

Finally with their arms full of parcels, Clara and Lizzie wended their way towards the head of the Moor and, looking down the long shop-lined street decided that they had walked far enough. Time was also passing and, if they were to catch the omnibus back to Malin Bridge to meet John, then they must turn back soon. 'Another drink and a bite to eat, that is all we have time for,' Lizzie warned, both of them being a little tired from the hustle and bustle of being amongst so many people.

As they sat, weary but happy, at a table in the window of a small eating house, Clara considered very tactfully how to raise the subject of Lizzie's future. 'I really have enjoyed myself today, there are so many varied and lovely shops that I could quite easily come here again,' she began.

Lizzie's eyes brightened. 'Would you really?' she exclaimed, then thought for a moment before speaking again. When she did her tone was thoughtful, almost sad. 'You know, today I too have seen a very different town in your company. Before I went to Worksop, which is a very small place, I had only been here occasionally with my Father, since Mother died, and he doesn't like to be in town very long. I can see that there is much to do, and perhaps now that I am older he may not object to my coming more often.'

'I'm sure he wouldn't. You are too young to be shut off from the world, and I think Edward is beginning to realise that things are changing. He is simply not used to rearing young women, that is why he sent you away, not because he doesn't care about you!' Clara smiled as she watched Lizzie, recalling how not so many years earlier, she too had been unsure and yet anxious to get on with life. 'Have you thought more about your future since you came back from Aldershot?' she asked, daring to dig a little deeper whilst at the same time feeling sorry for the young woman before her, who so obviously needed a mother's touch.

Lizzie looked at Clara with an almost defeated look. 'No,' she said lamely. 'It is all too much for me to organise; you are very independent but I fear I am not.'

'Rubbish!' Clara declared strongly. 'You have a good spirit and a strength of character to match. Poor Edward doesn't know how to go about solving your problems, but perhaps I may have a suggestion if you would like to hear it?'

Lizzie was beginning to realise that in Clara she had a friend and not an enemy. 'I have not been the kindest of people to you, have I?' she said meekly. 'I would ask you to forgive me my childish behaviour of the past.' Encouraged by Clara's gentle smile she said, 'It is a pity that you live so far away, for I would truly like to make up for my mistakes.'

Clara waved her hand as if dismissing the confession as unnecessary. 'I too have been young and in need of guidance—at least now you know that I am your friend and mean you no harm. However, the suggestion I have may not be to your liking. I only make it in case it is a good one.' She paused before continuing. 'Have you ever considered training to be a nurse? You came to the hospital with me and did not seem disturbed by what you saw there, in fact I was rather pleased by the way you offered words of comfort to those who were ill.'

'But I have no experience,' Lizzie interrupted. 'And what would Father say?'

'I don't think Edward would be a problem, but it would mean going away again, maybe to London. I have contacts at St Thomas' Hospital and could make enquiries if you were interested. Give it some thought for a while, there is no harm in thinking carefully about a very important decision such as this.'

'I really will consider it, and thank you for trying to help.' Then as an afterthought, and as if revealing some great secret, Lizzie said softly, 'I wish that you didn't have to go back to Aldershot. I love my father but I feel so isolated on the farm.'

Clara was moved by this heartfelt plea, and was aware that she herself might never return to the valley once having left it, if she did not marry Peter. 'That's why you need to consider a life beyond these confines. In some ways the freedom Edward has given you has paved the way for a fuller way of life, at a time when many women are struggling for recognition as worthwhile individuals, rather than being simply mothers and wives. Slowly attitudes will change, but unfortunately this may come about too late to be of full benefit to you and me. Nevertheless, we must play our part in the progression of women's rights.'

Having listened intently, and with considerable admiration for Clara, Lizzie asked, with no more ulterior motive than mere curiosity, 'Will you go to India with Peter? I should not see you then for some long time.'

There was a look of sadness in Clara's eyes and she replied, 'I will not be going to India, Lizzie. If Peter feels he must go then so be it. Perhaps I don't love him enough to go with him, but I can't go back there and live the life of an officer's wife. I would die of frustration, I am not one for social gatherings as you have probably realised. Peter is a man's man, as are many soldiers, my father included, whereas I must fulfil myself or wither as so many Army wives have done, through no fault of their own. Peter is a good man but in many respects I feel older, not younger than him. This is a problem with which I have been trying to come to terms for several months now.'

'But isn't Peter expecting to marry you?' Lizzie said in some bewilderment.

'That's just the point!' Clara said rather too loudly, drawing attention to herself from those at nearby tables. She lowered her voice, 'It's always what Peter wants in the end—but I am too independent just to accept his word as Master'.

'Does he know this?' Lizzie asked in a hushed, awe-struck whisper at the revelation.

'He must, otherwise he is even more insensitive than I thought. Whilst his mother was ill I have done my best to be supportive but it doesn't change anything in the long run. I came here because he needed me, not for a holiday.' She saw her companion's face drop and knew that she was in need of reassurance. Reaching over the table and placing a comforting hand on Lizzie's arm she softened her tone. 'Believe me, I have enjoyed being here far more than I ever expected and will be genuinely sorry to leave—and we can write to each other. I will keep my promise to help you if you want to take up nursing, and I would come to London to see you.' Suddenly realising how long they had been sitting at the table, she quickly gathered up her parcels, saying, 'Come, get your things together, I fear we may have missed the 'bus.'

By the time they reached the waiting area it was too late as their omnibus was already overcrowded, and there was nothing to be done but wait patiently until the next one arrived.

Edward, meanwhile, was making his way down to meet them at Malin Bridge, having spent the day thinking of nothing but Clara and the fact that she would be leaving the farm shortly. With Peter somewhere between the farm and Bamford he decided to collect the pair himself rather than send John. He arrived early as was his habit so that by the time the 'bus arrived he was cold, and then a little put out to find them not on it.

'It's market day, Sir!' the driver explained. 'The 'bus was full even before we left, and there was already a queue for the next one.'

Had Edward known precisely where the two were waiting in town he could quite easily have fetched them himself, but now there was no alternative to a further long wait.

By the time the pair arrived, shaken by the constant stopping and starting, Clara was feeling far from well. She was grateful to see Edward rather than John standing there and managed to smile weakly, although he could tell by her pale face and cold hands that something was wrong. He gently assisted her up into the trap and wrapped both of them in a warm blanket. He wanted to get home as quickly as he could before dark, but he was forced to go at a much slower pace out of consideration for Clara.

However, after a mile or so in the sharp fresh air she picked up sufficiently for him to increase the horse's speed so that they arrived back just as dusk was falling.

As the house was well lit, Edward assumed Peter had returned, yet he didn't come out to greet them and this was puzzling. Having helped Lizzie and Clara down from the trap, together with their parcels, Edward took it

208

immediately to the stable and put the horse away for the night. On walking back he saw Peter's figure through the lighted window and breathed a sigh of relief. On entering the house, however, he found the atmosphere rather gloomy and was immediately alerted into expecting trouble in some shape or form, especially as both women looked ill at ease. Peter, who had been standing with his back to the door suddenly turned round to face him, saying, 'It's nothing Uncle Edward, I'm fine, really I am—it just looks worse than it is!'

Edward gasped, 'Good God, man! Have you been in a fight?' he asked, looking directly at the bruised and bloody face of his nephew.

'Well, sort of!' Peter answered, his voice subdued.

'How do you mean, sort of?' Edward demanded, none too tolerantly. 'Either you have or you haven't, in any case you look a mess!' He shook his head in disgust. 'It's those brothers of yours, am I right?'

Peter sighed. His uncle's anger did not surprise him, and he was ashamed to admit that he'd lost his temper when provoked by Nathan. 'I know,' he admitted, 'I should have had more self-control, but it was as if all my years of anger suddenly exploded when Nat tormented me again. At least I got it out of my system but I shall never return to Bamford!'

Lizzie was about to say something when Clara gave her a quick look and a barely perceptible shake of the head.

Edward's initial anger was subsiding now, and he looked more closely at Peter's face. 'Well, my lad, you can't go back to Aldershot looking like that. It's obvious you've been in a fight rather than an accident, so what are you going to do? They'll not tolerate an officer fighting, not even with his own brother.'

'I've been thinking about that, but if I stay much longer than expected I shall be absent without leave. Then there's Clara to think of, she's needed at the hospital.'

Edward looked with less than sympathy at his face. 'You've created quite a dilemma for yourself, haven't you! As for Clara, she's not too well either, so you'd better put your mind to solving the problem.'

'Well I was wondering,' Peter began cautiously, 'if you could do me a favour by going down to the Barracks here in Sheffield, and asking them to telegraph a message to Aldershot saying I have, in fact, had an accident and that I'll travel back as soon as possible?'

Edward thought for a moment, 'Do you think they'd accept my word without some proof?' he asked, doubtful about the very suggestion.

'Is there a doctor in the village, then, who would vouch for my accident?' Peter asked hopefully. 'I could so easily have been thrown from my horse.'

Edward shook his head in despair, 'You can't fool a doctor, or expect him to lie, can you?'

'No, not to lie exactly, just to say I'm not fit to travel—I can feign a bit, surely. Otherwise this could mean the end of my career as an officer if I go back too soon. Mind you,' he continued 'I'm not proud it's happened either.' He turned to Clara, 'I'm sorry, it's nothing short of disgraceful I know, but I couldn't help myself.'

'I half expected something like this after the funeral,' Edward said. 'I don't want to know any more details, I've heard enough to know I'm best left in the dark.' Then, as an afterthought, he added, 'Just so long as Nathan doesn't come over here looking for you!'

Peter shook his head, a glint appearing in his troubled eyes. 'I doubt it, he looks far worse than I do and will think twice about challenging his 'little' brother again.'

'What did your father say?' Edward asked with some disgust.

'Fortunately he'd just left. I was also about to leave when it happened, so if Nathan's got any sense he'll say he's had an accident too.'

Edward tensed. 'I presume the horse is alright?' he asked, and was immensely relieved when Peter nodded reassuringly. 'I would have told you by now if it wasn't.' There was a moment of silence, then he turned to Clara, and in a quieter, softer voice asked, 'Did Uncle say that you aren't well? What's the matter?' He went up to her and was genuinely concerned about her, but Edward sensed withdrawal in Clara.

'I think it was a touch of travel sickness,' she said quietly. 'The atmosphere in the omnibus was fetid and unpleasant, and we seemed to be constantly stopping and starting in the traffic most of the way back. However, once we were in the trap I soon began to feel better.' Her face had now regained its colour, but she still felt drained and could have done without the strain of this latest development. 'A rest is all I need. Shopping is a tiring exercise and we've both done a considerable amount today.' She was more than used to the rumbustious behaviour of soldiers—and to patching them up, however, her respect for such men had gradually diminished with these experiences. 'I had better take a look at the damage,' she said, without displaying any signs of emotion. With that, both women escorted a protesting Peter into the kitchen.

While Clara tended to Peter's cuts and bruises, which he'd already attempted to clean up, Lizzie set about cooking the meal prepared earlier by Mrs Fox.

Peter winced and groaned like a child as Clara, none to sympathetically bathed the broken skin, and Edward in the sitting room smiled to himself at this. His anger now gone, he considered with a paternal view that Peter had come to no permanent harm, even if his pride was damaged. Perhaps if, as a boy, he'd stuck up for himself against his brothers he would simply have turned out like them, at least now he'd had a revenge of sorts. The only obstacle to overcome was the army side of things. Peter winced again and Clara slapped him playfully on the shoulder, saying, 'Just behave, you big baby!'

Hearing this Edward chuckled to himself and rose from his chair. As he entered the kitchen a domestic scene met his eyes. Lizzie stood by the oven half-enveloped in a large apron, and Peter squirmed and scowled as Clara appeared to be taking delight in tormenting the wounded soldier. What a pity such a family scene in his home could not go on forever.

'Ahem!' he said, clearing his throat, 'I see everything is back to normal again.'

There was a touch of humour in his voice to which Peter replied sarcastically, 'This woman's actually enjoying my discomfort'.

Clara said nothing, but Edward could see that she was in her element with Peter under her control. She was without doubt a very competent and shrewd nurse, with a knack of handling awkward male patients.

'I'm willing,' Edward said, 'to go the Barracks tomorrow and testify to your unfortunate accident. Let's just hope that they accept my word and your note to the Duty Officer.'

'Oh, that's jolly decent of you, Uncle, I'm very grateful,' Peter responded, his pain and discomfort suddenly disappearing as if by magic. 'I'd go myself if it wasn't plain to all that I've taken a punch or two.'

'I wonder,' Clara broke in, 'if I might ask a favour of you as well? This morning Lizzie pointed out a rather elegant hospital not half a mile from the Barracks, and I would very much like to go and see if I can look around. Our Cottage Hospital is very antiquated, and perhaps I may gain some useful ideas to take back with me.'

'Well,' Edward hesitated a moment, 'I had planned to ride there—but why not?' And so it was arranged that the two would go together in the trap, providing the weather was favourable.

Later, as Peter joined Edward in the sitting-room to await supper, Edward remarked with a wry smile, 'Well you do look a fine specimen, and no mistake.'

Peter hit the back of the chair with his hand. 'It's damned inconvenient, but how can I show my face anywhere looking like this?'

'I agree it's unfortunate, but no doubt you'll manage to occupy yourself until we return, and there are books on the shelf. In fact if you like you can clean my gun and make a few cartridges for me. I'm not sure if Lizzie is coming with us or staying here, but I don't want you to engage Mrs Fox in too much conversation as she's a bit nosy, and she'll never get her work done.'

With Peter and Edward in the sitting-room, Clara took the opportunity of being alone with Lizzie to ask if she'd had any thoughts on their discussion earlier in the afternoon. 'I have no intention of influencing you one way or the other,' she said, speaking in a low voice so as not to be overheard. 'But tomorrow would be an ideal time for me to sound out your father on the matter. If you remain here to amuse Peter, I could describe my experiences at St Thomas' and suggest it as a possible way forward for you. I have no idea as to his financial circumstances, but I get the impression that he is not without a little capital on which to draw for important needs.'

'Oh, would you, Clara?' Lizzie exclaimed enthusiastically. 'I haven't really had time to think too much about it, yet the suggestion has great merit and I would like to consider it.'

'Then that is settled, and I will be very careful to make it appear to be my idea, not yours.'

The idea of traipsing round the Barracks and then the hospital did not appeal to Lizzie, who felt there would be more to amuse her at home in the presence of her cousin. 'Knowing my father,' she said, 'you will be back in no time at all and so it would hardly be worth my while going. You go, I will keep Peter company.'

In spite of Peter's injuries he was in good spirits for the rest of the evening, due mainly to the wine of which he'd consumed a fair amount. Lizzie responded to his light-hearted clowning, whilst Edward attempted to browse through a newspaper which he'd collected that afternoon. Clara was not unaware of the lively atmosphere as she sat at ease, her long fingers sorting out the strands of wool needed to show Lizzie how to work a tapestry, and occasionally her own witty comments brought laughter from everyone. Edward was struck by her graceful poise, and the way she would, at times, glance up from her task and smile brightly, say something, then resume her work. Later, whether it was from the warmth of the room or the wine, Edward wasn't sure, but he began to feel quite drowsy. He did not want to mention this, in case he dampened the happy spirit around him, but eventually he decided to retire.

'Not yet!' Clara cried, with a touch of mystery in her voice, and dropped the wool onto her lap. 'I have a surprise for you all. Just sit and be patient for a moment.' Without getting up she placed the wool on the stool by her side, and produced several packages from their hiding place behind her chair. 'I have a small package for each of you.' she said, her eyes sparkling mischievously. 'But first you must make a guess as to what it might be.' Taking the largest she held it towards Lizzie, 'This is for you, to remind you of our day out,' and Lizzie reached over to take it. 'No, guess first!' Clara laughed.

'I have no idea,' Lizzie protested, eagerly trying to obtain the gift.

'Then I shall leave yours till last.' At that Lizzie's face fell and they laughed. 'Here, this is for you Peter, now guess!' She offered the small but solid looking packet to him.

'That's hardly fair, Clara. It's quite obvious what Edward's is,' he said, looking at the remaining gift and pretending to be put out.

'Then he shall be first and you shall be last.' She made to hand the flat oblong package to Edward. 'Do you know what it is?'

Edward smiled. 'A book,' he replied suspiciously, expecting it to be something entirely different.

'Ah, but which one?' she asked, enjoying the suspense she was causing.

He thought for a moment, 'Dickens?' he cried, thinking to outwit her.

'No!' Clara cried in triumph. 'But you may open it for trying! It is to say thankyou for your kindness in having me here.' He was forced to reach over to take the book, and had great difficulty in concealing the effect her thoughtfulness was having on his emotions. He took it almost gently from her hand and unwrapped it.

'*Far From the Madding Crowd*,' he exclaimed in amazement. 'I shall think of you when I read it.' His face betrayed none of his deeper feelings but he couldn't hide the quiver in his voice.

'Now, it's Lizzie's turn.' She watched as Lizzie almost tore the wrapping away. 'That is to repay you for being so patient whilst I did so much shopping.'

'The paisley shawl! Oh, how beautiful!' exclaimed Lizzie, springing from her chair and kissing Clara on the cheek. 'I have never enjoyed a day so much before, thank you for taking me with you.'

Peter waited, watching the exchange of affection between the two women and seemed a little mystified at the emotional atmosphere in the room, which seemed even to affect his uncle. He was quite hot and his head swam a little, maybe more from the wine than anything else. Finally, Clara held out the smallest parcel which he took and quickly opened. His eyes widened. 'Now that really is a splendid pocket knife,' he cried, as he opened out the separate blades in the shape of a fan. 'And a Joseph Rogers' knife at that! This will fit nicely into the pocket of my uniform.' Then, as if shy, he slowly crossed the room and kissed Clara on the cheek, much in the same manner as Lizzie had done.

Edward slowly opened his book, thinking to himself that his nephew was a cold-blooded young man in his lack of warmth towards Clara, and how much he himself longed to thank Clara more cordially. 'You must give her a coin in return, Peter, or you will cut your friendship—remember the old custom.'

'It's a load of rubbish,' laughed Peter. 'But, when I go to my room I will fetch one down.' He refilled his glass and as he sipped from it became suddenly elated, 'I have an idea,' he cried with excitement, 'Why don't Clara and I get married in Bradfield Church whilst we're here?'

Without hesitation both Edward and Clara gasped in unison, 'No!'

Peter recoiled in astonishment, and looked from one to the other. 'Why on earth not?' he demanded, looking at Clara in consternation and accidentally knocking over the glass of wine as he made to place it on the table.

Clara flushed and made an attempt to clean up the mess. 'I'll do that,' Lizzie offered, and ran into the kitchen for a cloth.

'You need to stay indoors where no one will see you,' Edward lied, in an effort to cover up his own outburst. 'Besides, you have to be a resident in the area for three weeks before a marriage can take place.'

'We could get a special licence! I'm not short of money, you know,' Peter argued. 'But as it appears to upset everyone, just forget the suggestion.' He turned to Clara who was red-faced and trembling, and then avoided everyone's eyes, considering it wiser to let the matter drop until they were alone together.

Edward was annoyed with himself for having spoken out so emphatically, and even more so because he knew he was guilty of not wanting Peter to marry Clara at all.

The earlier relaxed atmosphere had disappeared completely now, and he thought it best to excuse himself and retire for the night. Rising, he looked directly at Lizzie and with a conspiratorial look said, 'I think an early night wouldn't do us any harm, don't you Lizzie?' To his great relief she must have understood the urgency in his voice, and together they said goodnight and left the room.

For several minutes after the others had departed, neither Clara nor Peter spoke to each other, but by the time Edward reached his room he was aware that all was not well below. His heart was heavy in the knowledge that, after spending a pleasant evening in good company, he had contributed, no matter how unintentionally, to spoiling it. His bedroom was situated above the sitting room where Clara and Peter were talking heatedly and, try as he might, he could not shut out the sounds which penetrated the unlined ceiling. He couldn't make out the words spoken, nor did he want to, but he was nevertheless deeply disturbed by it all and couldn't sleep. Suddenly, everything went quiet and he was left wondering if the pair had settled their difference, or parted in anger. Eventually, after what seemed half the night had passed, he drifted into a fitful and restless sleep.

Chapter 11

All Edward's happy anticipation of the trip to the Barracks with Clara disappeared when he woke and remembered the disturbance of the night before. He made a sluggish start with his work, and dreaded returning to the house to change into better clothing for the visit. On entering the kitchen he was informed by Lizzie that Peter was sleeping off a heavy head, which didn't please her at all, and that Clara was 'a bit out of sorts'. So much for young love, he thought, as he removed his jacket, and coughed quietly before entering the sitting room to wish Clara a gentle good morning.

After breakfast, and with Clara seated by his side in the trap, they departed with no expectation of anything more than a bumpy ride on a chilly morning. Clara was unusually quiet and Edward knew she was deep in thought, seemingly unaware even of his presence. Having no idea of the outcome of the heated discussion she'd had with Peter he could do no more than try to divert her with comments on their surroundings, and suggest what he might say when they arrived at the Barracks.

After a while he began to feel the cold striking through his clothes and asked, 'Are you warm enough?' He glanced down at the blanket which covered their knees. 'Take more of the rug if you wish.'

Clara shook her head. 'I am warm enough, thank you. It is a coldness of spirit which disturbs me.'

'How so?' Edward asked, as if unaware of her real problem.

'You could not be oblivious to what happened last night,' she said sadly. 'Without thinking, and without any consideration for Peter's feelings, I bluntly turned down his suggestion of getting married.'

'No,' Edward admitted. 'I'm not unaware that there are problems, but perhaps it was merely the manner of his proposal which took you by surprise, rather than the question. After all, he had been drinking rather more than I have seen him do before due, no doubt, to the events of the afternoon in Bamford. That, together with the enjoyable atmosphere and your kindness, may have led him to become a little carried away.' As if considering his words, she said no more and, although he couldn't remove his eyes from the road for long, he did glance sideways and saw the crestfallen look on her face. Taking one hand off the reins he gently placed it on her arm and squeezed it, saying, 'When he wakes he'll probably not remember much about the incident at all, and you will be able to make light of it.'

'But it will not ease my mind,' Clara protested, 'because I meant what I said. I am fond of Peter, for he is a splendid young man, but I don't love him as I should. I thought I did but it isn't so. He is intent on going to India, I am not. He has known this for some time now and it was only because of his mother that I came here with him. I was about to tell him of my feelings when the Parson's message came, and although you may not realise it, Peter is not one to show great emotion in public, he was so beside himself at the news that I felt I had to give him all my support, and, in that, he may have read much more than was implied.'

His hands were trembling and he knew he should answer her. He didn't care about Peter now, and murmured, 'Then we may never meet again?' His voice was subdued with emotion, and he stared hard at the road ahead.

'No,' Clara whispered softly. 'No, we may not.'

He swallowed hard at these words, acknowledging the truth that she had only come for Peter's sake. He released her arm with a deep sense of loss. How foolish he had been to hope that in some way she might care for him. He took the reins with both hands and couldn't speak; his heart was too heavy with disappointment to trust himself to do so. What, pray, had he hoped would happen on this, their one day out together?

There seemed little more to say under the circumstances but he was filled with a powerful desire to stop the trap, to face her and tell her that he loved her and needed her companionship above all else, but it was plain she loved neither Peter nor himself. In front of him lay a desolate path down which he would be forced to travel in the years ahead, and he would always be alone with his thoughts. If that was to be so, he might as well be dead than grow old with only work to occupy his mind.

How long they rode on in silence didn't particularly worry Edward. Somehow there was safety in silence, and despair in speaking out. Instead, he chose to enjoy, while he could, the closeness of the intelligent and attractive woman by his side. What was she thinking? Only she and God knew that, and to enquire would inevitably spoil what was left of his hopes and illusions.

The Barracks loomed up ahead, and as he urged the horse up the incline to the gates, Clara spoke for the first time since her disclosure. Her voice was barely audible above the noise of the wagons and carriages on the road, and as he leaned to catch her words he saw there were tears in her eyes. 'Tell me later,' he said, lifting his voice against the racket around him. 'It's too noisy now.'

Remembering the routine of the Barracks, Edward halted the trap before entering the main entrance, and waited until one of the two sentries approached him to enquire of his business. Edward stepped down and asked if it was possible to speak to the Duty Officer of the Day, as he had a request for help from a fellow officer. Calling a soldier to lead the horse into the open yard, the sentry conducted Edward into the guard-house and explained the situation to the Sergeant Guard Commander. A runner was despatched to find the officer in question, and then both Edward and Clara, who had been helped down from the trap by the soldier, were invited to take a seat in the visitors' waiting room.

As the door closed, Edward spoke quietly to Clara, who had now regained her composure. 'I suppose you could say that this is a Model Barracks,' he said, looking out of the window onto the parade ground. Everything is contained within a square of land almost twenty-six acres in extent. It was here before the idea of Aldershot Camp was even conceived, and has a chapel, accommodation, in fact everything needed by a garrison, all neatly gathered together in one place. Aldershot, of course, has become so spread out that it is now like a large town in itself.'

Do you know the place well, then?' Clara enquired, her interest growing.

Edward turned from the window. You remember me telling you that I worked for a man gathering horses for the Army during the Crimean War? He was a farrier employed by the military and worked in the Barracks here. I also brought forage down from the farm for the horses when Abe was alive. In fact we still do supply fodder, so I have occasion to call in on business.'

Fortunately they didn't have to wait long before the door opened and an officer entered and introduced himself. Edward explained the situation, and handed Peter's letter to him which he read before going to obtain permission from his Adjutant to send a telegraph message to Peter's Depot. Before leaving, he enquired with great courtesy if Clara was comfortable, and instructed the Sergeant to arrange for more coal to be placed on the fire.

Edward thought it unwise to discuss personal matters at that time in case they were suddenly disturbed, but it was difficult to find a subject which was neither mundane nor an intrusion into their personal feelings. He knew from Clara's subdued demeanour that she too was finding conversation hard, and when the officer finally arrived back to say that a telegraphed message would be sent, Edward felt most relieved.

Having arranged to call back later for a reply, Edward helped Clara into the trap and set off towards the Infirmary where he offered to sit outside while she went about her business.

He watched her walk along the path to the entrance, her trim figure outlined against the stonework. She had a graceful movement, and he could imagine her gliding quietly down the long hospital wards.

He felt quite happy to wait, knowing that nothing she ever did would be a waste of time, and he appreciated her dedication to something she believed in. As to her dilemma regarding Peter, he was powerless to help except by commiserating. To do or say more might expose his inner feelings, and that would be a disaster which would end any possible friendship in the future. However, the longer he sat there waiting for her, the more pensive he became, and although she couldn't have been away for more than ten minutes, he was so pleased to see her that his face betrayed his pleasure.

'Would you like to come inside?' Clara asked, holding out her hand to invite him down. 'I would so much like to look round, and have been given permission to do so, but it may take a while.'

She awaited his answer, and in spite of the delay it would cause, he had no heart to refuse, saying, 'I'll just find somewhere to leave the trap, then if you don't mind waiting, I'll join you in the entrance as soon as I can.'

Several minutes later he returned and found her sheltering from the cold in the foyer. 'What a cold and uninviting building it is,' he observed, as they climbed the stone staircase to reach a small office where a man was expecting them.

'I heard your footsteps on the stairs,' he said, greeting them. 'Come in.'

Clara introduced Edward. 'This is my friend Mr Morton of Bradfield, of whom I spoke.' She turned to Edward as the two men shook hands. 'Mr Watson has kindly given us permission to look round,' she said. Then, addressing them both, added, 'As I told you, I am rather interested because the hospital in Aldershot is small and very old. There is the possibility of a new one being built and, as a nurse, I may see ideas here worth passing on, should I get the chance to influence the Hospital Board.'

'Come with me,' Mr Watson invited. 'I'll show you the medical and surgical areas first, and then you may visit the wards if you like. I will arrange for someone to take you round.'

'Thank you,' Clara said. 'I am most grateful. I understand the hospital was especially built for its purpose, am I right?'

Mr Watson nodded. 'It was built in 1797 as a Charitable Trust, the money being raised by subscription and fund-raising events. But we do have other hospitals in the town. There is the Royal in West Street, much newer than this one, and last year a hospital just for women was also established.' He saw Clara's interest at his last remark, and added, 'There is also a free hospital for children opening at Broomhill this year.'

To Edward, who had little need of either doctor or hospital, this information was of no importance other than general interest, yet he could see that to Clara it imparted a great deal. He was, therefore, gratified to know that, in some small way, by bringing her, he was contributing to her enjoyment. He followed behind Clara and Mr Watson at a small distance, and his admiration for her powers of observation grew; she was indeed a remarkable and astute young woman. The look on her face as she considered Mr Watson's explanations contrasted sharply with the tearful and vulnerable one at the Barracks only an hour earlier.

Having shown them the more restricted areas himself, Mr Watson led them to the wards where he intended leaving them. 'Oh, nurse!' he called out, attracting the attention of a small, stout and mature woman who was about to enter a side room. 'Would you mind showing Miss Burton and Mr Morton round some of the wards, if you're not too busy, that is?'

The nurse smiled, and replied obligingly, 'Certainly, Sir.'

'Do come to my office before you leave,' Mr Watson said, as he turned to leave them. 'I would like to hear your opinion of the hospital, Miss Burton.'

As they followed the nurse through several wards, Edward watched Clara; she spoke kindly to any patient with whom she came into contact, and he knew exactly what it was about her that, as her patient, Peter had fallen in love with. She was far too independent to merely follow in the shadow of Peter's demanding life in the army, and would never be content with the restrictions protocol would impose on her as an army wife. What then could he, Edward Morton, a mere farmer, offer her?

He was a little despondent at these thoughts, and Clara must have sensed it, for suddenly she said, 'You can see why the thought of being hospitalised is not a cheery one, and why visitors are reluctant to stay longer than necessary, can't you?' She looked around. 'I have seen enough, and this is taking up too much of your time. I have been a little self-indulgent, I'm afraid.'

'No, no!' Edward protested with sincerity. 'I find it very illuminating, it's just that…' his voice trailed off and he seemed downcast.

Clara eyed him keenly, and, ignoring his protest, said, 'Come, we have been here far too long, and you have work to do!' With that she took his arm and led him back to the office, where they thanked the Almoner for his time and trouble.

'Won't you have a cup of tea?' Mr Watson offered, smiling. 'It is almost dinner time and I am in need of a break.'

Clara turned to Edward, inviting him to answer. 'That would be very welcome,' Edward replied with enthusiasm, admitting to himself that he was not at all eager to return to the farm just yet.

Having had a pleasant chat with Mr Watson, and thanking him once more for his help, they left the hospital and went to collect the trap.

'I can see you're very dedicated to your calling,' Edward said, as she settled down on the seat and allowed him to tuck the blanket gently round her legs. 'Is that the real reason why you don't want to marry Peter, do you think?' He was standing by the side of the trap at this point still holding the blanket on her knee, and realised that his hand was trembling, although not from the cold.

Clara looked down at his bent head, unable to see his face. In many ways he was a difficult man to understand, sometimes quiet, always gentle, shy even; at others, when in the confines of his own environment, he was strong, self-confident and masterful. His hand on her knee was only inches away from her own, but she dared not touch him in case he misunderstood her motives. If only she…but no! She pulled herself together and said softly, 'If I loved Peter enough then I would give up the work and go with him. As I don't, I cannot.'

As if approving her decision Edward placed his hand on hers. 'You are wise beyond your years sometimes, and when you return to Aldershot, life here will be the emptier because of it.' He hadn't realised that as he spoke, his hand had tightened on hers so fiercely that she winced. 'I'm sorry,' he muttered, releasing her hand, then caressing her fingers as if to ease the pain he'd inflicted. In doing so he was almost overwhelmed by the powerful urge to tell her that if she no longer loved Peter, she might find someone like himself who did need her, and cared for her very much. He ached with the need to hold her hand gently and lovingly in his, and his throat was so constricted by emotion that he could not speak.

Fortunately his face was averted from her gaze, and so, saying nothing more, he slowly set her hand down and walked round to his side of the trap, patting the horse on the neck as he passed. He climbed up, and they set off to see if a reply to Peter's message had been received at the Barracks.

The Guard Commander handed Edward a sealed envelope addressed to Peter, and with this in his pocket he prepared to face the long drive home, wondering what he could say that would not overly expose his feelings. It was difficult to converse in the heavy traffic, the horse was inclined to be skittish when it felt threatened, and it wasn't until they reached Malin Bridge that a sensible discussion could take place.

'Has Peter told you much about the flood that devastated the area?' he asked, looking ahead.

'Not really,' Clara admitted. 'But I know there were many deaths and that much destruction took place.' She listened quietly as he told her of that night, and of his and Hannah's struggles in the aftermath. He was tempted to tell her the full story, leaving out Lydia of course, but then thought better of it.

'You would hardly believe such a dreadful thing had happened, to see things as they are now,' Clara said. 'But I have been remiss, I seem to have had so much on my mind today, that I have not talked about Lizzie, and I must do so before we reach home.'

'Has she a problem about which I am ignorant?' Edward asked in alarm.

'No, not a problem,' Clara assured him. 'However, in talking to her yesterday and asking if she'd come to any conclusions about her future, I was pleasantly surprised how much she appears to have matured since we last met.'

'She does seem more contented, I must admit,' he agreed thoughtfully.

'But she can't stay shut away from the world, Edward, she is too intelligent and too young to be just contented, so I made a suggestion which she promised to consider. Several times when in Aldershot she came with me to the hospital, and showed a compassion and fortitude there which was quite remarkable in one her age—I think she would make a good nurse!' To allow him to ponder on this, Clara said no more but simply waited patiently, watching the movement of the horse until Edward answered.

'Don't think I'm not grateful for your help,' he began, not unkindly. 'However, Lizzie is not used to hard work, and I would have preferred her to...' he stopped, a little reluctant to go on.

'To stay at home?' Clara interrupted.

He reddened. 'Please try to understand...', here again he paused, and then continued, 'It's just that—I suppose I'm being a little selfish, but she is all I've got.'

'I know that,' she said quietly, in an effort to soothe his growing agitation. 'Even so, you don't want her to be unhappy and grow away from you, do you?' His lips were pressed together now in a firm, determined way, and she felt that to push him further at this point might make matters worse. 'Lizzie may yet not even like the idea!' she added cautiously, knowing that if what she understood of him was true, he would eventually calm down and consider the matter more rationally.

'How would she get to town on her own?' Edward suddenly asked, as if he'd found a reasonable excuse as to why Lizzie couldn't become a nurse.

'Surely Jack, or John could take her, or at least go as far as the omnibus?'

'You seem to have it all worked out,' Edward said ruefully, as they left Low Bradfield and headed towards the farm, thinking that to be the end of the matter.

However, Clara knew that if she didn't tell him about the possibility of Lizzie going to St Thomas' before they reached home, it would certainly provoke an angry rejection which she must try to avoid. 'Please, pull in a moment,' she begged. There is something which I must say before we get back.'

Immediately he brought the trap to a halt Clara knew she'd made a mistake, for now she would have to speak directly to him, rather than to the front as she'd been doing. As a result of this she was unsure of herself and a little hesitant, not knowing how to begin.

Edward watched her, and although he suspected that she was nervous he couldn't help but admire her tenacity. He said nothing, however, and waited for her to speak.

In a subdued voice she said, plainly, 'I believe that if Lizzie does wish to become a nurse, then she should go to London to receive the best training available.' Edward opened his mouth to speak, then closed it again just as quickly. Clara waited, wishing he would say something, be annoyed with her if necessary, but not just sit there leaving her to agonise over what his response would be. Finally plucking up courage she said, humbly, 'I'm sorry, it really wasn't any of my business to suggest it.' Then she turned away from him.

'No, it wasn't!' Edward said coldly. Lizzie has enough fanciful ideas of her own without you giving her more, and by doing so you may have taken away what family I have.'

His tone was hurtful and it stung Clara, who wished she'd said nothing to him about Lizzie at all. 'That was unworthy of you!' she whispered, gathering up what dignity she had left, and longing to be back home in Aldershot. 'I had no desire to hurt you; you of all people!'

There was a catch in her voice which did not escape him, and he deliberately turned to look at her. He saw no arrogance there, no triumph either, only a subdued, forlorn figure.

'Oh, Clara!' he cried. Once you have left here, if Lizzie goes too, then I have nothing!' It was a simple statement and spoken with such intense feeling, that Clara raised her eyes questioningly to his. There was an agonised, almost pleading look there which she could not ignore, or turn away from. His face was flushed. I didn't mean to upset you,' he whispered, clasping her arm with his hand, his head so close that she could feel his breath on her face. She couldn't move, there was nothing she could do but wait and wonder. 'Oh, Clara,' he murmured, drawing back and looking at her. 'You are always in my thoughts; I am tormented by the knowledge that you are leaving and may never come back.' He lowered his head despondently, released her and seized the reins again.

Edward had spoken with such frankness that Clara was unable to speak, as she realised just how deep his feelings for her were, and knowing also that this strong, shy man was capable of turning her world upside down. Reaching out, she took his clenched hands gently in hers to let him know that she understood and was not offended by the outburst. Relieved by this, he looked up and, seeing the tenderness on her face, instinctively put his arm around her and drew her close; holding her tightly, half expecting her to draw away. She trembled at his touch so Edward released her for a moment but, once reassured that his affections were not unwelcome, he kissed her lovingly.

'I didn't mean this to happen,' he said, softly, when finally he released her. 'I found myself thinking Peter to be a fool not to have married you before now, and always at the back of my mind I dreaded that possibility. I know now that I was jealous of him.'

Up to this moment Clara had said nothing, she was so shaken by the suddenness of it all, then, before she knew it, she found herself confessing, 'Edward, I have loved you since that evening in Aldershot when you said that if you were a younger man you would challenge Peter for my affections. I feel so guilty because, when I came here, I knew it was not just out of sympathy for Peter, but because I wanted to see you again, to see if I was being foolish to think of you so often.'

At this mention of Peter, Edward stiffened, knowing his moment of joy was being spoilt a little by his own sense of guilt. 'Look,' he said gently. 'For the moment we mustn't let anyone know of our feelings, or they will believe we intended it to happen.' He kissed her again as she made to protest. 'Remember this, I cannot live without you, no matter how long it takes to sort things out.' He kissed her once more, with passion, not knowing when he would be able to do so again.

'Someone's coming!' she cried suddenly, moving away from him in the hope of not being seen, and blushed with embarrassment.

'It's no one I know,' Edward laughed. 'But this is dangerous and we must get back immediately, or they will wonder what has taken us so long. Mind you, I don't know how long I am going to keep this a secret, with you staying under my roof! We must be very careful.' His face took on a more sober expression, and he continued, 'I don't want to upset Peter, or Lizzie for that matter. In the end they must be left in no doubt that we haven't planned any of this.' He looked quickly at her. 'How I shall be able to conceal my feelings for you, I just don't know.'

Clara responded with a mischievous smile, 'I think perhaps that might prove a little difficult.'

'Don't you dare make it harder for me than it is,' he threatened, teasing her, as he took up the reins and urged the horse on.

'Good afternoon!' he called brightly to the workman who had caught up with them.

On reaching the farm, Edward drove straight to the stable instead of dropping Clara off at the cottage. 'What are you doing?' she asked, as they reached the stable door.

'Aren't you interested enough to see me put the horse away?' he replied with an air of mystery, as he helped her down and led the horse inside. Clara followed him and watched as he removed the harness. 'I have to wipe him down properly in a minute, but first,' he turned and put his hands firmly on her shoulders. 'It may be some time before I can do this again!' And so saying he pressed his lips warmly against hers. 'There!' he said, releasing her. 'That will have to do, and now you will have to compose yourself, if you wish to appear innocent before the others.'

'I am not dishevelled,' she laughed.

'No, but your face is not the colour of a demure maid, either!' he chuckled, a feeling of happiness stealing over him. 'Now, you go indoors and give this letter to Peter.' He gave her the envelope which he'd collected, 'I'll be in shortly,' he said, as he watched her go.

Jack then entered the yard and was most intrigued by the unusual sound of whistling coming from the stable. 'Who's there?' he called out with a puzzled look on his face.

'It's me!' Edward answered through the doorway. 'There's nothing wrong is there?' Jack shook his head and looked at his Master's happy face. Then, looking across to where Clara had just entered the house, he smiled to himself, and wondered what had happened to brighten Edward up so much.

To Clara, within the house, it seemed as if Edward would never return from the stable. Peter was asleep on the sofa and Lizzie was bombarding her with questions about the hospital, and what Edward's response had been about her going to London. Clara could hardly tell her that the discussion had fizzled out when he'd kissed her, and the memory of his touch thrilled her. 'He, too, is considering the idea,' she lied. 'But you haven't made up your mind yet, have you?'

'The more I think about it, the more attractive I find the prospect.' Lizzie replied, It was apparent that she had indeed been contemplating the idea, for she asked, 'Do you believe that once I'm qualified I could find work here in Sheffield?'

'There is no doubt a properly trained nurse could find work almost anywhere,' Clara replied. 'Only today I discovered that two new hospitals have opened here recently, and that a larger one for women will be built soon. I know for a fact that at the moment the Infirmary requires a nurse who can write, so there are jobs available and, if you train in London, you will see all the sights you want whilst you are living there.'

Edward's footsteps were then heard in the entrance, and Clara breathed deeply to disguise the quiver of excitement which she felt, hoping also that Lizzie wouldn't notice her distraction.

On entering the kitchen he smiled at them both. 'I see Peter is comfortable enough!' he remarked. 'I presume he hasn't got the letter yet?'

'No,' Clara smilingly replied. 'I was reluctant to disturb him. I did notice however, that his face is much improved now. Do you think I should wake him?'

'No, let him sleep, he must need it because it's not like him to idle time away.'

So began one of the most frustrating and difficult evenings of Edward's life.

When Peter eventually stirred himself he yawned prodigiously, then drew himself up into a sitting position and looked around. 'Good God! Is that the time?' he called out. 'I must have slept on and off all day. Why didn't someone wake me?'

'What does it matter?' Edward replied. 'At least we don't feel that we have lied completely to the authorities about you. How do you feel now?'

Peter started to rise cautiously, then, on realising there was nothing amiss, got to his feet. 'I'm fine, never felt better.' he said, stretching his limbs.

'Good!' Edward said, watching his nephew. 'Here's a telegraph message for you from the Barracks, your reply I think.' Edward gave him the envelope which he casually opened and read.

'I've got it!' he exclaimed, his face alive with excitement. 'I've got it!' he repeated, pressing the message to his lips in delight. 'I'm off to India,' he finally told the bemused and curious company. Then he turned and looked sheepishly at Clara. I know it's not what you wanted, and I suppose we'd better tell them our other news as well, unless you've already done so?' Without waiting for Clara to answer, he turned to Edward and explained, Clara and I agreed last night that we didn't love each other enough to marry, and would go our separate ways!' He paused, and Edward pretended to be surprised at the news.

Lizzie's face fell, 'Then you are to go away, and we may never see Clara again.'

'It's not that bad, Lizzie. You should be pleased for me, and there is no earthly reason why Clara should not remain your friend, is there?'

'No!' Clara butted in. 'And I wish you well Peter, you deserve more than I could give you.'

'Then you don't mind, Clara?' he asked, turning and waiting for her approval. She shook her head and smiled, to which he replied, 'You're a good sort, you know.' There was humour in his voice and his face reflected the pleasure the news of India had brought him.

'But we won't see you for years!' Lizzie moaned.

'But we can write, can't we? I should like to know how things are here in this country of ours. You'll keep me up to date won't you?'

At this Lizzie's face brightened. 'Of course I will, providing you bother to reply.'

While Peter and Lizzie talked excitedly about the future, Edward and Clara exchanged glances which, had the others not been so preoccupied would have given them more than India to consider. It was all Edward could do to stop himself from crossing the room to sit close to Clara, to make sure she wasn't upset by the news, and to reassure her of his love for her. If he gave the game away, then Peter's reaction to Clara's refusal would change drastically; all Edward wanted was to retain the friendship he had with his nephew. As it was, he must restrain himself and be content to gaze fondly at Clara when no one was observing him.

Clapping Peter firmly on the shoulder, Edward congratulated him. 'Well done! They say India is an extremely interesting place, for the young at least. How soon do you estimate it will be before you leave?'

'I'm not sure, it just says, "Return as soon as possible. Your application for India successful".' Peter replied. 'This does of course mean that I must return to Aldershot as soon as I can.' He fingered his bruised cheek, 'Another day here, and then by the time we get back I should get away with it, don't you think?'

'I would imagine so,' Edward agreed, his heart sinking at the knowledge that his time with Clara was almost at an end. He looked quickly in her direction and saw that she was listening intently to their conversation, a perturbed look on her face. 'Then you'll be leaving the day after tomorrow?' Edward said, his mind racing, and Peter nodded in agreement.

It was a sad moment, for they all realised that nothing would ever be quite the same again for them. It would be years before the good companionship which had been growing over the past few days could be repeated, if ever.

'You will keep in touch with Clara, won't you?' Peter asked with genuine concern. 'I still care for her, even though our future paths will not be the same.'

'Yes, of course we will,' Edward murmured, afraid to look at her again in case anyone noticed the love in his eyes. 'She has become dear to us both,' he added, with a catch of emotion in his voice.

Peter was as generous of spirit as he was lively, and it wasn't long before all signs of awkwardness and strain gave way to a much happier atmosphere. This was a relief to Edward, but he desperately needed to talk to Clara alone, and not in snatched moments when the others weren't aware of it. For some time he contrived to find a way to do just that, until finally, as though considering Peter's approaching departure from the valley, he suggested that he might appreciate a long ride before he left.

'Now that I would like!' Peter exclaimed happily. 'I'd better take it easy though, I don't want to do anything which might spoil my chances with India.'

Lizzie was not to be out done, and piped up, 'May I go too? I promise not to get in Peter's way, Father.'

Barely controlling his enthusiasm for this idea, Edward raised his eyebrows and looked at his nephew, saying casually, 'Do you mind?'

'No, of course not, but what of Clara? Peter asked, mindful that he owed her some consideration for the support she had given him, and because his admiration for her had not diminished.

'Listen, I have a suggestion to make,' Edward said. 'If Clara is in agreement, you two go riding and I'll take her up on the moors, if she'll come. The ewes are heavily pregnant and I need to check them. Perhaps you can lend her one of your walking skirts Lizzie, and a pair of stronger boots if they'll fit?'

Clara clasped her hands together, 'I should like nothing better, although I might find it difficult to keep up with you.'

'He won't let you lag behind,' Lizzie laughed. 'He used to make me walk almost faster than my small legs could go!'

'I stand admonished!' Edward protested. 'Now how about it, Clara, could you spend the day with an old tyrant like me?' His eyes twinkled playfully and she had difficulty in containing herself.

Thereafter, the prospect of a day on the hills with her left Edward in a state of euphoria which was difficult to curb and, although he chatted with her during the rest of the evening, their dialogue was full of subtle exchanges understood only by themselves. If they had need to pass each other for some reason, it was almost beyond his power not to touch her. He was grateful for Clara's quiet dignity which prevented him from revealing their secret, but every so often he saw a secret, happy smile on her face which delighted him.

When, however, they all finally decided to retire, he was allowed one brief opportunity in the hallway to squeeze her hand, just before Lizzie came bustling through.

It was a glorious sunny day, warm even, and Edward marvelled at his luck as he carefully prepared some sandwiches for his and Clara's outing on the moors. This, he felt, would be the day on which to prove his affections to Clara sufficiently for her to give up the many luxuries and conveniences which the military town of Aldershot provided. Here he had no gas lighting, the water supply and sanitation was almost primitive and indeed it would probably remain that way for years to come. He was much older than she, and when he eventually died, she would be left in isolation at the farm. Being in love with him was one thing, but would it be enough? These many questions had exercised his mind for some time before he'd finally fallen asleep, but never had his thoughts been selfish enough to want to mislead her into thinking that life in the valley was without problems. It was the combination of all these factors which made him a little nervous and apprehensive, at what was to follow.

Edward had wanted to make an early start but, by the time Peter and Lizzie were organised and despatched, time was getting on. Releasing Bella from her chain, he and Clara at last set off, and the sheer relief of being able to speak their minds freely was, in itself, a luxury, and strange in some ways, so that Edward hoped he hadn't expected too much of the day.

In spite of the clear weather the ground was soft and very muddy, and although the going was easy on the lower slopes, Clara, who wasn't used to such heavy boots found it a little more difficult. Her skirts frequently caught on withered bramble or dead nettle stalks, and Bella ran excitedly to and fro around her, so that Edward had to come to her aid. The dog soon grew weary of the game, however, and Edward talked of the need to replace her soon with a younger, livelier pup. This dismayed Clara, but he explained that Bella was, after all, a working dog and not a pet, though he wouldn't get rid of her, he was too attached to her to do that. This pleased Clara who fondled Bella whenever she caught up with them.

On reaching higher and drier ground Edward was able to take Clara's hand gently in his, but it wasn't until they reached a clump of rowan trees that he dared do more than that. 'You should admire my patience,' he said soberly, although she knew he was teasing her. 'A younger man would not have waited this long before taking you in his arms.' At that he drew her to him, 'I wanted to do this all last night!' he complained sternly.

'Then you shall wait a little longer,' Clara laughed, and with that she pulled away, caught up the hem of skirt and ran further into the trees.

He was, however, quicker and more sure-footed than she, and caught her before she could go very far, clasping her roughly to him to prevent any further chance of escape. 'Got you!' he said, as she struggled faint-heartedly. Suddenly the merriment ceased and with a surge of happiness she kissed him. Only when Bella barked jealously at them did Edward release her and guide her out of the trees towards the top of the hill.

Without his hand to pull or support her she would have fallen many times on the moss-covered boulders strewn in their way. They followed the narrow, centuries-old paths worn by countless sheep over the years, and Edward kept a watchful eye for ewes as he went. Fortunately here, the brown and withered bracken no longer hung over the paths as it did in summer, and the smell of the damp, peaty earth was unlike anything Clara had smelled before.

They could see for miles now, but Edward was aware that for all the seeming isolation there were many spots from which a rider could see them. Clara was now a little wind-blown and her face rosy from the unaccustomed exercise. 'It's not easy to walk up here,' he said as they paused for a while. 'The going's hard, but I love it!' There was pride in his voice which she recognised as one also of deep satisfaction.

As they stood there, Bella flopped at their feet, one paw pressed possessively over the toe of Clara's boot, and she bent to stroke the dog's head, saying, 'I can easily see why, being here on top of the world, you are unhappy in crowded places. You don't really need other people around you!'

He looked fondly down at her, pleased that she seemed to understand at least some of his feelings. Moving on, he found a large boulder in a more sheltered spot and, placing a sack on it which he'd brought from the barn, sat Clara on it. 'This,' he said as he sat beside her, 'makes a nonsense of bustling streets and dirty buildings, and I know how fortunate I am to be able to roam freely up here. It has taken all my life to find someone who can at least share and understand my feeling of oneness with these moors.'

They sat comfortably holding hands for some time, just looking at the surrounding hills, and taking pleasure in each other's company, but Edward knew that there was more to be discussed than the view. 'Have you given any thought to what happens now?' he asked, his voice suddenly serious. 'Tomorrow you return to Aldershot, and I...' his voice trailed off. 'Will you...could you come back?' He turned, taking both her hands in his. 'I know this is too soon to ask, but is there a chance that you could live here with me, as my wife?'

Clara slowly entwined her fingers with his. 'To say yes now, would be easy. So much has happened, and so quickly, that it is almost impossible for me to think of the future.'

'I know,' Edward agreed. 'I am a patient man,' he said softly, 'and have waited so long for this moment that there is no need to make a hasty decision which you may later regret. The contrast between here and Aldershot could not be greater, I can see that for myself.'

Clara seemed shy all at once, and lowered her head. 'Hannah, your wife,' she said softly. 'You seemed so lost without her when I first met you; did she come up here with you?' He felt her hand tremble and before he could answer she said, 'Perhaps I shouldn't have mentioned her, I'm sorry.'

'No! Don't be sorry!' he said, cradling her hands tenderly. 'I would never want to forget her, for she is Lizzie's mother, and it wouldn't be right not to talk of her. She was a gentle soul, and I like to believe that she would want me to be happy now she has gone.' He turned her face towards him. 'Hannah and I belong to a long story which one day I will tell you, but never doubt that I love you, and should you go away from me then I might as well be dead too.' He looked deep into Clara's eyes and, as if to reassure her, kissed her; tenderly at first and then more passionately, and held her tightly for fear she would go away. 'Hannah never came here,' he said huskily, 'nor Lizzie—this is our special place.'

'I will come back,' she said softly; then, raising her hand to his face, she touched him gently with her fingers. 'It would be so easy not to go,' she murmured, 'but I know there is much to sort out.'

'I can wait,' Edward said. 'And soon, once lambing is over, I shall come to Aldershot and court you properly in the old-fashioned way.'

Clara laughed fondly at him. 'I shall look forward to that time with great impatience,' she replied. 'I too can be as eager as the next person in certain matters.' There was an air of coquetry about her which she made no effort to conceal.

'Meanwhile I suppose we must make do with writing to each other,' he conceded and sighed. Then, holding her hand tightly, he removed something from his pocket. 'I have nothing better to offer, no ring to give, no book even, except this and a lock of my hair.' It was the little box from the writing desk, which he had cleaned and polished especially for her.

'Accept this trifle from a friend whose love for Thee will never end.' She read the words, and touched the hair with tentative fingers. 'Oh! Edward, it is beautiful, and I shall keep it with me at all times, even when I have your ring. Thank you so much.' Then she put it carefully into the pocket of her cloak, and kissed him tenderly.

'And now,' Edward said, pleased with her reaction, and taking the sandwiches from the bag by his side, 'we'd better eat before you wilt away.'

'It's damn gloomy in this place,' Peter exclaimed later that evening, as the four of them sat down after dinner. 'What on earth's the matter?' Having thoroughly enjoyed his day riding with Lizzie his mind was now stimulated and obsessed by the preparation for life in India. 'If we didn't have to make such an early start,' he added a little selfishly I'd take myself off to the *Plough* for a drink.'

'Oh, no you won't,' Edward spoke up sharply. 'You'll stay here and help Clara pack, because if there was another incident, India and all else could be out of the question!'

'I suppose so,' Peter conceded reluctantly. But why the sombre atmosphere?'

Lizzie pouted her lips. 'You may have exciting plans for the future,' she wailed, 'but we're left here to carry on as normal when you and Clara have gone!'

Edward was rather hurt by this outburst, yet he could do nothing other than agree with her, for the parting would be a painful one. There wasn't much for either of them to look forward to, for several weeks at least, but he felt that her misery was enough to bear without remonstrating with her.

'By the way,' Peter said, seeming not to notice Lizzie's despair. 'Whilst we were out I called in at the village and there is now no need to bother yourself tomorrow on our behalf, Uncle. I have arranged for a carriage to call here at seven-thirty in the morning to take us to the station in Sheffield. The earlier we leave the easier travelling will be.'

Edward and Clara exchanged glances, realising that they were to part sooner than expected, but it was Lizzie who spoke for them all, her voice choked with emotion. 'Then after tonight, this is going to be a sad and lonelier place.' There were tears in her eyes which she bravely tried to wipe away. 'And now I am not even going with you to Sheffield to say goodbye.'

'Never mind,' Clara said quietly, her heart going out to the unhappy young woman. 'I have promised your father that I will come and stay for a while in the summer, and you can always come and stay with me.'

'But that's too long to wait,' Lizzie complained. 'If I am to go to London I may not see you at all!'

Clara looked nervously at Edward, afraid that her statement would upset him, but in order to appease Lizzie, whose thoughts were only of an immediate nature, she'd done her best to find a quick solution.

Edward, however, merely shook his head. 'Is that what you really want to do Lizzie, go to London?' he asked, aware that if she did go he would need Clara more than ever. Lizzie nodded timidly, as if expecting him to be angry with her. 'If that is what you really want to do,' he said positively, 'then I will not stand in your way. Clara has convinced me that it is best for you, just so long as you don't later accuse me of sending you away again.'

The relief on Lizzie's face was a transformation. Her eyes lit up and she ran over and threw her arms round him in delight. 'Thank you, Father! Oh, thank you!'

Within minutes she and Peter were locked in a world of their own with talk of India and London, to the exclusion of Edward and Clara who slipped casually into the kitchen, to spend a quiet moment on their own before she had to pack and retire early, ready for her departure the following day.

Next morning, Edward was able to snatch one tender moment alone with Clara whilst the others were preoccupied eating their breakfast and, as the carriage finally rolled out of the yard, Edward stifled the rising wave of emotion he felt.

Lizzie waved energetically until Peter and Clara had disappeared then, gently taking Edward's arm, she said, knowingly but kindly, 'I saw you kissing Clara in the kitchen last night!'

Further Reading

The Great Sheffield Flood (Hillsborough Community Development Trust). ISBN 0-952533502

Amey, Geoffrey, *The Collapse of the Dale Dyke Dam 1864* (Cassell). ISBN 0-304293628

Cole, Howard N., *The Story of Aldershot* (Southern Books (Aldershot) Ltd). ISBN 0-950714704

Harrison, S., *A Complete History of the Great Flood at Sheffield on March 11 and 12, 1864* (S. Harrison, Sheffield).